THE PARSLEY KNIGHT

Dan Ackerman

Supposed Crimes LLC • Matthews, North Carolina

Published in the United States.

ISBN: 978-1-952150-27-2

www.supposedcrimes.com

This book is typeset in Goudy Old Style.

For David

ever. "You make a living."

A first quest was not a requirement for a knight, but it was an expectation for most of them. Some knights, well-heeled ones who could go back to their family's castles, would head home and take up their lives there, readying themselves to inherit their father's titles or aid their older brothers in managing the manor.

Others would set out for glory, or at least work.

Ainsley came from a line of respectable, but lesser, noblemen. He would have to work to keep his armor in good repair and his horse fed.

And he did need to keep Hadley fed. She had served him well, her build well-suited to his slim form, and more than that, she was his only horse.

She nuzzled against his hand when he greeted her that morning.

It took him longer than usual to get her groomed and tacked, each glint of sunlight off any shiny bit of metal an affront to his eyes.

He had a light breakfast, all his stomach could handle, said his goodbyes to the other knights, and headed south, towards the border.

The border always saw conflict and conflicts always had people in need of knights.

He slept beneath the stars that night, exhausted and still aching.

He spent the next night under the stars as well, but that night he was not so tired that being alone beneath the stars didn't unnerve him.

Last night he had been too tired to think about being alone, but tonight all he could hear were crickets and rustling branches. The world without a companion became enormous and overwhelming. He had squired for Sir Richard since he had turned fifteen and he'd been a page since the age of seven.

Some of the other new knights had set out in pairs, but Ainsley had wanted to strike out on his own. He had friends among his peers, but they'd had different aspirations than he. They had wanted glory or had harbored fantasies of finding some sweet-hearted maiden to bring home as a wife. Ainsley worried more about gold crowns than glory and he had never been interested in maidens, no matter how sweet.

If he'd been a bolder man, he might have invited Alfred to travel with him. He and Alfred had nearly gotten along too well. A few close calls had found them both agreeing to stay away from each other, for the sake of their reputations and their families.

The decision had been smart. Safe. Alfred's idea, mostly. No one had ever called Ainsley wise.

Once alone, though, he wished he'd set out with someone.

Especially when a crow called out from the tree above him.

In the morning, he woke to the cawing of a crow and he wondered if it was the same bird that had kept him awake for most of the night.

He glanced up and spied the creature sitting on a low branch, its beady eyes glimmering in the light. It watched him as he ate, and he tried to ignore it. Feed a thing like that once and soon there would be a flock of them scavenging around.

He left the bird behind without a second thought.

He slept that night in an inn to get himself and Hadley out of the rain. Spring had not yet moved far enough towards summer for him to tolerate a rainy night beneath a tree. He'd shiver himself half to death and his purse had not yet grown so light he had to suffer that thoroughly.

He listened closely for any sign of trouble, any bit of rumor that might set him in the right direction to make a bit of coin.

The closest thing he got to a lead was rumors of a witch a few villages over.

He pointed Hadley in that direction anyway; the path toward that village still took him towards the border.

The villagers confirmed that they had a witch in their midst, the cause of ill livestock. The lord of the manor offered him a few coins and a wedge of cheese to venture out into the dense wood beyond the village and take care of the crone.

Ainsley agreed and set out.

He had never encountered a witch before, though he'd heard rumors about all kinds of witches. Practitioners of low magic, untrustworthy things that could, in a pinch, be useful if there were no mages to offer an arcane spell, or if the mages charged too much for their work.

Mages, with all the prestige their profession offered, could charge more. The king himself was a mage.

Witches, though...witchcraft was barely tolerated and that meant you could buy witch spells for a third, a quarter, of the price.

Ainsley, so far, had been lucky enough to never need a spell, from a witch or a mage. He'd never been gravely ill or wounded, he'd never gotten in over his head with any enemies or gotten a girl with child when he shouldn't have. He'd never had anyone to impress with magical trinkets or been able to afford enchantments for his weapons or armor.

For a knight in the most magical kingdom on the continent, Ainsley knew hardly anything about magic, high, low, or natural.

He hoped it was that inexperience that dried out his mouth as he followed the villagers' directions out to the crone's hut.

He gripped Hadley's reins too tightly and his knuckles started to ache.

The trees thickened until Hadley could barely make her way through.

It started to grow dark, but too early, and too quickly.

The caw of a crow nearly scared him out of his skin.

He looked up to see a crow perched on a low branch to his left. Much closer than any common crow would get. It ruffled its wings and he glimpsed a flash of white beneath one wing. It squawked at him again.

He urged Hadley on, wanting to be away from what he feared was the crone's familiar.

After what felt like hours of slow, painful wandering he spotted a light in the distance, a flickering yellow glow.

Hadley trudged on, seemingly unconcerned by the oppressive darkness or the crow that called after him and hopped from branch to branch a few feet behind him.

Eventually, he came upon a clearing with a small thatched hut and a tidy garden. A cauldron bubbled above a firepit and a woman stood above the cauldron, stirring it slowly, constantly.

She glanced his way when he entered the clearing. "Lost?"

"No."

"Didn't think so." She continued to stir.

Ainsley dismounted, threw Hadley's reins over a branch, and took a few steps forward.

The crone didn't move from in front of her cauldron. "Villagers sent you I figure. What is it this time, sick goats or rotten crops?"

"Cows."

She nodded and continued to stir.

He wished she would stop stirring. "You bewitched them."

"No."

He drew his sword.

She didn't seem to notice. Or care.

A young girl, maybe ten, came out of the hut and looked him over. In her arms, she carried bundles of herbs.

The crone waved the girl over and began to throw in the bundles. She gave the girl a pat on the head. "And a crock, lovey, to put it in."

He tightened his grip on his hilt.

From behind him, a crow cawed.

The girl returned inside, giving Ainsley another sideways glance.

"Ain't me that witched 'em," the crone assured.

"Is there another witch in these woods, then?"

She nodded then jabbed one knobby finger towards something he hadn't noticed before, something that would have stopped him from entering the clearing.

From a gnarled tree beside her hut hung a body, cut into pieces. The limbs and head had all been severed from the torso of what must have been a lovely maiden, judging by what remained of her slender form.

"Were it Thomas Brown's cows?" the crone asked.

Ainsley didn't know.

"That's the one what broke her heart."

He couldn't stop staring at the body dangling from the tree, watching the pieces sway in the breeze.

The crow fluttered over to inspect the face of the corpse and he had to look away before it started to peck at her eyes.

"First his livestock, she said. Then his wife, then his wee ones," the crone said. "Wouldn't be her first time doing it either."

"The cows are still sick."

The crone nodded towards the cauldron. "We'll get the cows fixed or they'll keep sending knights after us, I bet."

The girl returned with a large clay crock in her arms, set it by the fire, then returned inside again.

"You stay the night, lordling, and you bring the brew back to the village when it's done. Tell them the bad witch is dead, huh? Best thing for all us, I think."

The crow left the corpse-riddled tree and landed on the thatched roof.

Ainsley thought he saw something glimmering on its beak but couldn't be sure and didn't look long enough to check. Bile rose in the back of his throat.

He glanced back towards Hadley, who had started to nose around in the witch's garden. He dropped his sword and rushed over to shoo her away from the plants, not sure what manner of wicked poisons the old crone grew.

"Naught but parsley over there. Good for stews or warding off too much drink, but harmless," the crone called.

Hadley snorted at him as if she had known all along that was what she'd been sniffling.

He held on to her reins more tightly and went to retrieve his sword. He sheathed it before he dropped it again.

"We've got a goat, you can put her in with her if she's got a good temperament," the crone offered and nodded towards a small pen that housed a spotted goat.

Not knowing what else to do at this point, he walked the mare over and untacked her.

"You hungry?" the crone asked.

He didn't answer until she fixed him with a stare. "Yes."

"Come over here."

He approached slowly, his hand on his hilt.

"Keep stirring. Slow but don't stop. And don't lean in too close, you don't want to breathe too much in."

Ainsley took the spoon and began to stir.

The crone went inside and didn't come back out for hours, not until his shoulders had grown sore and he'd had to switch arms several times.

The girl came out, handed him a bowl of stewed barley and roots, and took over stirring. She had to lean back and arch herself unnaturally to keep her face out of the way of the steam that rose from the cauldron.

He sniffed at the food, detected nothing foul, and took a cautious bite. It tasted safe. Better than that, it tasted good. He busied himself eating and the girl continued stirring, still twisted away to keep the steam out of her face.

He watched her for several minutes before his better nature took over. He shoveled down the meal, then told her, "Go on, I can do it."

She eyed him, her mouth downturned, but stepped back from the cauldron. She watched him stir for a while. "You really came to kill us?"

"I came to kill whoever bewitched the cows."

The girl looked towards the tree. "So you won't kill me or Nan?"

"No."

"You swear it?"

"On my honor as a knight," he vowed, not sure if he could ever lift his sword against a child, witch or not.

"What's a knight?" she asked.

"I'm a knight," he answered, not sure what else to say at first. "A knight is...someone who swears to defend the realm and its people, who serves the king and..."

"And goes about killing old ladies," the crone answered from behind him.

"I haven't killed anyone," Ainsley protested.

"I'm surprised you can even pick up your sword."

He didn't take the bait. All his life he'd been teased by the other squires for being small, slender, and more like something out of a ballad than someone suited to combat and questing. He'd made up for it by working harder than they ever had. He could keep pace on foot, horseback, or in water with most any knight, he could shoot a longbow, and he'd bested all the other squires he'd trained against at least once in single combat.

With practice weapons, of course. He'd yet to see real conflict. Sir Richard had avoided it. To a fault, some of the other knights had said. Richard had ignored them and told Ainsley that he'd know if he wasn't fit for battle the very first time he saw one and there was nothing he could do to change it.

He stirred until the crone and the girl both had eaten and his arms began to burn from the effort. He threw a few furtive glances in the old woman's direction, but she either didn't notice or pretended not to.

Uneasy and unwilling to risk her displeasure, he stirred for hours. He thought his arms would drop off his body before the brew finished.

By the time the witch shooed him away, his clothes had soaked through with sweat and his hair stuck to his scalp.

The crone came over a peered into the cauldron, then flapped her arms at him. "Enough of that."

He withdrew, his arms hanging like lead weights.

She filled the crock, placed on the lid, and sealed it with wax. When he stepped towards it, she warned, "Too hot to touch now. And you don't want to be out in the woods at night."

He glanced towards the trees as if he would see wolves sitting at the edge of the clearing.

"Room by the hearth if you don't fancy a night out here," the old woman offered.

"I..." He looked around once more and could almost feel the darkness of the surrounding forest staring back at him. "Thank you."

He retrieved his sleeping roll and followed the crone inside.

After he removed his armor and settled himself in by the hearth and the initial discomfort of the situation faded, he found himself glad for the warmth of the fire and a roof above his head. Though she was crooked and ugly, the crone didn't appear much more crooked or ugly than most old women. Despite the grisly omen of a dismembered corpse hanging out front, she had offered him no harm and didn't appear to have any intention to hurt him, unless she thought to wait until he fell asleep.

She wouldn't have to wait long if that was the case.

As soon as he shut his eyes, he fell asleep.

The pale light of dawn found him alive and well.

The child pointed him in the direction of the wash bin. He scrubbed himself of the previous day's sweat and dirt, though he couldn't wash away the herbaceous scent that hours stirring the witch's brew had imbued into his skin and clothing.

"Nan says to take the head when you go."

Those words, said in such a small, sweet voice, cut Ainsley to his core. He struggled back into his armor, his arms still stiff and sore, and went to retrieve the head and the crock.

Cutting the head down from the tree proved more of a task than he had anticipated and delayed his departure by some time. In the end, he had to scale the tree and slice through the rope with his knife.

The crow, Hadley, and the young girl watched him.

Once he had the head secured to Hadley's saddle, he hauled himself up onto the horse and the crone had the kindness to hand him the crock.

He cradled it carefully into his lap.

"Make sure to tell em ain't no more bad witches in the woods," the old woman said. "Mix the brew in with the cows' water."

"I'll tell them, you have my word," Ainsley vowed.

He steered Hadley out of the clearing, passing through the same uncommonly dark area as he had on the way in, though a glance upward showed that little more than heavy foliage above his head caused it. Last night, it had seemed such an ominous sign of things to come.

The villagers stared at him as he rode up to speak with the lord of the manor. He delivered the witch's head, explained the uneasy parley he'd had with the old crone, and accepted the two silver shields, as well as the promised wedge of cheese, from the lord.

On his way out, he learned that the villagers had long since discounted him as dead. He purchased a loaf of bread and returned to his southward journey.

After three days of being followed by the crow and several hours of it watching him struggle to light a fire and occasionally cawing what felt like jibes, Ainsley gave up on ignoring the creature and tried to shoo it away.

It cawed indignantly and fluttered up to a higher branch.

"Go on, leave me alone. Get out of here."

It ignored him, then went on to preen as he continued to struggle with the fire.

Rain had soaked them all the night before and made the wood too damp to burn. Ainsley resigned himself to a cold, dark night.

The moon, at least, sat fat and full in the sky.

The crow hopped down onto a lower branch and squawked at him.

"Go away."

It didn't, of course. It disappeared sometimes, but always returned and Ainsley had started to wonder if the damned bird spelled out ill luck in his future.

It flapped down from its perch and pecked at the handful of sticks he'd gathered.

"Too wet."

The small flame he'd managed had smoked horribly and set his eyes smarting.

The crow flapped around the pile of branches some more, then returned to the tree. It appeared to have settled in for the night because it didn't heckle him any further.

Hadley settled in on her side and didn't seem to mind when Ainsley nestled up to her to ward off the night's chill.

He'd be glad when summer finally showed its face.

The following morning, he found the crow still roosted in the tree above him.

When he took out his last hunk of bread and bit of cheese, the little beast stirred. It came down and hopped closer and closer. It carried a small, shiny bit of rock in its beak.

"Go."

The crow tapped at his hand with its beak.

"What?"

It tapped his hand again and when he extended his hand to the creature, it deposited the rock into his palm.

"Oh. Uh. Thank you."

It cawed viciously at him and snatched a chunk of bread out of the end of the loaf.

"Hey!"

The crow scarfed the bread and rustled its wings.

Ainsley stared down at the rock in his palm. "You know, rocks aren't money."

The crow eyed him, more intelligence than seemly glinting in its beady eyes.

Ainsley sighed and held out another piece of bread to the bird. "Might as well take it, it's stale anyway." He hoped to come across another village or tavern soon. He needed to restock his supplies.

And find another human being to talk to.

It had been one thing to chat with Hadley; she had been his steadfast companion for some years now and horses were respectable creatures.

This crow, though...it must have been an unnatural thing, following him around and croaking at him as it did. It would be best to get rid of it, but here he was talking to the thing and feeding it his last bits of bread.

The crow took the bread from his fingers and gobbled it down.

A few days later, when Ainsley came across a small town, the thing settled itself onto Hadley's rump and remained there, keenly watching as Ainsley made his way to a baker's stall and made his purchases.

He caught wind of a few rumors, including one about fires plaguing a town a day's ride away. He gathered as many details as he could and got the directions to the village. When he headed back on the road, he noticed that the crow had left its perch on Hadley.

Good.

Maybe the thing had found someone else to bother.

As he rode on, he found himself glancing over his shoulder, making sure that the thing hadn't returned.

When he made camp that night, a loud, rough caw from right behind him scared him enough to jump and yelp.

He swiveled to find the crow settled beside his pack.

"Go away."

The crow remained, though.

It hopped closer to him when he took out his evening meal. It cawed a few times.

When Ainsley flapped a hand to shoo it away, it pecked him hard on the wrist. He cried out and yanked back his hand.

"I'll get a priest to deal with you, I swear, next time I see a church."

The crow lifted something from the ground and deposited it into his lap.

He plucked it from his legs.

A penny.

The damned thing had found a penny.

He looked over and found it waiting expectantly. He swore it looked almost haughty.

The beast was too clever by far, but he handed over a bit of his food anyway.

The thing accepted it.

The town plagued by fires showed signs of it everywhere. Burnt patches of grass, charred buildings, and people with bright red burns on their skin.

He asked around about the burns and got a lot of scowls and curses in return, but a few people informed him that a wyrm lived in a cave by the nearby river and would come to town.

To what end, no one knew, especially because they'd never had any such trouble until a few weeks past, but the monster would scorch anything in its path.

They laughed when he asked for directions but pointed him towards the monster's cave.

Hadley plodded along without complaint for some time, but as they progressed further up the river, she began to snort and shy.

Eventually, he gave up coaxing her along, given the number of blackened patches of grass and trees with charred rings around their trunk. He dismounted, patted her on the shoulder, and continued along.

The crow took wing and Ainsley expected that it knew better than he did what sort of beast lay ahead of them. Animals always had a better sense about things like that, especially when it came to fire.

Instead of leaving, however, the thing settled on his shoulder.

Somehow it chilled him more than if the bird had gone. What sort of ill fate awaited him that the creature wanted to witness? Perhaps it wanted to peck at his face the same as it had pecked the face of that dead witch.

The eyes of the corpse had been missing, though if it was the work of this particular crow or some other scavenger, Ainsley didn't know for sure.

Given that the bird now perched on his shoulder, he didn't think he wanted to know.

The further he went, the greater the extent of the fire damage. Soot covered every inch of the entrance to the cave, the rock face blackened.

No ominous glow came from within the cave, no growls or puffs of smoke. No sounds filled the surrounding area, not a bird call or the buzz of a single insect, nothing but the quiet, gentle bubble of the river.

Ainsley kept his hand rested on the hilt of his sword, ready to draw it should the wyrm show its face.

He made it to the mouth of the cave without a single incident, aside from sliding a little in the mud and dunking his right leg up to the knee in the cold water of the river.

The crow on his shoulder pecked at his helmet and Ainsley could only assume the wicked beast had done so in retaliation for disturbing it.

It took him several minutes to gather the courage to enter the cave. As he moved further back, the cave grew warmer, contrary to what he knew about caves altogether. The air grew hotter and drier and had him sweating in his armor.

The crow ruffled itself several times.

At the back of the cave, Ainsley found two things. One was a dried-up husk of a beast about the width of a man and perhaps nine or ten feet long. The other was the same sort of beast, he guessed, but no larger than a grass snake. The little thing had coiled inside beside the husk, nestled between a clutch of unhatched eggs.

From what he could see of the larger, dead beast, they were the same sort of creature – smooth, burnished scales the color of copper, legless, and with a ridge of jagged, sharper scales along the back. The little creature had a broad, flat head with a blunt snout. The larger one had no head that Ainsley could spot.

It would be quick work to take care of a sleeping monster, especially one so small. And young, Ainsley suspected.

He stepped forward, drew his sword, and prepared to swing. A quick blow would take off its head.

In the end, though, Ainsley did nothing more than prod the thing with the flat of his sword.

Dragons, no matter their breed, were intelligent creatures and usually not troublesome, despite their reputation.

Some of the things could even transform into human shapes, at least, according to lore and Sir Richard's favorite barkeep.

Imagine if this wyrm were that type of dragon? Would cutting off its head be the same as taking the head from a human babe?

When he prodded it, it stirred, first sluggish then coiling even tighter upon itself. Its scales went from burnished to glowing, aflame like coals. It reared back its head and hissed, producing a few puffs of smoke.

Ainsley and the wrym stared at each other for some time, neither moving, both somewhere between uncertain and anxious.

The crow shuffled over to Ainsley's other shoulder and seemed to be peering at the little creature. It pecked at Ainsley once.

"I don't know what to do."

The crow pecked him again, though what it intended to communicate Ainsley couldn't fathom.

He immediately chided himself for talking to the crow again. He had long since stopped doubting that the thing had more intelligence than the average crow, but he couldn't shake the feeling that it was a wicked creature, some witch's familiar or unholy demon. It acted too unnaturally.

Another hiss brought Ainsley back to the situation at hand.

He couldn't leave the creature here to grow and cause more damage to the surrounding wilderness and towns.

Nor could he slay the beast, not when it was so small and helpless. This sort of slaying would have no more honor than plunging his blade into a wolf pup.

He sheathed his sword and went back outside to think. He retrieved Hadley from where he had left her and coaxed her towards the cave. He set up camp for the night and built a small fire, actively avoiding thinking about his problem.

The crow watched passively for a while. Once he had shed his amour, it flapped over to him and pecked at his hand.

He recoiled.

The crow pecked at him again, gentle but insistent.

"What?" Ainsley demanded.

It nodded its head towards a bush a few yards away.

Ainsley followed its gaze and saw a rabbit. He glanced back at the crow, not able to believe any of this, but tossed his worries aside. Fresh meat had not been easy to come across lately and he hastened to string his bow before the rabbit hopped away.

Within half an hour, he had the thing skinned and spitted, cooking over the campfire. The crow pecked happily at the guts, but Ainsley didn't doubt it would nose around for a share of the meat, too.

Maybe the crow wasn't as wicked as Ainsley had originally thought. What cause did it have to help him like this?

True, it had gotten food, too, but Ainsley didn't think that a creature meant to predict his ruin would do anything to keep him fed.

The rabbit hadn't been roasting for more than ten minutes before Hadley began to snort and stomp and Ainsley detected a crackling slither coming from the direction of the cave.

He looked over to spy the wrym snaking towards them, its scales shining but not glowing.

It came right up to the fire, slithering inside of the flames and reaching up for the rabbit.

The crow squawked and the wyrm shrank back, letting out a small hiss and puff of smoke.

The crow squawked louder and the wyrm coiled up, settled into the flames.

It stayed put, even when the rabbit finished cooking and Ainsley took it from the spit.

The thing did watch him pitifully, though, as he ate.

He took a sliver of meat from the rabbit and tossed it towards the wyrm.

It darted out from the fire and gobbled up the meat as if it hadn't eaten in days.

Maybe it hadn't. The dead one must have been its mother and maybe wyrms were the type of creatures who cared for their offspring.

Maybe this little thing had been struggling all on its own, no mother or siblings.

The crow handed over some of the organs to the wyrm and Ainsley continued to dole out bits of meat to both animals.

He should have been saving some of this for tomorrow, but he had some stores remaining. Maybe the crow would point him in the direction of another meal again soon.

Once the meal concluded, the wyrm returned to the flames.

Ainsley guessed it had fallen asleep.

The crow fell asleep, too,

Hadley eventually settled better, though she continued to cast distrustful looks towards the wyrm all night.

Ainsley didn't sleep much either.

He had no idea what to do with the wrym. Surely it couldn't stay with the cave. He had no desire to take care of it either. Having the crow following him around was bad enough. He didn't know anything about wyrms or caring for baby ones.

Morning came and he found that the fire had died during the night. He found the wyrm tucked up against his chest, pleasantly warm to the touch. He ran a finger along the ragged scales down its back and it nestled up against his hand.

It curled around his wrist and up his arm and refused to let go.

The crow cackled at him.

"Shut up."

The crow preened.

The wyrm remained on his arm, so he couldn't put on his armor, and Hadley refused to let him mount her with the wyrm on his person.

He sighed, took Hadley by reins, and began to walk into town.

People shied away from him when they noticed the wyrm and a few even threw things at him. He nearly lost control of his horse.

The wrym didn't loosen its grip on him even once until a blast from the blacksmith's furnace caught its attention.

It loosened from his arm and stretched towards the furnace.

No idea what else to do, Ainsley wandered in and held his arm as close to the fire as he could. The creature unraveled from his arm and slid into the fire, nestling happily among the coals.

The blacksmith wandered over. "What're you doing to my fire?"

"Uh...the wyrm..." Ainsley pointed. "It wouldn't get off my arm until we came by your fire."

"It was on your arm?" The blacksmith peered at him.

Ainsley held up his arm to show his arm, free of injury, though slightly sweaty from the heat of the wrym.

"What was it doing on your arm?"

"I fed it. It got...sort of attached."

"You fed it?"

Ainsley nodded.

"You can't leave it there," the smith told him.

"I'm not going to reach in there and get it out."

The blacksmith harrumphed.

"I think it's just a baby. I think it's been coming into town looking for food."

The smith grunted and rubbed his head.

"Maybe if you feed it..." Ainsley suggested. "I think it will stay put for a while, long enough for someone to write to the university so they can come fetch it."

"Mmm."

"You don't mind?"

"Figure not," the blacksmith said.

"I'm sorry. I thought I would do more but..." Ainsley rubbed his neck. "Well, it's so small, I couldn't kill it."

"Mmm." The blacksmith grunted and turned away from the wyrm. "George! Run up and fetch Master John. We need to send a letter."

Ainsley took his leave.

Hadley nuzzled his shoulder once he exited.

"No worries, old girl, just you and me again."

The crow cawed.

"You, me, and possibly a demon," Ainsley amended.

The crow preened.

Ainsley settled in beside the campfire, rummaging through his pack for the handful of oats he knew he had in there. They'd probably settled to the bottom. Things he wanted to find tended to do that.

The crow alternated between watching him and preening.

It had been preening a lot lately.

Maybe mating season grew near and he would lose its company.

He thought of it as a shame. He'd grown used to the bird.

Once he found the oats, he threw them into the pot to cook and set about cleaning his armor.

He paid no mind to the sound coming from the road. It wasn't so late yet that seeing other travelers would be suspicious. He came across plenty of others. Sometimes they had pointed him in a helpful direction. Other times they traded greetings and continued on their own ways.

For a few days, he had traveled in the same direction as a merchant. They had parted ways in a town with a werewolf.

The merchant had made his trades and Ainsley, instead of skinning the werewolf, had helped her gather enough wolfsbane to keep her transformation at bay.

So far, none of his quests had gone how he'd meant for them to go, but none had ended with blood spilled, on either end. That satisfied him and so did the handful of coins he'd earned.

The other travelers grew closer and he snuck a backward glance at them. Three men dressed in leathers and bearing swords on their hips.

Foot soldiers, maybe, or town guards out roving.

As they grew closer, Ainsley prepared to hail them. Night had almost fallen and he'd already set up a fire. He wouldn't mind company that could talk, either.

Except they approached before he greeted them. They approached with their hands on their swords.

Ainsley had the foresight to stand and reach for his before they were fully upon him.

"We can do it easy if you like," one of the men said.

Ainsley drew his sword. "I don't want trouble."

"Then hand over everything."

"I'm a knight, gentlemen. I trained with the best, I've been questing these months...Pick a wiser fight."

"Knight or not, three to one is odds I'll take," said another of the men.

Ainsley adjusted his grip and his stance. His training would hold against them, he knew. Three men in leather, who lacked training and conditioning, would stand little chance against a knight even without his armor.

Two swung at the same time and he easily sidestepped their attacks. One of the men left his entire left side exposed and Ainsley swung.

What would have left a bruise with a practice blade proved much different with sharpened steel. His sword bit into the man's neck, deep into the flesh and thunked against bone.

Ainsley recoiled as blood erupted from the man's neck, splashing and spurting all over Ainsley, into his eyes and mouth.

Never had he seen so much blood, not human blood, and not even during a hunt had he gotten soaked.

The world darkened and faded and Ainsley's whole body revolted. His stomach churned and he stared, frozen, as one of the man's companions turned towards him, sword raised.

It would have been his end except that, as Hadley screamed, a strange, dark figure drove a long knife through the second attacker, then whirled and impaled the throat of the third.

Ainsley staggered, then fell, overwhelmed by the stench and the blood, and the very real knowledge that he killed a man.

A flesh and blood man.

The dark figure dropped its knife and came to crouch beside where Ainsley had collapsed, retching on all fours.

A hand settled on his back. "Oh, poor thing," came a soft, husky voice, a voice like the whisper of wind through autumn leaves.

Ainsley heaved again, heaved until his stomach was empty, then heaved even more. His ribs ached and his throat burned.

The figure remained by his side. "You're alright."

Finally, emptied, Ainsley stared at the blood, the bodies, and began to shake. He couldn't make sense of any of it and he began to keen.

He had no control over the sounds and wails that escaped him. He could do nothing to rein in his sobs, horrible wrenching sobs that hurt his whole body.

Arms settled around him and a hand pushed the hair away from his face. That husky voice whispered to him, soothing comforts.

"Let me take you home with me, get you cleaned up."

Ainsley continued to sob.

"Clean and safe," the figure promised.

Through his sobs, through the haze and confusion, Ainsley could only nod. Clean. He had to be clean. Could he ever be clean again? Would this blood ever wash away?

He remembered nothing after that. He woke somewhere dim and warm. He must have fainted. He had thought he was going to, anyway, and it explained why he didn't know where he was or how he'd gotten there.

He found himself nestled into a bed, bundled in soft sheets that he slid away as he sat up.

His clothes...he skimmed his hands over his chest to make sure. Yes, his clothes were gone, all of them.

Ruined, probably.

He wanted badly to rinse his mouth and spied a pitcher of water on a table.

Carefully, he climbed out of bed, not trusting himself to retain control of his body. He made his way to the pitcher and rinsed his mouth, then splashed his face.

He shuffled back to the bed, checking to see if there were any clothes to be had. Before he found anything, the door opened and in stepped the same figure that had rescued him.

His wits now more about him, Ainsley saw that the figure belonged to a man, lean and sharp.

The man, his eyes keen and black, glanced over him, then took a robe from a peg on the wall and brought it over to Ainsley. He draped it around his shoulders.

Ainsley stepped back, clutching the robe. "I..."

He couldn't stop staring at the man. His skin...he had gray skin, a middling shade that reminded Ainsley of river stones, and long, sleek hair the same pale gray as a dove's wing.

The man smiled. "Not how I imagined I would introduce myself, no, but things come to pass in the strangest ways."

"Who...?"

"Call me Rue."

"But who *are* you?" Ainsley asked.

"Your savior, or do I misremember the evening past?"

Ainsley tightened the robe about himself, not just because of the godawful shiver that remembering the attack produced in him, but because it had started to settle in that this man couldn't be human.

Inhuman races and humans brokered an uneasy peace in Triviai, and Ainsley had encountered his share of vampires and demons. They had passed each other in towns or even settled in at the same tavern counter for a mug of ale.

But this man...he wasn't a vampire, nor one of the half-human bastards that the Devil had spawned on Earth. No, his colors were uncommon and his face had more angles than a piece of crystal.

This man had to be something more unearthly. Ainsley had heard rumors of people who'd encountered fallen angels and heard them described in similar terms. Odd-colored and strange to look upon.

Had he been whisked away somewhere by one of the Devil's loyal servants?

"What?" asked the man, his sharp, thin brows drawing down and the ends of his mouth tugging ever so slightly into a frown.

"Am..." Ainsley hugged himself, drowning in the overlong robe and feeling small. Smaller than usual. The thin, slippery fabric, made for finery and not warmth, offered him no comfort. "Where are we?"

Rue gestured around with one long hand, his fingers artfully crooked to show boredom, disdain, and haughtiness with one gesture. "Welcome to the summer abode of Balor and Corva, lord and lady of the Western Court."

Ainsley blinked, not sure what to make of that information.

"Ah, what confusion clouds that lovely face," Rue purred. "The Western Court lies not in the human realm. I've brought you to the Otherworld."

He could do nothing but shake.

"You don't look well."

Ainsley shook his head. He didn't feel well, his stomach weak and hollow, his head light.

Rue stepped closer and took Ainsley by the elbow. "Back to bed. More rest, I think, would do you well."

Ainsley allowed the man to walk him back to the bed and didn't have the wherewithal to recoil from the gentle intimacy of his touch as Rue pulled up the blankets and smoothed them over his legs.

"And nourishment, too, you lost a fair bit of food yesterday." Rue brushed his knuckles over Ainsley's cheek. "I'll return."

Ainsley nodded and found himself touching his face where the man's hand had lingered.

No, not a man. If this was the Otherworld, that meant that Rue numbered among the Fair Folk.

Ainsley shifted uncomfortably in the bed, unable to find a way to settle comfortably. His heart pattered unsteadily against his ribs and it only worsened when Rue returned bearing a tray.

"I appreciate it," Ainsley murmured, his eyes fixed on the bowl of porridge and fruit, drizzled with honey and cream.

"No trouble at all," Rue assured. "Lucky for us, Dora had the larders well stocked. The lord and lady of the house plan to take a holiday in the coming weeks."

"I...I don't want to intrude."

"They'll likely think less about your presence than my return."

That statement provided no comfort and it must have shown on his face.

"But nothing to worry about." Rue gave him a smile.

Ainsley stared down at the porridge, his mouth watering and stomach begging for food, but he couldn't make himself take a bite.

"Something troubles you."

"My horse."

"Safe and comfortable in the stables," Rue vowed.

"And..."

"What?" the fairy prompted.

He felt stupid and childish asking. "There was a crow, too, it didn't...I lost track of what happened, but I don't figure they would have gone after a bird. Did you notice a bird?"

Rue laughed, warm and rough, a sound that Ainsley would never forget. "The bird is quite safe. He'll be warmed to know you were asking after him."

Ainsley couldn't shake the feeling that Rue mocked him but knew better than to get prickly around a fairy. The Fair Folk had earned their reputation as capricious things.

"Eat. Then a bath, yes?"

The idea of a bath, no matter how strange the circumstances, spurred Ainsley to eat. It had been so long since he'd had a real bath, not a quick scrub in a river. Judging by the fineness of the robe and food, the plush mattress beneath him, and the beautiful embroidery on Rue's tunic, this bath would be steaming hot.

Not to mention, a quick inspection of his hands revealed that whoever had washed him had not managed to entirely scrub away the gore of that night.

"Who...?" Ainsley glanced up to find the fairy watching him. "My clothes..." He didn't know how to ask, but Rue seemed to catch his meaning.

"I tidied up as best I could, but I kept the intrusion as brief as possible. Perhaps not as thorough as I could have been, but I thought, well..." Rue's eyes, dark and hard to read, flicked over Ainsley's face, then to the strip of skin left down his chest, uncovered by the robe.

Ainsley adjusted the robe, his cheeks warming.

"We don't know each other that well, do we?"

"No," Ainsley agreed, unable to control the breathiness in his voice.

"Not yet." The fairy gave him a slippery smile.

Ainsley swallowed.

Rue stood and made toward the door. "Finish your meal. I'll draw you a bath." He left before Ainsley could mumble anything else.

By the time Rue returned, a thick fluffy towel draped over his arm, Ainsley had scarfed down his porridge and scraped the bowl clean.

"Come along."

Ainsley made sure to fasten the belt of the robe before he got out of bed. He padded along behind Rue, trying his best to be quiet, especially because Rue's feet, even booted as they were, made hardly a sound.

Rue led him down a lengthy hallway, passing many other rooms, though none of them appeared to be in use.

"Are we alone?" Ainsley asked, for the first time worrying about Rue's intentions.

"No. Dora and Letti are here as well."

Servants, Ainsley guessed. He didn't know what that would do to save him.

If he needed saving.

He shouldn't have had such poor expectations of Rue. The man had done nothing to earn such distrust.

He had come to Ainsley's rescue and offered him food, shelter, and a bath.

Rue pushed open the door to a large washroom but lingered in the doorway. "I'll allow you some privacy," Rue offered. His eyes flicked over Ainsley once more. "Unless you'd prefer otherwise."

"Privacy...some privacy might be in order."

Rue nodded and handed him the towel. "I'll see about some clothing. We should have something in your size. Somewhere."

Rue closed the door behind him when he went.

Once alone, Ainsley slipped out of the robe and hung it carefully on a screen beside the tub.

He climbed into the tub and sank in up to his shoulders. He washed and soaked, the heat of the water easing the stiffness in his muscles. It did nothing to clear the images from his mind. He dwelled on the images of the brigand's blood, the gaping wound in his neck...his stomach roiled.

God in Heaven, he was going to be sick, right here in this lovely bath.

He slowed his breathing, trying to steady himself. Anything to keep his porridge down. He sat up and brought his knees up close to his chest. He thought of his sweetest childhood memories, his mother's embrace, sitting on his father's knee, running through the fields with other children.

It kept the sick at bay, but his nerves remained frazzled.

A quiet knock disrupted his panic.

"Yes?" he called, voice wavering.

"I brought you something to wear. I'll come set it down if it please you."

"That's...that's fine."

Rue entered, set a small pile of clothes on a chair, and asked, "Do you require anything?" He hadn't placed himself overly close to the tub, but given his height, Ainsley felt as though he loomed over him.

Ainsley shook his head.

"You look troubled."

The fairy had taken two lives and seemed unbothered all together.

"I...I'd never killed anyone before," Ainsley confessed.

"It is a troubling rite, to be sure; to find it unenjoyable is normal."

"You don't seem upset."

Rue gave a horrible, wicked smile. "Perhaps I am abnormal."

Ainsley stared. He drew his knees closer, unnerved by the effect that smile had on him.

"Or more accustomed than most. I served some years in the king's army." Rue took up the towel and spread it open wide. "Come along, I'll show you something that soothed me when I was less experienced."

Ainsley stood without a second thought and stepped into the towel that Rue offered, too transfixed by the sharp planes of the fairy's face and the tranquility of his eyes. Looking into those eyes reminded Ainsley of bottomless water, unfathomably deep and devoid of color.

Rue folded the towel around his shoulders.

Ainsley swayed momentarily and resisted the urge to lean against the fairy. Wet and undressed, the action could be interpreted unfavorably. As an advance, even. He stopped himself and took hold of the towel.

He dried and dressed, though the clothes hung rather loosely.

"I was afraid of that...Here, I'll make some adjustments." Rue reached over and tugged and plucked at the tunic and hose in a few key places.

Not a moment later, Ainsley felt the tingle of magic jittering over his skin and the clothes settled more appropriately against his body. The feeling distracted him, leaving him to wonder about what else Rue could do.

The boots fit on their own.

Rue gestured for Ainsley to follow and he did so, guessing at their destination but also marveling at the suppleness of the boots, the easy comfort of the clothes. Somehow, the fabric captured exactly the right amount of heat, moved with his body so well he felt like he wore nothing without the discomfort of being exposed.

Rue led him over a small bridge that spanned a cheery stream and brought him to the stables.

Ainsley's heart leaped at the sight of Hadley.

Her ears pricked when he approached; she sent a warm huff of air against his chest when she nuzzled her face against him.

Rue placed a curry comb in his hand. "Here."

Ainsley frowned but began to groom Hadley. Within minutes, he understood why Rue had set this task before him. Once he'd groomed the horse and cleaned her tack, his nerves had altogether settled.

He hoped it would last.

While Ainsley had worked, Rue had busied himself visiting the half dozen other stabled horses. He spent the most time with a high-spirited and fine-boned mare who pranced about in her stall at the sight of Rue.

"I know, my love, who's been taking care of you while I was abroad?" Rue whispered to the horse, stroking her face. "We'll ride soon, I swear it."

Compared to the liquid black of Rue's mare, Hadley's brown coat, even freshly groomed, seemed dull. Her build seemed so heavy, earthly and slow, alongside these delicate steeds.

Ainsley gave her an extra pat and assured her that she was a good horse.

"Have you worked up an appetite?" Rue asked.

Ainsley nodded, not sure what else to do. Some numb and distant part of him felt hungry.

"Good. Come along." He extended an arm towards Ainsley, a gesture that could have been one meant to beckon him along, but also could have invited Ainsley to walk close beside him.

Ainsley followed a little closer than he had on the way out and this time he took note of the structure in which he'd awoken.

To call it a house or a castle felt wrong. It seemed to be a place made of earth and trees woven together to create a home. Large and meandering as the place was, Ainsley couldn't tell what was landscape and what was building.

From within, Ainsley had gotten no hint that he'd been inside anything so unusual. It hadn't been dark, cold, or dank, nor had it been crawling with beetles or worms.

"It's beautiful," he said, though the word did no justice.

"Ah, Wolfwood is a sight to behold, is it not? A living marvel of magic and nature," Rue proclaimed with soft pride. "My many-times-great uncle grew it."

"Grew?" Ainsley whispered.

Rue nodded to confirm what he'd said.

"Are..." Ainsley looked out over the lands and saw great expanses of wood in one direction, as well as rising land and the gentle curve of a mountain to the north. "Are there wolves in the forest?"

"Of course, 'twould be a silly name otherwise."

The grounds lacked any barrier that might keep the wolves at bay, not even a fence or small stone wall. Ainsley glanced towards the stables and couldn't help the worry that leaped into his heart when he saw how easily a hungry wolf could access the stables. Hadley wouldn't stand a chance against a pack of such beasts.

"Fret not, sir knight," Rue assured. "I cannot say that the wolves are tame, but they shan't offer you or your steed harm at present."

Ainsley wondered if all fairies talked like that but thought the question might offend Rue. He kept his silence and nodded in acknowledgment.

"After we eat, you may return to your rest, should you wish."

"I'm not tired." Truly, he didn't know if he'd be able to sleep easy ever again.

Other knights...not just knights, common foot soldiers, had taken lives, far more than he, and they all slept. If every man who killed didn't sleep at night, armies would be blown over by a fierce breeze.

No matter that grooming Hadley had soothed him, he doubted it would be enough. He stole a peek towards Rue, almost embarrassed to admit that things still bothered him.

Rue brought him to a large kitchen and settled him at the wooden table, large enough to seat five or six.

He inspected the pot simmering over the hearth, then disappeared into smaller room off to the side, calling, "Dora?" as he went.

In quiet voices, Rue discussed the pot with Dora, then came back out and asked, "Would you care for some barley soup?"

"Just a little, if you don't mind."

"No trouble at all."

Rue set a bowl before Ainsley and settled into a chair to eat his own meal, though he seated himself strangely, tucking one leg under himself and resting his other foot on the seat of the chair, his knee pulled to his chest. He took up a spoon and tucked in, seeming pleased with the barley and mushroom soup.

Ainsley should have been pleased, too, from the rich smell, but he could barely make himself take more than a few bites.

"Is something amiss?" Rue asked.

Ainsley opened his mouth to lie but thought better of it and shrugged. "I don't know."

Rue nodded. "Eat what you can," he advised. "We don't want you wasting away."

After their meal, Rue showed Ainsley a little more of Wolfwood. The library had shelves and shelves of tomes and beautiful stuffed chairs, but Ainsley had never been one for reading. He didn't have the head for it and even now, he struggled to keep the letters straight. A vast, empty hall boasted shimmering, life-like tapestries and Ainsley could have sworn they shifted when he looked away. He had never been one for dancing, either, never once enthralled with any of his partners.

Of all the things he saw, the garden impressed Ainsley the most. Large pools of water, some dark and deep, others shallow and clear called to him. Flowers, bushes, and trees grew freely throughout the area, not constrained by any attempt to organize them by color or species. It gave the impression he'd wandered into some perfect, natural paradise, a slice of what Eden must have been.

The sun trickled through the boughs and illuminated one pool of water, dappling the surface so it shimmered like a jewel.

The sun shone on Ainsley, too, warming his face and shoulders.

"Do you swim?" Rue asked.

"I do."

"We could, if it please you, go for a dip. The water is warm."

Ainsley hesitated.

"Or we could simply walk the grounds a little more."

"Maybe...maybe a different time. For the swim."

Rue nodded and didn't seem to mind either way.

Together, mostly quiet, they walked through the garden. Rue would point out a flower every so often.

They passed a more organized section, comprised more of greens than flowers. He spied a familiar looking bunch of leaves. Parsley.

"Ah, yes, Dora does keep an herb garden, too," Rue told him when he noticed him looking. "Bless her, too, no good fairy home should be without its herbs, but the lord and lady aren't here enough to keep their own...although, I'm sure they would grow fine without tending. Just a little wild."

"You...the lord and lady, you mentioned they wouldn't mind me being here," Ainsley reminded.

"They shan't," Rue assured.

"Shouldn't they, though? A perfect stranger in their home without their invitation."

"You have my invitation, that will suffice."

"Yes, but...but why?"

"Because this is my home, too," Rue explained. "My only home, as I'm not...well, court life doesn't agree with me. Or it agrees with me too well."

"What were you doing in Triviai?"

"My lord and lady sent me abroad in the hopes that it would do my spirit some good. Keep me well."

"Did it?"

With a smile, Rue said, "It did. I found a companion, went a-questing, encountered many a fantastic beast. You know, we haven't got dragons in the Otherworld anymore. They've all gone away, but no one knows where..."

Ainsley stopped walking. Slippery thoughts darted through his mind and he tried to catch them.

Rue continued for a few paces but stopped to look back when he realized Ainsley had left his side. "What?"

"What companion?"

"A gentle knight, with honeyed hair and eyes like moss."

Ainsley swallowed. Blond and green-eyed, like him.

"Fair of face and slight of form," Rue continued.

Warmth and nervousness began to curl together in Ainsley's gut. With Rue's eyes fixed on him like that, he couldn't be talking about anyone else. "I didn't have a companion."

"No?" Rue asked, his mouth tilting up. "What about the crow?"

"But it..." Denial wouldn't serve him here. The crow had been unusual for a bird of any species and the Fair Folk had a reputation for such things. "Why, though? Why were you following me?"

Rue turned away and plucked a flower from a bush. He examined it for some time. "I didn't know how to make introductions. Especially when I first presented myself as a crow. At the start, I thought nothing of it, one more mortal to watch and pester but...well, you conducted yourself admirably with the witches and I, I became quite curious. Interested."

Rue offered Ainsley the flower.

Ainsley took it, not sure what else to do.

"Then I waited too long. I had followed you too long for it to be seemly. But I found myself unable to leave."

"Oh."

"You tell me, how should a fairy go about courting a knight?" Rue asked quietly.

Ainsley's eye snapped to his face, unable to stop staring, to stop searching Rue's face for some hint of jest or mockery. He saw none, though, only warmth and patience.

"I've gone about it wrong, that much I know."

Ainsley took a few paces back, not knowing what to do with himself. He had never spoken of something like this aloud. Even he and Alfred had never given a name to the feelings between them. After the exchange of one too many longing glances, after straying too close to capitulation, they had simply agreed that it would be wiser to be apart, or only together in company.

But to admit to courting...no, that simply wasn't done. Anything to be had would be quick and secret, the cause for prayer and shame.

Except that Ainsley had never been able to summon the right about of shame.

Alfred certainly possessed whole barrels full of shame, but not him. Ainsley had been nervous and frightened, yes, but of being found out. Of being jailed or flogged, or worse, burned.

"That's sin," Ainsley protested weakly, staring at the flower in his hand. He should drop it, crush it beneath his heel, demand to be taken home.

"Not here." Rue kept his distance; he even seemed to be cautious about it, constantly checking over Ainsley to see his posture. "The love between the Green God and the Black is well known."

"Who?"

"The Green, the god of things that grow, and the Black, the god of dark soil, giver of life and warmth..." Rue gestured around the garden as if providing evidence for these gods' existence. "The Blue Lady, overseer of weather and water, and the White Woman..." He pointed to the sky. "The hunt, and light, and the living things that mate. Four eternal forces, and love between all of them in some way."

"I..." Ainsley shook his head.

"Things not of your world, not your gods, this much I know. But they are mine and I tell you, there is no sin here."

The idea certainly held a lot of appeal.

Much more than damnation and hellfire.

Still, he had a human soul, not an Otherworldly one.

Ainsley shook his head again but couldn't release the flower. "I don't know."

Rue regarded him for a moment longer, then dropped his gaze and turned away. "Should we walk some more, you and I? Or would you prefer to turn back now?"

"Let's keep walking."

The garden and the day were too beautiful to turn aside, and no harm had ever come from taking a stroll with someone. How could it?

Oh, yes, a determined priest could have counted a thousand things wrong with this walk, from the fact that Ainsley found Rue particularly captivating to the idea that a good Christian would walk so willingly aside a professed pagan, but Ainsley couldn't bring himself to care.

Ainsley twirled the flower stem between his fingers as they continued through the garden. "All that time," he announced.

Rue glanced his way.

"All that time and you let me go blabbering on like a fool, talking to a crow and a horse when I could have been talking to a person."

The corner of Rue's mouth tugged up. "Would you have welcomed my company?"

"I certainly didn't welcome the crow's! I thought it...you, were an ill omen."

That made the fairy grin. "And was I?"

"I'd have been dead, I think. Without you."

"Then I shall praise all the lucky stars in the heavens that our paths crossed. The world would be much dulled without you in it."

At that, Ainsley flushed so hot he knew his cheeks had colored.

Rue made no more mentions of courting for the rest of the day, not while they walked, fed the horses, or at dinner. He walked Ainsley back to his room when the sky began to darken. They parted ways at the door.

"You'll find me at the end of the hall, the third to last door to the east, should anything trouble you during the night."

"I...I'll be fine, I think," Ainsley answered. A room with a bed and a hearth outshone any tavern or campsite he'd encountered in the past months. Even some of the castles he'd visited had not been so fine; his own home had been clean and comfortable but paled compared to this.

The thought of home sent a pang through him. What would his mother think if she knew he'd found his way to the Otherworld? What would his father think of his reaction to felling a man? What could either of them possibly have to say about Rue?

The fairy nodded and stepped back, making his way towards the door.

"Rue?"

He glanced back.

"Hadley...Those wolves really won't bother her, will they?"

"Rest assured, sir knight, she is safe where she is."

Ainsley nodded. He'd been told all his life to never thank a fairy, but he felt he needed to say something. "I...This is all very kind of you."

Rue smiled. "Good night."

"Good night."

Ainsley couldn't sleep. No matter how deliciously comfortable he managed to get, no matter how warm and safe he felt, sleep wouldn't come because as soon as he shut his eyes, he saw only one thing.

That would-be thief spurting blood, his flesh cleaved and gaping. The gouts that had poured from the others as Rue had made quick work of them.

The attack replayed over and over in his head, interrupted only by worries about wolves and an overarching sense of dread when it came to Rue.

The flower he'd given to Ainsley sat on a small table beside the bed and each time Ainsley tossed and turned, his eyes lighted upon it. He wondered if Rue still intended to court him and knew he shouldn't have. The idea should have sent him running into the woods to take his chances with the wolves, but instead, he worried that Rue had lost interest in him. Especially after seeing him so undone by blood.

Somehow, he didn't think so. Rue had flattered him and more than that, he had looked at Ainsley, gazed at him with clear appreciation.

Maybe sins committed in the Otherworld didn't count against his soul. Maybe God didn't have eyes in this realm.

Ainsley wondered if even considering that counted as blasphemy. He certainly couldn't ask anyone, just as he couldn't ask anyone what it would mean for Rue to court him. He didn't know if the Fair Folk had different manners and rituals concerning such things, though he felt they must.

And like that Ainsley went from worrying about his soul and sin to worrying about what would happen between him and Rue. He worried that

Rue might grow disinterested or impatient, that he might expect things Ainsley couldn't give. A difficult worry, too, because Ainsley had no idea what he could give. He'd never been in the position to find out; anyone with whom he'd shared a mutual attraction had been firmly against investigating.

He even worried that he would be too unpracticed with letting his guard down. It took him by surprise to realize that he wanted to; he had always expected to marry some maiden of his parents choosing, produce a few children, and commit himself to their raising and the care of whatever household he might manage. His elder brother would inherit the family holdings and Ainsley had assumed he'd take up residence in a nearby manor house.

Dithering back and forth over such things wasted his night so that by the time someone knocked on his door, he had barely slept.

He dragged himself out of bed to answer the door.

Rue looked him over and from the look on his face, Ainsley must have looked as haggard as he felt. "Not nightmares, I hope."

Ainsley shook his head. "Restless is all."

"Ah. Might I enter?"

Ainsley hesitated, then stepped back to allow Rue inside the room.

"It is early yet. I could give you something to aid your rest."

"Like what?"

"Magic or herbs, whichever you desire." Rue's gaze skated over him. "Or—"

All his careful debates and considerations from the night vanished and Ainsley rushed to say, "No, no...maybe...maybe a walk will wake me. Especially if the morning still holds a chill."

"Of course." Rue nodded. "Shall I wait for you out of doors?"

"Please."

Rue nodded again and went.

Ainsley washed his face, pulled on his clothes, and headed outside, his stomach bubbling with nerves. He didn't know what Rue had been about to offer and maybe he had assumed too much from a glance, but the other man's eyes had held some unfamiliar look. Affection or something more carnal, Ainsley hadn't been able to tell.

When Ainsley arrived outside, Rue asked, "Shall we walk the garden again, or would you prefer something else?"

"What else is there?"

Rue grinned, then the expression faltered. "It would be a bit of a walk from here...'tis a sight, though."

"I'll survive a walk, even in my enfeebled state."

"Wonderful."

They stopped by the stables to feed the horses, then Rue led him upstream towards the small mountain. Ainsley struggled to keep pace with the taller man's long strides, especially as the ground began to slope upward. After a few glances back, Rue slowed himself to an amble.

The earth beneath them grew steadily more treacherous until, after about an hour, they came to a series of small cascades that fed the stream. Here the stream disappeared underground entirely, turning to a gently flowing spring that emerged from beneath a largish boulder.

"This spring is the source of the River Tadgh," Rue informed him. "If you followed it to its end you would reach the sea."

The steady sound of the cascades, the rush of the stream, and the calls of birds made Ainsley wish for a place to lay down his head.

Almost as if he'd read his mind, Rue gestured towards an enormous, ancient tree. "They say this is the first tree the Green God ever sowed. Whether that be myth or truth, no one knows, but it is the place where King Etriah first spied his bride as he weathered a night beneath its boughs."

Ainsley stared at the tree, taller than any castle and wide enough that were it hollow an entire family and their livestock could live within. He had never seen a tree so vast in his entire life.

Rue moved towards the tree, resting his hand on its trunk the same way he had rested his hand upon his horse's neck.

Ainsley approached more slowly, sure he walked on ground sacred to the Fair Folk. A twig snapped beneath his foot, shattering the peace of the moment, and his eyes snapped towards Rue, terrified to have offended him.

Rue smiled. "Only a twig. Would you like to sit a while?"

"I could."

They settled against the tree together.

"Do you think…" Rue began, quietly, then trailed off.

Ainsley looked at him, waiting, then wondering if he'd said anything in the first place. "Do I think what?"

"There are a great many beautiful things here. Would it please you to stay and see them?" Rue asked solemnly. "With me."

How many mortal knights got the chance to tour the Otherworld and with a guide to boot? At present, he had no wish to go home and return to bumbling his way through quests. Maybe staying here for a while would soothe his nerves enough so that he could pick up a sword with confidence again. "It would."

A smile broke on Rue's face. "It would please me to show them to you."

Comfortable beneath the tree and looking forward to whatever else the Otherworld might hold for him, Ainsley relaxed enough to move a little closer to Rue. He hoped the shift of his body was subtle, but Rue glanced towards him anyway.

Ainsley stifled a yawn with the crook of his elbow.

"Come here and rest your head," Rue offered.

Ainsley scooted a few more inches toward the other man.

Rue placed an arm around Ainsley's shoulders, the contact enough to send shivers through Ainsley. Not enough, though, to banish the sleepiness that settled over him.

A sleepless night, a long walk, and the lull of the spring were all enough to tug at the lids of his eyes; the warmth of Rue's body sealed his fate. Ainsley nestled further into his arm, rested his head against his shoulder, and closed his eyes. Within moments, he fell asleep.

When he woke, the sun had climbed high above them.

"Ah, our gentle knight wakes..." Rue murmured when Ainsley stirred.

Ainsley straightened up, what remained of his drowsiness chased away by embarrassment. "I'm sorry, I...has it been ages?"

"I consider the hours well spent."

Lounging against the tree with one leg bent and lolling to the right, his hair swept off to one side and over one shoulder, Rue looked...in truth, he looked beautiful. It was something more than that, too. He looked confident and utterly unguarded.

Ainsley wanted that confidence. He also wanted to be in Rue's arms again, in a different way this time, and for the first time in his life, he thought that he might be allowed such an indulgence.

Rue watched him, likely taking in each shift and fidget, maybe trying to puzzle out the expression on Ainsley's face.

Or maybe he knew all along what Ainsley meant to do because when Ainsley returned to his side and nestled up against him again, Rue adjusted himself easily. He even drew Ainsley in closer.

"From the top of the far mountains, you can see all the way to the sea on a clear day. A three day climb to the peak, though most pass through the Noor Valley. Safer and quicker..." Rue glanced up at the tree, his face dappled by sunlight. "Dora mentioned it might rain this afternoon. It might be wisest to head back."

Ainsley nodded and began to stand. It would be foolish to disagree but hated to leave this moment behind.

As they started back, Rue linked hands with him.

The barest bit of skin against skin made Ainsley's stomach flutter.

Was it all too soon? Too easy? Ainsley couldn't make himself care. Unreality shaded everything that happened here and made it easy to disregard a lifetime of doctrine and stigma all for the warm thrill of holding another man's hand.

By the time they made it back to Wolfwood the skies had darkened, but it had not yet started to rain.

Ainsley got his first glimpse of the other people in the house that day when, as they ate, a woman with patches of shimmering yellowish-green scales and something that looked like lakeweed and cattails for hair passed through. She glanced over Ainsley, asked Rue if he needed anything, and then went about whatever her original task had been.

The rest of the day they spent in the library. Rue sprawled in one of the stuffed chairs with a slim volume in a language Ainsley didn't recognize. Ainsley stared up at the framed map of Wolfwood and the surrounding area that hung on one wall.

He had never left Triviai before. He'd never even traveled the entire kingdom, truth be told, and he had thought that seeing it from border to border could serve as a goal.

Would anyone believe his tale when he went home?

King Jannes had a vast interest in magical and unnatural things, maybe he would even want to hear the story from Ainsley's own lips.

That idea gave him goosebumps.

King Jannes had always given him goosebumps, even when he'd been a page and Jannes hadn't yet taken the throne. Perhaps a decade older than Ainsley and wonderfully made with auburn curls, green eyes, and a rugged build not expected from a man who dedicated his life to arcane magic, it had thrilled Ainsley to see Jannes's eyes and know they shared something, even something as inconsequential as eye color.

"Are you with me still?" Rue inquired softly.

Ainsley pulled himself back to the present and realized he'd been gazing out the window overlong. "I was just thinking."

"Of something lovely, no doubt. Your face had such a dreamy cast to it." Rue set aside his book and left the chair, coming over to peer out the window. "Who is it that's captured your thoughts?"

Ainsley shook his head. "I was thinking of my king, is all."

"Do all knights in your realm think of him with such a look on their face, or should I be envious?"

He couldn't stop the smile that bloomed across his face. "Neither."

Rue returned the smile. "It brings me such relief to hear that."

Ainsley's stomach fluttered with nerves of the best sort. "You." He couldn't get the words out, too filled with butterflies.

"What?"

"You didn't mean that, what you mentioned before? About a fairy courting a knight," Ainsley said.

Rue began to answer, then hesitated. His gaze shifted to something outside. He seemed particularly focused on a songbird when he asked, "Did you mean it when you called such a thing sin?"

Without knowing exactly how to answer, Ainsley ventured, "If it is, then I...I don't think I care." When the words passed his lips, lightness filled Ainsley's chest. He'd waited years to utter that phrase, waited for someone who wouldn't curse him for saying it. "If it is, I'd do it anyway."

"Do I have your permission, then, to court you, sir knight?"

"Only if you'll stop calling me that."

"You dislike it?"

"Ainsley would do fine."

Rue slid his fingers across Ainsley's throat then up through his hair to cradle the back of his head. As he moved in, Ainsley thought that this might be some wicked trick, that the Devil had sent this creature to set him firmly upon the path of damnation. When their lips met, though, Ainsley didn't care. If this was the Devil's work, then the Devil could have him.

He moved in too eagerly, pressing against Rue like some wanton, desperate to make up for a thousand thoughts he'd never let roam free, for all the kisses he'd forgone in his life. He wanted every single one of those kisses and more immediately.

Rue pulled back, though, and gazed down at him. He seemed unaffected, cool and calm.

Ainsley knew he must have looked flushed and sluttish, easier to convince than a whore. Did Rue find him displeasing? Had his willingness been too much? He had no idea what a creature like Rue would want in a partner.

"Forgive me if I've been too bold," Rue said.

"You haven't."

"You mustn't think I expect anything of you. I've barely even declared my intentions. I know you must be..." Rue searched for a word and finally settled on, "Apprehensive."

Ainsley shook his head. The idea to be apprehensive had never even crossed his mind. "No. Should I be?"

"I was," Rue admitted. "It took me five, maybe six, cups of wine to work up the courage to invite my first lover to bed."

"Oh." Ainsley didn't think he would need even a sip of wine, just another kiss. The exact idea of taking Rue to bed hadn't crossed his mind, just hazy blend of need and warmth that had wanted to find some sort of release.

Now that he stopped to think about it, maybe he did need to consider things a little more carefully.

And maybe Rue needed time, too. He had been the one to pull back and that could have been out of concern for Ainsley or his own need to slow things.

The fairy certainly looked like he had something on his mind. Something unpleasant.

Ainsley hated to see it. He took Rue's hand and brought it to his lips. "Penny for your thoughts."

Rue shook his head. "Nothing just...a wisp of a memory, some spider-silk thing clinging where it shouldn't. Let's find a pleasanter subject."

Releasing the fairy's hand, Ainsley leaned in to rest his head against

Rue's chest. "What's it like to fly?"

"Hmm. Oh. Yes, as the crow you mean." Rue wrapped his arm around Ainsley's shoulders and rested his chin on his head. "In fair weather, it's lovely. To see for miles and miles around and float for hours on the right sort of wind. Would you like me to show you?"

"Oh. I...I don't think I want to be a crow."

"And I won't turn you into one. That sort of magic is best left unworked on mortals. It does things to their constitution. And sanity. I mean that I can share with you how I felt, should you wish it."

"Really?"

"It's a simple enough brew, valerian, mugwort, and mullein leaf, shared before sleep, and the right magical adjustments to the spirits of the sleepers."

The idea of his spirit being magically adjusted gave Ainsley some pause. "Uh."

Rue assured, "Safe enough but it can be unnerving...perhaps something better saved for another time, now that I think about it."

"Maybe."

"The map of Wolfwood interested you, yes? There's a volume of maps in here somewhere, I know there is. Perhaps some destination will catch your eye."

Ainsley itched to know what else the Otherworld had to offer and eagerly poured over the book once Rue produced it. He spent the rest of the evening soaking in the geography of the realm, not yet able to decide which he might want to see first. Or at all.

Some places bore terrifying names, like a vast range of mountains far to the north called the Spine of the Revenant, or an expanse of forest called the Lingering Wastes.

When he pointed it out to Rue, the man came over, peered down at the map, and nodded. "Ah, the Wastes are treacherous. The trees and creatures there are all somewhere in un-life. Once a university stood in the center but too many forays into necromantic works saw the thing burned and the lands so afflicted." Rue ran his finger over a black smudge in the center of the forest. "A place for the foolhardy and overconfident to test their luck."

The idea made Ainsley shiver and he searched for something pleasanter. His eyes lighted on a small hill ringed in white flowers. "The Western Court."

Rue touched that illustration, too. "You would see such sights there, a great many wondrous and terrible marvels, and such exquisite horrors. Not a place for the uninitiated. We need a tamer locale before I go exposing you to the Court. Perhaps the Singing Fields or the Cascades of Neve. Or there's a very respectable little town not so far from here."

"Wherever you think we should go."

"How about to bed?" Rue proposed. "Your head keeps nodding and I hope it isn't me boring you."

Ainsley blushed. "Maybe I could use some sleep."

Rue walked him to his room but this time, when he began to say goodnight, Ainsley stopped him.

"I'm worried I won't be able to sleep again." It wasn't the tiredness in the morning that worried him but the relentlessness of his late-night anxieties.

"I'll make you some tea."

"Or you could come lay down with me."

"I. Yes. I'll..." Rue stepped away from the door. "I'll make us both some tea, then."

Ainsley didn't know if he'd done something wrong.

Rue withdrew and headed towards the kitchen. He returned sometime later in a nightdress bearing two mugs of tea.

Ainsley had perched himself on the edge of the bed to wait for him, his own nightdress tugged over his legs so Rue wouldn't think him too immodest.

They sipped their tea quietly, a few words exchanged, but the more they drank, the briefer and more slurred their exchanges. Finally, Rue took the mugs, shuffled over to set them on the mantel above the fireplace, and shuffled back to the bed.

Ainsley turned aside the covers for him. He'd already burrowed himself in among the blankets and pillows. As soon as Rue laid down, Ainsley nestled up to him, too, filled with a lazy affection for the other man.

"Rue?"

"Hmm?"

Some half-formed thought floated through his mind but sleep-clouded as it was, Ainsley couldn't manage to articulate it. Instead, he pressed a kiss to Rue's shoulder, closed his eyes, and fell asleep.

Sleep, though, served him just as poorly as lying awake had. Instead of reimagining the attack, he dreamed of it.

He clawed his way from the dream, trying to rouse himself, and became caught in a strange half-waking state where he tried to sit up or to move but found himself too sluggish. He couldn't tell if he had entered another dream or not. He remained like that for some time, but for how long, he didn't know.

Several quick shakes brought him fully back to reality and his eyes snapped open to find Rue staring down at him, his face illuminated by a small, soft orb of light.

"I wouldn't have woken you except that you were, well, you seemed bothered by something. You were, ah, tossing about rather vigorously."

"I'm glad you did."

"Dreaming?"

"I think so."

Rue slid an arm around his shoulders and pulled him close. He whispered a few words Ainsley couldn't understand then pressed a kiss to his temple. When his lips made contact, warmth slithered across his skin, turning his tense muscles to puddles. "You'll sleep easier now."

Ainsley melted into the bed, oozing out of Rue's grip.

The light above them vanished and Ainsley disappeared into a deep, thoughtless sleep that saw him through until the morning.

A series of similar days and nights passed, the two of them traveling to small, pretty destinations within walking distance of Wolfwood and nestling together when it came time to sleep.

Tonight, when Rue leaned in to kiss Ainsley's temple and send him into a dreamless sleep, Ainsley placed a hand on his chest.

The appeal of sleeping beside someone dimmed when Ainsley couldn't stay conscious long enough to even enjoy the feel of Rue's skin or take in the other man's scent.

"Hmm?" Rue inquired.

"Maybe we could do something else tonight."

A small smile flickered over Rue's face, then disappeared. "Such as?"

Ainsley shrugged. "I don't know, maybe...just. Get to know each other a little better." For five days now, they had shared a bed and exchanged kisses, but not anything more than kisses, and sedate ones at that.

"Ah. Well. What is it that you wish to know about me? Or have me know about you?"

Ainsley moved in closer to the fairy and placed his hand on the other man's thigh.

Rue twitched away just like he always did when Ainsley put a hand on the right side of his body.

"Maybe you could tell me why, um, why you don't like it when I touch you in certain spots."

"I don't mind anywhere you touch."

"But you pull away," Ainsley pointed out. "And you pull away when I kiss you, too."

Gently, Rue explained, "It isn't that I mind. It's reflex, that's all. My right side is somewhat more sensitive. I hate that I've given you the impression I don't enjoy what's passed between us."

Ainsley pressed, "And pulling away from kissing, is that reflex too?" When he saw Rue hesitate, an uncomfortable weight settled on his chest. "I've never done this before. I want to know if I'm doing something wrong."

"You aren't."

"I'm not too...eager?"

Rue laughed. "No, not at all."

"So then...?"

"A fairy cannot lie."

"I know."

"When you ask me these things, do you realize how it holds me captive? To tell the truth, no matter what it is, or to answer not at all?"

"If you don't want to tell me, then that can be the truth," Ainsley offered.

"I don't want to tell you."

Ainsley kissed him and kept it gentle. He couldn't keep his hands from sliding over Rue's ribs, both sides.

Rue flinched but he grabbed Ainsley's wrist before he could withdraw his hand. "It doesn't hurt." He ran his hand up Ainsley's arm and drew him in. "It's been some time since I've taken a lover."

Ainsley nodded. That could explain his hesitance, as far as Ainsley knew. Not that he knew much.

"But I've never in all my life taken one without at least four drinks. Usually, it took more than four."

That explained much more. Ainsley had not seen a single cup of wine or mug of ale in his time here. Nothing but tea and water had passed his lips as far as Ainsley knew.

"Otherwise..."

Ainsley waited and when Rue said nothing else, he reminded, "You don't have to tell me. I only want to know that it's nothing I've done."

"No. I can swear to that." He brought Ainsley in even closer and kissed him, his arms twined around him. "But without my senses clouded, what I've done a hundred times feels different. Without my teeth and lips numb, without my head spinning, without my limbs stripped of all their dexterity...it's different, Ainsley, and I want to feel everything. I want to feel *everything* this time. I want to remember in the morning. What we did and who you are."

"I'd be terribly wounded if you forgot who I was."

Rue nestled his face against Ainsley's throat.

"If I promise to make sure you feel it, do I have your permission to do more than kiss you?" He rested his hand on Rue's knee, his belly quivering at the feel of bare skin, at the idea of moving his hand higher. He slid his hand an inch further up Rue's thigh.

Rue laced his fingers with Ainsley's and pulled his hand away. "Not yet." He kissed Ainsley and wrapped an arm around his waist. He guided Ainsley on to his lap, one knee on either side of his hips.

He continued to kiss Ainsley. His hands strayed all over, sliding over his thighs and hips, up his stomach and down his back.

Ainsley squirmed beneath his touch and soon enough found himself leaking. He resisted the urge to press his length against Rue's belly and writhe against him. His hips bucked forward of their own volition and he had to beg, "Please."

Rue nodded and pulled the nightdress over Ainsley's head. He sighed at the sight of Ainsley undressed. "Here he is, my beautiful knight." He flattened one hand against Ainsley's chest, then dragged it lower until his fingertips skated over Ainsley's shaft, from base to tip.

Ainsley shuddered. He could barely catch his breath when Rue wrapped his hand around him. It took barely anything to undo him, nothing more than half a dozen strokes before he was gasping and spilling over Rue's hand.

He struggled to clear his mind, to think of something to do or say, but the only action his mind could settle on was saying, "I'm sorry." He grabbed his nightdress from where Rue had tossed it and began to dab at Rue's hand. "I'm sorry, it's...it got all over you..."

Rue wrapped his hands around Ainsley's, keeping them still. "Shhh, now."

"I didn't mean—"

"Ainsley," Rue murmured.

Hearing that husky whisper, that voice made of woodsmoke and autumn leaves, speak his name made him shiver.

"Come here." Rue drew Ainsley against him. "Rest your head."

Ainsley burrowed against him, not sure what to do with the churning mix of emotions within him. Everything had been so needful and ecstatic a moment ago. The abrupt departure of that bliss left him somewhere between empty and sad.

Rue started to run his fingers through Ainsley's hair. His touch settled Ainsley until nothing mattered but the feel of his fingers and the beat of his heart.

"I'm sorry," Ainsley whispered again, somehow feeling that he had to apologize.

"It's not unusual, this sort of melancholy."

Ainsley had never heard a single person mention it. He'd made himself spill and never felt like this before. "It happens to you?"

"Not as such, no."

Ainsley didn't feel better.

Perhaps as consolation or a distraction, Rue offered, "The first time I ever touched myself...oh, I had seen, thirteen, maybe twelve summers, and I brought myself to the point of spilling and, well, no one had ever *told* me what would happen. By all the gods, I thought something horrendous had happened to me and I wept. Sobbed all the way through my bath, hoping that if I washed enough no one would ever know."

"I can't imagine you sobbing."

"I'm adept at it."

"What happened?"

"Oh, I kept my hands firmly out of my pants until my uncle took me aside and explained the making of children to me. Once I knew it happened to everyone, I was quite insatiable, as most are at that age."

Ainsley grinned.

Rue kissed his hair and patted him on the flank. "Go on, let's clean up, at any rate."

"Oh. Should I...would you like me to...?"

"Not yet," Rue assured, a hint of a purr slipping into his voice. He nipped at Ainsley's throat. "Shall I wash you or do you think you can manage on your own?"

"I can."

Once they had settled back into bed, Rue offered another snippet from his childhood, this one about the time he had gotten stuck to the web of a moss spider and his cousin had left him there.

"How did you get out?"

"I took off my clothes and ran home in my underthings."

He offered it with a bit of dry humor, but Ainsley couldn't find any amusement. "Are they dangerous, those spiders?"

"Moss spiders? Dangerous to rodents and birds. Maybe a cat or one of those small dogs. For people, their bite causes pain, swelling, nausea, fever. All the usual unpleasantries, I'm sure."

"And your cousin left you there?"

"Left me, forgot about me, what difference does it make? I survived unscathed."

Ainsley tightened his arms around Rue. "Still, it doesn't seem right."

"Right and wrong are such bothersome concepts for the Fair Folk," Rue sighed. "For everyone, from what I've seen of your world. Although maybe not for you, fair and gentle knight that you are."

Ainsley scowled.

Rue drew him in for a kiss, soft and sweet. "Rest. Tomorrow we've a ride ahead of us."

"Oh. To where?"

"The Ruins of Lothfey and the Barrow of Etriah."

"Oh."

"Treasure hunting," Rue added. "In all the tales handed from mother to son, we speak of the fifteen legendary relics, handed from god to fey. The Blue Lady granted Etriah, the king before the court, a lens through which the unknown world could be seen. He used the lens to track his love, seeing the traces her spirit left upon the world. When Baylin smote the king in Lothfey Keep, he shattered the lens. The Lady, in all her kindness, vowed that if recovered, the pieces would rejoin."

Ainsley shouldn't have yawned, but he couldn't stop himself and tried to stifle his yawn against his shoulder.

"So tomorrow we seek the Lady's Lens."

Ainsley nodded and wiggled closer to Rue and more cozily beneath the covers. "Hadley will be glad to get out and stretch her legs."

He drifted to sleep after that, content for a while, though he didn't sleep entirely easily. The man he'd killed still invaded his dreams, but this time so did Rue, and not in the way Ainsley would have liked. Despite Rue's assurances, the way he flinched still worried Ainsley.

In the morning, earlier than they had woken all week, Rue slid out of bed to answer the gentle but insistent knock at the door.

Ainsley refused to acknowledge that he'd woken and tried to fall back asleep as Rue carried out a hushed conversation with Dora then returned to the bed, perching on the side and pressing a kiss to Ainsley's temple. "Wake up," the fairy murmured.

His hand finding its way out from the blankets, Ainsley knotted his fingers in Rue's nightshirt. "A little longer in bed."

"Ainsley, 'tis a long ride from here to there and darkness meets strangers unkindly on these roads."

"What strangers?"

"You, my knight, you are a stranger. I want you safely encamped by the time the sun sets." Rue gathered Ainsley in his arms, bedcovers and all. He nuzzled against Ainsley's neck. "Don't make me carry you to the bath."

"What if I want you to?"

"Then you need only ask," Rue purred. "Anything I have and it is yours."

Deliciously pleased by the answer, Ainsley hummed and stretched. "Anything?"

"Perhaps I'd stop short of wholesale genocide," Rue answered. "Come."

Ainsley stretched once more, pulled on the robe Rue offered, then followed the other man to the washroom.

The fairy stopped in the doorway. "A few things require my attention—"

Ainsley stopped, too, and turned back to look at him. "You won't...you won't come in with me?"

Hesitance scrawled across his face.

"Please."

"You...you get started without me."

Every instinct demanded that he whine and beg to get his way, but Ainsley nodded.

"I'll return in short time, I swear."

Ainsley nodded, watched him go, then went about getting the bath started. He'd struggled to figure out how to fill the tub at first, unversed in magic as he was, until Rue had explained that it wasn't magic, merely plumbing.

The magic came when heating the water. A series of runes ringed the tub and they needed to be activated by touch and voice to function.

Gingerly placing a finger on each rune, he spoke their names as carefully as a priest spoke his prayers. Rue assured him nothing would happen if he misspoke, but at home, miscast spells could have disastrous effects. Ainsley had no wish to be incinerated, turned inside out, or otherwise maimed.

The wood of the tub groaned and creaked softly; the water began to steam after a few minutes.

Ainsley slid into the tub. He'd adjusted easily to life at Wolfwood. Soft beds, plenty of food, and hot baths daily. He could grow fat and lazy here.

He rested his head on the edge of the tub, though he should have been washing if Rue really meant to make haste.

They could make up time on the road, surely. Hadley wouldn't mind a good brisk pace after so long in the stable.

He peeked one eye open when the door creaked. "You should come in."

Rue padded over. "Alas, my gentle knight, there appears to be no room."

Ainsley scowled and sat up.

"Lean forward. I'll come in behind you."

While Ainsley made room for him, Rue came around the other side of the tub. Ainsley heard his nightshirt land on the floor and felt the water ripple as he stepped in. His knees bumped against Ainsley's back, then his legs slid around his hips. One hand found his shoulder and drew him back against Rue's chest.

"We shouldn't dally."

In response, Ainsley located Rue's other arm and drew both his arms around himself, nuzzling against him.

Rue tugged his right arm back and initially, Ainsley took it as his usual flinch, but he persisted and slithered his arm out of Ainsley's grip.

"Rue..."

"The water's hot," the fairy mumbled.

Ainsley began to turn around. "What's that got to do with it?"

Rue planted a hand against Ainsley's shoulder, preventing him from turning too much. "Nothing..."

Ainsley scoffed and tried to turn again.

"Don't."

"Why not?"

He didn't answer.

After some time passed in silence, nothing but the creak of the tub and the gentle slosh of water, Ainsley turned around, pushing past Rue's somewhat slackened defense.

The other man froze, one arm out of the water, his eyes wide.

"Oh." Ainsley shouldn't have stared, but he wanted to take in the extent of the scarring.

Vast swathes of Rue's skin on the right side of his body bore the distinctive discoloration and twisted pattern of burns long since healed. Gray and red melded together in smooth distortion over most of his shoulder and arm, down his flank, and over the outside of his thigh.

Ainsley had seen scarring like that before on knights and soldiers who had seen their share of sieges and on mages who had worked a spell poorly.

"Oh," he repeated and couldn't help but smile at the other man. "Rue."

Terse, the fairy reminded, "I asked you not to turn around." He drew in on himself, tucking his knees close to his chest.

"And I asked you why not," Ainsley countered. "You didn't answer."

"How does one say that? Don't turn around, you'll find me unsightly?"

"Well, no, because it isn't true," Ainsley answered.

Rue's lips twisted. "And capable of lies as you are—"

"Capable is different than actually doing something!" Ainsley snapped. "I'm not a liar."

Rue glared, his eyes burning but the rest of his face completely smooth.

"Besides, weren't...I mean, you weren't ever going to let me see you?" he asked.

"I."

"Rue."

The other man drew in a slow breath, his face softening, but his gaze turning from Ainsley's face. He stared over Ainsley's shoulder as he said, "I haven't let anyone see me undressed in years unless I was well into my cups. Further in than I should have been."

"Why?"

"Because how do you shed your clothes when you know what lies beneath? When you..." Rue swallowed. "When you know the face they'll make and their questions before you've even got one lace untied. Ugly things are unspeakable to the Fair Folk."

"Or maybe the kind of men who will take someone who is too drunk to bed are the kind of men who'll make faces at something out of the ordinary."

"Wings are out of the ordinary, Ainsley, and horns and tails and spots. Scars are wholly ordinary. Just ugly."

"Are wings that out of the ordinary here? Fairies always have wings in the stories at home."

"Don't make this about something else."

"What shall I make it about?" Ainsley asked. "What could I say to you to soothe your worries? That you're beautiful? Achingly beautiful. And kind to me. That you saved my life. That your voice alone is enough to thrill me. I can tell you that I don't see an inch of ugliness on you if that's what you want to know."

Rue had fixed his eyes on the water in front of him.

"Give me your hand." Ainsley held out his hand.

Rue's eyes darted up.

He wiggled his fingers a little.

With great hesitance, Rue placed his hand in Ainsley's.

"Did I make the same face as your past lovers?"

"No."

"And did I ask the same questions?"

"No."

Ainsley kissed his knuckles. "So then trust that my heart is different than theirs too."

Rue's eyes glittered; he blinked several times. "I." He drew in a breath. "I suppose I have no choice but to take your word."

As much as Ainsley hated that answer, he accepted it. He brought Rue into his arms, wrapping him up in the warmest embrace he could manage, hoping it could melt a little of the strangeness that had put itself between them. "I'm sorry."

"What?"

"I'm sorry that this was hard for you. I wish I could have made it easier."

"You shouldn't have turned around."

"I...Rue, if you'd just given me a reason, I wouldn't have."

Rue pulled back. "Will a reason be required for everything to which I don't wish to consent?"

"I didn't mean it like that," Ainsley rushed to say. "I mean...if you'd...I don't know. I didn't imagine that, that looking at you would be something I'd need permission for. I didn't know it would hurt you. I swear I didn't. And I'm sorry. And I won't..." A sting in his eyes and tightness in the back of his throat took Ainsley by surprise. "Are you very angry?"

"No."

"Have I ruined things?" Ainsley couldn't banish the idea that he had done some terrible damage to their relationship, new as it was. Whatever Rue had liked about him, whatever he had admired must have surely paled given this transgression.

Rue's face softened and he cooed, "Oh, my gentle knight, no. It would take so much more to make me think of you harshly. I forget your youth. And your innocence." He skimmed his fingers over Ainsley's cheek and leaned in to kiss the top of his head. "I forget that you act without malice or deception."

Ainsley wrapped his arms around Rue once more.

Rue returned the embrace, tightening his grip so fiercely Ainsley's ribs ached. He pressed his lips to Ainsley's shoulder, then released him.

By the time they had finished their bath, things had eased back to normal. A quick breakfast saw a smile on Rue's face and by the time they'd saddled their horse, Ainsley had almost forgotten the incident altogether.

Instead, now he focused on the sword Rue held out to him, gingerly held by the scabbard. His sword. He stared at the hilt. "Will it be dangerous?"

"I would rather be overprepared."

Touching the sword sent a chill and a small wave of nausea through Ainsley, but he fought it back and tied the sword down to his saddle. Better than strapping it to his hip but still accessible if he really needed it. He hoped he wouldn't.

He looked over to see that Rue had stored his knife in the same way.

"What sort of danger should I be looking out for?"

"Ah, dear Ainsley, that brings us to the most troublesome part. Your eyes, fair though they be, may well be useless when it comes to spotting danger. Vigilance will be my charge." Rue ran his fingers along the shirt of mail he'd given Ainsley to wear that day. This shirt had links of something other than iron or steel, judging by its lightness and purplish sheen. "But all this is precaution for something that will not come to pass so long as we make just a *little* haste and begin our journey."

Ainsley blushed at the teasing, gave Hadley's tack a last once over, then pulled himself into the saddle.

Rue swung up into the saddle with a slinking grace that made Ainsley seem half-drunk in comparison.

Between the light, jaunty gait of his black mare, his easy confidence in the saddle, and the beauty of his garments and form, Rue looked every bit the fairy of stories, come to lure unsuspecting mortals to the Otherworld. He urged his mount into a trot and Ainsley watched him, too enchanted to do anything but stare.

"Come along! Or have you forgotten how to ride?" Rue called back.

If it had been any other man, Ainsley would have said something boastful and challenging. Most men teased, though, because they took

Ainsley for an easy target, someone easily outstripped in most feats.

Instead, he followed him, unhurried but not dawdling. Once he caught up, he asked, "Tell me more about this place."

"Which place in particular?" Rue asked. "The summer estate, the Otherworld, our destination, the path we take to get there?"

"Any of them," After a moment, he amended, "All of them."

"Mmmm. Have I told you fully about Milt?"

"Who?"

"The mage-architect of Wolfwood?"

"No. Just that he built it."

"The youngest son of Petyn the Vain, Milt spent his childhood in the wilds of the Meridian Court, lost some thirty years," Rue began.

"Thirty years!"

"Mmm."

"It took thirty years to find him."

"Oh, no. It took thirty years for him to find his way home. Petyn wasted not his time searching for the youngest of his brood. By the time Milt came home, he was no longer the youngest of Petyn's sons five times over."

"But not to look for him at all?"

"His father was called Vain, not Tender-hearted," Rue pointed out.

Ainsley thought that a parent should have gone looking for their child, no matter how vain.

Rue continued, "Forever touched by his time in the wilds, Milt struggled to find a home for himself among the Western Court. Finally, he struck out on his own and, one night, as he slept beside the Tadgh, he slept without dreaming for the first time since his return. Thus, he decided that place would be his home. First, it was one room, then it was two...Wolfwood grew slowly over years. He bequeathed it to a niece upon his death and she was shocked to find that her mad uncle had built something so beautiful. They'd all imagined him living as a hermit, not as a lesser god of the wood."

"How'd he decide who to give it to?"

"Oh, I don't think he had any particular fondness for her. She happened to be getting married around the same time that he started to plan his suicide. I suppose it made sense to him."

Ainsley's gaze snapped over to Rue.

With a small smile, he said, "You didn't think a man abandoned and alone for most of his life would find a happy ending, did you?"

"I...I suppose I had assumed."

"No. Milt took his life. On the west wall of Wolfwood, you can find the last room he built. You can...in the design of the room itself, you can see him give up."

"Oh. Well."

"But regardless, that is how Wolfwood came to be the summer estate."

Ainsley rubbed his nose. "Do all the places you mentioned have a sad story to go with them?"

Rue thought for a moment, his nose wrinkling slightly and his lips somewhat pursed. "A great many places in the Otherworld have somewhat dolorous tales in their histories, but cannot that be said of most places in every realm? Wolfwood's origins may be disheartening, but many wonderful things have come to pass within its walls. Lothfey Keep saw bloodshed, but before that, it was home to happy families, the sight of many weddings and births...It's all...the world cannot be all happy stories. The apple tree where you break your arm may also be the tree beneath which you receive your first kiss."

"So then tell me a nicer story this time," Ainsley requested.

"Maybe it's your turn to tell a story."

"I don't know any stories."

"I'm sure you know many stories. You refer to them all the time. Tell me what a child in your realm learns at his mother's knee."

"Um. Well. My mother used to tell me about the goose that laid the golden egg."

"Sounds a wondrous tale. Relate it to me."

"Uh, once there was a farmer who had a goose that laid a golden egg every day. He thought that the goose must have some large piece of gold within it. He decided, then, to kill it and get all of the gold all at once. Except that when he slaughtered it, he found that its guts were no different than any other goose."

Rue remained quiet for some time, then looked over and asked, "Is that it?"

"Hm?"

"The farmer didn't...I don't know, try to find some witch to bring the goose back to life? Or scour the world looking for another?"

"No, I don't. I don't think so."

"Were they solid eggs? Or was it just the shells?"

"I don't know."

Rue said nothing again, keeping his silence for much longer than he had last time. Finally, he announced, "I think it must have been just the shells. Geese don't lay eggs that are shell all the way through, so it wouldn't lay an egg that was gold all the way through. Do you think he ever tried to hatch the golden eggs?"

"I've never thought about it that much."

Rue went quiet again, then demanded, "Tell me another one. I think I need to hear more of them before I can unravel it."

"Uh. Once there was a fox stuck in a trap outside the farmer's henhouse. When the cock—"

"The what?"

"The cock," Ainsley repeated, then looked over to see a wicked smile on Rue's lips. He scowled.

"Please, go on."

He sucked in a breath, sighed, then continued, "When the cock saw the fox trapped, he looked upon him for a bit. The fox said that he had been on his way to visit a sick friend and needed to be on his way, but the cock knew better and went on crowing, rousing the whole henhouse and the farmer himself. And that was the end of the fox."

"Ah. I understand this one. The fox wasn't a clever enough liar," Rue announced. "One more."

Ainsley grinned. "The swallow and the crow argued over their feathers. The swallow declared that his were fine and bright and downy, that the crow should have pride and care for himself better. The crow said that the swallow's feathers did well by him in the spring, but he'd never seen the swallow in the winter and that, said the crow, was when he enjoyed himself best."

Rue frowned and didn't speak for a long time. In the end, he demanded, "Tell me the answer. This one is lost on me."

"They aren't riddles."

"Well, they aren't very good stories either," Rue sniffed.

Ainsley laughed. "Then it's your turn."

Rue told him more of the battle that had occurred at their destination; Baylin had acted against Etriah hoping to win his crown. Baylin had felled the king and rule for some years until Etriah's daughter had reclaimed her rightful throne.

From what Ainsley had heard of the battle at Lothfey Keep, he expected to see ruins weathered by centuries, the broken edges softened, the grass regrown, the soot marks washed away. Instead, the castle looked as if it had been besieged a few days ago. He thought he still saw blood soaked into the grass in places.

A large heap of fresh earth ringed with a vast garland of white flowers loomed to the south of the battlefield.

"When Baylin realized the lens had been shattered, he called together all the mages he could find and had them freeze the keep in time. Here it has been ten days since the battle ended," Rue explained.

"It's..." Ainsley breathed. "Has it really been standing still for so long?"

"The spell has begun to weaken." Rue slid off his mount. "New flowers are blooming." He offered a hand to help Ainsley down from his.

Ainsley didn't take it. He didn't need help. He did link his fingers with Rue's, though, once he had his feet on the ground.

The sun lingered above the horizon.

Rue went to set up a tent along the shore of the lake beside the keep. Not within the ground of the battlefield, though; far enough that the grass had regrown, that new trees had sprung up. While he pitched the tent, Ainsley made towards the woods to search for firewood.

He hadn't made it far enough into the woods to crush a single leaf underfoot. He whirled when he heard a rush of footsteps behind him.

Rue threw his arms around him, dragging him close. Pulling him away from the woods. "No, no, not into the woods, never into the woods alone, please."

"I...I. I thought we'd need firewood."

Rue smoothed back his hair, cradled his cheek with one hand. "I know. I'll get it. You see to the tent."

Ainsley nodded, shaken, still, and hating the trembling in his limbs. He wiggled his way out of the mail shirt, finished the tent and gathered the largest stones he could find in the surrounding area. He dug a shallow hole and lined it with stones. By the time Rue returned, his arms full of branches, Ainsley had untacked the horses and tethered them.

He felt useless watching Rue and the feeling sat in his gut as the fairy knelt and began to pile in tinder and twigs to make a fire.

He forgot to feel useless when Rue leaned in close and whispered life into the fire. The kindling took and Rue fed larger sticks into the flame. He kissed the top of Ainsley's head and said, "Mind that for me."

He took up a long stick from the pile and dragged it in the sand behind him as he circled around the tent and horses.

"What are you doing?" Ainsley asked, watching him circle three times clockwise, then three times counterclockwise.

"Staking my claim." Rue set the stick aside by the fire and settled into the sand beside Ainsley. He wrapped an arm around Ainsley's waist and rested a head on his shoulder. "How do you feel?"

"I haven't spent that long out of the saddle in years."

"Sore?"

"A little. But in a good way." He leaned against Rue. His stomach rumbled. They'd eaten a light breakfast and Rue had hurried their midday meal, too. He didn't move, though. He liked being in Rue's arms too much.

Rue started to get up. "I'll—"

"Don't go anywhere."

"We should eat."

"Mmm, not yet." He tightened his arms around Rue. "I could stay like this forever."

"You'd waste away."

Ainsley ignored that warning and turned his head, nipping at Rue's ear.

The fairy squirmed a little and at first, Ainsley thought he'd provoked discomfort in the other man again. Instead, Rue turned and sealed his mouth over Ainsley's. He raked his hands through Ainsley's hair and dragged him in.

And then Rue was pushing him back, on to the sand, and straddling him.

They locked themselves together, hands roaming, arching against each other. When Ainsley slid his hands inside Rue's clothes, though, he pulled back.

"I'm sorry," Ainsley offered immediately.

Rue shook his head and began to work Ainsley out of his clothes without shedding any of his.

"Wait, Rue, wait a moment."

"What's wrong?"

"It's...I've got sand all over me."

Rue laughed and gave him one last kiss, then pulled him up. "I did suggest we eat."

Ainsley waffled between what he wanted, but the sheer amount of sand that trickled into his clothing put a damper on his mood. He hadn't even gotten fully undressed; he didn't want to think about what it would be like trying to do anything with sand grinding into his more sensitive parts.

"I'll move the tent tomorrow night, we can make love on the grass, and you can complain of twigs and leaves instead of sand."

Ainsley flushed at the idea, well aware that Rue was teasing. "I'm not complaining."

Rue swooped in for one last kiss. "I find that blush of yours so appealing. Does that make me a wicked creature? Tormenting you for my own pleasure?"

A shiver, so strong it was nearly violent, shook Ainsley.

Rue turned away from him to tend the fire and set up a cooking pot over the flame. He put barley, water, and onions in the pot. He then set about cutting apples and hunks of salted meat with a treacherously sharp and wicked looking blade that Ainsley assumed had not been created as a cooking knife.

When he noticed Ainsley watching, he held up the blade so it flashed in the firelight. "I present to you Falconclaw, handed these generations from father to son. Now it is yours. May it serve you as well as you serve your king. Go, Brightling, and do not disappoint." He gave Ainsley a grin. "I'd already disappointed him mightily, though. My father. He wanted an alchemist for a son, to follow in his footsteps. Instead, he got a man who trembles at the sight of a flask."

"I...Oh." Words eluded Ainsley and he gaped somewhat.

Rue resumed his cutting of ingredients, tossing them into the pot as he went. "While my mother birthed me, my father walked the halls. He stepped out for air, bothered by my mother's screams. He waited for me and the world eclipsed the moon. He watched the eclipse and as he did, while the world went dark, a shooting star passed across the sky. He took it as a sign that I would be like him. He called me Brightling and knew...my father *knew* without a doubt that passion for fire would burn in me as hot as it did in him."

Unease began to grow in Ainsley's gut.

"I never loved the flame as he did, but I loved my father." He tipped the last of the salted meat into the pot and fixed his eyes on the campfire. "I loved to work beside him. That he trusted me in his laboratory better than he trusted his assistants made my heart swell and overflow. No matter how the wine fouled his breath or slurred his words. 'Good work, Brightling.' It was all I needed."

Ainsley shifted, rapt but anxious.

"I was eight. A flask of a new formula for alchemical fire hadn't been corked properly. 'Fetch the new one for me, Brightling,' said he and I scampered to do it, climbed up on to the stool to reach it as a squirrel scurries for acorns. One sway and then..." Rue brought his fingers together and made a gesture that imitated a flame's ignition. "And then..." he murmured.

Without thinking about it, Ainsley moved in and slid his arms around Rue. He didn't expect Rue to fold so easily into his embrace, but he did, burrowing into Ainsley's arms.

"Queen Corva called for me to come to court when I was nine. Her son was four years my senior and she thought he needed a companion. My parents gladly sent me. I saw my father again when I reached twenty. He gave me the blade and relinquished me to the king's army without a single 'be careful' or 'come safely home to me'."

His words wrapped around Ainsley's chest, tightening so that he couldn't breathe. How could Rue relate all this so coolly, without a sniffle or a stutter? Compelled by the ache in his heart, Ainsley kissed the fairy's temple and softly offered, "Thou art altogether beautiful, my darling, and there is no flaw in thee."

"My darling," Rue echoed. "I could grow accustomed to that. I could grow accustomed to you reciting poetry to me, too."

"It's from the Song of Songs."

"What's that?"

"It's part of the Bible. The word of God. It's about the love between a man and his bride."

"And you know all of it?"

"My mother does. She loves the Bible, loves our Lord, but she loves the Song of Songs best. More than she should, everyone says, but I never understood that. I've heard people say that my parents love each other too much, that it's unseemly. Love is...foolish, I suppose. Distracting and irresponsible," Ainsley shared. He had never seen a lord and lady so enamored of each other, so public with their affections.

He continued, "Marriages are for children and brokering deals between families and so many people are unhappy I think they hate that my parents aren't. 'I delight to sit in his shade, and his fruit is sweet to my taste,' Mother always says when people tell her she's being unladylike. Doesn't that give you shivers? 'Sweet to my taste'."

"Hearing you say it nearly makes me tremble. Perhaps I could eat the words from your very mouth and have naught but that to eat for a thousand years and I would be plump and happy as a bear before winter," Rue pronounced.

Ainsley tightened his arms.

They remained snuggled together while their dinner cooked, one of them moving every so often to stir the stew. After they ate, both sedated by a long ride and hearty meal, they retired to their tent and curled together beneath their blankets like cats in the sun.

Before they fell asleep, though, Ainsley covered Rue with lazy kisses and worked his hands inside his clothes.

Maybe comforted by Ainsley's assurances that his scars held no ugliness, or maybe too drowsy to worry, Rue allowed Ainsley to caress him to completion, rolling his hips and pressing close.

The fairy nodded off not long afterward and Ainsley, hating to disturb him for something as petty as washing his hand, used his tunic to wipe up as best he could.

In the morning, he woke before Rue and washed himself and his clothes in the lake.

He didn't realize Rue had come out of the tent until the other man gave a shrill, lecherous whistle. He startled and whirled around, then scowled.

"Ah, don't pout, you might break my heart."

"I'll pout less if you come in with me," Ainsley answered.

Rue hesitated, a harried look of calculation flashing across his face before his eyes flicked over Ainsley's body once more. After a full battle played out on his face, he tugged his tunic over his head and headed towards the water.

Ainsley sloshed up to the shore to embrace him.

"Oh, it's *cold*," Rue gasped.

"I'll keep you warm." Ainsley kissed him and drew in deeper into the water.

"You're cold, too."

"Then you can keep me warm."

In the end, it took them a while to get to the actual washing, but they managed to clean and feed themselves before the sun rose too far above the horizon.

The ruins of Lothfey had not crumbled with age but had been thoroughly battered in a siege. Walls tumbled to the ground and whole towers sat in piles. While Rue poked around in the rubble, Ainsley combed through what remained of the keep. Most of it had burned and he sifted through ash and charcoal more than actual furnishings.

They searched for a shard of glass about the size of a man's hand, Rue said.

Ainsley wanted more detail than that to go on before he discounted anything, so he gathered up all the pieces of glass he came across, no matter how small. He finished up his search of the northernmost tower and returned to find Rue shifting chunks of stone from one of the larger heaps.

"Any luck?"

Ainsley showed him the few pieces of glass he had found.

Rue peered at them, then shook his head. "Ah, alas, none of these be what we seek."

"I didn't think they were. Not really." He glanced out over the enchanted area. "I don't think we'll look through everything in a day."

"Two days. We depart on the third morning."

"Oh."

"Unless you'd prefer something else."

"No."

Rue gave him a quick smile and returned to sifting through the rubble. After a minute, though, he looked up and asked, "What?"

"Nothing."

He held out a hand and when Ainsley took it, he pressed his lips to the back of Ainsley's hand. "Would you rather do something else?"

He looked down at the soot that had worked its way into the creases of his fingers. "I'm going to wash my hands."

Rue nodded.

Ainsley made his way to the nearest part of the lake and dunked his hands in the water, scrubbing them as best he could.

The burial mound to the south caught his eye and he wandered that way. He paced around the barrow, carefully keeping away from the fresh-turned ground and flower garland. An unpleasantly large and spindly spider crawled out from beneath the garland and made its way on to the dirt.

Revulsion and fascination wrestled inside him. He had never seen such a large spider before, nor one that boasted such bright colors. Its fat blue abdomen glittered in the sunlight, yellow stripes winking. It settled onto the center of the mound, a leg twitching every so often.

He leaned in a little closer, but not too close.

The spider wiggled its front legs somewhat.

"What manner of beasty are you?" he asked.

He expected no answer, of course, but he got a bloodcurdling screech in return. He leaped back from the barrow, his heart in his throat. As he scrambled away, Rue sprinted to his side.

Rue immediately skimmed his hands over Ainsley, checking him over and asking, "Are you well?"

"That wasn't me." He gestured to the spider, which hadn't moved.

"Oh, well, what are you?" Rue asked, frowning at the spider.

It emitted the same screech.

Rue flinched from the sound, his hand tightening on Ainsley's arm. "Gracious."

"Do you know what it is?"

"It be a most monstrous spider so far as this humble explorer can discern."

Ainsley wrinkled his nose.

Rue gave him a wide grin. He extracted himself from Ainsley's side and crouched beside the barrow. "What sort of thing be ye to so sully the barrow of the king before the court?" Rue demanded.

The spider let out another shriek and seemed to waggle a leg towards Rue.

"Keep an eye on our friend. I'll return in a moment."

When he returned, he came bearing a cracked and singed plate upon which he had set a small cake and a glass vial.

From the golden color of the liquid, Ainsley thought it was ale, but when he uncorked it and drizzled it over the cake, Ainsley caught the thick, sweet scent of honey.

"'Tis my share of the cakes, worry not," Rue comforted when he noticed Ainsley watching. He placed the plate atop the mound, asking forgiveness from the deceased king under his breath.

He withdrew his hand and the spider approached the plate and began to nibble at the cake. Once it had gotten a good taste, it proceeded to eat the entire cake, shoveling hunks into its mouth.

It finished its meal and then stood up on its last pair of legs and stretched upwards. Its shape changed somewhat; the thing became less arachnid and more humanoid, creating an unholy looking little beast the size of a child's forearm.

Rue gave a small nod of his head.

The little creature titled up his chin.

"Thine feet be upon the grave of the father of my line."

At that, the spider-thing bowed.

"I seek the lens."

The beast nodded, crouched, and began to dig into the barrow.

Rue flinched at the sight and drew in a small breath.

Finally, the spider straightened up, a sliver of glass grasped in what passed for one of its hands. It handed over the shard to Rue with a bow, then scuttled away, returning to its spider form as it went.

Rue carefully held the lens in his hand and stared at the barrow.

"Would you like me to fix it?" Ainsley asked, worried the pale glimpse of something he saw poking out of the soil might be the fallen king.

Rue nodded without taking his eyes from the shard in his hand.

Carefully, Ainsley moved aside the garland, pushed the dirt of the barrow back into place, and patted it down. He returned the garland and then, feeling it necessary and good manners, said a small prayer for the king.

He found Rue at their tent, wrapping the shard in a length of cloth. "You look upset."

"Shocked. I didn't think we would find it. People have looked for generations."

"Would you rather not have found it?"

"No. I'm glad. Relieved."

Ainsley sat beside him. "I know we'll have to camp here for another night, but..."

"Two days. Dora needs to finish preparing for the lord and lady and it is easier to do without anyone underfoot."

"Oh, have we been underfoot?" Ainsley asked. He hadn't gotten the impression that Dora even noticed him much.

"We would have been had we stayed. Cleaning to do and rooms to get ready." Rue knotted a length of twine around the cloth bundled and stored it in his pack. "She'll need to ready the guest rooms, too. They won't be coming unaccompanied."

"And I've been staying in one of the guest rooms?"

"Yes. You're welcome to it, though, they won't turn you away. Unless they've brought a great many courtiers with them, in which case you may have to move to one of the smaller rooms...though that depends on who they've brought with them. I'm not sure how a human knight ranks compared to members of the Court..." Rue made an apologetic face. "Although."

"Although what?" Ainsley prompted.

"You could leave the guest rooms altogether. My rooms have space enough for two."

Ainsley nodded. "I'd like that."

"You wouldn't prefer to have your own quarters? I don't want you to feel set aside."

"I don't think I will."

Rue set his hand on his pack again.

Thinking about the shard, Ainsley guessed. He gave him a moment longer to think before he asked, "What should we do with the rest of our day?"

"Unless my ears fool me, it sounds as though you have an idea as to what you'd like to do?"

Ainsley blushed to know he'd been so obvious. "I want to swim out to that island." Grassy and green, like a jewel on blue velvet, the island had called to him since he'd spied it from the north tower that morning.

"It's far."

"I'm a good swimmer. As long as there isn't anything unsavory in the water."

"Not in these waters. Here 'tis the woods that should cause concern. Elsewhere in the Otherworld, I'd warn of kelpies and selkies, naiads and nokken...but this lake is tame. I learned to swim in this lake."

Ainsley took his hand. "Then let's go."

Rue hesitated.

"Unless you're worried that a mortal might outswim you."

"No such worry has ever darkened my heart," Rue assured.

Ainsley tugged on his hand. When he didn't come along immediately, Ainsley exited the tent and started to work off his boots. By the time Rue had joined him, he'd stripped entirely. Without waiting, he headed towards the lakeshore, delighted to hear rustling and huffs coming from behind him. A glance back told him Rue had started to shed his clothes as well.

He sloshed out up to his hips by the time he heard Rue make his way into the water as well.

He glanced back once more to confirm Rue's location but saw nothing but ripples. He swung his head the other way and still couldn't catch sight of the fairy.

A hand, wet and cool, flickered across his back and he leaped and shouted. "How...!" he demanded when he found Rue standing beside him.

"Mortal eyes are easy to deceive."

Ainsley crossed his arms and snorted. "You probably turned into a fish."

Rue clasped a hand to his chest, indignant as anything. "I? A fish? You think I would so shame myself?"

"You were a crow."

"Crows are clever. Fish are not."

"So?"

Rue didn't answer, just grinned, and leaped away into the water, disappearing beneath the surface with hardly a splash. His dark form streaked through the water, barely visible except for his pale hair and the occasional hint of pink from his scars.

Ainsley followed him, endeavoring to catch up with him. Once he had, he wrapped his arms around the fairy.

Neither of them hastened towards the island, both stopping to splash the other or float in the water. Slow, lazy strokes brought them to the grassy shore within the hour though. They lay in the grass, the heat from the sun soaking into them.

Ainsley hooked one leg around one of Rue's and wiggled closer.

The fairy had his face turned toward the sun, his eyes closed. "Hmm?"

"Mmm." He kissed Rue's shoulder.

Rue peeked at him with one eye. "That sounded melancholy."

"There were so many times just like this when I was young, except that it could never *be* like this at home. Friends but never anything more."

"Ah."

"I wish it could have been."

Rue brushed his fingers over his cheek. "I wish your world was kinder. And mine too. There is always some reason to be unkind to one another. Not you, though, you were never unkind."

"I'm no saint."

"There were so many creatures you should have slain, but you were gentle, Ainsley. And that's more beautiful than your eyes, though they be gems, or your hair, though it be gold."

"Flatterer."

"I cannot lie," he reminded.

Ainsley, to his own surprise, let out a soft, hungry growl; a voice should not have so much power over him. Though, he imagined, it helped that the voice belonged to such a splendid creature as Rue. He rolled half on top of him and slid his tongue inside the other man's mouth before he'd even thought about it.

Rue responded in kind, wrapping his arms around Ainsley and pulling him more fully on top of him.

Without having to fumble with any clothes, things moved quickly from kisses to caressing. Having so much Rue's skin against his made his own skin flush, overly sensitive and wantonly desperate for more.

"In whichever manner you might wish to proceed, Ainsley, I would have few objections."

Ainsley didn't know how Rue had the wherewithal to put together such a long sentence let alone utter it so calmly. He paused in his shameless kissing and wiggling against Rue and tried to process what the other man had said more fully. "I." He realized a little better what Rue offered. "Yes. I think we should."

Rue chuckled. "Should what, my love?"

"Lay together."

"Mmhm. Like this?"

"I...no." Ainsley licked his lips. He had no idea what to do, nothing to guide him but instinct and buried fantasies. One whim floated to the top of his mind. "On, on your belly. If you want."

Rue grinned up at him, his eyes flashing. Somehow, he managed to seamlessly maneuver himself from his back to his stomach.

Ainsley wouldn't have been able to manage it. He could scarcely manage most basic movements in his current state. Over and over, the vastness of his inexperience stilled his hand. The sight of Rue laid out before him, the firmly muscled expanse of his back and rear begging to be touched, overwhelmed him. He had to ask, "Can you tell me what to do?"

Rue had propped himself up on his elbows and glanced over his shoulder, still grinning. "I absolutely can tell you what to do. I should very much *like* to tell you what to do. Give me your hand."

Ainsley leaned forward.

Rue drew his hand in closer, kissing Ainsley's palm, then whispering into it so softly that Ainsley couldn't make out the words. It tickled, though, and he almost pulled back. He jerked his hand back when something warm and slick oozed into his hand.

Rue didn't release his wrist, though. "I'll teach you the spell some other time."

A spell. Ainsley didn't know if he could learn a spell, but it was better than thinking that Rue had spit into his hand without warning.

"Put it on yourself. And on me."

Ainsley wasn't so naïve that he didn't understand what Rue meant, but still, he hesitated. All the urgency and heat had gone, leaving him uncertain. It seemed such an intimate place to touch and he had to remind himself that of course it was, that laying together was an intimate thing, that not everyone ended up shagging away in a haystack with a tavern girl or the butcher's daughter.

When he'd been young and newly agitated by all the changes of maturing, he'd envied the people who'd found release so easily. After a while, he'd stopped wondering what all the fuss was about. Now he didn't know how the other lads had managed.

He started with himself then eased into touching Rue. "Is that…is that right?"

"Yes."

It wasn't until Rue gave long, delicious hum and lifted his hips to meet his fingers that Ainsley felt he was doing anything correctly, though. After that hum, though, a roll of heat moved through his belly and he worked to provoke other such sounds.

Rue rasped a few other instructions from time to time and soon enough, Ainsley found himself just as eager as he had been before. When Rue granted him permission to enter him, he had to stop himself from moving too fast.

"Gently," had been Rue's request and Ainsley made sure to be gentle. He would have guessed slowness to be maddening from the way other squires had boasted, but it proved wonderful.

He had the chance to feel everything as they moved, every subtle shift in Rue's body, every flushed inch of his skin. As his heart thudded in his chest, a steady, unhurried pressure built inside of him, inside more than just his body, inside the core of his being.

Rue lifted himself from his belly to his knees. He uttered things Ainsley couldn't understand and let out husky cries. His most plaintive plea came when he breathed, "Touch me."

Ainsley wrapped his arms around him, nipping at his throat and shoulders. He molded his hand over Rue's length and stroked him slowly.

After a while, the pressure inside of him became too much to bear. He spilled, gasping and holding on to Rue for dear life.

Rue arched against him, writhing and pleading for release.

Ainsley gave it to him, his heart still thundering as Rue spilled over his hand. He kissed Rue's shoulder and rested his cheek against his back.

Rue extracted himself from his grasp and Ainsley nearly whined at being left so cold and alone. He returned within moments, this time facing Ainsley. He drew Ainsley close so that they nestled together in the grass.

Part of him thought that he should say something, but he couldn't think of anything worth saying. His whole mind had emptied.

Rue combed his fingers through Ainsley's hair and cooed, "What a sweet thing I've found, this lovely knight."

"Rue?"

"Hmm?"

"I'm going to close my eyes."

Rue chuckled and gathered Ainsley further into his arms, giving him a kiss. "Go ahead, my love."

Ainsley, as he nodded off, couldn't stop his fingers from seeking more of Rue's skin. He trailed his fingertips over the edge of Rue's scar, for some reason desperate to touch that spot in particular. "I'm not going to sleep."

"No, of course not."

He buried his face in Rue's side.

He dropped into a light sleep, waking slightly from time to time, and getting a few grunts and hums from Rue in response to his movements. Eventually, the sun had beat down on them for too long and Ainsley started to grow overwarm.

And hungry.

He prodded Rue awake, carefully at first, but then harder when the other man didn't stir. "Rue. Are you awake?"

"I am now."

"I'm hungry."

"Then we should feed you."

Ainsley glanced behind them. They hadn't made it further than the shore and he had genuinely wanted to look around the island.

Rue followed his gaze. "We can linger a little longer. It wouldn't take any longer than...half an hour, I think, to walk the entirety of the island."

Hand in hand, they made a small foray into the island, passing by a few fallen trees and a handful of saplings. Ainsley spotted a toad upon a stump and a vividly purple cluster of mushrooms sitting in the shade of a log.

The sound of whistling wind caught his ear and he began to look around. No breeze blew that day.

"Look." Rue pointed to a small brown bird settled on the branch of one of the taller saplings.

It took Ainsley some time to realize that the sound he heard was not the wind but the bird's call.

"When it's going to rain, the whip sparrow's call will grow louder and louder with how much rain she expects. Hang a chime of her bones outside your window and a storm will never take you unaware, but only if she loved you in life."

"How do you get a bird to love you?"

"Raise her from an egg. Bring her seeds every day. Shoo away the boys from her nest when they come barreling through the wood with their sticks and rocks," Rue offered.

"I can't imagine fairy boys being as cruel as human ones."

"Imagine them being so much crueler."

That sent a shiver through Ainsley and he tightened his hand around Rue's.

Rue tugged him back towards the shore. "I'd like to eat, too, and it's not a short swim."

They made it safely back to their camp, gathered up their clothes, then ate. They spent the rest of the day lazing about and after dinner, Rue presented Ainsley with a cake identical to the one he had given to the spider-creature.

Ainsley broke it in half. "Here."

Rue blinked at the cake. "You're certain?"

"Of course."

"You give it freely?"

"Of course."

Rue took the cake cautiously.

Ainsley darted in to give him a kiss then popped his share of the cake into his mouth. Apples and cinnamon, heavy with honey. Dora, or whichever servant had cooked this, ranked among the best cooks Ainsley had encountered. Everything he'd eaten here had been delicious, sometimes bordering on exquisite. He wondered if King Jannes ate so finely or if fairy kings supped on better fare than mortal ones.

Rue ate his cake more slowly, making Ainsley wonder if he'd been rude to scarf his down. As much as he'd been told that fairies were finicky creatures, he'd managed not to offend Rue yet.

Or...

He glanced over at Rue. "Do I have bad manners?"

"You have human manners."

"I mean...your lord and lady, they'll...I don't want to offend them."

"You've yet to break any of the most important tenants of fairy manners," Rue assured. "No names, no thank-yous—"

"I've told you my name!"

"Not your true name," Rue said.

"Ainsley *is* my true name."

"But not the whole thing, surely?" Rue asked, worry creeping into his voice.

"No," Ainsley agreed. "Not the whole thing."

"Keep it that way."

"Why can't I tell you my name?" Ainsley asked.

"I could control you with it."

Ainsley wrinkled his nose. "I don't think it's the same with humans."

"Still. I don't want to risk anything."

"Is Rue not your name?"

"That would be a rude question," the fairy pointed out.

"Oh, I. I'm sorry."

Rue combed his fingers through Ainsley's hair. "I know you didn't mean it." He kissed his temple. "Everyone calls me Rue. My true name is known only to my parents and myself. When I went to Court, they impressed upon me the importance of keeping that secret."

"Oh." He leaned against Rue. "No names, no thank-yous..."

"No oaths. No gifts. Either given or received, unless you know they're offered freely."

Ainsley rubbed his fingers, still sticky with honey, together. A distant childhood memory tugged at his thoughts and he couldn't quite grasp it. It floated so close yet remained intangible and he started to grow distressed. "There's something about food."

"Ah. Yes. The food," Rue agreed. "Never eat or drink anything from the Otherworld."

Panic settled in his gut. "I've eaten."

Rue grinned. "And drank."

Ainsley sat up straighter, desperate to recall what had been so important. Was he trapped here now? Or had that been some Greek myth? Did he owe someone something?

"Peace, Ainsley," Rue soothed. "For thieves or mortals wandering on their own or for those who hold no favor with the Court, consuming anything here can produce a terrible curse of one sort or the other. You could be trapped for a while or it could come to pass that all other food or drink that passes your lips will leave you unsatisfied, still hungry, with the taste of ash on your tongue."

"I don't hold favor with anyone," Ainsley insisted, shamefully close to tears.

"You hold favor with me, my love," Rue reminded. "You are here under my protection."

Despite Rue's assurances, tears slipped down Ainsley's cheeks.

"What's wrong?"

"I don't know."

Rue slipped his arms around Ainsley and drew him against his chest. "Shh, now. What is it?"

"I don't *want* to be cursed."

"You haven't been cursed."

"No, but...but I know I'm going to end up cursed. I'm going to do something wrong." He tried to scrub away his tears.

Rue rubbed his back. "When I brought you here, I brought you under my protection. That means anyone who tries to curse you or hex you—"

"Hex!" Ainsley squeaked.

"Or offer you harm in any way would have to cross me to do it."

Ainsley continued to sniffle, unable to fathom what would have happened if he had followed any other fairy but Rue into the Otherworld. Or what would happen if they were separated. "I don't belong here."

"I." Rue faltered. "I can take you home, Ainsley, if that's what you want."

He didn't want to go home, not yet. This place still had so much he hadn't seen and of course, at home, he could never have what he had with

Rue. Not without keeping things secret and putting himself in peril. He didn't understand the panic that had come over him.

"I'm not cursed?"

"No, you lovely thing, you are not cursed." Rue nuzzled his throat. "Cold iron, red berries, a rowan bough. These things will ward off fairies of all sorts. Bells and pure silver will sort out the wicked and warn them away. Swift and humble apologies should comfort any who take offense at your manners."

The rasp of Rue's voice calmed his heart and settled his nerves. His panic now seemed childish as well as unexplainable. "I'm sorry."

"No need. Imagine my terror in your world. Iron at every turn and church bells ringing to mark the hours. Disorienting even once the terror had faded and I had...better come to my senses."

Leaning against him, beneath unfamiliar stars and with the crackling fire to keep the darkness at bay, Ainsley thought he should ask, "Were you sent away from home?"

"I told you already, my lord and lady sent me abroad."

"But I mean..."

"Was I sent away in shame? Will they be furious at my return?" Rue asked. "I was not disgraced, but nor was it with good cheer. I think I had irritated them, inconvenienced and embarrassed them too many times, but they did not exile me. My return will be well taken or ignored. Or that's my guess, at least."

Ainsley stretched and yawned.

"To bed, my love?" Rue asked.

Not for the first time, Ainsley wondered if Rue knew him significantly better than he knew Rue. Some part of him shied away from the idea that Rue had watched him for months, a silent observer, and capable of more intelligence than Ainsley had ever guessed. A larger part didn't care; that part cared that Rue had saved him, been kind to him, and offered him passage to a fantastical world he never would have seen otherwise.

Funny, Ainsley thought, what he willingly ignored in exchange for a like-minded companion. And for no small amount of pleasure. He had allowed himself to be led into damnation for sure, but he didn't care about that either.

He stretched again and nodded.

They found Wolfwood bustling upon their return. Voices rang out across the grounds and the scent of cooking fruit drifted out as far as the stables. When they returned their mounts to their stalls, Ainsley saw eight horses he didn't recognize, one of them so small he mistook it for a foal at first glance.

Rue peered down his nose at the small horse, which bared its sharp teeth and snorted at the stable boy attempting to groom it. "'Tis Godwin's or Rayla's?"

"Lord Godwin, my prince," the stable boy answered.

Ainsley's head swiveled towards Rue.

"A lesser prince." Rue dismissed the title with a wave of his hand as if being a lesser prince discounted his royalty altogether. "Come." He strode off towards the house.

Ainsley collected himself then hurried after Rue. "You're a prince?"

"I'd have to outlive my aunt and uncle, my cousin, and my father before I took the Barbed Throne."

"That's only third in line."

Rue didn't answer.

Ainsley caught up with him just inside the building and hesitated at the sight of half a dozen strangers heading towards them.

Each of them dazzled him, beautiful men and women in slippery, elegant clothing. None of them looked alike and half of them barely looked like people, but they all had the same air of grace and mischief about them. He saw one among them no taller than a five-year-old and thin as a sapling.

The man who walked at the forefront had silver-blue skin and shining white hair that fell into his eyes. Upon seeing Rue, the fairy grinned and cried, "So it's true! I hardly believed Dora when she said you'd come home to roost."

Rue barely smiled. "Did she learn to lie while I was away?"

"I thought you wouldn't dare show your face for years and years. Maybe even never." The man swept Rue into an embrace.

Rue slid out of his grip like smoke.

His eyes scanned over Rue, lingering on his face. He turned his attention to Ainsley. "And what mortal morsel have you brought home with you?"

"This is my cousin, Prince Tadgh. Tadgh, this is Sir Ainsley, a knight from the mortal realm."

Ainsley gave his best bow, though he knew he must have looked ungainly.

Tadgh laughed, light and glittery. "Just like you, Rue, to be sent away and come home with a stray." He gestured languidly to the people behind him. "We'll be in the gardens if you wish to share how you spent your time abroad."

They streamed out the door, tittering as they went.

Without a word, Rue took Ainsley by the hand and led him to his room.

Their room.

Ainsley had never set foot in here before.

"We'll want you in something a little finer before your presentation to the lord and lady."

"Too late," came a voice from the doorway, musical and deep.

Ainsley whirled to see a woman in the doorway.

Her gown floated about her body as if made of clouds and its pale gray drew out the warm pink undertones to her ivory skin. She looked like a thing made of softness and air, but he needn't see the tiara perched on her head to know her as a queen. She had feathers in her gray hair, pale like Rue's, and entirely black eyes, no whites to speak of at all.

He bowed instantly.

"Auntie," Rue greeted her. He kissed her cheek, then drew back.

"You look well."

A smile twitched across his face. "Triviai suited me."

"Which makes me question your return."

At that, his face fell. Rue swallowed.

"He saved me," Ainsley pipped, feeling like a child interrupting an adult conversation.

They turned to look at him.

"I'd been traveling, and bandits set upon me. He saved my life but I...my nerves failed me. Rue offered me a safe place to recover," Ainsley continued.

"Are you recovered?" the queen asked.

His mouth dried at the question; her voice moved through him like a stone through deep water. "I suppose only another fight would tell."

Graciously, she offered, "I can arrange that."

"Auntie, please," Rue insisted.

"Is he so fragile?" she asked.

"I've offered him my protection," he said.

"Hmm. Your uncle expects you at dinner tonight. Your guest is welcome as well."

Rue nodded.

Ainsley nearly thanked her but bit back the words quick enough that no more than a half-choked syllable came out.

They both wrinkled their noses at him; he cleared his throat.

"Do you need water?" Rue asked.

"If you don't mind."

"I'll leave you to it," the queen said. She floated away as quietly as she'd come.

Rue pressed a cup of water into his hand.

Ainsley sipped instead of thanking him. He set the cup down when he'd drained it, unsettled by Rue's careful attention. He shifted, then asked, "What?"

"Never have I needed to introduce anyone to my family before. Never has anyone stayed so constantly by my side."

"Ah. Well." Ainsley shifted as he thought of the months they had traveled together. "It was you staying by my side, wasn't it? I thought you were a bird. Or possibly a demon."

"Oh, sweet knight, you *definitely* thought I was a demon. And that aside, I referred to the time since you came to know me as a man instead of a bird."

Less than a fortnight, Ainsley realized.

"Usually only as long as it took to move from seduction to completion did they linger in my company," Rue explained, then added haughtily, "And praise all the gods that they left as soon as they did. I wanted release, not companionship."

Ainsley rubbed the back of his neck and tried not to worry that Rue would speak of him someday with such distaste.

His worry must have shown on his face, though, because Rue circled in close and told him, "Fret not, my love, I enjoy you for so much more than your cock."

God, that rasp in his ear! Hearing Rue utter something indecent made Ainsley's guts start to burn.

His fingers trailed through Ainsley's hair as he continued, "And I enjoy yours much better than theirs, too. What a fool I was, thinking that their careless humping could serve as a replacement for the eager wiggles of a sweet thing like you."

After a glance to make sure the queen had closed the door on her way out, Ainsley turned to face Rue. More than he was moved by his words, the urge to show Rue how much he liked him had Ainsley maneuvering Rue towards the bed.

"Ainsley—"

Ainsley checked his initial urge to shush him and asked, "Is it dreadfully important?"

"After a full day of riding, a bath might not be unwarranted."

True, they had worked up a sweat and the scent of horse lingered on their skin, but Ainsley didn't mind. "Does it bother you?"

Rue hesitated.

"If it bothers you, we'll stop."

"'Twould be wiser, methinks."

Ainsley nodded and stepped back, though not before he gave Rue a kiss. "I'll defer to your wisdom, then."

"Mmm."

Ainsley took him by the hand and led him out of the room. "For now, anyway. You'd better watch out once I know what I'm doing."

"Oh? What will you do to me then?"

Whatever clever, risqué answer he had died on his tongue at the sight of someone making her way down the hallway. She carried a bottle of wine and two goblets in her hands and she called for someone behind her to hurry.

Ainsley released Rue's hand.

The woman's eyes flicked over the two of them. She had surely seen their hands clasped, but she continued on her way with nothing more than a greeting to Rue.

Ainsley kept his head down as he walked towards the bath. He shucked his clothes and climbed into the water before it heated.

"Something the matter?" Rue asked.

Ainsley shrugged.

"Would you mind company?"

He shrugged again and started to scrub himself, wishing the hard lump of fear in his belly would go away. It had come on suddenly.

Rue approached the tub and rested a hand on Ainsley's shoulder. "Whatever it is that troubles you, I cannot aid in the solving of it if you remain silent."

"You truly intend to introduce me to your family?"

"Doing otherwise would be rather rude of me."

"Introduce me how?"

"Oh, well, I don't know your whole name, my love, you don't have to worry about them hearing it from my lips," Rue soothed. "I thought Sir Ainsley would suffice."

"No, not that. I mean, *how*...what sort of person will you introduce me as?"

Rue frowned. "Likely just as I did to my cousin. Sir Ainsley, a knight of Triviai. Did you wish me to say something else?"

"And people won't wonder about us?"

"They'll likely wonder a lot. Are you worried about the courtiers? I can certainly make my intentions with you clearer if you fear their advances. A lovely thing like you will catch someone's eye without a doubt."

Ainsley hated how fully Rue had misunderstood his worry. He splashed water on his face.

Rue flinched from the splash. "Water's cold."

"It's fine."

Rue activated the spell to heat the water anyway. He tugged his clothes off and climbed into the water just as Ainsley stood to exit.

Ainsley passed him the soap and Rue took him by the wrists. "I'm done," Ainsley said.

Without releasing his grip on Ainsley's wrists, Rue said, "You missed your back."

He didn't want to pull away. He waited, hoping Rue could say something to make him feel better. An awful burden to lay on someone else, but he needed it.

"Tell me, Ainsley, what it is that has made it so you can't even look at me anymore?"

"I'm afraid."

"Afraid of what?"

"That people will find out about us."

"Find out? My love, I'm going to tell them," Rue told him. "You think I've been taking lovers in secret all these years? That we would share a room without tongues wagging?"

"I..."

"You must be a perfect fool, Ainsley. I already told you, it isn't a sin here."

"I'm not worried about sinning, Rue. I'm worried about what people will do to us."

Rue slid his fingers under Ainsley's chin and made him look up. "I don't understand."

"It isn't always the Church that riles prejudice. Being different can get you stoned just as much as devilry can."

"Ah. Well. When you see the others who've come to the summer estate with our lord and lady, you'll understand better I think. Until then I can only offer my assurances that no one will do anything ill-intentioned to you because we share a bed." Rue cradled his cheek. "Does that comfort you at all?"

It didn't but he kept that to himself.

"Let me wash your back."

Together they sank back into the water, now warmed. Ainsley relaxed a little beneath Rue's attentions.

By the time they had to dress, dread filled him less. He badly wanted to cling to Rue but didn't dare. First, because he still couldn't shake the feeling that no one should witness them so openly together, but second, because Rue looked too beautiful to touch.

He'd dressed them in similarly colored, though differently styled, tunics. The cream-colored fabric and burnished copper embroidery of their tunics looked wonderful on Rue. On Ainsley, he thought the colors brought out too much pink in his skin. "I look like a piglet," he muttered when he caught a glimpse of himself in a mirror.

"You look delicious," Rue corrected. He gave Ainsley a kiss on the cheek and glided away.

He wore a tunic much shorter than Ainsley's and seeing his long legs in such gloriously tight hose made Ainsley want to pull him into the nearest room.

A different type of wonder replaced that, though, when Ainsley got a full view of the Fair Folk who had come to Wolfwood with the king and queen. He spotted Tadgh and his company laughing together and among them saw two women with their arms circled about each other's waists.

The queen sat at a head table and by her side stood a tall, broad-shouldered man with ink-black skin. Upon his head sat a crown of something so thin and fine Ainsley thought it to be spider silk, frozen somehow. The king wore a floor-length garment, not a robe or a tunic, but something that was unmistakably a gown.

Ainsley tried to rationalize it but found no other way to explain the wide neckline that left the king's shoulders exposed, nor the gossamer skirt slit up the side to reveal the king's bare leg.

While he stared, Rue took the opportunity to nuzzle against his jaw and ask, "Do you understand a little better now why you have nothing to fear?"

"He's..."

"He's spotted us," Rue said.

He took Ainsley's hand and brought him over to the king.

They both bowed, though Ainsley did it less gracefully and with far more staring than seemly.

"Your Majesties, I present Sir Ainsley, a knight of Triviai. Ainsley, this is Queen Corva and King Balor, lord and lady of the Western Court."

Ainsley continued to stare at Balor, fascinated by a king that could go barefoot and still look prepared to make the entire room bend to his whim.

"Your guest looks shocked. Perhaps he would do better among his own kind," Balor chided.

"Oh, forgive him, Uncle, he's never—"

"I've never seen anyone so beautiful in all my life," Ainsley answered, cutting off Rue's explanation.

"Never?" Balor asked. "Perhaps you are not sure what you gaze upon so ardently. Perhaps at home you prefer women with strong frames and the veil of the expectation has twisted what you see into something else."

Ainsley shook his head. "If a gown were enough to confuse me, my parents would have seen me happily wed by putting a maiden in a tunic and hose."

He didn't know why he could speak so boldly when moments ago he'd been terrified of what this night would hold. It had to do with the king and his gown, and the women holding each other, and the fact that he, for once, would have felt as safe holding Rue's hand as he would have if they were alone.

Balor laughed.

Corva raised an eyebrow at Rue, who shrugged in response.

"Welcome, then, Sir Ainsley, to Wolfwood. We hope you enjoy your stay," Balor said. He offered his hand.

Ainsley took it and pressed a kiss to his ring, thrilled to hold the king's warm and heavy hand in his own. The king smelled like flowers and good earth, like rain and honey.

He did the same when the queen offered her ring.

From within his tunic, Rue drew out a small bundle of cloth. He dipped his head and held it out to the pair. "My companion and I traveled to Lake Moon these days past."

Queen Corva took the cloth from him. "What do you bring me?"

"The last shard of the Lady's Lens, lost all these years."

She raised an eyebrow and unwrapped the bundle. She lifted the shard and inspected it. "So you have. We'll reunite the pieces when the summer ends and we return to the Western Court."

Rue straightened up.

Corva placed a hand on his shoulder. "Many sought it. You did well to find it."

Rue grinned.

Corva returned his smile, though hers was not so joyous, and she turned away to greet someone else after a few seconds.

Rue escorted Ainsley away as his aunt greeted another and softly murmured, "There you went flirting with my uncle. And I thought you so shy."

"I...! Rue, I wasn't. I wasn't flirting."

"I saw the look on your face when you thought of your king. Is it a partiality of yours? Powerful men?" Rue asked.

Ainsley began to insist, "I didn't mean to overstep. I just—"

"And now you're so flustered you can't even recognize that I'm teasing." Rue chucked Ainsley under the chin and drew him in for a kiss. "Seeing you flustered does do something spectacular to me."

Ainsley let the kiss happen in full view of all the courtiers, though he didn't know that any of them paid attention. Rue brought him in slowly enough that he could have pulled back, but he didn't want to. The knowledge of their safety filled him up with an unexplainable lightness, the same as when he'd been able to confess that he didn't care if their intimacy made him a sinner.

Did his mother feel this way when she kissed his father?

He threw himself into the kiss, surely pressing too close to be seemly, even if the Otherworld did allow kisses between men.

No appeared to pay them any mind, though.

Rue approached a set of chairs, one empty on either side of a woman in a garish, plaid-patterned chiton. He placed a hand on her shoulder, leaned in to whisper into her ear, and she moved down a seat.

Tadgh himself poured them wine, setting two glittering crystal goblets in front of them with a beneficent smile on his face. "Summer wine. Enjoy."

Ainsley dipped his head and reached for the goblet, taking the first sip without a second thought. The taste bloomed on his tongue, heavy and sweet, and it warmed him all the way to his toes.

"Careful with that. Fairy wine always hits you harder than mortal swill," Rue warned.

Tadgh clucked his tongue. "Shall I water it for the two of you?"

"We'll manage on our own, fair prince. I wouldn't want to trouble you."

Tadgh smiled as he left, but Ainsley trusted it less this time.

He waited until he had food on his plate to take another sip.

Rue's hand twitched towards the goblet. He picked at his food.

A few more sips of wine started Ainsley thinking about how Rue had talked about wine in the past, from the stink of it on his father's breath to how much of it he had needed to undress before a lover.

How his family had sent him away to recover.

He finished his wine, trying not to ruminate too much. He didn't want to spoil the mood.

"Vintage not to your liking, my prince?" Dora asked quietly on one of her passes to collect plates. She glanced towards Rue's untouched goblet. "I'll fetch you something else."

People would see her carry away a clear goblet full of wine.

Without a second thought, Ainsley grabbed Rue's goblet before he could answer and downed it in one painful swallow.

Rue raised both his eyebrows. "Something weak would be best for this one, I think, Dora."

She filled their goblets with what amounted to little more than tinted water.

Ainsley tried his best not to knock anything over or slide out of his seat. The second cup of wine had hit him all at once.

The rest of the night passed in a hazy blur. Even the watered wine affected him. People around him laughed and caroused. Rue participated, more sedate than the other fairies, but he smiled and kept his hand over Ainsley's for most of the time.

The urge to relieve himself became pressing and Ainsley heaved himself out of his chair. He braced himself on the table and wobbled.

"Are you well, my love?"

He nodded. "Right back." He staggered a few steps before Rue slung an arm around his shoulders.

"Where are we headed?"

"Piss," he managed.

"Mmm."

Rue escorted him to a chamber pot and had the courtesy to hold him steady, so he didn't make a mess. He brought him to bed and helped him out of his clothes. "You'll want to start sleeping this off now."

"Mmm fine." He fell, naked and eyes closed, face-first into the bed.

"There's an empty pot by the bed if you need to be sick," Rue informed him.

He nestled into the pillows, his whole body unsure and heavy. "Good."

Instead of leaving, Rue remained by his side, settling him under the covers and gently stroking his back. "You needn't have done that. With the wine. I…" Rue hesitated.

Ainsley peeked one eye open.

"I brought you here with no intention to burden you with troubles not your own."

"None of, of the rest of them talk like you."

Rue smiled. "Ah, well, every family has its odd ducks."

"Rue?"

"Yes?"

Ainsley nodded off.

"Ainsley?"

"Hmm?"

"Did you need something?" he asked.

"You can burden me."

Rue leaned in to kiss his temple and smooth back his hair. "Of course."

Ainsley launched into an incoherent ramble about how they'd had contests to see who could carry the most and how Sir Richard had made him carry around saddles and heavy packs for weeks to help him prepare. He never got to the end of the story because the world began to spin and he threw up.

He remembered Rue wiping off his face with a damp cloth and little else.

He woke in the middle of the night, queasy but desperate for water. He struggled out of bed, tangled in the sheets. He found the water, rinsed his mouth, and carefully slurped down a few mouthfuls.

As he picked his way back to bed, he realized that Rue must have returned to dinner. He crawled back beneath the covers and tried to go back to sleep, but it eluded him, as restful sleep sometimes did after overdrinking.

The part of him not preoccupied with combatting nausea and disequilibrium worried about Rue. He could hear laughter still, beautiful voices ringing through the halls. He wished they would be quieter.

He faded in and out for some time.

Finally, once the voices quieted, the door opened. Rue's taut figure slipped through. He moved without a sound.

Ainsley let out a small grunt. He had meant to call to Rue, but the words had gotten caught in his throat.

"I thought sleep would have you well in her grip by now," Rue susurrated. The scratch of leaves, the whisper of grass, the rustle of fabric. He had such a beautiful voice.

Ainsley cleared his throat. "Woke up."

"I see."

"You left."

"Yes, my love, but you excused yourself before dessert and among the Fair Folk we can almost never resist sweetened cream and summer fruits."

"Oh."

The sounds of rustling fabric and boots thumping against the carpet reached Ainsley's ears. Rue slid into bed beside him. He draped an arm over Ainsley's waist and snuggled up against him, his chest against Ainsley's back.

His hand splayed over Ainsley's stomach and somehow that abated the disquiet in his gut. Ainsley didn't know if he'd used music or if his touch alone brought enough comfort.

Within moments, the fairy's breathing evened out and he stilled, deep asleep.

Ainsley lingered awake a little longer but eventually dropped into a fitful sleep.

Morning brought its own challenges, namely a throbbing headache.

Before he could even sit up, Rue pointed to steaming mug on the table beside him. "That will help."

He pushed himself up, bit back a groan, and took up the tea. He sipped it, finding it perfectly warmed and somewhat bitter.

The room he now shared with Rue sprawled more than the guest room he'd previously occupied. Rue had enough room for his bed and a desk, as well as a plush chair similar to the ones in the library in front of the hearth, and a large, tall wardrobe. Rue's clothing never varied much, usually a tunic and hose in a muted tone, so Ainsley couldn't imagine why he needed such a large wardrobe.

Other smaller furnishings dotted the rooms, a small table, a bookshelf, things like that.

He took another sip of the tea and allowed himself to savor the sight of Rue lounging in the armchair beside the fireplace. His bare legs stretched in front of him and he balanced a slim volume in one hand. The robe he'd donned slipped over his shoulders and pooled in his lap, more enticing than if he'd been altogether undressed.

Ainsley would have acted on those feelings if only he thought he'd make it over to the chair without dying. He'd been ill the morning after drinking before, but the fairy wine had thoroughly incapacitated him. He wondered what would have happened if he'd taken a third glass.

He leaned against the headboard and sipped the tea, content to watch Rue read as his stomach settled and headache retreated.

By no means did he feel ready to run a footrace, but he would survive the day.

"Not as good as moderation, but the tea helps, doesn't it?" Rue asked.

"Yes. Thhhh. Yes. It does."

Rue glanced up from his book, half a smile on his face.

"Did your family enjoy having you back?"

"To say they enjoyed it may overemphasize the importance they place on my presence. But they were not displeased." Rue pulled his robe up over his right shoulder and twitched it over his leg. Casual, subtle movements that suggested a slight breeze more than his discomfort with his scars.

"I can't imagine placing anything but the utmost importance on your presence."

"Flatterer," Rue accused.

"I think you might enjoy being flattered."

Rue grinned. He marked his page and set aside his book, then crossed the room to settled into bed beside Ainsley. He leaned against him and pressed a kiss to his shoulder. "My auntie liked you."

Such a simple, uncomplicated statement.

"I didn't think I lasted long enough to leave an impression," Ainsley admitted.

"More than she's seen of anyone else."

Ainsley took the last sip of his tea and set aside the mug. He twisted, then, to nestle into Rue's arms. "Can I ask you something?"

"Yes."

"Those others, the ones you didn't want to spend time with, I think I understand that. But why do you want to spend time with me?"

A look flitted across Rue's face, impossible to read. "Your virtues I can extol if that's what you wish. The kindness of your eyes, the gentleness of your spirit..." He shrugged.

"Is that enough?"

"Enough for what?"

"I don't know. Enough so you'll want to keep spending time with me."

"I don't know. I hope so," Rue admitted. "I enjoy this."

Ainsley burrowed against him. "So do I."

Rue pulled him closer. "You should rest, I think. You tossed and turned all night. I can't imagine you actually slept."

"No, I...whatever you had planned, I could come along. I'm not that out of sorts."

"Presently, I plan to stay in bed. 'Tis early yet. The house wakes later than we have been. Court life is a life of lazy mornings and long nights, as I remember it. Only Balor rises this early."

That didn't sound so bad, at least not right now. "But we'll still go to see things?"

"Yes, of course," Rue assured. "I have a whole world to show you."

The idea fixed a contented grin on his face. Ainsley slept easier and well into the afternoon.

Though he and Rue dined with the Court every night they were home, Ainsley managed to avoid intoxication and the resulting sickness in the weeks that followed. Dora had taken to serving him and Rue their drinks first and always serving them goblets of wine so watered it barely tasted of wine at all. For that, Ainsley counted her among the saints. Whether she did it out of affection for either of them or because she didn't like cleaning sick out of chamber pots, it didn't matter. Ainsley went out of his way to be nice to her.

Because they imbibed less than the others, Rue and Ainsley almost always woke before them. Wolfwood in the morning had a strange air to it now, subdued and indolent, and Ainsley tried his best to move as silently as Rue.

This morning, they had stepped outside Wolfwood planning to go for a ride, but the air sat so heavily that Ainsley didn't want to do anything that required effort.

When he voiced the idea, Rue agreed, saying, "I did think the weather a bit too oppressive." He squinted up at the sky.

Sweat had already started to dribble down Ainsley's back and the sun had barely climbed above the horizon.

Rue took him by the hand and pulled him towards the gardens. "We should swim."

The idea of sinking up to his chin in cool water had enormous appeal and he followed along eagerly.

They passed Balor on his usual morning stroll and he raised a hand in silent greeting.

Rue brought him to a wide pool of water overhung by a large tree whose branches cast shade over a broad swath of the surface. They stripped and slid into the water.

Ainsley hummed contentedly and allowed himself to float for some time. "I could stay in so long that I'll prune all over."

"You'll what?" Rue asked, an unusual note of worry in his voice.

"Prune," Ainsley repeated, thinking the other man must have misheard him.

"You'll *prune?* What do you mean you'll prune?"

Ainsley righted himself in the water. "When your fingers wrinkle? From the water?"

Rue shook his head.

Ainsley swam over to him and held out his hand palm up to show the wrinkles that had already started to form.

The fairy stared openly and demanded to know why his hands did that.

Ainsley had no answer to give but did enjoy Rue's bewilderment.

They alternated between swimming and lounging in the grass for hours.

Balor passed them once and stopped to speak with them at length about the tree beneath which they sat. He informed Ainsley that his wife's parents had planted that tree when she'd been born.

"It's a lovely tree," Ainsley said. "Was she born here?"

Balor nodded. "And born early. I remember the fuss of all of it...the midwives running around and Queen Lilia screaming, in such a complete panic. Corva was her firstborn..." Balor surveyed the tree again. "And such a small baby, too."

"You were here?"

"Corva and I were betrothed since before she was conceived, let alone born."

Ainsley nodded, not overly surprised to find out that royal marriages here worked much the same as they did at home.

Balor stood quietly for a while longer, looking at the tree mostly, then bid them farewell and wandered away, his hands clasped behind his back.

"Balor was promised for marriage to the royal family as soon as he was born, so highly sought was he," Rue informed him.

"Hm?"

"Born the perfect incarnation of the Black God, he is blessed among us."

"Does that happen often?" Ainsley asked.

"Every so many generations there is a fairy born who uncannily resembles one of the four. Legend speaks of a time when four will be born in the same generation and the world will know unparalleled peace and prosperity."

"And your gods..." Ainsley thought about how best to phrase the question without offending. "Tell me more about them."

"What do you wish to know?"

"Anything. The beginning, maybe."

"Ah." Rue settled back against the tree. "Before the gods, magic ruled this land, untamed and purposeless. The Black God rose first, born from magic and the land itself. He lived for some time on his own, long enough to grow from a boy to a man."

Ainsley moved in close to Rue and nestled into his arms, happily prepared to listen to him talk for hours.

"He walked the land and found it dark and scoured by the magic that had born him. He tried to tame it but it broke free each time. The third time he was defeated, he wept, out of shame, out of loneliness. His tears birthed the sea and from there came the Blue Lady. She stepped from the waves and put her arms around him. She showed him friendship and gave him strength."

"Just friendship?" Ainsley asked.

"The Blue Lady loves deeply and powerfully, but she takes no lovers. Her love is not the love of flesh," Rue explained. "Though it's been the lament of many a sailor..." He remained quiet, lost in thought.

"What happened next? That's only two."

Rue continued, "Together, they were enough to contain the world's forces. They bound it in a single mass and placed it in the sky. They felt the warmth of the sun on their faces and smiled because for once it did not burn to feel magic against their skin. They reached up and the light reached back. The White Woman left the sky to walk with them. For lifetimes they walked together and born from their companionship finally emerged another life. The Green God grew up from the soil, the youngest and most vibrant. They all doted upon him, though the Black God loved him the most."

"But not as a parent."

"No, certainly not as a parent. The Black God had grown solemn and quiet and the Green God, youthful and pliant, drew out joy in him again. He buried himself deep in the Black God's warmth and from their love came the first plants."

"That's...surely that's not..." Ainsley sputtered. "Buried himself!"

"Those are the exact words passed down in the myths and songs. They laid together and good, green things covered the world," Rue told him as easily as countless priests had told Ainsley about Christ. "The green life grew unchecked, though, and choked the earth. The White Woman shaped another kind of life. Life that mated. The animals ate the plants and fed the soil with their bodies when they died so that more green things could grow...and so the world has been ever since."

Ainsley thought idly that he could worship deities like this with more ease than he'd ever worshipped God. He struck the thought down immediately and put it aside. One story shouldn't make him turn away from a lifetime of learning. He forced his thoughts to something else. "Are you hungry?"

"It's too hot to eat."

Ainsley kissed his jaw. "Come back in the water then."

"Mmmm. Alright."

Back in the water, they floated together, talking about nothing in particular. Hunger stirred in Ainsley, but distant enough that he could wait. He floated on his back, eyes closed, and Rue trailed his fingers over his chest, singing softly.

Ainsley had never heard him sing before, not even when the other courtiers had raised their voices and taken out their instruments after dinner had ended.

True, Rue's voice lacked the sweetness and airy lilt of the others, but Ainsley liked it that much better because of its difference.

"We spilled the cream and burnt the cake and still he doesn't cry," Rue crooned, "A boy so sweet, a boy so fine, he'll be his mother's pride..."

Rue trailed off when he realized Ainsley had opened his eyes.

"What were you singing?"

"Some nonsense song, half a lullaby," Rue answered shortly.

"It was pretty."

Voices approached, accompanied by laughter, and Ainsley needn't turn around to know that they came from Tadgh and his companions. He glanced over anyway, just to confirm, and turned back to look at Rue when he heard a great deal of sloshing.

Rue must have scrambled out of the water because he already stood beneath the tree, his tunic over his head. He struggled into his hose, the fabric snagging against his wet skin.

"Rue."

"Let's eat."

Ainsley climbed out of the water more slowly, wondering if he should ask what was wrong. He didn't have to, though, once the others approached bearing bottles of wine and plates of finger food.

"Rue! Come, back in the water. We've enough to share," Tadgh insisted.

"That's kind of you, cousin, but I find myself more in the mood for privacy," Rue declined.

Ainsley pulled his tunic over his head and gathered up the rest of his garments, not bothering to put them on. His stomach bubbled uneasily, not sure what this interaction would bring. Something about Tadgh put Ainsley on edge and the prince always managed to provoke a strange, curt nervousness in Rue after they spoke for any length of time.

"You haven't got to hide, you know." Tadgh pulled off his clothes to reveal a smooth, willowy form rivaled only by artistic ideals. His silver-blue skin bore not a single blemish that Ainsley could see, not even a freckle. "Everyone knows you were burnt, and the scars aren't half as hideous as rumors say."

Rue's cheeks darkened.

"I'm sure we'd be over the shock in hardly any time at all."

"We had other plans," Ainsley said. He reached for Rue's hand and wiggled his fingers between Rue's. "Private ones."

"By all means, stay. We could use a spectacle," Tadgh offered.

With false concern, Ainsley answered, "I wouldn't want to shock you or your friends, Your Highness; if you can be undone by something so slight as a scar, I can't imagine what lovemaking might do to such delicate sensibilities."

He pulled Rue away after that, not sure what Tadgh might say back and not wanting to have to come up with another response that walked such a fine line between insult and manners.

Once alone in their room, Ainsley stripped off his damp tunic. He glanced at Rue, who had leaned against the door, looking almost ill.

"Are you alright?" Ainsley asked.

Rue glanced up then dropped his gaze without answering.

"Well, come get changed at least. You'll feel better without soggy hose," Ainsley advised. He hung his tunic to dry and opened the wardrobe, passing by dozens of beautiful, gossamer garments. He stopped to examine a few of them. "How come you never wear any of these?"

"They show my scars. Gifts from Tadgh."

Ainsley pulled out one thin, short shirt, flimsy enough to be transparent. The silver embroidery would have shone like constellations against the dark cast of Rue's complexion. "They're beautiful."

"Wear them if it please you."

Ainsley set the tunic aside and selected something Rue usually wore. He laid the garments out on the armchair. "You'll catch a chill in wet clothes."

Rue huffed and stripped out of his clothes with a few grumbles and glowers. He threw his damp clothes into a pile on the ground and snatched up the tunic from the chair.

Ainsley caught him by the arm and sidled in closer. "You haven't got to get dressed so fast."

"Ainsley, leave me be."

He let him go but stayed in proximity. "I'll only ask once and then I'll really leave you alone."

Rue glanced his way, eyes narrowed with suspicion.

"Let me kiss you, just once, so I can show you how beautiful you are."

"Plenty of people have kissed me without making me feel beautiful," the fairy challenged.

Nervous flutters filled him and poured out his throat as a question, "Did any of them love you?"

Rue met Ainsley's gaze, his face briefly impossible to read. Then the smooth mask fell away and his face crumpled. Tears filled his eyes.

Ainsley hadn't expected this response. "Rue...I."

"No one loves me."

"I do."

He shook his head.

"I do. I love you," Ainsley said.

Rue wrapped him up in an embrace and buried his face in the crook of Ainsley's shoulder. He squeezed him so tight that Ainsley had trouble breathing. "Say it again."

"I love you," Ainsley whispered, not having enough air in his lungs to say it any louder.

Rue stayed in his arms for a long time.

Ainsley rubbed his back and pressed a few kisses to his throat and jaw.

Rue leaned further into his arms, pressing their hips together. He caught Ainsley's mouth with such force that it hurt. He continued relentlessly, maneuvering him towards the bed and straddling him. He moved desperately against Ainsley as he never had before. All his usual composure disappeared along with his amusement at Ainsley's yearning. Now he rocked against him, all hands and kisses, just as voracious as Ainsley had ever been.

He looked so wild and abandoned, so recklessly lovely that Ainsley forgot whatever paltry plans he'd had to show him his own beauty.

The heat of the day penetrated the room, making their skin bead with sweat and slide beneath each other's hands.

When Rue took Ainsley inside of him, he did it with a throaty gasp and his head tossed back. He splayed one hand over Ainsley's chest, holding him still as he rolled his hips, slow and careful.

Ainsley couldn't stand to be held away from him, though, and he took him by the arm and drew him down, wrapping his arms around him and nipping at his throat. The salt of his skin sang against Ainsley's tongue.

Rue spilled first, hot and sticky over Ainsley's belly. He came without a sound, rigid for a moment as Ainsley made his final thrusts, then he collapsed, trembling, when Ainsley finished.

Ainsley kissed his hair.

"Don't say anything," Rue murmured as he lay motionless against him.

Without taking offense, Ainsley remained silent until Rue began to stir, first just nuzzling against him, then sitting up and stretching.

"Maybe," Ainsley suggested, "We should have given your cousin that spectacle he wanted."

Rue snorted. "He's stumbled in on me being humped enough times…"

"But was it like that?"

"No," the fairy admitted. He swooped in for one more kiss. "That was much nicer." He extracted himself Ainsley's limbs. "Besides, careful with Tadgh, he'd take something like that as an invitation to start an orgy."

"Not a fan of orgies?" Ainsley guessed.

"I find them disorienting, but I've never been to one sober."

Ainsley washed up and ventured, "Your cousin, he…it seems like I might want to be careful with a lot of things around him."

"Yes. You'll want the utmost caution when dealing with Tadgh. Do you…I'd like to have a bath. By the stars, I haven't sweat like this since I served in the army."

A bath and a small meal saw them through the first part of the afternoon. They spent the latter part in the library, watching heavy, dark clouds roll in over the gardens. Rue sat in one of the stuffed chairs to read and Ainsley settled into his lap. He watched the rain dribbled down the windows.

Tadgh and his company twirled through the rain when it started to pour down but hurried inside when lightning cracked through the sky above their heads.

The heat broke with the storm and the rain outlasted the thunder.

"Where should we go tomorrow?" Ainsley asked. "If the rain breaks."

"I don't know about tomorrow. Dora thinks the rain will last. In a week or so there's a local festival. It promises song and dance and a bounty of summer fruits. I enjoyed attending as a youth."

"Will you sing?"

"I avoid singing when others are about."

"You shouldn't," Ainsley said. "I thought your voice was lovely."

"Shh, no need for flattery. You've already gotten me into bed once today."

Ainsley huffed. "Do you believe anything I say?"

Rue let out a soft hum that buzzed through his chest. "I cannot say for sure." A beat later, he added, "I want to, though. I desperately want to believe every word."

"I could prove it to you."

"How?"

Ainsley had no real answer, so he shrugged and suggested, "I don't know, wear your ribbon at a tourney."

Rue snorted. "Is that what passes for love in your world? No wonder mortals live with such misery in their hearts."

"What do the Fair Folk do to prove their love?"

"Those who've lost favor, or never had it in the first place, often entreat to be sent questing. Their love sets before them a task, the difficulty of which ranges from paltry to impossible. The quest giver may request a ring that shines like starlight, easy enough to find, or might send the asker out to seek a unicorn's horn. If the proclamation is truly unwanted, or even untoward, the usual quest is to retrieve the staff of King Minea."

"Who?"

"'Tis a curséd object and one that might not even exist at that."

"Cursed how?"

"Minea ruled the Meridian Court in the ancient days, long before the Obliteration. He ruled cruelly and delighted in it, but his cruelty tormented him as well. He was a man of two minds and finally, he sought the help of the Hags. They worked their magics and forged him a staff that would ease his troubles, which it did. It removed all his passion and torments and made him empty. Any who touch it finds themselves similarly afflicted."

Ainsley shivered at the idea. "That's horrible."

"Mmm, such a quest is usually reserved for those who have made their love unseemly or threatening."

"If I asked for a quest to prove my love, would you give me one?"

"Only if I could think of one that would keep you my side in the doing of it," Rue answered. "I couldn't bear to be without you for too long."

Ainsley liked that answer. He wouldn't have wanted to send Rue away either. He'd seen plenty of his fellow squires embroiled in infatuations with fair maidens and he'd seen it fade to ashes just as quickly as it had flared. Somehow, though, he didn't think this love would burn out.

Of course, none of the other squires had thought that about their love either; the older knights had warned them not to make fools of themselves over nothing, but their warnings had gone unheeded.

Still, Ainsley hoped he had found something more enduring than calf-love. He didn't know what more he could ask for from a companion. They had their adventures and their lazy days, they had easy silences, long conversations, and moments of laughter. Rue offered passion and tenderness and he offered himself as well, revealing the side he never showed around anyone else.

What, Ainsley wondered, could be better than that?

Most immediately, the answer seemed to be time by themselves.

The sounds of Tadgh and his friends neared the library and Ainsley hoped they would pass by. They turned into the library and dashed the quiet peace between Ainsley and Rue.

Tadgh flopped into the chair nearest to them. "Cousin," he pronounced severely.

"Yes?" Rue asked.

"You fled from me before. You don't know how it wounds me."

Rue raised an eyebrow, but he answered, "Such was not my intent."

Tadgh pursed his lips. "You return from your travels with a new lover and surely many tales to tell, but you don't bother to tell me about either of them."

"You've been to the mortal world, Tadgh, I didn't think my tales would interest you."

The prince scowled. "You never used to keep secrets from me."

His eyes flashed like bits of glass when Rue snapped, "I have reason to since then."

Ainsley shifted and sat up. He wanted to leave. His instincts demanded he get away from Tadgh and his beautiful friends. Their beauty held a different quality than Rue's; something sinister lurked beneath their laughter. As far as Ainsley could tell only flowery proclamations and a hint of melancholy lurked within Rue.

"What reason?" Tadgh asked.

His lips pressed to a thin line, Rue stared down his cousin.

"That's what I thought," Tadgh sniffed. "Blaming others for your own weaknesses. As though it's my fault you can't handle yourself. Just as you always were, Rue."

Ainsley stood and tugged on Rue's hand. "Let's go somewhere else."

Rue didn't move.

"And after all the fingers you've pointed at me, I ask you about your travels, about this mortal foundling you've brought into our home, and you don't have the decency to answer me," Tadgh accused.

Ainsley gave Rue's hand another tug.

"What do you want to know, Tadgh?"

A wisp-thin woman draped herself over the back of Tadgh's chair and combed her fingers through his white hair. It slipped through her fingers like water. "Where did you kidnap him from?" she asked with a nod towards Ainsley.

"He didn't kidnap me," Ainsley interrupted.

Tadgh and all his friends laughed.

"What kind of glamour have you got on?" another of the courtiers asked, their eyes raking over Rue's body, over parts hidden by clothing.

"I'm not glamoured," Rue answered with a scowl.

The courtier raised an eyebrow.

"What's a glamour?" Ainsley asked.

"A glamour is an illusory spell," Rue answered. "Fair Folk often use them to pass more easily in other worlds."

"And to draw in unsuspecting mortals," Tadgh answered. He gestured to a creature with the torso of a youth and the legs of a goat. "A faun like Ilso might use a glamour to hide his hooves so he doesn't send all the maidens squealing away."

"Oh." Ainsley glanced towards Rue. "Are any of you using a glamour?"

"Other fey almost always spot a glamour, so the only point to them here is decoration, unless you have uncommon talent for them," Tadgh explained. "Jori, your eyes are glamoured. Show him."

A woman with iridescent orange eyes waved a hand over her eyes and they changed to a dull blue. She waved her hand once more and they returned to orange.

Ainsley's eyes slid towards Rue again. He yanked them back, but Tadgh had noticed.

"Which means that if my dear cousin tried to hide anything..." Tadgh shrugged. "Paint on a sow doesn't hide the fact it's a sow. It just makes it a little easier to bring it to bed."

Rue's cheeks darkened.

"Although...he probably *has* hidden them from mortal eyes, hasn't he? That does explain how nonchalantly you dismissed me earlier. You think I meant some paltry little mark."

Ainsley protested, "No!"

"How bravely he lies for you, Rue. You should keep him," Tadgh advised merrily.

"I'm not lying," Ainsley insisted.

Tadgh and all his friends laughed again.

The sound of it inflamed him. "I won't be called a liar."

Tadgh sobered. He straightened in his seat. "No? What course do you plan to take, then?"

Ainsley drew himself up to his full height and jutted out his chin, though he must not have looked impressive judging by the others' faces. "I'll have an apology."

"And if I won't give it?"

Rue met Ainsley's eyes and gave a small shake of his head.

His heart still hammered in his chest and his hands had started to shake from the indignity of it all. A true knight would never let his lover be so besmirched, not even by a prince. There was no honor in turning tail.

But the pleading in Rue's eyes stayed his temper. "If a prince so fine as you lacked the good manners to soothe the wounded honor of a guest to whom the king and queen extended their welcome..." Ainsley shrugged. "Perhaps customs are different here but, in my realm, hospitality surpasses pride."

"Things are gravely different here," Tadgh warned.

"Not on this," Rue reminded quietly. "You called him a liar and he hasn't lied about this. He's seen me, all of me, as I am."

Tadgh narrowed his eyes and curled his lip. "I beg your forgiveness, then, Sir Ainsley. I thought you fooled by a glamour but now I see he must have done much more to so endear himself to you." He stood. "You should take care with my cousin. If you knew him as I do you might not be so quick to leap to his defense."

"It wasn't him you called a liar," Ainsley reminded.

"Cousin, maybe I'll find you in a better mood some other time. I do still wonder what trouble you got into in the mortal world." Tadgh breezed past them.

His courtiers jostled Ainsley as they streamed past.

Once the others had left, Rue quietly pronounced, "That was dangerous."

"His waist is the size of my thigh. I'd best him in single combat."

"Tadgh doesn't shake at the sight of a sword," Rue reminded.

With his face hot, Ainsley stared at the floor. He hadn't drawn his sword since he'd come to the Otherworld. He'd avoided touching it if he could.

"Think of that before you try to challenge anyone."

Swallowing past the hard lump in his throat, Ainsley asked, "I...When you served in the army, how did you manage to pick up a blade after the first time?"

"I managed it because my choice was to draw my knife or to let a war-cat rend my face from my skull."

Ainsley didn't know if he'd choose his sword even then. Panic might stay his hand forever.

Rue returned his book to the shelf and didn't speak much for the rest of the evening.

The following dawn found Rue asleep and Ainsley trying to slip out of bed without disturbing him.

He didn't manage.

"What are you doing?" Rue asked, his eyes still shut, his face turned into the pillow.

"I've been idle too long."

"It's still muddy out. We'll go somewhere once it dries," Rue promised.

"No, not...you were right. Yesterday. I can't be a knight if I can't draw a sword." He searched for a tunic and pair of hose that wouldn't be ruined by a morning of training.

Rue pushed himself up and made a show of stretching and rubbing his eyes.

"Go back to sleep."

"You plan to train alone?" Rue asked.

"I." Ainsley hadn't thought that far ahead. He searched around for his sword.

"There are practice weapons in the shed. Here, wear this." Rue placed a roughspun set of clothing in his hands. "I'll see about breakfast."

What started as nervous flutters in Ainsley's stomach turned to nausea as Rue led him to an area of hardpacked dirt beside the stable. He regretted the small breakfast he'd eaten, plain as it had been.

The mud slid beneath his feet slightly as he trod out onto the training yard.

Rue disappeared into a shed and came back with two dulled blades, a sword not quite the same as Ainsley's and a long knife. Thankfully, he set them aside and began to stretch.

Momentarily, Ainsley stood transfixed, then regained his wits and started to stretch as well.

For a good hour or so, Rue led him through a series of exercises. The fairy moved so effortlessly and never once labored to breathe. He could not, Ainsley noted, throw a stone quite as far as Ainsley could, nor did he try to lift the largest of the stones set out for this purpose.

Ainsley eyed the largest stone, which had deep channels that had been filled with gold. "Why's that one gilded?"

"'Tisn't gilded, my love, 'tis weighted with gold. It requires two men to move it. An exercise in cooperation."

Ainsley paced around the stone. No larger than a horse's skull, Ainsley thought he might be able to lift it, though he didn't know how much weight the gold had added. "Have you tried to lift it?"

"Most everyone tries to lift it," Rue informed him. "Balor can move it alone, but he's possibly a god incarnate."

Ainsley wrinkled his nose and put his hands on his hips. "You couldn't move it?"

Rue shook his head. "Go ahead."

"I'll feel a fool if I can't." Still, he squared up with the stone and tried to figure how to best grip it. He squatted, gripped the stone, and readied himself.

"I like it when you wiggle like that," Rue commented.

Ainsley shot him a look, then turned back to the task. An odd warmth and slight hum moved through the rock. He glanced up at Rue. "It's humming."

"'Tis enchanted as well," Rue explained. His dark eyes had settled on Ainsley, his expression somewhere between amused and doubtful.

"Enchanted to do what?"

"To be heavier."

"Oh."

With great effort and a lot of grunting, Ainsley managed to clutch the stone to himself and lift it. He could not lift it higher than his chest and had to drop it after a few seconds, dancing back to avoid dropping it on his feet.

Rue let out a lecherous hum and declared, "No wonder I feel so safe between your thighs."

Ainsley blushed.

"Should we set to the task for which we started this endeavor, or would you like to find other ways to show off?"

He glanced towards the practice blades. "We should."

Rue retrieved the blades and held out the sword to Ainsley.

He took it, but it felt unnatural and heavy in his hand. It had a different weight and shape than his sword, a slight curve to the blade, but nothing to which he wouldn't grow accustomed. He rolled his shoulders and tried to acclimate to the feeling of holding a weapon again.

Rue moved through a series of forms with his knife. He kept his eyes away from Ainsley, perhaps purposefully.

Slowly, Ainsley began the easiest form he knew. The first one he'd ever learned. He remembered Sir Richard's criticisms of his grip and stance. He'd been just as nervous all those years ago.

With time, his arm remembered the weight of a sword and he began more complicated forms.

When he realized Rue has started to watch him, he faltered.

"You moved well."

Ainsley shook his head.

"I have to say, it surprises me. All those months watching you *not* use your sword made me wonder if you could."

Ainsley titled up his chin proudly. "I held my own against everyone I fought."

"Mmm."

"I did," Ainsley insisted.

"I do not doubt it. Did it win you admirers?"

Ainsley thought, then answered, "I don't know." From time to time, some of the young ladies had been nice to him, but he didn't know if they'd admired him. Maybe he had been oblivious.

"Did crowds cheer for you?" Rue asked, but he didn't seem to want an answer, because he continued, "I would have cheered wildly for you if I had seen you in my youth. Thrown flowers before you. Swooned if you had looked my way."

Ainsley snorted. "That doesn't sound like you at all."

"If you saw me as a youth, you would not recognize me." Rue leaned against the fence. "I mean...I looked much the same. A little softer in my features, perhaps, and my hair was not so long, but I mean I was...I was quiet."

"You're still quiet."

Rue frowned.

"Do you mean you were timid?"

"Perhaps that's a better word," Rue admitted. "I. I worried what others would think of me. I wanted badly to be one of those beautiful creatures of the Court. Oh, they laughed like light and danced like petals in the wind. If you saw them, you would think me unsightly."

"Never."

"And they would love to play with you, too, such a sweet mortal thing."

Ainsley didn't know what to make of that. He swallowed, then cleared his throat. "You."

"Hmm?"

"I hate hearing you sound so melancholy." He hated to think of a young Rue, baby-faced and unloved, among the members of a Court like the one he described. He hated to think of him with only Tadgh to guide him. For all the kindness Balor and Corva had shown their guest, they also remained aloof from their nephew.

He had been brought to court to serve as a companion for their son and he no longer served that purpose.

Ainsley set aside his sword and approached Rue, sliding his arms around his waist. "Let's go inside before it gets too hot."

Rue nodded and slipped out of his arms. He returned the weapons to the shed and headed inside.

Ainsley scurried after him and snatched his hand. He pecked his cheek. "I'm glad you came out with me."

"We can make a habit of it," Rue offered.

"Let's. I don't want to get fat yet."

"When do you want to get fat?"

"When I'm old," Ainsley answered sensibly.

Rue laughed.

"So fat that I'll need three servants to roll me out of bed in the morning."

After a bath and a more substantial meal, Ainsley and Rue lazed about in their room. Ainsley looked through Rue's things, with his permission of course, in an effort to find a way to amuse himself.

They'd spotted Tadgh and his friends about and had decided to wait for them to go elsewhere.

He found a lap harp, beautifully carved of dark wood. He plucked a string.

Rue looked over. "You play?"

"No. You?"

"For my own amusement."

Ainsley ran his fingers over the engraving on the harp. A crow. It stirred a question and he asked, "Was the crow a...one of those spells?"

"A glamour? No. The ability to change my form is a gift from my mother," Rue answered.

"Any form?"

"No." He didn't elaborate.

Ainsley left the harp behind and sat on the bed. He crossed his legs, smoothed a wrinkle in his hose, and stared at Rue.

"What?" the fairy asked.

"You get cagey when I ask you direct questions."

"Ask and see if I'll deign to answer," Rue suggested.

Ainsley fidgeted a little longer, but finally managed to ask, "Were you going to use one of those to hide your scars? I know you hadn't wanted me to see them that day in the bath."

"I considered it."

Ainsley waited because the look on Rue's face said he had more to say.

"Had you not tried to turn around, I likely would have. I would have done it sooner, but I fretted so much about even getting undressed around you that I lacked the presence of mind to cast it."

Ainsley nodded. He'd suspected as much; he also suspected that Rue would have hidden them forever if he could have.

"It bothers you."

"Not..." Ainsley sighed. "Not the way you think. I...I'm sad for you, Rue. For the person you were."

"Then you're sad for the person I am, my love, because little has changed."

Ainsley licked his lips. He didn't like that idea. He didn't like this conversation and wished he hadn't broached it. He searched for another topic. "Tell me about the festival."

Rue set aside their previous topic just as easily. "It begins at dusk on the equinox and lasts till sunrise. It commemorates the victory of Abdalla over the Moonlight Uprising."

"And who was he?"

"She," Rue began pointedly, "Was the mayor of Bramble. She had turned a necromancer out of town for playing too freely with the deceased."

"Playing?" Ainsley asked, put off by the strange inflection in Rue's voice.

"Aye. At first, the townsfolk turned a blind eye, not caring what he did with the corpses of the unloved. However, the day came when Mayfel rose the corpse of a young bride, a sweet, fair thing who had passed on her wedding day. Her groom found that Mayfel had...enjoyed the girl's corpse in a way even he had not."

"Oh, how vile," Ainsley whispered.

"Abdalla cast out Mayfel and he swore his revenge. On the equinox, he rose all the dead of Bramble and set them against their living kin. Abdalla led her people to victory without a single person falling to Mayfel's wickedness. The necromancer's skull still rests upon a pedestal in Bramble's hall."

"Sounds grisly."

"Mmm," Rue hummed in agreement.

"Will Tadgh be there?"

"Not likely. He doesn't care to walk among the common folk often."

That comforted Ainsley. "No, I didn't think he would."

Flutes and drums and the voice of one jubilant bard had whipped the townsfolk into a frenzy. Dozens of them had paired off as the sun had started to sink. They danced in circles around the unlit bonfire in the town square.

The fire wouldn't be lit until the moon reached its zenith, Rue had explained.

They had watched for a while, standing on the fringes. Rue kept his hand on Ainsley's shoulder, patient and quiet.

Ainsley fidgeted.

"If you shuffled around much more you'd be dancing," Rue pointed out. "You might as well join them."

"I don't know how to dance like that." A thousand miles separated the courtly dances he'd been taught from the boisterous whirling of the dancers. They moved with unnatural grace and fervor. Ainsley couldn't match that.

Rue rolled his eyes. "You can vault onto a horse, but you can't dance?"

"Not like that," Ainsley insisted.

"Your body is well-trained. It will do as you tell it."

"I." Ainsley felt his face get hot. The music did call to him, as did the movements of the others. "I don't know how."

Rue slid his arms around Ainsley and spun him to face him. He pressed a kiss to his mouth. "I can show you."

Ainsley melted momentarily and by the time he came back to his senses, Rue had taken him by the hand and led him towards the dancers.

He didn't pull him into the thick of the crowd. He settled his hands onto Ainsley's hips and swayed gently to the music. He gave Ainsley time to adjust to the movement then changed the pace, their movement slightly more complicated and quicker.

"Not so hard, hmm?" Rue asked.

As long as he had Rue steering his movements, the dance didn't seem so complicated, though they didn't match the fervor of the others.

Not yet.

After Rue had twirled him a few times, Ainsley spun away on his own and threw back his head, laughing.

Rue chased after him and swept him off his feet, spinning them around together. He kissed Ainsley and nuzzled his throat.

They danced together song after song until Ainsley's throat grew dry. He voiced it to Rue, who clasped his hand and brought him over to a drink merchant.

He guzzled down half the crisp, cold ale Rue handed to him, then paused. "Is...is this as strong as the wine?"

Rue laughed and wrapped one of Ainsley's curls around his finger. "No, my love. Not anywhere close."

He took another, slower sip. He offered the mug to Rue, who hadn't brought anything for himself. The fairy had tolerated watered wine without issue and Ainsley didn't think a sip of ale would hurt him.

Rue swallowed a mouthful of ale, then returned the mug.

As soon as he'd emptied it, Ainsley took Rue by the hand and pulled him back among the dancers.

The pattern repeated itself. Dancing, then a drink, on and on, until suddenly a roar went through the crowd.

Rue drew him in close and they watched the crowd part for a young girl carrying a torch. She held it high, her chest proudly puffed out as she touched the torch to the bonfire.

It caught with a great rush of air and heat.

Another cheer moved through the crowd.

Ainsley nuzzled against Rue, but the other man didn't respond.

He had his gaze fixed on the fire. The flames reflected perfectly in the blackness of his eyes.

Of course. He'd been burned and horribly, too. If a fight where he hadn't even been hurt had unnerved Ainsley, he couldn't imagine what such a terrible burn had done to the mind of a child.

"We can go," Ainsley offered.

Rue glanced down and seemed to understand the offer. "I'm not afraid of the fire. It wasn't fire that burned me, or...it wasn't natural fire. Strange how the mind makes such divisions."

"Then what's that look for?"

"I don't want to go home."

Ainsley blinked, not sure what to say. "Why not?"

"Because I...I don't have the gift of Sight, you mustn't mistake my mewling for premonition, but I have this...stone in my gut, Ainsley, there's such fear in me that something will ruin this."

"The festival?" Ainsley guessed even though he knew it was wrong.

"Our love. I spent so much of my life as a wretched thing and a scant few months in your world cannot erase that. It does not change who I am. Nor does loving you."

"No," Ainsley agreed. "But...but every day you get a little further from that, don't you? And maybe love doesn't change people, but having a, a...an ally helps. Battles are easier fought together."

Rue raised his eyebrows.

"You think I grew up around knights and didn't see a few who relied too much on drink?" he asked. "Some rotted because of it but others...if you reach out for help, you'd be surprised how many will pull you out of the mud."

"You're so sweet, Ainsley, someone could mistake you for a fool."

He jutted out his chin. "Better a fool than the fool who loves him."

Rue snorted, slung an arm around Ainsley's shoulders, and kissed the top of his head. "I want to dance."

Ainsley could not have denied him anything. He clasped Rue's hand and they dove back into the crowd together.

They didn't dance the whole time, though. At one point, Ainsley rocked up on his toes to kiss Rue and couldn't make himself stop.

Rue dragged him away from the others, out of the firelight, and behind a building.

They grasped at each other furiously, tearing each other half out of their clothes, and coupling roughly. Sloppiness and desperation marked their union and they collapsed upon each other once they had spilled.

Ainsley buried his face in Rue's chest, sweaty and exhausted. He clung to him, obsessed by the warmth and scent of his skin.

Once they had redressed themselves, they returned to the festival, but to watch instead of dance. Ainsley nodded off in Rue's arms and woke the following morning in a bed with Rue sprawled beside him.

Undressed, with the sunlight dancing over his skin, Rue nearly broke Ainsley's heart. How, he wondered, could someone else so firmly control his emotions? He understood all the irrational danger of love and why the world so firmly condemned romantic notions. Love, unchecked, might drive a man to destroy the world.

He rolled over and kissed Rue's shoulder.

Rue buried his face further into the pillow.

"Wake up."

"'Tis early still, the sun's not yet shown her whole face," Rue protested.

"The curtains are half-drawn, my love."

Rue groaned, then rolled over and caught Ainsley in his arms. He kissed and nuzzled him so fondly that Ainsley gave up any wish to get out of bed and greet the day. They murmured sweet nonsense to each other and enjoyed each other more tenderly this time.

They spent one more day in Bramble, a quieter one. Most of the townsfolk they encountered seemed quieter, too.

They left early on their second morning away from Wolfwood and arrived home just after midday.

As they brought their horses into the stable, Tadgh turned away from his friends to watch them. Ainsley hated the feeling of the prince's eyes on him. Everywhere they went that day, Ainsley couldn't shake the feeling that Tadgh watched them.

Tadgh kept his distance, though, until after dinner.

The evening meal had been sedate, and Ainsley came to understand that the courtiers would return to the Western Court soon. He wouldn't miss them. The lord and lady had shown him hospitality and he couldn't begrudge them their own home, but he wouldn't miss the courtiers.

He especially wouldn't miss Tadgh.

The prince rapped on their bedroom door and when Rue opened it, he came in with three wooden cups and a bottle of wine.

Severely, Tadgh pronounced, "The first birthday we spent apart since you came back from the war."

Rue shifted uneasily. "I don't spend my birthdays the same way I did."

Tadgh handed over the bottle. "From Noor Valley, fiftieth year of Balor's reign."

A small smile flickered across Rue's face. "First thing you ever got me drunk on."

"You got yourself drunk, cousin," Tadgh corrected. "I didn't force your hand."

Rue snorted.

Ainsley cleared his throat.

The two fairies looked at him.

"It was your birthday?"

"The equinox," Rue admitted quietly.

"You didn't tell me."

"I didn't want a fuss." Rue glanced at Tadgh. "Or trouble."

"No fuss, no trouble," Tadgh promised. "One cup of wine. Between cousins. Between *friends*."

Still, Rue hesitated.

"And your foundling is here to keep an eye on you," Tadgh insisted.

Compelled by the sadness etched into Rue's face, Ainsley said, "One cup."

"See!" Tadgh cried. He patted Ainsley on the head. "Good pup. Can you sit and beg as well?"

Ainsley scowled but bit his tongue.

Rue uncorked the bottle and poured them all wine, though he served Ainsley and himself considerably smaller portions.

"To eighty-nine more years, Rue, hopefully kinder ones, too." Tadgh rose his cup.

Ainsley tried not to show surprise at Rue's age, sure it would cause offense if he demanded that Rue confirm his years. Eighty-nine! Older than even Ainsley's grandfather, had he still lived.

Rue snorted and clinked his cup against his cousin's. "You can sit."

Tadgh settled himself into the stuffed chair.

Ainsley sat on the edge of the bed and Rue leaned against the desk.

"You'll stay at Wolfwood for the rest of the year?" Tadgh asked.

"Yes."

"You don't worry about the snow?"

"Snow doesn't bother me."

"Mmm. The Snow Hag wakes this year, though," Tadgh reminded gently.

Ainsley glanced towards Rue. "Who?"

Rue dismissed the idea with a wave of his hand. "The Snow Hag. A child's tale."

"Undwyn lived in the Noor Valley. She bore many children, but she loved her youngest daughter the best. She loved her to a fault, though," Tadgh began. "She crafted each moment of the girl's life, every dress and meal and moment. The girl lived happily beneath her mother's doting, until...and doesn't it always go this way? Until a boy came along. She fell in love one winter. A snow sprite saw her dancing in the show, her cheeks rosy, her eyes shining, and he danced with her."

Ainsley found himself entranced, despite his dislike for Rue's cousin.

"Do the stories go like that in your world, Ainsley?"

"A lot of them."

Tadgh smiled. "They fell in love and Undwyn could not abide it. She could not share her beloved daughter and especially not with some sprite. She forbade the girl ever see him again, locked her indoors and stoked the fire so hot that no snow sprite could bear the heat. And what do you think the girl did?"

Caught off guard by the question, Ainsley sputtered, "I-I suppose maybe she ran away?"

"You suppose right. She slipped her mother a sleeping draught and ran out into the snow, into the arms of her lover. She became his hoary bride and ran away to the mountains with him to live with the snow prince in a palace of frost. When Undwyn woke, she ran out into the worst blizzard the Noor Valley had ever known. She looked and looked, she climbed the peaks looking for the sprites, but she never found them. She looked so long that her heart froze up with sadness. Her whole body froze and only the hottest of summers can wake her."

"A summer like this one?" Ainsley guessed.

"Clever pup."

"A child's tale," Rue reminded.

"After a hot summer, Undwyn wakes and freezes our valley so she can look for the frost palace again," Tadgh concluded. "Rue, don't you remember that fall? It snowed three days after the seasons changed and we couldn't get out for a week!"

"Some years the snow is heavy," Rue agreed. "It doesn't worry me."

"Court isn't the same without you."

"I'm sure it's tidier."

Tadgh groaned. "It's *boring*. Besides, don't you want to show your foundling where you grew up? Deflower him in your childhood bed?"

Ainsley raised his eyebrows and took a slow sip of his wine. He saw no reason to correct the prince and, it seemed, neither did Rue.

"You still haven't told me what you even *did* in the mortal world," Tadgh whined.

Rue asked, "What do you want to know?"

"Start from the beginning!" Tadgh's face lit up and he leaned forward eagerly in his chair. "Oh, you always tell my favorite stories, Rue."

Rue related a few tales of what he had done in Triviai.

Tadgh hung on to the words, seeming particularly fascinated with the tale of the wrym. He even went so far as to praise Ainsley for his cleverness in bringing the wrym to a blacksmith.

Tadgh drank the rest of the bottle of wine and teetered out towards his room after a few hours.

Rue and Ainsley finished their own wine more slowly. It left both rather affected, though not quite enough to be called truly drunk. Rue pulled Ainsley into bed and curled around him, fully dressed, and held him like that for some time without speaking.

Or, at least, without speaking any words. He stroked Ainsley's hair, rubbed his back, and pressed an ear to his chest to listen to his heart. That spoke volumes.

The court departed within a week. Balor and Corva both kissed Rue on the cheek in farewell. Tadgh pulled his cousin into an embrace, repeating that court was dull without him. None of them paid Ainsley much mind with the exception of polite farewells and that suited him well enough.

The days at Wolfwood remained warm and gave the two of them plenty of time to continue their explorations. They journeyed through the Noor Valley to visit the Singing Fields and struck out south to see an ancient bridge made of living wood.

By the time the nights did begin to cool, Ainsley had nearly forgotten about Tadgh and his tales of the Snow Hag.

It wasn't until Rue stood at the door of Wolfwood, watching the sky darken over the mountains to the north that Ainsley wondered if the story had any truth to it.

Dora passed them on her way indoors, her arms laden with herbs. She, too, looked northwards and declared, "Undwyn's awake."

"'Tis a bedtime story, Dora."

"You've not even a full century under your belt, little crow," Dora answered. "She's awake."

Ainsley slipped an arm around Rue. He hadn't known Dora to be wrong about the weather yet. "Will the horses be alright in the stables?"

Rue nodded.

For several days, no snow came, though the clouds remained, and the temperatures started to drop. Dora continued to bring things in from the garden and Rue gave the horses more feed and water than necessary one night.

Rue paced around the gardens restlessly the next day and frowned when a few light flakes of snow started to trickle down.

Ainsley watched them touch the surface of one of the garden pools, dissolving as soon as they made contact.

The ground quickly collected a dusting of snow and Ainsley amused himself in the first snowfall of the year. He traced shapes in the snow, tried to pack a few snowballs, and kicked up drifts of the powder to watch it dance on the wind. He'd enjoyed being out of doors in the winter as a child, building snow forts with the other children of the manor. His older brother, who broke out in hives when the weather got too hot, had always been more companionable when the temperature dropped.

"We should go inside," Rue informed him.

"It's hardly even snowed yet. Did you ever make snow castles when you were young?" Ainsley asked.

"Go inside."

Ainsley frowned at the harshness of his tone. Not a moment later, an enormous gust of wind rocked him so hard it almost ripped the cape off his body. He immediately forgave Rue's shortness.

Rue grabbed his arm and pulled him indoors. The wind slammed the door behind them, and Rue latched it shut.

"Bit blustery," Ainsley declared.

Rue finger-combed his curls back into order. "She's awake."

"I thought you said the Snow Hag wasn't real."

"I said she's a children's tale. So many things are."

Ainsley rolled his eyes. "You sounded awfully convinced that she wasn't real."

"Whether the hag's real or not, I know that there's unpleasant weather on the horizon." Rue combed his fingers through Ainsley's hair one more time. He frowned and wandered away.

Ainsley followed.

They watched the snow roll in together from the library window. It piled up for hours and hours. When the snow covered half the window, Ainsley started to worry.

He wandered over to the window and peered outside. The only thing he could think to say was, "That's a lot of snow."

"It'll be sometime before we can go outside again."

"Mmm," Ainsley agreed. "Do you think the horses will be alright?"

"The barn is warded against the cold."

The first few days indoors passed with an indolent sort of ardor, late mornings spent in bed, long baths, and warm meals. They learned each other's bodies well, played several games of chess, though it took them some time and several arguments to come to the understanding that chess had different rules in each realm.

On the third day, boredom started to settle in.

Ainsley found Rue better equipped to handle this kind of boredom. He sat and read for hours, seemingly unbothered by the lack of movement or intrigue. Ainsley, on the other hand, paced and wandered through Wolfwood, exploring all the rooms he could enter.

When the snow had continued well into the third night, Ainsley attempted to open the door and encountered a snowbank that stood taller than he did.

Rue poked his head out of their room. "What's that draft...my love, what are you doing?"

"I'm worried about the horses." He had been worried about the horses for some time now, truth be told.

"The horses are probably fine. Close the door."

Ainsley hesitated then closed the door. He didn't move away, though.

"I gave them extra food and water."

"Three days ago."

Rue studied him. "You're right." He left the room and tied his robe tight about his waist. He headed down the hall to towards the kitchen.

Ainsley padded along behind him. He watched as Rue let himself into the pantry and pulled open a trap door on the ceiling. He leapt back from the vast pile of snow that fell through, then pulled down a ladder of rope and vines.

He shed his robe, then started to climb up, the wind whipping down through the trapdoor and showering him with even more snow. "Wait down here. The roof isn't safe."

Ainsley retreated a few feet.

Rue disappeared through the door, leaving Ainsley to anxiously await his return.

He watched the door for a while, then stoked the fire for a warm drink, knowing Rue would likely be frozen when he came back. He found a jar of cider and set it to warm, heady scents wafting up.

The slightly alcoholic tinge to the smell made him worry, but he figured cider must have been like ale. And either way, it was only one mug. Most of the occasional details Rue let slip about his past troubles began with four or five glasses of wine, not one mug of cider.

After a long wait, something small and dark tumbled through the trap door, landing on the floor with a graceless thump.

Ainsley rushed in to find the crow, bedraggled and speckled with white. On instinct, he seized Rue's discarded robe and scooped up the crow, swaddling the thing. He brought it into the kitchen, set it on the table, and then rushed back to the pantry to close the trapdoor.

When he returned the crow had gone, replaced by Rue, equally as bedraggled and his gray skin turned pink by the cold. He forced shivering limbs through the sleeves of the robe. He had his jaw clenched so tight that Ainsley feared for his teeth.

"Here, to bed, right away," Ainsley insisted, hurrying him toward the door.

The fairy went without protest, perhaps too stiff and numb for it.

Ainsley put him in bed, wrapped him in blankets and stoked the fire, then remembered the cider and dashed away to take it off the heat. He presented one mug to Rue upon his return and, almost too embarrassed to get the words out, asked, "How were the horses?"

"They're well. I fed and watered them, double checked the spell to keep the stable from growing icy. The stalls need to be mucked, though."

"Th." He bit his tongue. "I made you cider."

Rue smiled. "You want so *badly* to thank me."

"It feels so rude not to!" Ainsley whined. "I'd have gotten switched bloody if I didn't when I was little."

"But it doesn't mean anything."

"It does, though," Ainsley said.

"Educate me, then, while the feeling in my limbs returns," Rue requested.

Ainsley sighed and settled onto the bed across from him. "Sometimes it doesn't mean anything, it's just what you say to be polite, but it's...I mean, it's also what you say when you someone did something just for you, that they really meant what they did, and that you *know* they did it for you. Thank you is, it's like a promise. It's saying that I understand you helped me, that I'll help in return when you need it."

Rue rolled his eyes. "Sounds just as empty as it did before. A hollow way to dismiss a deed. I acted for you and your words are to be sufficient repayment? No. Fairies don't work like that. Our world is not a world of repayment. You cannot do something out of obligation for a past favor."

Ainsley reached out and gave his arm a squeeze, checking to see if he'd warmed up. "Drink your cider. It'll help you get warm."

Rue sipped his drink. "Honey?"

"I know how much you like it."

The fairy grinned his wicked smile.

"Do you have to get undressed to become the crow?"

Rue shrugged. "I'd look silly as a crow flapping about in a robe ten times too large for me."

"Don't you get cold?"

"Oh, well, you don't think I started following you around *just* because of how beautiful I found you, do you?" Rue asked. "The ability to start a fire had close to equal appeal."

"You'll hurt my feelings one of these days."

That only made Rue grin again.

On the fifth day, after Ainsley had completed his exploration of Wolfwood's cellar, he stopped by the library to check in on Rue, maybe invite him to lunch, and found him reading in exactly the same position as before.

No. Not exactly the same. On the small table next to him sat a wooden cup.

So he had gotten thirsty. What did it matter?

Ainsley approached and placed a hand on his shoulder. He couldn't help but peer into the cup.

"It's watered," Rue told him.

Ainsley's face burned. "I."

"I understand."

"I'm sorry."

"Don't be sorry," Rue said.

"I should trust you."

"You should not trust me," Rue answered. "A wicked fairy prince and a drunkard to boot. Never trust me."

"You watered it, though," Ainsley pointed out. He squeezed Rue's shoulder. "I trust you."

Rue took his hand and kissed his knuckles. He tugged Ainsley onto his lap and buried his face in his shoulder. "You should try reading a little. It might still your pacing."

"I'm not good at reading."

"Then to the maps. You can plot our course come the spring."

That idea held tremendous appeal. "In a little while." He nestled more comfortably into Rue's lap. "Rue?"

"Hmm?"

"Maybe in the spring, before we head anywhere else, I should go home for a little while."

Rue closed his book on his finger and looked at Ainsley. "Home?"

"To see my parents. I haven't seen them in a while. I don't want them to worry."

"I forget that's something parents do."

Something didn't sit right with Rue's tone and suddenly, stories of human spent a year among the Fair Folk and returning home a century later leapt to the forefront of Ainsley's mind. "And...Rue. If I were to go home, how long would it have been?"

"However long I decide it should have been," Rue declared. "The days pass nearly the same here as they do in your world, give or take a few months or weeks. But I can, when we pass between the worlds, slide through time to bring you back any point from the moment of your departure to hundreds of years after it."

Ainsley swallowed.

"'Tis a wicked trick to play and time sliding is difficult. I never had much of a knack for it," Rue shared. "And, of course, I have no wish to distress you so. Home you shall go."

"And you'll come too, right?"

"If you'll have me."

"Of course, I will. What a silly thing to say."

Rue smiled easier then and returned to his book.

"We won't go for too long. I want to see *everything*, Rue. The whole Otherworld. I only wish I had time."

"Why wouldn't you have time?"

"I'll probably be old before we get through half of it. The Western Court alone is vast."

This time Rue marked his page with a ribbon and set his book aside. "Time does not touch you here, Ainsley. You will not wrinkle or gray or stoop while you live in the among the Fair Folk."

"Like you?"

"A little different," Rue said but didn't elaborate.

"So I could stay here for...fifty years and never get any older than twenty-one?"

"Yes. You have as many years as you want to explore every inch of this world."

"Oh." Ainsley hadn't thought about that. He hadn't noticed himself not aging, but he didn't think he'd ever noticed himself getting any older at home, either.

After two more days, the snow stopped, the highest banks reaching all the way to the roof of Wolfwood. Rue and Ainsley joined forces with Dora and Lettie to dig their way out to the stables, then to muck out the stalls.

The horses trotted back and forth on the path they'd dug, nosing at the snow walls and occasionally shying away from a bit of snow that tumbled towards them.

Hadley practically refused to go back into her stall. Ainsley had to sweet talk her the whole way. He promised her half a hundred times that he would come and let her out again tomorrow.

It took about a week to clear out enough snow to allow their lives to resume any semblance of normalcy.

Ainsley rejoiced at taking Hadley on long rides in the snow, bundled up and pink with the cold. Rue accompanied him on most of his trips but seemed to enjoy these excursions less than their fair-weather ones. Ainsley tried a few times to tell him that he didn't need to come if he didn't want to, but the fairy persisted.

The strangest thing about the snow, Ainsley decided, wasn't the fury with which it had descended, or its sheer volume, but the fact that an hour's ride away, the snow barely reached to his knees. Half a day brought them to more seasonable fall weather with no snow at all.

"Does it always snow like this? Uneven in places?" Ainsley asked as he looked over the merrily bubbling river and flaming foliage.

"It snows the worst by Wolfwood during hag winters."

"And it will snow again?"

"Likely soon."

Ainsley's skin crawled at the thought of another two weeks, or maybe more this time, trapped indoors. He turned his face up towards the sky and relished the feel of the sun on his skin.

"Will you be able to stand it?" Rue asked.

Ainsley opened his eyes and looked towards him. "What?"

"Being trapped indoors with me again?"

Ainsley snorted. "You're so morose sometimes, Rue."

As if to prove his point, Rue blinked slowly and steered his horse away from Ainsley. He didn't speak much for the rest of the night, though he answered, "No," when Ainsley asked if he was angry with him.

His mood persisted for a few days though, no matter how Ainsley tried to soothe it.

Finally, in desperation, he begged Dora's help and baked a cake. He topped it with whipped and sweetened cream, then crept down the hall to the library.

Rue had heard him coming anyway; he almost always did. He turned towards the door when Ainsley entered. "I thought you'd be out of doors. 'Tis warm out today. Probably our last warm day, given the cast of the sky above the mountains."

"I thought this was more important." He handed over the plate to Rue.

"A cake?"

"I made it. Well. Dora helped."

Rue tilted the cake here and there, studying the confection. "You made it?"

"Dora helped," he repeated to assure Rue that the cake was edible and not some half-hearted concoction. He leaned down and kissed the top of Rue's head. "You haven't got to eat it now if you don't want, I won't be offended. I just, well, you seemed so sad, I thought it might boost your spirits a little."

Rue set the plate on the table beside his chair, kissed Ainsley's hand, and said, "Go get your last bit of sunshine, my love."

"Are you sure?"

He nodded. "Yes."

"I won't be gone too long. I want to let Hadley stretch her legs, especially if you think it's going to snow again."

"Of course."

Ainsley headed to the stables and took Hadley for a long ride, groomed her, and double checked that the horses had food and water aplenty. As he headed inside, the wind nipped at his clothes and the first flakes began to fall.

He tried to pretend it didn't bother him. He pretended well through dinner and grinned when he saw that Rue had saved his cake for dessert. The sight of him relishing the cake lifted his spirits and Rue seemed happier too.

Their good mood persisted until the following morning until Ainsley saw how much snow had fallen overnight.

The sight of it alone tightened his throat. He scrubbed the tears off his cheeks and wiped his nose, hoping Rue wouldn't see. He felt reasonably certain that Rue hadn't, until that night when Rue wrapped him up in an embrace and said, "This time when the snow clears, we'll depart Wolfwood."

"To go where?"

"Likely the Western Court is our only option," Rue said. "We'll have to take care, but it's better than being here, isn't it?"

"I'll be careful," Ainsley promised. "I won't even *think* about saying thank you to anyone."

Rue snorted and pulled him even closer, pressing a kiss to his shoulder. "You'll have to withstand a few more days trapped in here with me."

"As far as company goes, I wouldn't pick anyone else to be trapped with."

Rue didn't respond to that, but he didn't move much either, so Ainsley guessed that he had fallen asleep. He had been sleeping a lot lately. Ainsley chalked it up to the weather.

On the fourth night of travel, as Ainsley pitched their tent and Rue stoked a campfire, an idea struck Ainsley. He'd left their travel plans for the rest of the year at Wolfwood. It would be safe enough in the library, he knew, but he hadn't had the chance to show all his ideas to Rue yet.

He'd have to do it in the spring after he visited his parents. He didn't think he'd visit Triviai for too long. Oh, long enough to catch up with his parents and show Rue around his childhood home, but not long enough that anyone started to wonder too much about Rue or what kind of adventures Ainsley had gotten up to in the Otherworld. He doubted his parents would take too kindly to him spending nearly a year away from the mortal realm.

"Love?" Ainsley called when he'd hammered his last stake.

"Yes?"

"Do you need help with anything?"

"No. Company wouldn't hurt, though."

Ainsley sat beside him, watching him stir their dinner. "Will they be happy to see us?"

"Happy is such a relative term."

"Are you ever able to give a straight-forward answer?"

"I'm capable of it," Rue answered. "I don't think they'll be angry. Does that suffice?"

Ainsley leaned against the other man. "I suppose it must." He had his reservations about visiting the Western Court, but he had survived the courtiers' visit to Wolfwood well enough. Rue had never faltered, either, proving himself perfectly capable of moderation.

"Ainsley?"

"Hmm?"

"I love you."

"I love you, as well," Ainsley answered. He took Rue's hand. "My mother says two are better than one. Well. She says it, but it's from the Bible."

"Common sense, then, in that text."

"You'd like my mother, I think."

"I doubt you would care for mine," Rue answered. "She's twice as slippery as anything you'll meet at the Western Court."

Ainsley didn't respond. He didn't want to speak ill of his companion's mother, especially if he'd never met her. Still, her slipperiness had less to do with the distaste stirring in him than the fact that she hadn't seen her son since he'd turned twenty.

He'd once thought that Rue hadn't seen his parents in maybe six or seven years, but now he knew it meant he hadn't seen them in nearly seven decades. He could barely fathom it.

He tightened his hold on Rue's hand.

Sleep came easily that night. He hadn't dreamt of the man who'd attacked him...the man he'd killed for a while now. Sometimes the fight did surface in his thoughts or dreams, but they didn't unnerve him as badly as before. His mornings practicing sword forms had helped, as had Rue's advice on managing shaky nerves. He found himself in no way eager to fight anyone again but thought that he'd be able to stand his ground should it become unavoidable.

And now, of course, he knew to aim his blows with care.

Part of him wished Sir Richard had doled out this kind of advice before he'd sent Ainsley off on his own, but he'd never overheard any knights exchanging such knowledge.

He woke with the sun, refreshed, and shook Rue awake.

The fairy rolled deeper into his bedroll.

"Rue," he whined. He pressed his forehead to Rue's back. "I want to sleep in a real bed tonight. A warm bed."

"Spoiled," Rue accused, his face still turned away.

"You're the one who's spoiled me. You've only got yourself to blame."

"Should I have been cruel to you instead?"

"I don't think you could," Ainsley pronounced.

"You think you know me so well. What can mortals know of fey hearts?"

Not put off by Rue's scolding, Ainsley insisted, "I think it would hurt you more than it would hurt me. Now get up."

Rue let out a long, dramatic groan, but rolled over and pushed himself up.

As the sun sank towards the horizon that evening, Rue reined in his horse and held up a hand, indicating Ainsley should do the same.

Ainsley brought Hadley to a halt and looked in the same direction as Rue but saw nothing. He remained quiet, listening hard, and put off by the tight expression on Rue's face. "What is it?" he whispered.

"I swear I heard something."

Ainsley's hands tightened on the reins.

They waited a few long, tense moments, then Rue shook his head. "I'll feel safer when we're away from here."

Ainsley urged his horse into a trot and Rue followed, both men glancing over their shoulder from time to time. Nothing emerged from the trees. Slowly, the road before them turned from dirt to a hard-packed sparkling white gravel. Still, each rustling branch made Ainsley snap his head in that direction, every gust of wind made him flinch. His stomach bubbled. He forced himself to focus on his breathing. He recalled his fondest memories.

The high, thin sound of a flute reached his ears. He barely registered it at first, but as the music grew louder, he slowed Hadley to a walk.

"Ainsley?" Rue asked.

"I know this song," Ainsley said. He could have sworn he did, anyway. The lyrics sat right on the tip of his tongue and, even though he couldn't recall them, he knew he loved this song. He had sat by watching others dance to it, wishing he could join in. Wishing for a lad to take his hand and pulling him towards the others swirling around the dance floor.

"What song?" Rue stopped his horse alongside Hadley. "All I hear is the wind."

"Flutes," Ainsley insisted.

The music had grown so loud that he didn't know how Rue couldn't hear it. The players must have been just off the path.

He slipped off Hadley before he'd even thought about it. How beautiful would these creatures be? And what beautiful boys would be among them? He had been so young when he'd first heard it, no more than fourteen, and his cousin had urged him to ask for another boy's hand. He'd been too frightened then, but he wasn't now. He wasn't afraid of anything, as drunk on these flutes as he'd ever been on wine.

He rushed towards the woods, barely aware of the footsteps behind him.

Someone seized his wrist and he spun to find a tall man with a severe face staring down at him.

He yanked his wrist back, but the man grabbed him again, this time holding firm onto his arms. "Ainsley, there isn't any song."

He tried to pull back again. "Let me go." Words came from his mouth, words he didn't remember generating. "I want to dance with someone."

The stranger stared at him.

"Tadgh said someone might dance with me. Maybe one of the wodnik, they aren't picky." Something in the back of his mind stirred, something about his cousin.

"How picky can someone covered in slime be?" the stranger said, the same words Tadgh had said earlier. His grip tightened. "Come back, 'tis a trick, my love."

He shook his head. He didn't know this man. He was too *old* anyway and being called a pet name by an old man made his skin crawl. "I...I need to go. I need to find my cousin." He wrenched himself out of the stranger's grip, surprised at his own strength. He hesitated a moment, then bolted for the woods.

Toward the music.

Tadgh would be there. He always had someone to dance with.

Branches snatched at him, stinging as they whipped against his skin. He heard someone slipping through the trees after him and he ran harder.

The flutes played so loud now. He must have been practically on top of them.

The person behind him didn't slow.

He kept running until his sides and lungs started to burn with the effort. His legs, heavy and tired, started to fail him.

The flutes played loud enough to hurt. He threw up his hands to cover his ears. He stumbled and fell, slamming his knees to the ground.

The wet, sticky ground.

In front of him, dozens danced around the fire, none of them bloated, slimy things like the wodnik his cousin had urged him towards. One lovely boy, his hair shimmery copper curls, caught his eye and grinned. The boy beckoned him over, so he stood.

The stranger caught up with him and grabbed him by the elbow, dragging him away from the fire, away from the boy.

"Stop, stop it," he begged, tears in his eyes.

"Ainsley."

That wasn't his name.

"Ainsley, look at me," the stranger demanded. He wrapped a hand around his face and forced his eyes upwards. "There is no music, it isn't real. Listen to my voice."

"Let go of me." He squirmed.

"Ainsley!" the man finally barked.

He flinched and stilled.

"Look at me."

He raised his eyes to the man's face, severe and strange.

Black eyes caught his. "You are Sir Ainsley, a knight of the mortal realm," the stranger insisted. "You grew up in a castle, you have a horse named Hadley, you squired for a man named Richard. You had a friend named Alfred and...And your mother's name is Elaine."

Something stirred, something in the back of his mind.

"You are human. Your king is Jannes."

"Human!" he scoffed.

"Ainsley," the man repeated, his grip loosening. "I'll unveil your senses, but you mustn't flee from me."

He didn't dare move.

The man traced his fingers over his eyes, nose, ears, and mouth. "You are Ainsley."

Magic tingled over his face, tickling and itching. He scrubbed at his face, scrubbing at his eyes and ears, pressing desperately against his nose to make the itch go away.

When it did, he heard no music. He had smeared sticky grime all over his face and the smell of something fetid wound its way up from the ground, assaulting his nose.

He glanced over his shoulder. No more fire, no more dancers. And no stranger.

Only Rue.

"What..."

Rue pointed up. In the branches of a tree a few yards away sat an enormous bird, not an owl or a vulture, but some grotesque combination of the two. It had massive eyes, bulging and round, and a long scraggly neck. It watched them, then ruffled its wings, and clicked its beak.

Ainsley looked down and saw bundles of bones and hair beneath his feet. Tiny round skulls and short little ribs.

The bird watched them, never blinking.

"A boughguide," Rue murmured. "We're too large for it to eat, so we should be able to go. If it startles, though, run, because the beast can do quite some damage."

The bird had talons as long as Rue's knife and Ainsley had no desire to find out how well it could use them. He clutched Rue's hand as they backed away from the bird. It watched them go, unperturbed by their departure.

"Normally, their call only affects children," Rue informed him quietly, though not without a hint of dark amusement in his voice.

"I...I wasn't remembering my childhood, though."

"I know. I can only assume it sensed us passing by and tried to call to me, but I was too old to be lured and its magic found you instead."

"Was I remembering your youth?"

Rue shook his head. "No. A dream. You experienced my dream from last night. That's what a boughguide does. It takes your dreams and makes them real. Or it makes them seem real."

"That's terrible."

"I'll have to let my aunt and uncle know. They'll want to get rid of it before it moves any closer to the court and the wee ones start going missing. We have so precious few children."

The grime on Ainsley's face itched as it started to dry. He did his best to scrub it away with his sleeve. "Why did it affect me?"

"Perhaps because you are young, or because you are human, or because you have no magic to protect you from the charms of fey creatures. I cannot say why."

When they emerged from the wood, Rue took the waterskin from his pack, wet a bit of cloth, and began to dab the grime off Ainsley's face. He did it gently, carefully grasping Ainsley by the chin and tilting his face from side to side to make sure he didn't miss anything.

"There he is, my lovely knight," Rue finally pronounced.

Ainsley rocked up on his toes and pressed a kiss to Rue's lips. "My savior, yet again."

"I'll save you as many times as you need saving."

"I'm a knight, I don't think I should need saving!" Ainsley protested. "Besides, I'm stronger than you."

Rue grinned and let out a small purring hum as he nuzzled his face against Ainsley's throat. "So very strong."

Ainsley gave him a quick squeeze then stepped away before they ended up doing something foolish.

Rue pulled him back in for one more kiss, then nudged him towards Hadley.

Despite the delay, they reached the Court before sundown. A large, spiny throne sat beneath an enormous oak tree, not quite the same size as the tree beside the spring that fed the Tadgh, but still so large it felt unreasonable. Neither king nor queen sat on the throne presently, though a few courtiers milled around the area.

A small girl, perhaps ten years old, scurried up to them and bowed. "Your Highness, I'll take your horse, if it please you."

Rue handed over the reins.

The girl looked over at Ainsley. "And your pet's?"

Something flickered over Rue's face. "You may take my companion's horse, too. Treat it just as you would mine. Have our things brought to my room."

The girl flushed, took Hadley's reins, and hurried away with both horses.

Rue linked arms with Ainsley and escorted him towards the hill, which stood as tall as three men. "Don't step on the flowers."

Ainsley carefully stepped over the ring of white flowers.

With a few words to the hill, Rue opened the entrance to the Western court. A portion of the ground melted away, exposing a set of stairs that descended into the space beneath the hill. Orbs of light hung in the air and lit the way, making the idea of descending into a hole in the ground a little less foreboding. Still, if Rue hadn't been holding his hand and guiding him along, Ainsley likely wouldn't have entered.

As they descended, the ground sealed up behind them. However, Ainsley got no sense that he was underground. Indoors, yes, but the walls and floor weren't made of dirt. No roots poked out; no worms wiggled through. At the bottom of the stairs, they entered a small concourse that branched out into five hallways.

"I'm going to get lost," Ainsley declared.

"You'll learn." Rue brought him down the center hallway.

They passed dozens of people as they made their way through the halls. Ainsley lost track of the turns, too enraptured by the courtiers. They came in so many colors, some sported wings, antlers, or tails, or entire limbs altogether inhuman. Others seemed to be made of something other than flesh, be it flora, water, or flame. All of them emanated a wonderous, terrible beauty that raised the hair on the back of his neck.

One fish-eyed man smiled at him, exposing sharp teeth.

Rue met the man's gaze and tightened his grip on Ainsley's hand.

The man only smiled wider, impossibly wide. "We're all so excited to see what spectacle your return brings, Your Highness."

Rue's lips peeled back from his teeth in the most aggressive smile Ainsley had ever witnessed.

The courtier continued past them, apparently unbothered.

Hoping to soothe Rue, Ainsley balanced on his toes and pressed a kiss to his cheek.

It didn't produce the desired effect. Rue scowled at him, an expression Ainsley could read all too well. The same scowl that had affixed itself on Sir Richard's face when Ainsley had lost at something. A scowl that spoke of disappointment, of being stuck with the runty squire because his father had done you a good turn once.

"This was a mistake," the fairy growled.

A lump in his gut, Ainsley struggled to find a response. He feared he might vomit if he opened his mouth.

"They'll probably eat you alive."

The rumble of that husky voice, usually so comforting, rolled through Ainsley like thunder over a man in an open field. "Uh. Literally?"

"Don't try to be clever," Rue spat. He gripped Ainsley's hand even harder and pulled him along so roughly he jostled Ainsley.

Giving in and going quietly might have been the wiser course, but Ainsley would never earn a reputation for wisdom. He dug his heels in so Rue had to stop short.

The fairy turned to glare. "If you're going to run—"

Ainsley redoubled his hold on Rue's hand and pulled him in. He pulled hard enough that Rue stumbled into him. "I thought I was here under your protection."

"You know you are."

"Does that mean so little? You offered it as if it had weight."

Still scowling, Rue answered, "It does."

"Then I am protected," Ainsley declared.

A few passers-by gave them strange looks. Why wouldn't they? A mortal holding a fairy like this in the heart of their Court must have been uncommon if not outright offensive.

"I'm not weak, Rue. Just small. You haven't got to worry about me."

The taller man stared down at him, eyes appealingly wide. He looked somewhere between shocked and sheepish, with just the right amount of affectionate thrown in. He licked his lips. "Well."

"And what were you going to say about running? Do you expect me to run?"

Rue blinked a few times. "Whatever you found in the boughguide's lair still sullies your skin. I'd wash it away if you let me. Replace it with oils and perfumes."

Although Rue hadn't answered his question, Ainsley couldn't refuse his offer. He nodded.

Rue guided him to a room.

Ainsley nearly forgot about his promise to wash him, too busy soaking all the fineness of the chambers.

At Wolfwood, Rue's room had been comfortable and fine, but these were truly the quarters of a prince. The first of the rooms held a large desk made of black wood and a heavy, ornate chair made of the same dark wood and sleek, scaled leather. Books, nearly as many as had lined the library shelves at Wolfwood, looked down at them from shelves that reached the ceiling and even had a ladder tucked away in the corner. In the center of the room, a thick fur rug from some monstrously large creature lay over the slate tiles; the fire crackled merrily, throwing orange and yellow licks of light across the room.

The scent of citrus and lavender laced the air, the evidence of a quick airing out, because beneath Ainsley could still detect a hint of dust and staleness.

"The bath is over here." Rue gestured towards another room.

"What animal is that from?" Ainsley peered at the carpet.

"A war-cat."

The fur had to be the size of two bears at least. "A cat!"

"Well, not any war-cat. The brood queen of the troll chief's stables," Rue explained mildly.

"And you fought it?"

Rue laughed. "No! Not at all. I wanted to keep her. But Ptholo poisoned his whole stable when he knew the war was lost. Poisoned himself and his family, too. He worried what we'd do to him. He wasn't wrong, either."

Ainsley bobbed his head in mute agreement. Conquered peoples didn't often thrive. "Trolls?" he asked instead.

"Mmm, just one of the southern clans. By the stars, if we had warred with all the troll clans we would have lost. We barely won out against Ptholo."

Rue had never offered so much information about his time in the army and Ainsley took the opportunity to ask, "What sort of dispute was it?"

Rue snorted. "A paltry one. Born of fairy pride and troll stubbornness. Ptholo's son wanted to wed one of our cousins, Erdia. Her father asked for a dowry, which of course, the trolls refused to pay."

"Why?"

"Dowry isn't a troll custom. Normally, fairy parents scoff and grumble when these kinds of matches come about, but they don't press the issue."

Ainsley guessed, "But her family did?"

"Of course, they did. Erdia eloped with her troll and her father called it kidnapping. He went to the Ptholo and tried to bring his daughter...who was the troll boy's wife, by now, too, he tried to bring her back, which the trolls saw as kidnapping. And they had the right of it, Erdia wanted to be with her husband." Rue let out a bored sigh and rolled his eyes. "So then the father and Ptholo came to blows. Erdia's father died and then, of course, our hand was forced. A six-year war, a miserable and stupid war. No one really won in the end. We breached their final defenses and found the whole troll chief's family dead at the dinner table."

"People..."

"Hmm?"

"People are fools, through and through, aren't they? No matter what kind of people."

Rue grinned. "Sir Ainsley, you never mentioned you dabbled in philosophy. I thought you far too pretty for such insights. Oh, don't scowl at me like that!" Rue scolded when Ainsley crossed his arms and huffed. He scooped Ainsley up into his arms. "The bath is this way. You can inspect the furnishings later."

Rue made quick work of removing their clothing and hurried Ainsley into the tub, twice the size of the one at Wolfwood and made of beaten copper. All that haste disappeared, though, once Rue had sunk into the water beside him. With agonizing slowness and care, he washed Ainsley then wrapped him in a towel soft as kitten's fur.

He carried Ainsley to the bed and massaged him with sweet-scented oil, the combed his hair and carefully arranged each curl. Any sense of lustfulness had long since faded, replaced with a slow, quiet sleepiness that settled into Ainsley's very bones.

He yawned into a feather pillow too warm and soft to be made of mere goose down. The feathers had probably been gathered from some obscure bird that ate only honey and perfectly ripe berries and lived on the northern face of hills that grew evergreens.

He mumbled this into the crook of his arm, stifling a yawn.

Rue chuckled as he wound his arms around Ainsley. "Is that what you think of my realm? That it's full of ridiculous things?"

"Well, you're here, for one," Ainsley teased. He made sure to soften it with a kiss immediately, before even a hint of melancholy could ghost across Rue's face. "And I did almost get eaten by a gigantic bird that gave me your dreams."

Rue kissed his shoulder instead of answering.

"You didn't answer me before," Ainsley reminded. "Where do you think I'm going to run to?"

"I...I pray you have the sense to flee from danger," Rue answered quietly, "But I also pray you won't go anywhere."

"I just got here and I haven't even gotten a good look at your rooms yet, I'm not going until I get a better look at the rest of this place at the very least."

"Is spectacle all the Western Court hold for you?"

"Well," Ainsley answered, "You're here, for one."

Rue rolled his eyes.

In response, Ainsley wrapped himself around him. "I'm going to fall asleep, I don't think I've got any choice in the matter. If you're not here when I wake up, I'll be heartbroken. And if we don't get something to eat immediately *after* I wake up, I might weep."

"You're a fool."

Ainsley let the statement stand; it had been said with affection instead of insult and he'd never expected to become a sage. He burrowed closer to Rue, beneath blankets that carried the smallest hint of staleness. He stifled another yawn and then almost immediately fell asleep. The journey, and the encounter with the boughguide, had taken more out of him than he'd expected.

He woke to the quiet murmur of voices. Through his haziness, it took him a moment to recognize the other speaker, but once he realized it was Tadgh, his mood soured. He pushed himself up, angrily scrubbing the sleep from his eyes.

Rue sat at the end of the four-poster bed, a heavy brocade robe draped around his shoulders as he spoke with his cousin.

"Oh, you're awake!" Tadgh whispered with quiet enthusiasm. "Come here and look."

The prince had a bundle of blankets clutched in his arms and, as Ainsley scooted towards the end of the bed, he fully expected Tadgh to unwrap them to reveal an angry badger. Instead, though, he unveiled a small infant. It lacked any uncommon qualities, just a nutbrown babe with dark hair and pouty lips.

"I'm calling her Merremia," Tadgh informed him with quiet pride.

"Is she...?" Ainsley saw no resemblance between the babe and the man who held her. Then again, Tadgh didn't look much like Corva or Balon in terms of build or coloring. Inherited traits seemed to work a little differently among the Fair Folk. Not for the first time, Ainsley wondered what Rue's parents looked like.

"In a week's time, she will be officially a princess of the Western Court. Presently, she's just some wench's cast off. But isn't she beautiful?"

"Very sweet," Ainsley agreed.

Beaming, Tadgh offered the babe to his cousin.

Rue slipped her out of the prince's arms. "What do our lord and lady think of her?" He brushed his fingertips over the baby's forehead.

She barely stirred.

"Who cares what they think?" Tadgh demanded. "They think of her what they think of *everyone*. We're so far beneath them they might as well ascend to the stars and get it over with."

Rue clucked his tongue. "You'll make her just as bitter as you are if you aren't careful, cousin."

"Better than having her be a morose wretch like you, cousin," Tadgh returned mildly. He didn't take the baby back, though. "Have you eaten?"

"Not yet."

Tadgh nodded and walked away. He activated the runes beside the bedroom door and, when a servant appeared, ordered a meal for three.

Rue cooed to the baby, soft, tender things in another language.

"Get dressed," Tadgh told Ainsley. "Or don't. It wasn't an order, just a suggestion."

By the time food came, Ainsley and Rue had secured robes around themselves and Tadgh had set Merremia down in a delicately woven basket. He set the basket on the fur rug and settled himself in beside it.

Rue and Ainsley joined him on the rug.

The servant came, set food and wine before them, and disappeared in the blink of an eye.

Tadgh took up his cup of wine and raised it. "To the health of babes."

"And to the health of family," Rue added.

Tadgh beamed, his thin, sharp face glowing in response to Rue's toast. It must have meant something Ainsley didn't understand, some acceptance of the child or the proclamation of new peace between cousins.

Either way, they all drank.

Rue warned his cousin of the boughguide that had taken up residence nearby.

Tadgh updated Rue on the various happenings of Court since the royal family had left Wolfwood. He also cackled mercilessly when Rue admitted the severity of the snows that had driven them out of the summer estate.

By the end of the meal, Ainsley had softened somewhat towards Tadgh, though he still wouldn't have trusted him to keep an eye on a dead dog. Maybe the fondness came from sharing wine, or seeing him without his usual band of courtiers, or maybe because he seemed so genuinely thrilled by Merremia's birth.

Tadgh took his soon-to-be daughter away to be nursed and changed before the night had grown late.

Rue watched his cousin go and almost as soon as the door closed, he wrapped his arms around himself and pulled his knees close to his chest.

Not how he usually sat, Ainsley noted. "Are you cold?"

"No."

Ainsley sidled a little closer to him and set a hand on his shoulder. "What's wrong?"

Rue shook his head.

"Should we go back to bed?"

"You go ahead, I'll join you in a little."

"You're sure?"

Rue nodded. "I want a little time alone."

Fuzzy as his head was, Ainsley didn't know if he should insist on staying by his side or if Rue would benefit from time alone. He hesitated, contemplating that the fairy couldn't lie. He kissed Rue's cheek, and said, "Don't be too long."

He returned to the bedroom and could hear Rue moving about in the other room. Not too long had passed before Rue came to join him in bed. He wrapped himself in blankets and didn't make a sound for the rest of the night.

Ainsley woke alone late the next morning and a steaming mug of tea waiting for him on the bedside table. He sipped at it, needing the relief from his mild headache and nausea it would bring, and shuffled out of the bedroom. He shuffled out from the bedroom and he almost didn't notice Rue sitting in a stuffed chair, already sipping his own mug. He looked just as wan and miserable as he had last night.

"Did you sleep well?" Ainsley ventured.

Rue glanced at him, a cagey look on his face. Caught between silence and a truth he didn't want to tell.

"You don't have to tell me," Ainsley reminded. He slurped down some more of the tea.

"Silence speaks volumes."

"Mmmm. That's the kind of answer I thought I'd be getting out of you," Ainsley said. "When all this started."

"More details I'll have from you, my love, or let your silence speak volumes, too," Rue requested.

"Twisted answers, half-truths, webs of things unsaid and things said in just the right way to tangle up my heart and my mind. All the stories say that fairies can't lie but the truths they tell are worse."

Rue watched him, unblinking, from the stuffed chair.

Ainsley came to perch on the arm of the chair, knowing it had been built sturdily enough that his weight wouldn't throw it off balance. "You haven't been like that with me. I've heard you talk to other people, so I know you can twist things up just as well as any of the other Fair Folk."

Rue finally blinked.

"I...I think I want to say that I know who you are with them will be different from who you are with me." He combed his fingers through Rue's hair, smoothing out how sleep had rumpled it. "As long as you love me still, that's all that matters. It's just a little while."

"Ainsley." Rue's voice came out so soft and pained that Ainsley knew he hadn't helped at all. He might have made things worse.

"I'm here, Rue, that's all I wanted to say. I'll help as best I can, but you...you might need to tell me how."

"Is that the sort of statement that would provoke a thank you in your realm?"

Ainsley shrugged.

"I understand a little more about the mortal realm now." He said it without wonder or flattery.

Ainsley chewed his lip and gulped down the rest of his tea. "Do you want to show me around the Court today?"

"No." Rue let out a sigh, set aside his mug, and pushed himself out of the chair. "Come, I'll show you the wardrobe. Anything you like can be made to fit you."

Ainsley followed, appraised his choices, then settled on one of the plainer choices available. Rue had many more outfits like the gossamer and glittering ones that went unworn at Wolfwood. Part of him did badly want to see Rue dressed up in something so enticing.

Maybe Rue would want to see him dressed up, too.

He didn't voice that now, just pulled on green hose and a tan tunic. He linked arms with Rue and walked hip-to-hip with him through the halls of the Court until they reached an enormous hall swarming with people of all shapes, sizes, and colors. A long table laden with sausage, fruits, porridges, and sugared pastries drew in the courtiers, all of them sliding in and out among their peers and retreating with laden plates and filled goblets.

Carafes of wine and cider sat among the food. Ainsley couldn't imagine indulging again so early in the morning.

Judging by the pinched look on Rue's face neither could he.

They both came away from the table with cups of spring water and bowls of porridge, though Rue had loaded his with berries and cream, and a healthy dollop of honey.

Tadgh, surrounded by twice as many courtiers as Ainsley remembered being part of his entourage, called over to them. He had the babe cradled in one arm and three of the courtiers leaned over the girl, cooing sweetly.

The girl fussed, though.

"Ainsley, you're young," Tadgh pronounced.

Ainsley sat in one of the empty chairs. "Compared to some."

"She's fussing."

"I'm not a baby," Ainsley reminded with as much gentleness as he could muster.

Rue asked, "Have you fed her?"

"Fed, changed, and swaddled," Tadgh confirmed.

"Maybe she could do with fewer sycophants breathing her air," Rue suggested mildly.

The trio of courtiers gathered around the babe glared at Rue but withdrew from the princess-to-be.

Merremia continued to fuss, though more quietly.

"And what do you know about babies, anyway, Rue?" one of the courtiers asked.

"I know about babies what I know about people, Alia."

"Well, skies help us if you get your hands on her after a few cups of wine, then," Alia returned.

"Alia, my plate could use refreshing," Tadgh said.

The woman's face smoothed over. She took the prince's picked-over plate and headed towards the banquet table.

Merremia let out the softest of whimpers, her face scrunching.

Tadgh looked at his cousin, eyes pleading.

"Give her your finger," Ainsley suggested. "That's what Nurse does for my brother's babes."

"How closely did you consider this arrangement?" Rue asked.

Tadgh offered the babe his little finger to suck. "I considered it as much as I could, given the circumstances."

Merremia quieted and closed her eyes almost as soon as she took the finger.

"You tell me, cousin, you come across a mewling babe left out with the rubbish, what would you do?"

"Find her a better guardian. We have precious few children; it would be best if good men saw to their raising."

Ainsley scanned the crowd. He saw maybe twenty children and only three toddlers among the crowd of hundreds. Tadgh held the only baby that Ainsley could see.

Maybe that explained why fairies stole mortal babes so often.

Tadgh let out a long, miserable groan. "You know, if this is the sort of mood you're going to be in, there's wine on the table. Get started now so you're tolerable by dinner."

Rue didn't speak for the rest of the meal.

A fog of gloom surrounded him for the rest of the day as he showed Ainsley around some of the Court and introduced him to a handful of people.

Ainsley tried as best he could to lift the other man's spirits and, even if it didn't work, Rue seemed to appreciate the effort.

"I'm tired," he said around midday. "I'm going to lie down, if you don't mind."

"Of course not."

While Rue slept, Ainsley better familiarized himself with the rooms. There were plenty of drawers to open and chests to rifle through, so he didn't lose himself to boredom.

After his nap, Rue emerged looking in better spirits. Dinner found him quiet, but not melancholy.

Three nights in a row, dinner found Rue somewhere between quiet and melancholy. Each night, Tadgh called them over to dine with him, which meant they ate with his courtiers as well.

After dinner each night, musicians began to play and almost everyone in the hall surged up from their seats. Not all of them danced, some sidled off into the halls or made their way above ground to get up to whatever mischief they could find.

Tadgh remained seated and cradled the babe for most evenings. He seemed utterly unperturbed by the lack of merriment and mischief-making in his life. He did, however, frequently urge his cousin to leave the table.

Ainsley felt responsible for that, in part. He couldn't stop watching the others, his eyes trailing after each pixie, sprite, and spriggan that passed by.

Tadgh nudged Rue's calf with the toe of his boot. "Take your foundling dancing before someone else asks him. They're all atwitter about this mortal."

"No, that's...I wouldn't want to dance with any of them," Ainsley insisted. "I don't know what they might do to me."

"Oh, shhh, you could stand to be played with a little," Tadgh teased.

Ainsley returned to watching the dancers. He had a hard time *not* watching them.

A hand snagged his. A blue-silver one.

Tadgh had deposited his daughter in his cousin's arms. "He holds my daughter, so you can rest assured you'll return to him with all your pieces."

"I." Ainsley glanced towards Rue.

"Go." Permission, neither pleased nor angry.

Tadgh pulled Ainsley to his feet and wrapped an arm around his waist. "You might even have fun. I'm not so terrible as my cousin makes me seem."

Together they slid in among the other dancers. At first, Ainsley thought only of going back to Rue, but Tadgh proved himself not just a good dancer but a fun partner. He whispered scathingly funny comments into Ainsley's ear and kept close, but not too close, to him, guiding him along with polite, chaste touches.

He also brushed his lips across Ainsley's cheek a few times, though it seemed more companionable than flirtatious. When he buried his face in Ainsley's throat, Ainsley didn't move back, not wanting to cause a scene.

He did say, "I'm not—"

"I'm not either," Tadgh interrupted. "I don't go for that sort of thing even in the most ideal circumstances. And entertaining my cousin's foundling hardly counts as ideal."

"Oh."

"Even if you are pretty." Tadgh pressed a little closer. "And unattended."

Ainsley swallowed.

"What easy prey you'd make, pup. I bet I could make you beg for all the things I'll never give you."

The prince's voice, slippery and sweet in his ear, made Ainsley almost want to squirm, though against him or away from him, he couldn't tell.

Tadgh chuckled, his breath warm against Ainsley's neck. "Watching you please yourself would please me, too. Would you like to please your prince?"

A whine escaped Ainsley's throat, a whine that had almost been a desperate yes.

Tadgh leaned against him, only for a moment, then stepped back. He looked over Ainsley. He swallowed, smoothed a hand over a shirt that held no rumples or wrinkles, then forced a grin. "Is this sluttishness what my cousin finds so appealing about you? You'd best take care, pup, or you'll get passed around the Court so fast you won't be able to count them all."

"You started it," Ainsley sulked.

Tadgh laughed and took his hand again. "One more dance. I'd hate to part on a sour note."

Ainsley acquiesced to another dance, but relief swept through his body when Tadgh led him off the dance floor and back to Rue.

Rue returned the babe to her father and took Ainsley by the arm, leading him right back into the crowd. "He didn't worry you too badly, did he?"

"No."

Rue looked doubtful, his face easier to read than ever.

"I'm entirely unscathed," he assured. He tugged at the front of Rue's tunic, bringing him down for a kiss. "Are you going to worry or dance with me?"

"Such are my talents, dear knight, that I can do both at the same time."

Rue didn't seem to worry, though. He led Ainsley through dances both wild and arranged, and from time to time, would bring him cups of wine and water and even a few morsels of food.

Any time Ainsley kissed the fairy, he tasted faintly of wine, but more strongly of whatever sticky, honeyed treat he'd retrieved from one of the servants. His mouth curved into a smile beneath each kiss, too. Ainsley could condone a little bit of indulgence, in wine or in sweets, if it had Rue smiling again.

That night, while they tumbled into bed together, both perhaps having had close to too much wine, Ainsley nuzzled up against Rue's throat and pressed his lips to the soft strip of skin just behind his ear. Hair tickled his nose and made him giggle.

"I missed this," he murmured against the fairy's skin.

Rue stilled a little and pulled back enough to look at him. "If I've left you unsatisfied—"

Ainsley caught his meaning before he even finished the sentence. Yes, they'd been less intimate of late, but he desperately needed to clarify, "No, no, sweet thing, no. I missed you smiling. I missed you laughing."

Rue regarded Ainsley with quiet distrust.

"I care for you in your entirety," Ainsley reminded, drawing Rue back into his arms. "Not just because you take me to bed."

The fairy didn't melt sweetly into his arms. "It helps, though."

Ainsley couldn't help the snort that escaped him. "How do you manage it, bending things the way you want to see them? Following me around as that crow, telling me there's no sin to be had in our intimacy, *courting* me, then sulking because you think it's all I care about."

As he spoke Rue pulled away from him entirely. He pushed himself upright and crossed his arms across his chest, a scowl firmly settled across his mouth. "Do you accuse me of improper conduct?"

Too disbelieving to be angry, Ainsley told him, "I accuse you of being morose, of being that same sad, shy boy too afraid to ask anyone to dance. I accuse you of not wanting to be loved because you think you shouldn't be loved."

Rue moved so quickly and so furiously that Ainsley flinched, throwing up an arm as swiftly as he would in a brawl. Rue did nothing more than hurl a pillow, though, and tear his way out of the bed, kicking at the sheets and bedcovers. He stalked away from Ainsley.

Ainsley caught him before he reached the doorway, blocking his way out of the room. "Tell me it isn't true."

"Move."

"No."

"Ainsley, move, or by the stars—"

"You'll move me?" Ainsley guessed, not impressed. "I'm stronger than you, remember?"

A bit of lightning whipped past his face, close enough to sting. A warning, but not a threat, no matter how coldly Rue demanded, "And how strong are your magics?"

Ainsley stood his ground and lifted his chin. "Answer me, Rue, and I'll move. But you won't lay a hand on me, nor I on you."

Rue shook his head but paced back a few steps. He gaped at Ainsley a little, then let out a huff and scowled at him.

"Tell me I'm wrong," Ainsley urged quietly after several long, uncomfortable moments of silence.

"How many years do you think it took me to give up wanting someone to love me?"

"More than it took me to realize that I could never love someone the way my mother loved my father," Ainsley answered. "I was eight."

Rue blinked.

"The other boys cheered, you know, when they dragged the pair of them out. Some foot soldier and the kitchen gardener. The same kind of spectacle you'd get if someone was caught swiping from the larder. Stocks and lashings. Didn't even let them get dressed first, left them out for days."

"Ainsley." All the spite and fire had gone out of the fairy.

"You forget that you are not the only one who thought he would meet death having never been loved. Loneliness is not unique to you or me. The world is full of lonely people. I'm not asking to know your full name, or for any...any promises or vows, Rue. I don't want you to undertake some impossible quest. I want to be around you and make you laugh and yes, I want to lay with you, which apparently damns me in your eyes as much as it does in the eyes of God."

"I..."

Ainsley raised an eyebrow, waiting.

"I was...I was just." Rue sighed and scrubbed a hand over his face. "I was wrong. And I regret implying that you had intentions to use me."

"You did a little more than imply."

"And I regret it!" Rue insisted, somewhere between snappish and whining. His next words came out slow and painful, "I fear that I cannot make you happy."

Ainsley frowned. All the irritation and resentment that had started to gather in him slid away with that confession. "I don't expect that."

"Oh."

"Come back to bed." Ainsley stepped out of the doorway.

"I."

Ainsley took his hand and guided him back. "What an awful burden to lay on yourself, Rue. Another person's happiness. Most of us can barely manage our own emotions. Oh, I understand the urge to lend assistance when another struggles. I'm not discounting goodwill and decency...but is that really what you've been worrying about this whole time? No wonder you've been so melancholy."

Once they had settled into bed, Rue rested his head upon Ainsley's chest and said, "The next time I call you a fool, you have my permission to trounce me."

"I don't think I need your permission to do it," Ainsley teased. He ran his fingers through Rue's hair, enjoying the way the locks slipped through his fingers. "I enjoyed dancing with you tonight."

Rue curled closer to him. "I enjoyed it, too. Maybe tomorrow I won't embarrass myself so badly between dancing and getting undressed."

"I did offer to take you in one of those little closets."

With a snort, Rue informed him, "I've had my share of trysts in tight spaces. Usually, someone ends up with a cramp."

Ainsley clucked. "No orgies, no tight spaces, how are we ever going to have any fun? Next thing it'll be no mud pits or haystacks."

"I take it back. Ainsley, you're a fool," Rue declared fondly.

"And you're the fool who loves me."

They both lingered in bed late into the morning. Rue stayed behind when Ainsley declared his intention to find something to eat. The fairy had been drifting in and out of sleep all night and could barely keep his eyes open long enough to warn Ainsley, "Don't talk to anyone if you can help it."

Ainsley heeded the warning with less severity than he would have if he'd received it months ago. He'd learned how to navigate the Fair Folk a little better and didn't fear them nearly as much.

He made his way to the great hall without a single wrong turn and scavenged what he could from the banquet table. Once he had filled his plate with as much as he could carry, he turned to find a slender youth standing just behind him.

"Oh, did I startle you?" the youth asked, his voice sweet as a lark's song.

"I didn't expect you there," Ainsley admitted.

The youth smiled; red crept across his snow pale cheeks. He snagged a bunch of grapes from the table and fidgeted with them. He looked like a plaster statue come to life. "It's not every day that a human is brave enough to wander the Court alone."

Ainsley shifted, not sure what to say to that. The boy had a comely face and fine clothes, but he didn't number among Tadgh's entourage nor had Ainsley seen him with the king and queen.

"We were all atwitter when the prince brought you here. He's never brought anyone anywhere, except somewhere private to grant a bit of a favor." When Ainsley didn't look properly scandalized, the youth clarified, "To muddy his knees."

"Oh, that."

"Kneeling or bending over," the fairy continued.

"Yes, I understand."

The youth had the decency to look a little ashamed. "It's common knowledge, that's all."

"Are you common knowledge, too?"

The boy flashed him a smile. "No, I'm harder to get to know. You can call me Marl, though."

"I can call you anything I like, I imagine."

A pink tongue darted out to wet pale lips. "You might know what would make a proper gift for the little princess. The joining ceremony is soon."

Ainsley shook his head. "I don't know much about fairy custom."

Marl nodded understandingly. "Ah. Shame. The little girl looks so sweet, we thought we should give her something. What's her name again?"

"You'd do better asking her father. Is that him now?" Ainsley asked, looking over Marl's shoulder.

Marl froze up, then risked a peek over his shoulder. "Oh, no, looks like someone else. Maybe I ought to go find him."

Ainsley gave the fairy a smile, doing his best to keep it open and friendly.

The smile Marl gave in return was likely just as fake. He turned and walked away, vanishing down one of the halls.

Balancing his laden plate carefully, Ainsley returned to Rue's rooms. "I brought food," he called.

Rue appeared, blankets wrapped around his shoulders, and selected one of the pastries. He hunkered down in front of the fire. "Did you talk to anyone?"

"Exactly one person."

"And?"

"You worry too much."

Rue bit into the pastry, a puff of sugary powder smattering across his face. "Don't smile at me like that."

"Can I ask you something?"

"You may."

"Why is one of your desk drawers full of rocks?"

The fairy's cheeks darkened. "They're the shiny ones."

Ainsley's smile widened. He set down the plate on the hearth and settled onto the fur beside Rue, an apple tart in hand. He thought about making a proclamation of love but decided to scoot closer and press a kiss to Rue's cheek. He wiped the powder from his face.

After a few bites of his pastry, Rue admitted, "My head hurts."

"A bath might help. And water. I don't think either of us drank enough water last night."

The fairy grunted his agreement.

That night when they made their way towards dinner, they found the hall nearly barren and the table sparsely laid out.

Rue frowned, then realization dawned on his face. "The full moon shows her face tonight. Come." He took Ainsley by the hand and led him through the halls.

For all the twists and turns that Ainsley had learned, he hadn't yet found his way back to the Court's entrance. He tried to memorize them this time, though he didn't think he'd have much luck.

Rue tiptoed carefully over the circle of white flowers around the hill and, instead of warning Ainsley to do the same, circled his hands about Ainsley's waist and lifted him over the flowers.

Ainsley squawked in surprise then gave Rue a small push. "Scared me!"

With a grin and a chuckle, Rue nuzzled against his shoulder. "Only a little." He kept his arm around Ainsley's waist, his grip tightening possessively as they made their way towards the throne.

The court had roused itself tonight as Ainsley had never seen. It made the music and dance of other nights seem mild in comparison.

Corva sat seated upon the Barbed Throne. Balor reclined at her feet, picking through a bowl full of cherries. Every so often, he passed one to his queen. Spots of cherry juice spattered across their gowns, but somehow instead of looking messy, the stains looked like decoration.

Tadgh lounged nearby, his daughter in his arms. He was closer to his parents tonight than Ainsley had seen all fall.

"What is all this?"

Rue shrugged. "A little festivity. The full moon tonight and Tadgh's joining tomorrow. Such events, they call for merriment, don't they?"

Ainsley nodded his agreement, twisting his neck so he could see the moon. As ever, it loomed bigger here than it did in the mortal world. Tonight, it had an uncommon sheen to it, like frost on glass.

"Snows will be starting here, too, soon," Rue declared.

The air nipped his cheeks and without any spoken agreement, they both moved towards one of the many small fires scattered around the oak tree.

Thick, heady smoke emanated from this fire, bringing the scent of too many herbs for him to name.

"Don't breathe too deeply," one woman advised. "You never know what's been set to burn."

Rue scowled at her and steered them away from her, heading towards his cousin, who had a small fire all to himself.

"Oh, how honored are we by your presence, sweet cousin?" Tadgh gushed.

Rue scowled at him too. "Better to seat myself with someone whose nonsense I understand."

Tadgh flashed a smile. He gestured with one hand to the assortment of food and drink laid out between him and his parents.

Upon the table, in a small gilded cage, resided a bird, bright pink in color and no larger than a lady's thumb. Ainsley peered into the cage and cooed softly to the little bird. He'd never seen anything so small and sweet in his life. It hopped frantically about the cage, its little black eyes flashing.

He offered it a crumb of bread, but the bird paid it no heed.

"Wiser to leave it alone," Rue advised.

"Why?"

"Because it knows its fate."

"Speak plain for once."

"'Tis part of the evening's games," Rue offered soberly.

Ainsley didn't like the sound of that. He took a bit of bread and mushrooms in gravy, glancing back towards the bird even as he settled in to eat. "What games?"

"Cleverness, athleticism, courage," Tadgh explained. "Each game has a winner and each winner receives a prize."

"What sort of prize?"

"Depends on what the losers have to offer," Tadgh said with a glint in his eye. "They what win may ask anything they like of the those what lost."

"Well, I'll sit out any games of cleverness, if that's the case," Ainsley decided. He looked peered down at the sleeping babe and found her gurgling quietly. "Someone asked me her name today."

The prince looked up with all the fury of a river that had flooded its banks. "And what did you say?"

"That he'd do better asking you."

The fury faded somewhat, but wariness remained. "You didn't tell?"

Ainsley shook his head. "I've got enough brains in my head not to do that."

Tadgh's eyes narrowed, searching over Ainsley for some hint of deception or weakness.

"I didn't tell, on my honor. I've got nothing against the girl."

Tadgh turned his eyes to his cousin. "His honor? That means something?"

"It does," Rue assured. "Besides, you haven't told anyone her true name."

"Nor do I intend to."

Ainsley used his bread to scoop up a mouthful of mushrooms and tuned out the conversation of the princes. Half the time when they spoke to each other, he couldn't follow half of the twisted-up things they said to each other. Things he found incredibly bad-mannered, Rue took as jokes, and statements Ainsley had taken as complements, Rue had received as terrible insults.

Instead, he watched the little bird and its desperate exploration of the cage. "What if we let it out?" he asked.

"Don't," both princes said together, the same steel and panic in their voices.

"What would happen?"

"I don't know what they'd come up with this time," Tadgh answered.

Ainsley looked to Rue for a better explanation.

Rue sighed, then offered, "I was..." He glanced at Tadgh. "Fifteen?"

"I was fifteen," Tadgh answered. "You were eleven."

"All those years blur together," Rue admitted. "I was eleven, then, and I'd seen little birds like that ripped to bits during the game. The winner always ended up with a handful of pulp and feathers. I didn't think it could bear it again. My sweet cousin offered me a cup of wine as comfort, but it brought none. Clumsy and stupid, but emboldened, I heeded his suggestion—"

"I didn't think you were that stupid," Tadgh protested.

"And opened the cage. The poor little thing flew away fast as a lightening bolt. With nothing to catch, the courtiers nearly rioted. My aunt offered me as recompense."

Ainsley's guts twisted.

Rue continued the tale with none of his usual flowery prose, his voice a little raspier than usual, "I ran and flew and hid as best I could, but I was young, weak, and...oh, I was so frightened. Imagine being chased by...three dozen grown people, at least. It took three days, but one of them caught me. I thought Darien would tear my arm right off."

"That's not half the things he would have done to you," Tadgh reminded darkly. "I had to trade him my three best horses *and* my star-silver tack to get you back. Family heirloom, that!"

"No one made you," Rue huffed.

"And no one made you open that stupid cage," Tadgh growled. "Always blaming someone else. I could have let him keep you."

The two fairies glared at each other, the air thick between them.

Ainsley fidgeted, cast his eyes out over the crowd. He reached for Rue's hand, but the other man reached for a cup of wine instead.

The mood between the cousins lingered so strongly that Ainsley could have sworn he could taste their bitterness whenever he breathed through his mouth. They remained silent through the games of cleverness and courage, which consisted of riddles and allowing the Court's jester to lead one about blindfolded.

Most people didn't allow the jester to lead them for more than half a minute. The winner lasted only twice as long, which prompted Ainsley to ask what the jester had done to frighten everyone so.

"You don't want to know," Tadgh answered.

Ainsley believed him.

So far, the winners had claimed a sword that could cut through anything with a single blow and a pair of boots that let the wearer walk upon water.

"Provided that's all you're wearing," Tadgh informed Ainsley.

Corva retrieved the little bird from its cage as Balor cast a glimmering dome that expanded to cover a wide span of land, large enough for a jousting match. A dozen courtiers followed as Corva entered the dome.

One man leered at Rue as he made his way towards the room. "You sure you don't want to play this year, birdie?" he asked.

Rue bared his teeth and tossed his wine at the man.

"One of these days, we'll finish our game," the man vowed, licking wine from his fingers.

Ainsley stood.

"Don't," Rue warned.

Ainsley paid him no mind, marching after the courtiers and making his way into the circle.

Rue tried to catch him, but Ainsley slipped through the barrier before Rue could get a hold on him.

"Get out of there," Rue demanded.

"No one may leave until the game has ended," Balor reminded calmly. "Have a seat, nephew, enjoy the contest."

Tadgh, carrying his baby in one arm, looped his other arm around his cousin's waist to stop him from following Ainsley in. "If he loses, he has nothing to forfeit but dignity."

"And whatever task someone might set before him," Rue reminded.

"He's grown, he takes that risk on his own. Sit, cousin."

"Go sit, Rue, I'll see you in a little while," Ainsley urged.

Rue went but went with a horrible grimace.

"Are we ready all?" Corva asked.

The courtiers, and Ainsley, chorused, "Yes."

"You may begin when I have left the circle." She released the bird.

None of the courtiers moved, all of them lined up against one side of the dome.

Ainsley rummaged through the pockets on his belt.

The bird tried to fly away, taking wing but coming up against the barrier Balor had set.

Corva made her way out, sliding through the dome with ease.

As soon as the last inch of her gown passed the barrier, the courtiers exploded with motion, rushing towards the bird.

Ainsley ran with them, shoving several people aside to move towards the front of the pack. He sunk his teeth into the fingers of one woman who grabbed at his shoulder, feeling no shame in harming this lady, as she had claws and jagged, pointed teeth that dripped with something dark and sticky.

He spat her blood from his mouth, straight into the eyes of the person closest to him.

The two of them howled at him.

He paid them no mind, worming his way around two men who had stopped to brawl with each other.

The little bird still fluttered around against the far side of the dome, letting out shrill, pathetic keens.

Only one courtier remained in front of him, a slender woman who streaked forward so fast Ainsley didn't think he'd be able out to outstrip her.

Corva had set no rules, so Ainsley improvised with what he had available. He scooped up a stone and hurled it towards the woman, hitting her square in the back. Lithe as her frame was, the blow was enough to make her stumble.

He used the opportunity to surge in front of her. He shoved a fist into one of the pouches and scattered a handful of salt before the woman.

She let out an awful screech and stopped to count the grains as if her body acted against her will.

Ainsley drew a bell from another pouch and set to jangling it as forcefully as he could.

Almost all the fairies stopped short in their rush forward. Some of them clapped their hands over their ears. One even fell to his knees and curled in on himself; with some satisfaction, Ainsley saw that the fairy most wounded by the bell's ringing was the same that had threatened Rue before. That one had blood trailing down from his ears.

Two fairies, identical in face and body, continued to move forward, but they did so with hesitance. "What else has it got?" they asked together.

Ainsley slipped his knife from his belt and brandished it towards them. At home, the knife had no value as a threat, it was only a fruit knife like the one carried by nearly everyone. Here, though, the blade held enough iron to burn the skin of any who touched it.

Rue had learned that by accident when he'd borrowed the knife to open a letter. The burn it left had smarted for days and Ainsley had never left their rooms without it since.

"I'll strike a bargain," he offered the twins.

"What's it offering?"

"What do you want?"

They smiled together. "The name of the princess."

He almost rolled his eyes at them. With her newness and Tadgh's infatuation, Merremia must have been the focus of so many schemes. "When the bird is in my hand, I'll answer."

"Swear it."

"On my word and honor," he vowed.

They nodded, accepting his promise.

He returned his knife to his belt and looked up at the bird, which had nearly beaten itself ragged against the walls of the dome. Still ringing the bell, he reached up his hand and told the bird, "I won't hurt you."

He didn't think it understood and it certainly didn't settle into his hand. He shoved his bell into his belt and leapt up, caging the bird with his fingers.

As soon as his feet touched the ground, the other contestants surrounded him, calling him a cheater. They hissed and jeered at him but parted with Corva entered.

"Sir Ainsley, the winner," she declared. "What would you have as your prize?"

"The star-silver tack that belonged to Tadgh."

"Is that all?"

He nodded.

"It will be delivered to your quarters before the week is out," she said, her eyes settling on Darien.

Still clutching the bird to his chest, Ainsley made his way out of the crowd and back to Rue.

Balor stood beside his son and nephew. He offered the gilded cage to Ainsley. "Admirable."

"They all think I cheated," Ainsley pointed out as he returned the bird to the cage. He took the cage from Balor's hands. "I'll return the cage once I've got one of my own."

Balor raised an eyebrow.

"With your permission to borrow it, of course."

"You may borrow it as long as you need," the king granted.

The twins sidled up to him, waiting expectantly.

Tadgh recognized them immediately and snatched up his daughter from her basket with enough force to make her squall.

"Her name," they said together.

"The princesses name is Elinor."

They withdrew, horrible smiles on their faces.

Tadgh stared at him. "What did you do?"

"Elinor is the princess of Triviai, but she's been dead for three years, so they can do what they want with that," Ainsley replied. He nodded towards Rue, who leaned against the oak tree. "Is he alright?"

"He...he drank quite a bit. And he drank it very fast," Tadgh informed him.

Rue made what Ainsley could only assume was a crude gesture towards his cousin.

"You made him nervous," Tadgh scolded Ainsley. "And me as well, stars help me if I have to deal with him heartbroken, of all things."

"But I won." Ainsley couldn't help flashing a smile.

Rue straightened himself up. Or, at least, he attempted to. He wobbled, took a few steps forward, then sank to the ground.

Trying to keep his voice low, Ainsley asked Tadgh, "How much did he drink?"

"Oh, I wasn't counting."

"Tadgh."

"That's Your Highness to you," Tadgh reminded sharply. He glanced towards his cousin. "Maybe a bottle."

"I was barely gone!" Ainsley squawked.

"My cousin may not have many skills, but he does have a prodigious talent for drinking wine."

With a shake of his head, Ainsley walked away from Tadgh and went to sit beside Rue. "Hello."

"Hello," the fairy returned, his head resting on his knees.

"I caught the bird." Ainsley showed Rue the cage.

Rue turned his head to the side and eyed the cage. "Oh...you. You caught him." He ran a finger along the bars of the car. "Surprised to see either of you in one piece."

"Do you want to go lay down?"

"I don't want to move."

"You can lay down here."

Rue took him up on the offer, oozing on to the ground.

Ainsley gathered him close so that Rue's head rested on Ainsley's outstretched legs. He tucked a bit of stray hair behind his ear. "You didn't have to worry so much."

"You don't know the what of things...that what those...what." Rue sucked in a breath. "You don't know what they can do."

"You don't have any faith in me at all, do you?"

"Because you're simple."

"If you weren't drunk, I'd resent that," Ainsley grumbled.

Rue nuzzled his face against Ainsley's thighs and after a long stretch of silence, he said, "You're simple even when I'm not drunk. And I don't want any less time with you than I'm getting."

"I'm not going anywhere."

Rue snorted and grumbled something derisive under his breath.

Ainsley didn't quite catch it but thought better of asking him to repeat himself. Instead, he waited, asking Rue if he wanted to go to bed every so often.

Finally, Rue consented to go back to their room and leaned heavily against Ainsley as they walked back. He leaned against him in a particular way, one easily interpreted as propositioning. He also somehow navigated them flawlessly back to their room.

"Not even a single wrong turn," Ainsley praised him.

Rue didn't take the compliment. Nearly as soon as the door closed, he had his hands inside Ainsley's clothes, pushing him up against the wall.

"Oh!" Ainsley jumped back a little, putting one hand against Rue's shoulder. He still carried the birdcage in the other hand. "Oh, wait, Rue."

Rue pulled back.

Ainsley set the bird down and told it, "You'll be alright in here, friend." He'd put a little bread and water in the cage, but the bird hadn't moved much since its return to the cage. Exhausted, Ainsley assumed.

Rue sidled up behind him, pressing himself against Ainsley's backside. "Come to bed." He wrapped his arms around Ainsley, nearly dragging him closer.

Ainsley wiggled out of his arms. "I think you should lay down."

"Laying down, bending over, what's it matter?" the fairy muttered, reaching for him again. "Just get it done."

Ainsley sucked in a breath, then sighed. He tried to think of a way sidestep this, certain that if Rue lay down for a few minutes, he would fall asleep. "You go ahead, I'll be in."

Eyes narrowed and frowning, Rue looked him over.

"I promise." He pressed a kiss to the other man's lips and stroked his cheek.

Rue went.

Ainsley puttered about for a little while. When he went to check on Rue, he found him sprawled facedown on the mattress, half-dressed. Ainsley got him out of the rest of his clothes and under the blankets before shedding his own garments and joining him.

Rue slept like the dead.

Ainsley couldn't sleep at all. Coming to the Western Court might have been a mistake. Habits were hard to break and one decades in the making must have been even harder. He should have endured the winter at Wolfwood. They couldn't go back now, of course, but now he knew for another year.

After what felt like an entire night of lying awake and worrying, Ainsley finally drifted off.

He woke to someone kicking him, climbing over him to get out of bed. He opened his eyes to find Rue scrambling for a chamber pot.

The fairy collapsed in front of it and vomited.

Ainsley slipped out of bed to crouch beside him, sweeping his hair out of his face, and rubbing his back.

Rue vomited until his stomach held nothing, then continued to heave. His muscles strained beneath Ainsley's hands.

Ainsley started to worry he might hurt himself.

The heaving subsided, though, and Rue hung over the chamber pot, spiting every so often. Finally, he leaned back and wiped his mouth on his wrist. One hand skittered over his chest. "Where's my clothes?"

"On the floor."

"Did I stay awake the whole time at least?"

Ainsley assured, "You fell asleep almost as soon as you laid down."

A stormy, pained look flickered over Rue's face. "You enjoy that, then?"

Ainsley caught his implication. "I put you to bed. And stay up half the night worrying about you."

"You didn't fuck me?"

"Rue!" The curse itself didn't shock Ainsley, he'd heard it often and uttered it enough times, but the accusation did. The disbelief. "You were *asleep*. And drunk off your ass. I wouldn't take advantage like that."

"Swear it."

"Of course, I do."

"Ainsley!" Rue whined. "I don't remember. I need you to say it."

"I didn't bed you last night. On my honor and my word and the graves of my ancestors," Ainsley vowed. He expected more disbelief and accusations but instead, Rue buried his face in his hands and started to cry.

The fairy curled in on himself.

Ainsley rushed to pull him into an embrace. "What's wrong, love?"

"I'm sorry."

He didn't know what to say, especially not when faced with the ache growing in his chest.

"I'm so sorry, Ainsley, I. I didn't want it to be like this. Not with you."

"Shh, now, it's alright. It is."

Rue shook his head, still shuddering with sobs.

Ainsley tightened his arms and kissed his hair. "We all overindulge. It happens. It doesn't mean—"

"I've ruined it."

"You haven't ruined anything."

"Ruined everything."

For the better part of an hour, though, Rue continued to weep apologies.

Ainsley offered the best comfort he could, but nothing he said seemed to make Rue feel any better.

Rue didn't calm down so much as he wore himself out. Hollow-eyed, he let Ainsley bring him to the bath.

They soaked in the tub together, not speaking. Just existing, both uncomfortable and gloomy.

That day, they kept to their chambers. They watched the fire and check in on the bird, which had pecked at some of the bread.

"I didn't think you'd catch him," Rue said. "Especially not whole."

"You told me everything I need to keep the Fair Folk at bay when I don't want them near," Ainsley reminded. "I wish you didn't think me so useless."

"Not useless. Delicate," Rue corrected. "Delicate and sweet and—"

"Stupid," Ainsley supplied.

Rue's face contorted. "That...no. Not stupid. I don't think you're stupid."

"Last night you called me simple. You've never been shy to call me a fool."

"Still. I. That's not what I meant."

"Well, it must be true, since you can't lie," Ainsley pointed out.

"No, there's a nuance to these things. I don't think you're stupid, Ainsley. You have my word on that," Rue said. "I think you're wonderful. And I love you."

"I love you, too."

The sooner they could get out of this place, away from free-flowing wine, sharp-tongued courtiers, and whatever else it was about Court that made Rue so uncomfortable, the better.

They dragged themselves to the joining ceremony that night. With the moon fat and bright above them and all the court dressed in their finest and most wonderous attire, Ainsley knew he should have been blown away by the beauty and spectacle of it all. Instead, though, he couldn't stop staring at Rue. As a member of Tadgh's family, he had a part to play in welcoming the babe to the family.

Ainsley didn't understand a lot of the ceremony. A woman in blue robes stood between the family members, passing the baby from person to person. Each of them held Merremia in turn, swiping their thumbs over her forehead and then leaning in to kiss the smear of oil they left behind.

The woman spoke briefly, though Ainsley couldn't hear much of what she said from his position in the back of the crowd. Rue had stationed him there, away from others, and warned him to stay put.

Warned, or begged. Ainsley hadn't been able to tell.

Throughout the ceremony, Rue sagged and swayed dangerously a few times. Even the usual tea to cure the symptoms of a rough night hadn't eased all his illness.

After the third time Rue faltered, Tadgh reached over and swiped his hand across the back of Rue's neck and whispered something into his ear. Rue stood straighter for the remainder of the ceremony.

The joining concluded with the family huddling in close for a short song, one in a tongue Ainsley couldn't understand. He easily picked out the rasp of Rue's voice from the hum of Balor, the effervescent bubble of Tadgh, and the deep, sweet sound of Corva.

Once the song ended, the family drifted away from each other and the woman in blue made left, heading out away from the Court.

Rue returned to Ainsley's side.

Ainsley pressed a kiss to cheek and told him, "I love your voice."

"That might be the first time he's ever heard that," Tadgh chimed from just behind Rue.

Ignoring the prince, Ainsley looped his arms around Rue's waist and nuzzled against him. "You seem better."

"Tadgh has more than enough experience nursing me back to health."

Ainsley cocked an eyebrow.

"Difficult to tell, given how easily he lends himself to the misery of others, but my sweet cousin has a disposition towards healing magic," Rue informed him.

Ainsley laughed.

Tadgh scowled at him. "Misery might be a strong word."

"His trouble with the discipline lies in a difficultly with touching others," Rue continued.

"I can touch people," Tadgh snapped.

Rue flashed a smile, pulling Ainsley closer to him. "For how long?"

Not interested in their spat, Ainsley interrupted, "Can you help our bird?"

"What?"

"If you can heal things. Our bird, it's...well, I don't think last night did the poor thing any favors," Ainsley explained.

Shifting his daughter more comfortably in his arms, Tadgh gave a loose shrug. "Help the bird. Why not?" He snagged Ainsley by the elbow.

Ainsley grabbed Rue by the hand as Tadgh dragged him along back to Rue's chambers.

Once there, Tadgh handed the baby over to his cousin and swept his way over to the bird cage. He peered inside of it. "Oh. I can heal his body, but I can't fix his heart."

"Hmm?"

"Bell finches mate for life and this little boy is missing his mate."

"That's not a bell finch," Rue protested. "Bell finches are..." He trailed off once he leaned in to get a closer look at the bird.

"Bell finches are what?" Tadgh asked.

"Pink," Rue finished quietly.

"Ohh, you were bad off, sweet cousin. You could have asked for help," Tadgh clucked. He opened the cage door and eased his hand in.

The bird shied away.

"Shh, shh, little friend, you'll be well again," Tadgh cooed. He moved his hand a little closer and caught the bird. He cupped it in both hands and clutched it close to his chest. He whispered to the little bird, weak, gray light emanating from between his hands.

The bird cheeped desperately, but when Tadgh returned it to the cage, the bird hopped around with more vigor.

"He'll still be missing his mate," Tadgh said.

"Does he live far?"

"Bell finches live around the Lake of Neve," Rue said. "They're nocturnal, actually."

"We should bring him home," Tadgh proposed.

"What, right now?" Ainsley asked.

"I'm up for a jaunty midnight ride if you are," Tadgh agreed. He looked at Rue.

Rue asked, "You'll leave your daughter on her joining night?"

Tadgh sighed. "No. I don't suppose I should take a baby on horseback either. Should we walk, then?"

"It's a long walk."

"Mmm, we'd have to bring a nurse, then..." Tadgh mused. "Well, fine, then, I grant you permission to depart from the joining without any ill will."

"And our lord and lady?" Rue asked.

"If they even notice you're gone, I'll tell them I gave you permission to go."

"You're not king," Rue reminded.

Tadgh rolled his eyes. "And all the stars know that if they have any other get that I never will be, but for now I remain Crown Prince of the Western Court and I lay before you this quest, Sir Ainsley, Prince Rue: Return the bell finch to his native lands."

Rue let out a sigh. "I hate it when you do that."

His cousin flashed a smile. "Have fun." He took Merremia back from Rue's arms. "Oh, and we're calling her Acorn as far as everyone's concerned. She can pick a better name when she's older. Merremia will be for family only. And, I suppose, pretty mortal foundlings."

When Tadgh had left, Rue started pulling off the fine garments he had worn to the ceremony and replacing them with plainer clothes.

Ainsley followed suit. "What happens if we don't go on this quest?"

"Depends on Tadgh's mood."

"Is Rue...is that a name you picked yourself?" Ainsley asked.

"No, my mother gave it to me when I was young. Before the fire," he said. "Not the kindest of names to lay upon a child but a son takes what a mother gives."

Ainsley chewed his lip and debated whether to ask his next question. Rue's mood had been so sensitive lately and he didn't want to spoil things. He decided not to ask if he'd been named for the plant or for regret. He took Rue's hand in his and carried the bird's cage in the other.

They saddled their horses without any words passing between them.

Hadley rubbed her face against Ainsley's chest.

He felt bad for having left her alone for so long. "How far is it?"

Rue remained quiet.

Ainsley glanced over to see his face twisted with contemplation instead of melancholy.

Finally, he answered, "Half a day until we reach the marshes. We can release our friend there. They'll be flooded this time of year, so getting in any further would be...unpleasant." He swung himself into his saddle.

His horse, a liquid splash of night, pranced beneath him, throwing back her head and letting out a pleased whinny.

He patted her neck and told her, "Oh, shh, I know they've not left you to rot in your stall. Don't act like no one's been taking care of you."

Ainsley pulled himself into his saddled, always feeling clumsy and heavy after watching Rue practically dance onto his horse. "Is there anything to watch out for in this lake?" He secured the bird's cage to his saddle and double checked to make sure he'd tied down his sword.

"Kelpies, nokken, swan maidens," Rue recounted. "And don't eat anything. Most everything that grows around the Lake of Neve is poison in one way or another."

"So I take it no one lives around there?"

"No one but the kelpies, nokken, and swan maidens and a handful of hermits who live off marsh roots. You'll want to watch out for them, too, they're all mad."

"Ah."

"Usually harmless, but you never know what they might see instead of the two of us."

Ainsley became less sure about this midnight quest the more he learned. "Not exactly a pleasant place, then, is it?"

"It is as all things in the Otherworld."

"Mm."

The quiet between them returned, punctuated by the sounds of the bell finch.

Ainsley worked up the courage to ask, "Rue?"

"Yes?"

"Maybe the spring is too late to return to Triviai. Maybe it would be better to go sooner."

Rue glanced at him, his face smooth and unreadable. "We have a quest before us."

"Oh, I didn't mean right this moment, of course. But soon."

"Perhaps."

"I just...things have been..." Ainsley stopped himself and tried to gather his thoughts better. "You seem so unhappy. It might be good for us both. A little time to, to recover."

Rue didn't speak.

Ainsley started to fidget and couldn't stop licking his lips, though his mouth had gone dry.

After a lifetime, Rue said, "I'll take you back to Triviai."

Reaching across the gap between their horses, Ainsley snagged Rue's hand and kissed his knuckles. "I think we need it."

Rue tightened his fingers around Ainsley but didn't answer.

"I'm not blaming you for anything."

"Did I utter any such suggestion?" the fairy asked.

Ainsley sighed and kept his answer to himself. "It's a beautiful night."

Rue glanced up at the stars and moon above them, then sighed.

They followed a well-traveled road due west from the Court. Eventually, the crunch of gravel beneath their horses' hooves gave way to the steady, quiet sound of dirt. Despite the lateness of the hour, Ainsley's head never drooped. The bite in the air, coupled with a day spent mostly in bed, kept him alert.

The further west they went, the cheerier the bird became. Eventually, it began to sing, and Rue said, "He's calling for his mate."

By the time the ground grew soft and muddy, the sun had yet to rise.

Ainsley could make out the glimmer of moonlight on a vast expanse of water in the distance and several smaller glints closer. Twisted trees with sparse foliage spotted the land, but tall grass dominated the landscape. Riding into a deep puddle or getting stuck in a mucky bit of marsh had likely claimed many travelers.

Dyed blue by the darkness, grass swayed in the breeze, blades rustling together.

"Is this far enough?" Ainsley asked.

Rue nodded.

He took the cage from his saddle and gave the bird one last look. "Safe travels, friend, and stay clear of the Court if you can."

The bird trilled and ruffled its wings.

In the distance, another bird returned the call.

Ainsley opened the cage door.

The bell finch shot out and flitted over the swamp, stilling trilling.

"Oh, look." Ainsley pointed when another small pink bird burst up from among the grass and met their bird in midair. "Do you think that's her?"

Rue didn't answer. He scrubbed at his face with his sleeve.

"Did you want to keep him?"

"No." Rue rubbed his nose. "I'm tired."

"Do you want to sleep awhile?"

"Not..." He sighed.

"I know we didn't pack any supplies but...I mean, if you wouldn't mind, I could hold you. I can lead your horse as long as she'll tolerate it,"

Ainsley offered.

"Hadley wouldn't appreciate us riding double, I don't think."

"She wouldn't mind if one of us was a crow."

Rue pursed his lips as though offended by the idea. He turned his horse and started east without another word.

The ride back dragged, especially because Rue wouldn't talk to him. The sharp light of the sun as it rose made things worse. Ainsley resorted to riding with a hand held in front of his eyes for nearly half the journey home.

By the time they'd handed over their horses in the stables, both Ainsley and Rue had accumulated all sorts of unwarranted foul feelings spurred on by irritated sighs and cutting looks thrown toward the other. They barely spoke and, when Ainsley headed towards bed to sleep, Rue didn't follow him.

Ainsley paused and demanded, more sharply than he'd meant, "Aren't you coming?"

"When I'm ready."

"Suit yourself." Ainsley threw himself into the bed and curled himself in the covers as though it would do anything to help.

He woke alone but lighter in spirit. He gave his face a quick wash and rinsed his mouth, then gave their chambers a quick search.

He didn't find Rue until he pulled his boots back on and made his way to the banquet hall. The remains of a light midday meal lingered on the table and Ainsley snagged himself a bit of bread and cheese. He headed towards Rue, spying him sitting with Tadgh's usual group, though the prince didn't number among his companions.

"There you are," Ainsley said. He took a seat behind him.

"Here I am," Rue returned.

"Did you come to bed last night?"

"Neither of us went to bed last night," Rue reminded tartly.

"You know what I meant."

"Meaning is such a slippery thing."

Ainsley understood the answer as bait and ignored it. Instead, he asked, "Where's Tadgh? Should we tell him we brought the bird home?"

Rue paused in bringing his cup to his mouth. "He knows."

Already tired of this, Ainsley concentrated on his meal. He did his best to ignore the meaningless, sharp-tongued chatter around him, but the rasp of Rue's voice joined in so often that he couldn't tune out the conversation entirely.

"Did you eat already?" Ainsley asked when he noted that Rue didn't have a plate in front of him.

"We aren't all so interested in getting fat."

One of Ainsley's eyebrows arched of its own accord, but he held his tongue. Rue's breath had been heavy scented with wine. "What do you want to do today?"

"It's snowed this morning," one of the courtiers said. "They're building an Ice Palace."

The image would have enchanted Ainsley any other time. Mages at home could have built something like that, he knew, but common courtesy kept them from gathering in great numbers anywhere but in armies and the university. Too many mages, too many magic workers of any sort really, in one place made regular folk nervous.

Rue slid his hand over Ainsley's, twining their fingers together. "The Otherworld holds a few more wonders for you yet."

As soon as Ainsley had finished his meal, Rue ushered him back to their rooms to don warmer clothes.

They joined the others to the north of the Court. Dozens milled about the half-built structure, an intricate palace in miniature.

The gaggle of children waiting off to the side, tossing snowballs and chasing each other, made Ainsley realize that the adults had not built this palace for themselves.

"The wee ones will choose their own regents and those two will rule over the Ice Palace until it crumbles or melts. This is likely to be a short reign, so the older children will likely let the littlest ones take their turn," Rue informed him. "If you think the Western Court holds terrors, wait until you see what becomes of the Ice Palace."

"What do you mean?"

"Oh, rare and mighty is the parent that can get their wee one to sleep in a bed made of feathers instead of snow while an Ice Palace stands."

Rue stayed by Ainsley's side for some time, their arms linked as they watched the palace grow.

Some of the other courtiers started fires and brought out cauldrons, setting wines and ciders to mull.

Tadgh appeared by their side at one point and handed Merremia over to Ainsley. "Rue, come along, we need someone tall."

"Get Laslo."

"We've got Laslo. We need someone to sit on his shoulders." Tadgh tugged on his cousin.

Rue went.

Ainsley stared down at the baby. "Hello, there. How are you?"

The baby squirmed a little.

He continued to coo nonsense to her, which is what he had always done with his brother's children. She didn't seem to mind, quiet and chewing on her fist.

Tadgh returned and took his daughter back. "Ah, here she is, little Acorn. Someday when you're a sapling you can be a queen of the Ice Palace. What a wonderous queen you'll be."

"Where's Rue?"

Tadgh nodded towards one of the cauldrons with mulled drinks.

Ainsley dug his teeth into his lip.

Tadgh casually assured, "You don't have to start worrying until he's had a few more."

"I don't even know how much he's had."

The prince clucked his tongue. "Well, do something so he's not angry at you anymore and he won't skulk off to drink."

"I don't know what I did. He'll barely even talk to me." Ainsley didn't like the note of whine that crept into his voice.

Together they watched Rue surreptitiously drain a mug, then make his way back to them.

"He's still walking alright, so less than five," Tadgh noted quietly.

Upon his return, Rue slung an arm around Ainsley's waist and pressed a kiss to his neck.

Tadgh caught Ainsley's eye and mouthed the word, "Three."

Ainsley bobbed his head slightly in acknowledgment and appreciation.

"Do you want to go somewhere?" Rue murmured.

"Go," Tadgh mouthed, his eyes wide with emphasis. "Before he gets upset."

"Alright," Ainsley agreed.

Rue wrapped him an embrace and lifted him off his feet. "Should I carry you?"

"Only if you promise not to hit my head on any doorposts."

Rue laughed and set him back on the ground. "That I cannot promise, dear knight." He kept his arm around Ainsley as they walked back inside the hill, carefully stepping over the unbroken snow that marked the circle of flowers.

The walk back to their rooms felt real and warm, the sweetest things had been between them in a long time. Rue kept him close and purred tender promises into Ainsley's ear, making chills run down his spine.

Guilt tugged at the back of Ainsley's mind. It leapt to the forefront once their door closed and Rue started to kiss him in earnest.

His body responded eagerly, though, and he couldn't help but return Rue's kisses and touches almost as earnestly. He struggled to let himself go any further, though, so reminded of how Rue had acted the night of the full moon.

"What's wrong?" Rue asked.

"I..." Ainsley searched desperately for something that wouldn't be patronizing, confusing, or upsetting to the other man. "I. I want you to tell me what to do." He swallowed, not sure how the request would be received.

Rue pulled back, concern scrawled over his face. Concern and something else, though.

Ainsley thought it might be intrigue, so he pressed, "You've been so careful with me, love, and good to me, but...but isn't there anything you've been wanting?"

"You mean it?"

Ainsley nodded. "You can tell me."

Rue skimmed his fingers over Ainsley's cheek and drew him in for another kiss. "I'll tell you exactly what to do."

The warm, glowing way he promised it made something in Ainsley stir, some need to please that hadn't exactly been satisfied before. Rue had never asked him for anything intimate, nothing other than preparation before they lay together and a climax after Ainsley had finished. A twinkle of disservice had always fluttered on the edges of Ainsley's awareness, but the hungry look in Rue's eyes forced the realization that Ainsley had been inconsiderate.

"And you'll tell me if you don't want to continue," Rue said. "You're still so new to these things...Are you ready?"

Ainsley nodded.

"Good." Rue led him to the bedroom and watched carefully when Ainsley undressed. He directed Ainsley to undress him.

Ainsley obeyed, letting his hands stray as he did so.

"Show me how you please yourself."

Ainsley pulled back. "What?"

"Touch yourself."

He hesitated, wondering if this could be some trick, but the quiet intensity of Rue's expression made him think otherwise. He lay on the bed, curled his hand around himself and began to stroke, awkward and clumsy at first.

Rue knelt beside him.

Ainsley fell into a rhythm then hesitated. His free hand scrambled over his thigh, desperate for something to do. He glanced at Rue.

Rue was waiting for something. He took Ainsley's free hand and whispered into it, just as he had their first time and so many times after. "Show me how you please yourself, my love."

Ainsley slicked his length with what Rue had conjured, stroking himself faster. Though he'd done it before, this time he had to work up the courage to slide a single finger into himself. Doing it alone, far away from others, had been one thing and his heart had always pattered in his chest, afraid to be caught polluting himself in this way particularly.

He threw back his head and closed his eyes, giving himself over to the act.

"Stop."

He stopped moving but kept his hands in place.

Rue leaned in to kiss him, long and deep, his hands skimming over

Ainsley's flushed skin. When he moved away and stood beside the bed, Ainsley nearly pulled him back.

"Come kneel," Rue said.

Ainsley swallowed, sure he knew what Rue would request next, and went, sliding clumsily on to his knees before the other man.

Rue combed his fingers through Ainsley's curls. "Start as slow as you like."

"What if I don't want to start slow?"

Rue threw back his head and laughed. He crouched down and kissed Ainsley. "Start slow, my love. Trust me."

At first, Ainsley felt coddled, but once he began and nearly gagged, he heeded Rue's advice. He struggled, though, to adjust his lips, teeth, and tongue all at once.

Rue, however, purred encouragement and soft sounds of pleasure, which gave Ainsley all he needed to carry on until the fairy murmured, "Stop."

Ainsley pulled back and wiped his mouth.

Rue crouched beside him again. "How we go from here is up to you. You know what you are ready for far better than I."

With so many options sprawled before him, Ainsley didn't know where to go. He wiggled his jaw to ease some of the ache. "If. If you were inside of me, would it hurt?"

"I would be careful and slow so that it wouldn't. It is a delicious sort of thing, if it is a thing that you enjoy," Rue answered. "And you can always tell me to stop if you don't enjoy it."

His heart fluttered so fast Ainsley worried it would tear out of his chest. The idea had its appeal, but more than that it terrified him. Would he disappoint Rue? Was it wrong of him to shy away from something that Rue had offered him so willingly?

Rue kissed his forehead. "I don't think tonight is that night for you, sweet thing. Come on to the bed, we can find our way together." He took Ainsley by the hands.

They tangled together on the bed, slowly caressing each other. It took Rue less time to spill and once he did, he devoted himself fully to Ainsley.

"I can use my fingers, if you like," he offered.

"Please."

He did it with the utmost care, coaxing Ainsley to spill with such intensity that his mind momentarily went blank.

They remained cuddled together for a long time afterward, lazy and exhausted.

"I'll miss this," Rue confessed quietly into Ainsley's shoulder.

"Why?"

"You want to go home," the fairy reminded.

"Oh. Right." Ainsley pulled him closer and tried not to think about how difficult a return home would prove. How could he keep so much from his family? Unrequited desires he could contain within himself, but he couldn't imagine keeping the depth and strength of his feelings for Rue a secret. "It won't be long."

Eventually, they parted and cleaned themselves. They stayed in, calling for a servant to bring them dinner.

For the following day, things felt more normal between them. Rue woke bright and early, singing to himself while he prepared for the day.

Ainsley grinned at the sight of him in better spirits. He threw his arm around him and nuzzled into his throat. "How did I ever get so lucky?"

"I stalked you across miles of countryside."

"And thank all the stars you did."

Rue kissed him.

They spent another day watching the completion of the Ice Palace and the election of its monarchs. Two small children, perhaps four, won the crowns this time and Tadgh placed them upon their heads.

"Rule well, your reign is the first of the season."

The children giggled, clasped hands, and ran away into the palace. The other children followed and soon enough, shouts and laughter made their way out of the palace.

In bed that night, Ainsley asked, "Do you think tomorrow would be a good day to go?"

"We'll have to see what tomorrow brings," Rue murmured. He wound his arms around Ainsley, his embrace growing tighter and tighter. Into Ainsley's skin, he whispered something too quiet to hear.

It sounded sad, whatever he said, so Ainsley didn't try to wiggle out of his too-tight embrace or squeak a protest. "We'll back to adventures and questing in no time. Wasn't that wonderful? Have you been to the sea?"

Rue didn't answer.

"I've never been. Triviai doesn't have any coast."

The fairy's grip relaxed a little.

"This is the farthest I've ever been from home, but it...it doesn't feel far at all. This feels like a place I'd go in a dream. Like I might wake up anytime and be back. Like this could have never happened."

"Shush."

"Hmm?"

"It's bedtime. We should be sleeping," Rue said.

"Oh." Ainsley snuggled under the covers. "Love you."

"You too."

Ainsley easily dropped off to sleep, warm and cozy, but he woke cold and alone.

Waking alone immediately filled him with dread. He pulled on a robe and padded out into the other room. He found Rue lounging on the fur before the fireplace, a poker in one hand and a cup in the other.

"Rue?"

"Hmm."

"Are you…" Ainsley wrinkled his nose, trying to think of what to say. "Are you drinking?"

"One does usually drink from a cup."

"It's morning still."

"A bit of wine with breakfast isn't anything unheard of."

Ainsley came to sit beside him, his stomach churning to see that Rue had an entire carafe of wine beside him. "You aren't eating anything."

Rue rolled his eyes. "Then call for breakfast."

"Rue."

"Or don't call, I don't care either way." Rue drained his cup and refilled it.

Ainsley sighed and reached across to move the carafe away from him. "You shouldn't drink anymore, not without eating."

"How do you plan to stop me?" Rue asked, a dangerous purr in his voice.

"By asking you not to, Rue. I can't force you to do anything."

"You could force me to do a lot of things," Rue told him.

Ainsley took his hand. "Will you tell me what's bothering you?"

"Why does something have to be bothering me?"

"Why else you be drinking first thing in the morning?" Ainsley demanded.

Rue didn't answer. He left, taking his cup with him. His robe flared out behind him as he left.

Ainsley clambered to his feet and hurried after him, but by the time he popped his head out into the hall, he saw no trace of Rue. "Rue!"

The fairy didn't answer or come back.

He hurried into something less revealing, not too keen on wandering around the Court with his body so easily accessed.

Ainsley didn't give up looking for Rue so much as he exhausted his options short of going into every closet, chamber, and nook in the Court. He asked Tadgh and some of the other courtiers, but they had no answers to give. Or, at least, no helpful ones. Tadgh, at least, appeared reticent that he couldn't steer Ainsley in the right direction.

"If my cousin has changed very little, and I fear he has, despite your tender ministrations, remained the boy with whom I grew up," Tadgh told him, "Then he is likely cozied up to the most unworthy fellow he can find."

"And who's that?" Ainsley asked.

"Maybe you don't want to see him like this," Tadgh cautioned.

"It doesn't matter how I want to see him."

"He makes mistakes, Ainsley. A lot of them. If you're too proud to bear his mistakes..." Tadgh trailed off.

"It's not about me, Tadgh. You know he doesn't like..." Ainsley trailed off, not sure what he wanted to say.

"Me? Himself? The men he lays with?" Tadgh guessed. "Find me something Rue does like, and I will grant you the most magnificent boon."

"He likes me."

"Oh, no, foundling. He loves you. If I see him, I will tell him you search for him."

Ainsley sighed and nearly thanked the prince. Instead, he walked away. He checked a few closets on the way but worry sat in his gut.

He returned to their chambers, shouldering open a door that felt ten times heavier than it had when he'd left.

His ears pricked at the sound of clattering and hushed voices.

"Rue!" he called.

He got no answer but heard the hisses of people shushing each other.

He made his way to the bedroom, not surprised at all to find Rue and some youth pawing at each other. He recognized the youth as Marl.

Rue kept eye contact with Ainsley as he wound himself around Marl.

"Rue, stop it. I want to talk," Ainsley said.

Marl hesitated, glancing between Ainsley and Rue. "Should I go?"

"Yes," Ainsley answered. He took the youth by the arm and pulled him back, then gave him a push towards the door. "Go, quick, before I get out some iron."

Marl scampered after that.

Rue scowled at Ainsley. "You haven't got to be mean to him."

"I looked everywhere for you."

"And you found me." Rue gave him a louche smile.

"Why are you doing this?"

Rue didn't answer. "Do you want to finish what he started?"

"I want you to talk to me."

"And what could I say to a simple fool like you?"

Ainsley bit his tongue to keep in the first words that came to mind. He closed his eyes and waited for the swell of anger to fade. "I know something is wrong."

"You know!" Rue cried. "What do you know, Ainsley? You...you stupid knight. Traipsing in and out like you own the fucking place. Telling my guests to go."

"Marl? If you want him back, you go get him, but you better goddamn bring me back home first."

Rue stared, his face icy and still until it broke. A heaving sob tore through him.

A wave of irritation rolled through him and Ainsley immediately felt bad. He forced himself to say, "I can't help if you don't let me."

"I'm sorry."

Ainsley came to sit beside him, easing himself onto the bed. "How sorry can you be without changing something?"

Another sob, then tears.

"Things aren't getting any better here, Rue. It's time to go."

The fairy curled in on himself.

Ainsley couldn't help but bring him in close. He waited until Rue had stopped crying before he said, "You said you would bring me home."

"I can't like this."

"When you're sober."

"When I'm sober," Rue agreed.

"You promise?"

"I do, Ainsley, I'm sorry. I am."

"I know." Ainsley pressed a kiss to Rue's temple. "Sleep it off."

Rue didn't sleep it off, at least not right away. He threw up and wept a little more first.

The problem, it turned out, was how to get Rue sober. Each time Ainsley turned his back on the fairy to do anything, he found his way into a bottle of wine. It became a cycle. Ainsley spent each day finding him or waiting for him to come back to their chambers, coaxing him through his sobs and bearing his insults. Then he would fall asleep, or think Rue had fallen asleep, and find Rue gone.

Sometimes Rue came back with another man, thought their visit never lasted long. When infidelity failed to provoke a fight, Rue tried other things.

Sometimes they fought, sometimes they made up. Ainsley lost track of whether they were on good terms or bad. He couldn't remember if the last thing had been an insult or a plea for forgiveness. He did his best to get Rue to eat and didn't like the way Rue avoided it. The other man's body began to show that it suffered: blood shot eyes with circles under them, too thin through his ribs and chest, but his gut puffy, and his face almost always ruddy.

More and more often, Ainsley slept somewhere other than their bed. A chair, the rug before the fire, once or twice even in Tadgh's room when Tadgh happened upon him and took pity. The depth of Tadgh's pity surprised Ainsley, though it usually came in private moments.

Ainsley didn't bother to keep an eye on Rue, so Rue started to keep an eye on him. Wherever he went, Rue followed, doing something ostentatious in a bid for Ainsley's attention.

One night after perhaps the most wine Ainsley had ever seen one man put away, Rue climbed up onto the banquet table and began to dance, to the cheers and encouragement of the other courtiers. In no time, he had a dozen others with him.

"This is bad," Tadgh announced to Ainsley. He'd come to stand beside him.

"I don't care."

"Oh, foundling, of course, you care," the prince chided.

Ainsley sighed, forced himself out of the chair, and approached the table. Hands scooped him up and dragged him onto the table.

He could see Balor and Corva watching, aloof and cool, but with none of the mild amusement they usually had for Courtly antics. The Court had gotten rowdy before; in fact, it did almost every night. Their eyes followed their nephew, though, as though they watched thunderclouds on the horizon.

Ainsley wove his way through the tight-packed crowd to Rue. "I think you've had enough."

"Enough what?" Rue asked.

Ainsley frowned.

Rue grabbed his chin and pressed a sloppy kiss to his lips. "What's wrong? Forget how to talk? You are a stupid thing, Ainsley. Would I even be surprised?"

"You've had too much to drink. You need to stop."

"Why?"

"Because I hate you like this."

Rue paused, just for a moment. "What's changed, then, my sweet, idiot knight? At least now I'm having fun."

"You aren't."

"I cannot lie, pet. I'm having fun."

"And later when you're getting sick all over the floor and weeping? Will you be having fun then?" Ainsley pressed. "Come to bed. Sober up."

"So I can go back to holding your hand through the most banal fucking I've endured? Children play with each other better, I'd put my money on it. Or! Or So you can cry about curses and hexes, or mewl about your mother some more? Shall I listen to another lament of how boys can't go jousting with other boys at home?" Rue sneered. "Watch you make a fool of yourself after a few ales?"

"You're drunk and—"

"I'm drunk!" Rue crowed. "I'm drunk and I'll grant a wondrous boon to anyone who can out drink me."

Ainsley gave Rue a shove, not half as hard as he wanted to, and hopped down from the table. He returned to where he had left Tadgh and demanded, "I need air."

The prince raised an eyebrow.

"Tadgh! I need to see the fucking sky. Weeks it's been and I can't find my way out of this accursed place."

"I need to see the fucking sky, Your Highness," Tadgh corrected. He handed his daughter to her nurse and took Ainsley by the elbow.

Outside, sitting in the snow, away from the noise and wild heat of the Court, Ainsley could think again.

Tadgh crouched down beside him. "I don't even know where he got you from, pup, or I'd offer."

"I know."

"You know?" Tadgh arched an eyebrow.

"You look like an ass, you know, when you make that face."

Tadgh grinned. He plopped into the snow beside Ainsley. "I've been told I look like an ass almost always. Tell me how you know I cannot bring you home."

"Because I asked him. And I asked your parents."

"You asked my parents?"

"I thought they might care about how much of a mess this is. Balor didn't seem bothered. I thought Corva was going to laugh at me."

Tadgh put a hand on Ainsley's shoulder. "If you wait long enough, they'll get sick of him and likely scoop you both up and toss you back."

"I don't want to wait that long."

The prince kept his hand on Ainsley for a moment longer, then slipped an arm around his shoulders and pulled him in. "I don't hate to touch people, you know. Not all of them, anyway. Not the ones I've grown accustomed to. But with most people touching like this leads to touching in other ways."

"I'm not about to try anything. I'm a little too heartbroken." The words came out, an easy confession that Ainsley hadn't even let himself think yet.

"I know you are, pup."

"It wasn't supposed to be like this."

"Things don't go how we want them to most of the time."

As his chest tightened and throat closed, Ainsley managed, "I hate it here. It was...it was so good and now..."

"Oh, shh, now, I know." Tadgh put his other arm around Ainsley and rocked him gently. "Go on."

Unwanted, unbidden, the tears came. Ainsley couldn't stop them. "What am I supposed to do?"

"Pup, if I knew a way to heal whatever drives my cousin to these things, I'd have done it."

"What did I do?"

"He gets like this."

Ainsley pulled away from Tadgh and shoved him. "And you don't help things! Bringing him wine."

"A cup or two of wine is not what has my cousin undone."

"Goading him!"

"Name me a person without flaws, Ainsley, and I'll grant you any boon I can."

"You're rotten, you know that. All of you. This whole place." Ainsley buried his face in his hands again.

Tadgh put an arm back around him and rubbed his back.

He sobbed his way to a clean, clear emptiness. He wiped his face on his tunic when he finished. "I need to go to the kitchen."

"Now?"

"If they have herbs."

"Oh. I'll do you one better. I'll take you to the apothecary."

The apothecary, a short, round woman that reminded Ainsley of a soap bubble, furnished Ainsley with the herbs he requested.

Once he had his hands full of greenery, he hesitated. He didn't want to go back to his room. He didn't have any interested in fighting with Rue, or cleaning him up after he'd been sick, or fending off his drunken, sloppy advances.

Tadgh tugged on his sleeve. "Come along, foundling, you can weather the night again in my quarters."

They retrieved Merremia from the banquet hall. Ainsley tried not to watch as Rue stumbled his way around the room.

"Something's going to happen to him," Ainsley murmured.

"Hmm? Well. Certainly, something's going to happen to him. Things happen to people all the time," Tadgh agreed.

Ainsley pursed his lips, still watching Rue. No matter his recent cruel streak, Rue had saved his life twice. He couldn't let anything happen to him.

Tadgh tapped his daughter's nurse on the shoulder, then nodded towards Rue. "Make sure he doesn't end up hurting himself or going off with anyone. He's got a few more glasses in him before he blacks out, but you can probably get him back to his room sooner than that."

The nurse bobbed her head. "Your Highness." She peeled away from them and headed towards Rue.

For the rest of the night, Ainsley stayed awake and made use of the herbs he'd procured. He slept burrowed into a pile of lounging pillows Tadgh had set up for him and he slept like a dead man. All the discomfort and sadness seeped out of him that night, but so did everything else. He felt quiet and empty.

He waited for hours until the night had ended and the wee hours of the morning had begun. He forced some food down his throat, tucked his herbs inside his tunic, and struck out to find Rue.

Tadgh walked with him to the hall. "Good luck, Ainsley."

He nodded.

The prince hesitated, then slid his hand behind Ainsley's head. He pressed his lips to Ainsley's forehead, then pronounced, "You have my blessing, for what it's worth."

Ainsley nodded again, swallowed, and went to find Rue. He found the other man swaying as he spoke to a group of courtiers.

"Rue."

The fairy spun, his eyes narrowing and wine sloshing over his hand. "Here he is, whore of a knight."

"I accept your challenge."

"What?"

"To outdrink you."

Rue laughed. "You can barely handle one cup."

"Then it will be an easy win, won't it? Same stakes on my end. If I lose, I'll grant you whatever you like."

Rue licked his lips. "Yes. Fine."

"Rules?"

"First to fall, or be sick, or pass out loses. First, who fails to finish a glass loses," Rue proposed.

"No magic."

"No magic," Rue agreed.

Ainsley offered his hand.

Rue shook his hand, but his expression of smug, drunken confidence faltered when Ainsley met his eyes.

In no time, the courtiers cleared one of the tables and set out two goblets. Ainsley and Rue sat across from each other. Two courtiers assumed the roles of drink servers and leaned across to pour their drinks.

Before he took his first sip, Ainsley took the crown he'd woven from his tunic. The lemony scent of the herbs tickled his nose, as the leaves had gotten a little crushed.

"What are you doing?" Rue asked.

"It's not magic." Ainsley lifted his goblet and took the first sip.

Rue scowled. "A bit of grass won't help you."

"Drink or forfeit."

Rue drank, deep and long from his goblet.

Ainsley swallowed his wine, the taste less sweet than he remembered, the high of it less heady.

When they had drained their goblets, their attendants poured another. Then another.

Then a fourth and a fifth. In between each drink, he plucked a leaf from his crown and chewed it.

Rue had begun to flag after the third. When he reached for the fifth, he nearly knocked it over. He clasped on to it with two hands.

"You can forfeit," Ainsley reminded. His tongue sat heavy in his mouth and he desperately wanted water to wash away the sticky residue the wine left in his mouth. A parsley leaf could only do so much to clear the taste.

"Fool of a knight, idiot boy, he thinks I need his advice."

Ainsley sighed.

"If I wanted the counsel of..." Rue stopped, burping and gagging. He pressed a hand to his mouth. "If I wanted—"

"Drink or forfeit," Ainsley pressed. He drained the last sip from his fifth goblet.

Everyone turned to watch Rue. He still hadn't sipped from his fifth goblet. He brought it to his lips, but as soon as the first swallow passed his mouth he gagged, then threw up all over the table.

Ainsley jumped back, startled by the force of the other man's retching.

Rue slumped back in his chair and vomited again, this time all over the front of his tunic. Not much more than pure liquid.

The courtiers laughed and cheered, several of them congratulating Ainsley on his victory.

Tadgh placed his hand on Ainsley's shoulder. "You won."

Ainsley sighed. "Help me carry him."

They slid their arms under Rue's arms and hoisted him to his feet, dragging him along to his bedroom. Every so often, he would burp and spew up a little more sick. They cleaned him up and tucked him into bed.

Ainsley sat on the side of the bed. "My boon."

"Can't wait?" Rue grumbled.

"You'll grant me this: tomorrow you'll be sober and you'll return me to Triviai. Proper time and place, no leaving me three hundred years in the future," Ainsley said. "Or the past."

Rue moaned.

"Rue, you'll grant me this. I won it fair and square."

"You cheated. No magic."

"What's magic about parsley?" Ainsley asked.

"Cousin, grant him the boon before the lord and lady get involved," Tadgh warned.

"You fuck him?"

Tadgh leaned over and smacked Rue on the back with the flat of his hand. "The boon, you horrible morose bastard! Agree to his terms."

Rue groaned and let out a few cries. "Fine. I agree."

"That's a good lad, Brightling." Tadgh gave Rue's hair a gentle ruffle. "We'll be back. Try to rest up." To Ainsley, he said, "Your chambers or mine?"

"I'll wait with him. I need to pack, anyway."

"And will you come to say goodbye to your beloved Crown Prince before you go?" Tadgh asked.

"Likely not. But I'll say it now. Goodbye, Tadgh. I like you better than I did."

The prince grinned. "I like you, too, pup." Tadgh gave him a pat on the head and took his leave of the room.

Ainsley gathered the few things he had and then settled into a stuffed chair for a little sleep. He had hours before Rue would even stir and hopefully, agreeing to grant the boon would keep him from drinking himself into another stupor.

Ainsley granted Rue permission for a bath and a meal before their journey. He looked so wan and pathetic that Ainsley might have granted him just about anything. He barely spoke and never raised his voice above a whisper when he did speak.

He shuffled after Ainsley to the stable and waited in the shadows as Ainsley readied Hadley for the trip home.

The whole time, Ainsley felt somewhere between sick and afraid. He had to force himself to face Rue. "I'm ready to go."

"I have to touch you."

Ainsley held out his hand. He didn't remember how he'd gotten to the

Otherworld. "Will it…"

"It's just like walking," Rue assured.

The fairy went still for a few minutes. He whispered to himself then waved a hand. An archway of shadow and ash appeared. Together they walked through the archway, the air sliding thick and heavy over them.

When they passed through, they stood beneath a tree.

The same tree where Ainsley had killed that man. No sign of the fight remained, no corpses, fresh or rotted. Not even a bloodstain. Snow up to his ankles. He wished he had warmer shoes.

Rue lingered. He cleared his throat.

"No tricks?" Ainsley asked.

"No. No tricks, Ainsley, I promise. You are home, when and where you should be."

"Good." Ainsley nodded. "Good." He looked around. Home. He needed to see his parents. He needed to sleep. He needed it desperately.

"You'll be happier here," Rue told him.

"I'll be miserable here, Rue," he snapped. "I didn't…It wasn't supposed to be like this."

"I. Before…before I go." Rue clenched his hands. "When did things…when did we fall apart?"

"Around the time you decided to stay too drunk to bring me home."

"No, I mean. Ainsley, when…? Before that?"

"What do you mean before that?" Ainsley demanded.

Rue shook his head and pleadingly reminded, "You wanted space."

Ainsley sighed.

"To come back here," the fairy insisted.

"Space from the Court. From wine. From whatever it was that was making you so miserable. And you wouldn't let me have it."

"Things were good before, weren't they?" Rue asked.

Hadley tossed her mane and stamped a foot.

"Before you kept me prisoner!" Ainsley reminded.

"Any task, any feat, name it and I'll—"

"No."

"Please."

"Rue, you kept me prisoner, you know that, don't you?" Ainsley asked.

"I regret it. I do. I just…I didn't want you to go. I still don't want you to go," Rue said.

"You should have thought of that before you called me a whoreson three dozen times over."

Rue licked his lips. "Hawthorne Gilrhys Escher."

"Rue."

"Call and I'm bound to come. Anything you order."

"I don't want your name."

"You already have it."

Ainsley rubbed his face. "Rue! Go. I can't do this. Not now."

"Can I come a different day?"

Ainsley opened his mouth to ask if he could stop him, but the weight of knowing Rue's name settled over him. Anything he demanded and Rue would have to give it to him. How worn raw did a fairy have to be to freely hand over his name? "Not tomorrow. And not the next."

"But the day after?"

"The day after you can come."

Rue nodded.

"And I don't want you following me around as that crow and spying on me!" Ainsley reminded.

The fairy nodded again. He went, walking away.

Ainsley hastened onto his horse to put more distance between them. He urged Hadley into a gallop until he felt he'd put enough space between himself and the fairy. Right now, he wanted to be away from him. Soon, he thought, the numbness in him would fade and he worried what would replace it.

Each night, Rue appeared as Ainsley made his camp. Each night, Ainsley told him, "Not today," and the fairy would slink away into the shadows. Ainsley didn't know how far he went or what he did.

The sight of the other man made his stomach hurt when he appeared tonight. Ainsley barely glanced up and began to say, "Not tonight," but some part of him wanted to see Rue.

Things had been good once and he had always relished the sight of the other man. He'd liked to watch him sleep or laugh, he'd liked to watch the water bead on his skin and the way he moved. A few bad weeks didn't erase the months that had come before. It worked in reverse, too. He couldn't simply will himself into forgiveness for the sake of what had been.

He didn't want to be alone, either, and that need for companionship made him look at Rue.

The fairy looked awful. Shadows beneath his eyes, his hair a tangled mess, his clothes...his clothes had somehow stayed clean. Plain and black, but clean. If Ainsley changed the angle of his head, he thought he saw Rue's body through them.

"Is that a glamour?"

Rue nodded.

"Why aren't you wearing clothes?"

"Can't carry them around with me."

"I told you not to—"

"To follow you around, or spy, but...but being something else makes it easier not to drink. Animals are less complicated."

Ainsley couldn't fault him for that. "Are you well?"

"Other than the shakes, nausea, and headaches."

"You should go home."

"Wolfwood is under ten feet of snow at least. And the Court...Tadgh has a daughter. He can't go keeping an eye on me. No. Here is better for me. I dried out last time, I'll likely dry out again," Rue said.

Ainsley didn't say anything more to him. He poked at the fire and chewed on a bit of dried meat. It tasted stale and pallid, but he'd been dining at the table of fairy royalty for months. He wondered if the mortal realm had been spoiled for him entirely.

Rue lingered at the edge of the campfire. His hands shook unless he clasped them together.

"I don't want your name. Can't you take it back?"

"I don't do mind magic. I wouldn't recommend you find someone who can, either. 'Tis dangerous, that."

They lingered, silent and uncomfortable.

"You should go," Ainsley finally told him, unable to tolerate this strangeness between them any longer.

Rue went.

"Wait."

Rue paused and glanced back at him.

"Take care of yourself, Rue."

"And you."

The fairy went.

Ainsley continued to chew his stale meat, sitting as close to the fire as he could. He tightened his cloak about his shoulders. He'd brought it with him from the Otherworld, one of the few things he'd taken from the Court. If he'd been smarter, he would have taken enough of value to get him home in comfort.

Or at least warmer pair of shoes.

Maybe Rue hadn't been far off the mark calling him an idiot all the time.

Hadley huffed. When he looked over at her, she twitched an ear.

He reached up to rub her nose. "You're a good girl, you know."

She let out a warm chuff of air into his hand.

As Ainsley traveled northwards, toward home, he kept his eyes peeled for anything to hunt. He saw little more than a few small, winter birds, nothing worth killing. He spotted a handful of rabbit tracks one morning, though. They must have been fresh because snow still drifted down from the clouds.

He slipped down from Hadley and strung his bow as he followed the tracks. He came across a rabbit snuffling around in the snow.

It seemed to turn to look at him. Its pink little nose twitched.

He drew his bow, his heart in his throat, hungry and worried that rabbit would bolt before he could release his arrow.

It didn't bolt, but it did turn into a man.

Ainsley nearly fired anyway but aimed away and sighed. "You can become a rabbit?" He relaxed his bow. "Have you been following me around like this?"

With a small gesture, Rue clothed himself in illusion. "Sometimes. It's warmer with fur than feathers."

"How many animals can you turn into?"

"Three...two. Three? Are spiders an animal?"

Ainsley smiled, unable to stop himself. "They're not a plant."

"Then three."

"I'll see you tonight, I guess." Ainsley turned and headed back to his horse. When he glanced back, Rue had gone, no sign of man or rabbit.

As darkness fell and Ainsley struggled to light a fire from wet wood, Rue emerged from the woods.

"I couldn't tell if you'd invited me or if you said it in jest," the fairy confessed.

"Well, you spent too much time with those sharp-tongued harpies at Court," Ainsley told him. "Makes your head muddled."

"There's a reason I drink. Do you want help with that?" Rue gestured to the fire, or the pile of twigs Ainsley wished was a fire.

"If you don't mind."

Rue approached the smoldering pile of wood. He crouched and blew into the fire. It leapt to life and crackled merrily. "Oh. And. Here." He handed over a rabbit. "You looked so disappointed when you didn't shoot me."

Ainsley took the rabbit.

Rue stood and began to withdraw from the fire.

"You might as well stay," Ainsley said. He regretted the words almost immediately but knew he would have regretted it more once Rue slunk away, back out into the cold and snow. "You've got to be hungry."

"Hunger is relative." Rue sat beside the fire and held out his hands to warm them.

Ainsley took out his knife and set about spitting the rabbit. Almost as soon as it started to cook, grease spattering onto the fire, Ainsley's stomach rumbled; he wanted to scarf it before it had even finished cooking.

Rue stared at the rabbit.

They ate in near silence, both uncomfortable, the meal full of aborted glanced between the two of them.

Quietly and after what felt like an eternity, Rue said, "None...Ainsley. Those others, the other men, they didn't mean anything."

"I know they didn't."

"I just. I thought I should say it."

Ainsley wiped his fingers on his tunic. "What is that you think I'm upset about, Rue?"

"My behavior."

"Specifics."

"The...the other men. The way I spoke to you. How messy I was. Refusing to bring you home."

Ainsley nodded half-heartedly. "I'm not pleased with any of that, you're right. But the thing that hurts most is you wouldn't tell me what made you act that way in the first place. I thought we were going to see the world together, every inch of it, and then you're slobbering all over strangers and calling me an idiot. What changed?"

"You were going to leave me."

Ainsley looked at Rue so sharply he flinched. Unable to keep the disbelief and indignation from his voice, he snapped, "No, I wasn't."

"All your talk of going home."

"I invited you."

"But then you wanted space."

"Space between you and wine, Rue, not space between *us*. And I'm the one you were calling an idiot!" Ainsley huffed.

"I."

"But you don't trust me, Rue. You never have. And now I don't trust you either." Ainsley rubbed his eyes. "I think it's time for you to go."

Rue nodded and stood.

"Go somewhere far this time," he suggested. "Don't come back tomorrow."

Rue nodded again and slunk away into the woods.

Once Ainsley knew he had gone out of earshot, he curled up on himself and pressed his face into fistfuls of his cloak. He dug his teeth into his knuckles to ward off the tears. He'd exhausted himself crying so many nights, the wind freezing his tears and snot to icy trails down his face.

He screamed into his cloak and lay awake all that night, unable to calm his mind for more than a moment at a time.

He would have given anything to cut all the rot out of their relationship, but he didn't know how to fix this. He couldn't hammer out the dents and buff away the scratches, he couldn't return things to that gleaming shine they'd had.

He couldn't even ask for advice from anyone. Not a single soul could be trusted with this secret and if he asked anyone for counsel about a woman who'd behaved as Rue had, he'd been laughed out of the room and told to beat the nonsense out of her.

When Rue resurfaced a few nights later, Ainsley told him, "If I want to see you, I'll call for you."

"Ainsley."

"Please, Rue. Go. Let me breathe. Let me think."

"One question. Please."

And, of course, Ainsley said, "Go ahead," because he didn't think he could deny Rue anything.

"Is there hope?"

He asked it so tremulously that Ainsley couldn't stand it. He thought he'd become immune to the other man's tears after watching them so many times, but this was different. This wasn't some maudlin, self-pitying sob of a man who didn't know how else to demand attention, it was the constraint of a man too close to the edge.

"If I say no?" Ainsley asked.

"Then you'll never see me again." Not a threat. A promise.

"Rue."

The fairy watched him, his dark eyes dulled.

"I don't know, Rue, I don't."

He nodded and began to walk away again.

Ainsley hated everything about that walk. He'd seen that walk before, haunted and hollow and lifeless. He'd seen how it ended. "Hawthorne Gilrhys Escher."

Rue paused.

Keeping his voice even took all of Ainsley's will. "Don't hurt yourself and don't get anyone else to do it for you."

The fairy swallowed and nodded, the barest acknowledgment.

"Promise me."

"I promise," Rue managed.

"I need to think. If I don't call for you in a month, you can come to ask again."

Rue didn't nod that time. He walked away, swallowed up by the night.

Ainsley stared after where he'd disappeared, wanting to call him back just to make sure he was alright. He knew he needed distance between the present and his time at Court. He needed to sort out his feelings, to decide how he felt about Rue and how he felt about the things Rue had done. Right now, they blurred together and he didn't know how to pull them apart.

Maybe, if he worded things exactly right, he could ask his mother what to do. She loved his father so deeply and his father was not a man without flaws.

The depth of how badly he needed to go home had not sunk in until then.

He'd been away for far too long.

No grand celebration welcomed him home. He had not written to give his family ample enough time to prepare any such thing and their family's means had never amounted to much. Enough for comfortable living for the lord and lady, but no luxury or splendor.

Ainsley didn't mind. He hadn't come home for luxury or splendor. He had come home to see his family. As soon as he laid eyes on his mother, the numb weight that had settled on him eased.

She opened his arms and he embraced her, tightening his arms around her as tightly as he dared. Sometimes he wished he'd never gone away to become page, that he'd stayed all his years by her side. An impossible thing to wish, of course, but he wished it all the same.

"Ainsley!" she laughed.

"I missed you," he said into her shoulder. He stood taller than her and her alone in his family. A few times his father had blamed her for breeding small stature into his family.

She pulled back and touched his cheek, her palm scraping over the stubble. "You need a shave. A bath." She waved over a servant and told them to start heating water. "You look...haggard."

"Not much luck questing?" his older brother asked.

A childhood of teasing and inferiority came back to him at the sight of Warren. It made him lift his chin and boast, "Plenty of luck, dragons and everything."

"You slew a dragon?" Warren asked, his eyebrows raised.

Ainsley faltered. "No, I...I saved it. It was just a baby."

Warren laughed and clapped him on the back. "Scraped together enough for a new cloak at least." He examined the fur lining, his face drawing into a frown. "What is this? Wolf?"

Ainsley shook his head. "Uh, not quiet. It's from a fetchgroat."

"A what?"

"They're sort of..." Ainsley tried to recall how Rue had described the beast. "A giant, carnivorous deer. But that's not a good explanation."

Warren peered at the fur a little closer. "Where did you get it?"

"The Otherworld," Ainsley answered, neglecting to say that he'd appropriated the cloak from his lover on his way out.

"Ainsley!" his mother scolded. "Don't tell me you went messing around with fairies."

"I had a guide," he assured. "And here I am all in one piece."

His mother tutted.

"Where's Father?"

"Oh, off somewhere with Domenic, you know how they are." His mother waved a dismissive hand. "Busy as bees, as always."

Ainsley nodded. His father and his castellan hardly ever left each other's sides. The nature of their positions, he supposed.

When his father did appear for supper, he pulled Ainsley into a big hug and said, "Not an inch taller, either. I thought you might grow a little more."

Ainsley rolled his eyes.

"Oh, don't roll your eyes at me, lad, you might be knighted but I'll still knock some respect into you," his father said, the warning rumbling up from his broad chest.

"Victor," his mother scolded.

His father growled at her, too. "Don't tell me how to mind the boy, you heard him."

She clucked her tongue.

"Don't give me that, either."

The look they exchanged made Ainsley smile. Victor might have been surly, critical, and ready to fight with most everyone, but he'd never raised a hand against anyone in their family. The first time Ainsley had gotten his ears boxed as a page, he'd cried pitifully.

After dinner, they all sat around the fireplace in his father's solar. His mother and sister-in-law had their knitting, making clothes for the babe that grew in his sister-in-law's belly. His brother's other children, a boy of four and a girl of two, toddled around, playing with wooden horses and rag poppets. Warren, Domenic, and his father had fallen into some discussion that Ainsley couldn't follow. It had to do with peasants and taxes.

He sat on the floor and tried to play with the children, listlessly moving a wooden horse across the rug.

"Maybe you should get some sleep," his mother suggested.

"Hmm?"

"You seem out of sorts."

He shook his head. "No, I'm not tired."

"Then what is it?" she asked.

He sighed, fidgeted with the horse a little longer, then turned to face her. He felt like a child again. "There's...While I was away, I met." It felt so wrong to pretend Rue was anything else. "I met this girl."

Everyone quieted and turned to look at him.

"You met a girl?" Warren asked, a smile blooming on his face. A disbelieving sort of a smile. "Don't tell me you came home to ask permission to marry."

"No, no, nothing like that."

"Ah." His brother nodded understandingly. "That sort of girl. Better not to talk about it, hmm?" He glanced at the women and children.

"Not like that either," Ainsley protested. "She was...she was highborn. But things went ugly."

His father laughed. "Then forget about her. There are other maidens out there to marry. If you want, I know a few lords who have got daughters a plenty."

"No."

"Finding a new maid will get the old one out of your head," his father promised.

"Victor, leave him alone," his mother said.

Ainsley sighed. "You're right, maybe I should get some sleep." He sighed and made his way to his room, climbing the long stair up to the tower.

His mother and father had their own chambers, as did Warren and his family. Ainsley had inherited this small room as his own when Warren had wed. Before he'd left to become a page, he and Warren had shared the bed, though Warren had often pushed him out for tossing around too much.

Small, dark, and cold. A hard, wooden chair and a small table, along with a chest and a narrow bed furnished the space. A far cry from what he'd grown used to, but it had its own comfort. The comfort of familiarity instead of luxury.

He wallowed in that comfort for a few days, feeling he deserved it.

One afternoon as he walked the narrow corridors where he'd played as a boy, his mother came to walk with him.

"You still seem out of sorts," she told him.

"I still feel that way."

"Did you really love her?"

For a moment, he didn't understand what she meant. "Oh, right. Right. Uh. Yes."

"But you don't plan to marry her?"

"Ah. No."

His mother remained quiet, her hands in her sleeves. The weight of her judgement pressed upon him.

"It's...it's not that easy."

"Why not?"

"She's..." He tried to think of how to explain this. "She's not the kind of girl I can marry."

"What kind of girl can't be married? Have you been involved with someone else's wife?"

"No!"

"You're being so mysterious, Ainsley, that's not like you."

He shrugged. "Maybe I'm not exactly who I was."

She put a hand on his arm and kissed his cheek. "Don't be silly, Ainsley. You'll be always be who you are."

"I don't know."

"Tell me why it can't work with this maiden, if she's not a peasant and she's not already wed."

"Because I don't trust her anymore. And she doesn't trust me."

"I see. There are other women, then."

He hadn't expected his mother to dismiss things so readily. It must have shown on his face.

"A wife you cannot trust is useless. And a trust you won't rebuild must not be worth having."

Ainsley stopped walking.

His mother didn't.

A little more than three weeks had passed since he'd asked Rue to keep his distance. The fairy had stayed away, as far as Ainsley knew. He could also take other shapes, but Ainsley hadn't noticed any crows or rabbits acting suspiciously. He hadn't seen any spiders either.

He'd tried, and tried hard, not to think about Rue. It hadn't been an easy feat and most days he'd failed. He didn't want to think about Rue, how he missed him and hated him all at once.

He hurried to catch up with his mother. "What about when you and Father fight? What do you do when you're angry with him?"

"I forgive him."

"How?"

"Because the alternative is ugly, Ainsley. A family that feuds is a family that weakens itself. We forgive each other, always, because we never act against each other with intention."

He walked alongside her, thinking.

"What did this woman do to spoil your trust in her?" his mother asked.

Ainsley didn't know how to begin to explain things.

"And who she? Who are her parents?"

"You don't know them."

His mother turned to look at him, one eyebrow raised. "A foreigner?"

"I didn't say that."

"Our family knows every noble house in Triviai."

He sighed.

"I can't help you if you won't talk to me, Ainsley," his mother reminded.

Her words hit close to home, given that he'd said exactly that to Rue when the fairy had been distraught. Whatever had bothered Rue, he'd guarded it closely. Now, being told that exact thing about something he had no choice but to guard closely, he felt his resentment weaken a little.

What secrets had there been between them, other than wine?

"And if you won't talk to me, I wouldn't advise asking your father. He'll tell you to be firm with her. He thinks everyone needs to be coerced. And I wouldn't ask your brother, either. He'll tell you to get her taste out of your mouth with another woman."

"I didn't plan on asking them," he said. "One more thing."

"What?"

"Why do you love him?"

"Your father?" she asked. "Because on our wedding night, when he tried to start barking orders at me, I slapped him across the face and he cried. Because he gave me two beautiful children and a good home. He's barked at me, yes, but he's never done anything without my permission. He's gruff because he doesn't know any other way to be. If you'd known your grandfather, you'd understand."

He nodded. They walked together a little longer in silence.

He tried to make himself content at a home. He told his family of the wyrm he'd saved, of the witch, and the werewolf. He even told him a few of the things he'd seen in the Otherworld, though they didn't seem to believe him about most of what he said.

Only his nephew took any of his stories to heart. Ainsley couldn't help but gloat when the boy started to ask Warren if he'd ever met a dragon and why he hadn't.

Although he'd never had much interest in books, Ainsley spent most of his days in his father's solar, looking through the handful of volumes his family had collected over the years. No books of magic, not that they would be of any use to him. He didn't know why he had gone looking for them, though.

He had lived for months in land inundated with magic. He had grown used to the barely-there hum of it all around him.

The runes that had lined the tub at Wolfwood lingered in his mind. He'd seen them so many times he thought he could put them to paper if he tried.

The world around him felt empty.

His brother's voice started him. "Ainsley!"

He turned to find Warren, bundled half as much as a regular man might have been for the weather. "Hmm?"

"Get your horse. We're going hunting."

"Hunting?"

"You know, that thing people do when they want to eat," his brother said.

"Hunting what?"

"Whatever moves, it's winter," Warren said with a shrug. "Father's already in the kennel."

Ainsley nodded, returned the book he had to its shelf, then hurried away. He grabbed his cloak, then broke into a run once outside, past the kennel and stable and into the woods.

"Rue!" he called into the woods. "If you're skulking around out here, you better turn into something we won't hunt!"

From nowhere, a voice answered, "Would the crow suffice?"

"Where are you?"

Rue stepped out from behind a tree, clothes weaving around him as he moved.

Relief and irritation mingled. "You know, following me around isn't exactly what I had in mind."

"I don't have anywhere better to be. And if you had called for me, I wanted to be near enough to answer."

Ainsley made a face. "Still. I hate that you're watching me."

"I'm not watching you. Not usually anyway," Rue told him. He tucked a bit of pale gray hair behind his ear; his fingers caught in a snarl and he shook them free.

"So what do you do all day?"

The fairy shrugged. "What any other animal does. Food, water, shelter."

Ainsley sighed. He almost didn't want to offer, but he didn't like the look Rue had about him. "You don't look well."

Rue shrugged again.

"You can come stay in the castle."

"It's not my intention to impose. Or make you uncomfortable."

"I wouldn't have offered if I didn't mean it."

Rue looked him over, lingering near the tree.

"You look awful, Rue. Come inside," Ainsley insisted. He had been a fool to think that he hated Rue. He didn't think he could; he didn't know if pitying him was worse. "We should talk."

The fairy nodded and followed Ainsley towards the castle, trudging through the snow clad in nothing but illusion. Ainsley glanced back to see him shivering.

He removed his cloak and threw it over the other man's shoulders.

"No, I—" Rue protested.

"It's yours anyway."

They passed by the stables. His father and brother, already on their horses, called to him. A hound trotted over to him, nosing at him and Rue.

"Who's that?" his father asked.

"Aren't you coming?" Warren asked.

"Uh, Father, Warren, this is Rue, a prince of the Western Court. Rue, my father, Lord of Cresthill, and his heir." Ainsley felt faintly ridiculous making the introductions, especially given the way his father and brother looked down at him and over Rue's haggard countenance.

"A prince of where?" his father asked.

The hound pushed its snout inside Rue's cloak.

Ainsley pushed the dog away. "Of the Western Court. In the

Otherworld," he said. "He's...we have things to discuss."

"Oh."

His father and brother looked at each other.

"Are you coming hunting?" Warren asked.

"No, I...it's important."

Cautiously, Ainsley's father said, "Make yourself at home, Your Highness. If I'd known you were coming...Well. It's a surprise."

Rue nodded. "I understand."

Ainsley awkwardly lingered a moment longer, then brought Rue back to the castle. They thankfully didn't encounter his mother on their way to his room.

Inside, Rue looked around at the sparse furnishings.

"Not what you're used to, I'm sure—"

"I've been sleeping out of doors for weeks, it's better than that," Rue answered.

Ainsley gestured to the chair. "Do you want a bath? I can have one drawn for you."

"I'm not here to impose."

"Rue, I'm." Ainsley rubbed a hand over his jaw. "I didn't invite you in just to tell you to go away."

Rue watched him, his black eyes trained on Ainsley's face, cautiously hopeful.

He kept his voice quiet, knowing how well secrets could travel in a castle. "You've been on my mind a lot. And I still don't know what to tell you. But I, uh. We really do need to talk, don't we? But not yet. You look awful. Do you want a bath?"

"Please."

Ainsley had the servants bring the tub to his room and as they went back to fetch the water, Rue told them, "I can manage from here."

The servants stared.

"You are dismissed." The fairy turned to the tub and, with a few gestures, conjured a small rainstorm above the tub.

Ainsley grinned despite himself. "I didn't know you could do that."

"Yes, well, at home we have plumbing."

In half the time it would have taken the servants, Rue filled and heated the tub.

Ainsley sat on the edge of his bed, his heels resting on the frame and one elbow propped on his knee so he could hold up his chin.

Rue shed the cloak and the glamoured clothes, then stepped into the bath. He melted into the water with a small, sweet sigh.

"How are you feeling?" Ainsley asked. He tried not to think about how the fairy had thinned out too much. The slight puffiness in his gut from over drinking had faded, replaced with sharpness about his hips and ribs.

Not that Ainsley looked his best either. Too much cold and too little nourishment for both of them.

"Mmmm. Empty, I think. And tired." Rue leaned against the tub. "Like an old tree trunk that's been rotting for years."

"Oh."

"What about you?"

"Sort of." Ainsley squinted. "Numb. I know there's something there to feel, I just can't feel it." He handed Rue a hunk of soap. "I know I should be mad at you."

"Aren't you?"

"I should be. I want to be. I want to...I don't know. I don't know what I want." Ainsley sighed and slumped forward, burying his face in his hands. When he straightened up again, he asked, "What about you?"

"I don't remember much. I mean, I remember how I acted, but not the details. It's a haze. I shouldn't have behaved as I did, but I did it out of fear, not...not strictly out of malice."

"Oh, then there was some malice?"

"I thought you were going to leave me. And you did. I wasn't wrong."

"Don't try to blame me for this," Ainsley growled.

"I'm not blaming you. You left because I made you. From your first mention of going home—"

Ainsley interrupted, "I wanted you to come with me."

Rue's face twisted. "At the start."

"I wanted you to come with me until the moment I had to force you to take me home," Ainsley told him. "Believe me or don't, Rue, but I had no intention of leaving you behind."

The fairy regarded him warily. He looked faintly ridiculous doing it, since he had lathered his hair full of suds.

"Is that what had you so miserable?" Ainsley asked.

"In part."

"Why did you think I would leave you?"

"Everyone does." Rue dunked his head underwater to rinse his hair.

Ainsley came over to the tub, dragging the chair closer. He sat beside the tub. "I asked my mother what to do."

The fairy's eyebrows shot up.

"I mean. I asked my mother what to do about the girl she thinks I was in love with," Ainsley clarified. "She said a trust that isn't worth rebuilding isn't worth having. I don't know if she's right, but she's the only person I know that actually loves anyone and has enough of a mind to articulate it."

Rue stared, not saying anything.

"But I don't know if there's anything to rebuild. You've never trusted me."

"I."

"You don't trust anyone."

"I want to."

Ainsley thought and thought, but he didn't have anything worth saying. He'd run out of ideas.

"Miles, I've followed you, through snow and storm. Do you know why?"

"Why?"

"Because you haven't told me to go away. If you tell me to go, I will, but if you don't, then I'm left to hope that there is something to save."

Again, Ainsley had nothing to say.

"I've given you my name," Rue reminded gently.

He said it with such weight. Ainsley knew he would never understand what it meant to him, not fully.

Ainsley sighed, got up, and turned away from him. "You haven't got any clothes?"

"No."

"I'll lend you something. If I can find anything that fits."

"A glamour will serve me."

"Don't be stupid. It's freezing." He rummaged through his things and at the bottom of his trunk, he found a few things that had belonged to his brother. Hand-me-downs into which Ainsley had never grown. He shook them out and held them up. They'd have to do. He tossed them onto the bed. "I can find you shoes."

Rue remained in the bath. Whisper quiet, as he washed himself, he sang, "To and fro the laddie runs, hither thither away from fun."

Ainsley stopped himself from looking over. If Rue knew he'd heard, he'd stop singing and Ainsley craved the sound of his voice.

"He knows not where the maidens lie, nor nothing of between their thighs. Winter comes, he's warmed by wood but by his hearth there's no one stood. As for me, I'm blessed to catch his mother's eye, I'll help myself to what comes by."

Ainsley sniggered at that.

Rue quieted; the next line of the song never came.

"I wasn't laughing at you," Ainsley clarified as he turned his attention back to the bath.

Rue, lips pursed, said nothing. He scrubbed the soap over his arms, both of them smooth and gray, the flesh utterly whole.

Ainsley crouched beside the tub. He folded his hands over the lip and rested his chin there. "You want to trust me."

"Yes."

"And you want me to trust you."

"I do."

"Don't hide from me, then." He skimmed his finger over Rue's right arm, the arm that should have been scarred. He'd memorized every inch of the scar, knew its exact bounds by heart.

Rue swallowed.

At the slightest contact, Ainsley's guts burned just as they had when he'd been untouched by any hand but his own. Nerves and desire tangled together. "Go on."

The glamour over his skin faded to reveal the scar that spanned most of the right side of his body. Rue slid further beneath the water to compensate. "And when there are others about?"

"Do as you will then."

Ainsley dipped his fingers into the water, knowing he shouldn't want to touch Rue as badly as he did. Touching the water provided a safe go-between. "If I said I like it when you sing, would you believe me?"

"No."

"I do, though. Maybe..." He cocked his head, thinking. "Maybe you have to let yourself believe it."

Rue wrinkled his nose.

"Go ahead, call me a fool again."

The fairy let out a breath through his nose. "A million apologies I can give if it please you."

"Apologies mean less than changing."

"A crow, a rabbit, or a spider, those are your choices if you'd like me to be something other than what I am."

"Rue, if you aren't going to even work at this, then you can go home," Ainsley told him.

Sheer panic swept over the fairy's face. He lurched forward in the bath. "No, I...'twas a jest, Ainsley. Whatever you set before me I'll accomplish."

Ainsley held out a towel to him.

Rue clambered out of the bath and grasped the towel as if it would offer him salvation. Dripping on to the floor, he insisted, "Anything. However you want me to be, that's what I'll become."

"Dry off."

Brusquely, Rue scrubbed the cloth over himself.

Ainsley sat on the edge of his bed and held out a hand to Rue.

The fairy twisted his fingers with Ainsley's.

"I'm not asking you to change who you are, Rue. Just what you do." It felt so good to have Rue's hand in his again and such a large part of him wanted to capitulate; the easiest thing in the world would be to nestle into his arms.

"Tell me what to do."

Ainsley gave him a tug and he came to sit beside him on the bed. "I want you to tell me when you're upset. And what you need when you are."

The apple of Rue's throat bobbed, but he nodded.

"Let yourself believe me, believe anyone when they say something kind to you."

"I thought you didn't want to change who I am."

"You're so morose," Ainsley said. He tightened his hand around Rue's. "No more than two glasses of wine, if you must have wine. Can we start there?"

"It would be easier if you would just send me to fetch some obscure artefact."

The corner of Ainsley's mouth tipped up. "What would that do? I'd have some piece of rubbish I don't want, and we'd fall apart again."

"What if I retrieved a wonderful artefact?"

"I don't want an artefact, Rue. I want us. I want you."

Rue licked his lips, his tongue fantastically pink compared to the darkness of his skin. "If I kissed you..."

"No." The last kiss between them had been sloppy. Rue had tasted of wine and sick and despair had sat heavy in Ainsley's gut. Too many kisses like that had passed between them. "I'm not ready for that yet."

Not to mention, if Rue kissed him, Ainsley suspected that he would be consumed by it. They'd tumble into bed and into some heady, confused mess. Ainsley had had enough of messes for a while.

Rue looked heartbroken though, so Ainsley assured, "I didn't say never again. I just said not yet."

"'Tis a wise stance to take. Far be it from me to ever call you a fool again."

Ainsley gave his hand one last squeeze. "Get dressed. People are going to start getting curious about who's visiting."

Rue shuffled into the ill-fitting clothes Ainsley had found for him, fussily tugging at them. Ainsley sent someone to fetch a pair of shoes for him, but the leather turn-shoes did nothing to diminish the ridiculousness of seeing a fairy prince clad in the hand-me-downs of a lesser nobleman.

Rue fidgeted in the clothes and peered at them with a degree of distaste. "If you insist I must, I'll wear these, but must they look as they are?"

"No, I don't care what they look like, I just don't want you to freeze."

"Mmm."

"And I don't want anyone to look at you sideways and get an eyeful."

Rue's cheeks flushed and a shy smile grew on his lips. "I'll be surer when I cast a glamour from now on. Most mortals can't peer through them so easily."

"Maybe I spent too long in the Otherworld for you to pull the wool over my eyes."

That got a chuckle from the fairy.

He tugged at his clothes, changing the plain hose and tunic to something that appeared fine and better fitting. By the time he finished his adjustments and found a comb for his hair, he looked the part of a prince again.

Ainsley didn't know how he'd taken Rue for anything but royalty. The subtle fineness of all his possessions, the hint of languor and boredom that persisted in his movements, and the shadow of haughtiness in his attitude.

And his beauty! Even as uncommon as he looked, Rue brilliantly outshone all but the finest of mortal men.

"Oh, he stares with such a look in his eyes, this gentle knight, and tells me I cannot kiss him," Rue casually pronounced as he wove braids into his pale gray hair. He said it with the smallest of glances and the ghost of a smile on his lips.

"Maybe you should have been a troubadour," Ainsley said.

At first, Rue's face tugged into a scowl, as if Ainsley had offered him offense. Then he sighed, closed his eyes, and stilled for a moment. "A harp sits beside my bed for reasons beyond passing interest."

Ainsley recognized it as an attempt at openness, stilted as Rue sounded.

"At home we call them nightingales, they're different from standard entertainers. They're...record keepers, of a sort, they're tasked to go out and take account of any new customs, poems, or songs, then bring them home for the lord and lady."

"What happened?"

Rue shrugged. "Many things interfered. The quality of my voice, my youthful indiscretions, the war, the state in which I returned home."

"Well, I think your voice has a lovely quality."

Rue smiled, strained but making an effort.

Ainsley forced himself to recognize how much of an effort Rue made. Not half an hour had gone by and already, the fairy had started to bend himself to Ainsley's requirements.

Someone rapped against the door, quick and light.

Ainsley pulled it open to find his mother.

"I'm told we have a guest." She barely moved her eyes but managed to peer into the room nonetheless. "I can't imagine your father had time to greet him properly, if at all."

"Father saw him." Ainsley tried not to glance over his shoulder. "The visit is a little unexpected."

His mother waited.

Ainsley stepped aside. "This is Rue, a prince of the Western Court and my travelling companion of some months. Rue, this is my mother, Lady Elaine."

His mother curtsied and Rue dipped his head.

"Much have I heard of you, my lady, and long have I desired to meet you."

"Oh? I cannot imagine what my son has told you, Your Highness." His mother graced Ainsley with a peculiar look.

"There's a song he told me of..." Rue glanced towards Ainsley, his expression indicating he hoped Ainsley could remember the song. "His taste is sweet to me?"

"Oh!" Ainsley cried, the sound strangled as it escaped his throat. "The Song of Songs. The Bible, Mother, they haven't got the Bible in the Otherworld."

"No Bible?" His mother sounded scandalized.

"Maybe you could tell me more of it. That song sounded sweet as lark," Rue said.

Dread twisted through Ainsley's veins; he had no idea what a discussion about religion between these two would entail.

"It would be my pleasure to tell you whatever you want to know about the Bible. I can fetch our priest, too, if you have questions I cannot answer. I'm not as learned as him, but I have devoted myself to Our Lord," his mother answered. "I once thought to take my vows, but that was..." She glanced at Ainsley. "That was before I met my husband."

"Anything you have to say will capture my attention."

Consumed with nausea, Ainsley followed behind his mother and Rue as she began to explain the Christian faith to her otherworldly guest. The longer he listened, the more Rue began to falter. He threw several concerned glances towards Ainsley.

When Ainsley's mother began to explain the crucifixion, the blood drained from Rue's face.

"And I thought the Fair Folk could be ruthless..." he whispered.

"Mother, you don't have to be gruesome."

"Our Lord died for us, Ainsley, if he can bear the crucifixion, you can bear hearing about it."

He knew better than to say anything back. He waited for a more natural lull in the conversation before he steered the conversation towards something that he knew would enrapture his mother even better. "Is Alys far along?"

"Oh, the babe should be here by the spring," his mother began, then launched into a lengthy recount of nearly every development her grandchildren had undergone in their entire lives.

Rue listened patiently, nodding or adding a small comment when appropriate. At one point, he added, "My cousin recently took in a daughter."

"He what?" Ainsley's mother asked.

"He took her in."

She blinked at him. "He legitimized her?" she guessed.

"No, I don't...I don't think the ceremony made her any more legitimate but..." Rue trailed off, his face contorted thoughtfully. "You know, the truth of it escapes me, my lady. I don't know if she's even a bastard."

"The babe's not his daughter," Ainsley explained to his mother.

"Brave would be the man who dared to say that to my cousin's face," Rue warned.

"Not his daughter by blood," Ainsley clarified.

His mother continued to stare at them.

"Things are a little different in the Otherworld, Mother, when it comes to heirs."

Rue added, "And marriages, if I'm not mistaken."

The amount of sheer panic that shot through Ainsley nearly made it so he couldn't change the topic before Rue brought up something he couldn't explain away. Ainsley hadn't asked much about marriage, as he would likely never wed, so he didn't know what practices the Fair Folk had regarding it. "I!" he squeaked.

They both turned to look at him.

"Father and Warren will be back soon, won't they? God, I could eat!"

His mother scowled. "Language, Ainsley. Or have you forgotten all your manners?"

"I'm sorry, Mother. I am. Too long traveling. A few more months and I would have come back to you a wild-man."

She chuckled at that, at least.

He extracted himself and Rue from the conversation, saying that Rue had traveled so far and must want to rest before they ate.

Rue followed along quietly until his mother had gone out of earshot. "Does talk of marriage always provoke such a reaction in you?"

In barely more than a whisper, Ainsley said, "Only when I'm worried that you'll tell my mother something that will shock her to death."

His head tilted to one side and his eyes carefully narrowed, Rue asked, "And what would do that?"

"You know exactly what."

"Assumptions I can make, but without a careful explanation, I may err. Most grievously, too, considering how fearful you looked."

"We can talk about it when no one can overhear us."

Rue glanced around the narrow hallway. "So out of doors?"

"And deep in the woods," Ainsley added. "We can ride out tomorrow."

"Until then, my mouth shall guard its words as though they are precious."

Ainsley snorted. "You must be in a better state these days if you're talking like that again."

The fairy shot him a sharp look, but the corner of his mouth tipped up the slightest bit.

That night, long after darkness had come, when they both began to yawn and rub their eyes, Ainsley offered, "I'll get a pallet for you."

Rue shook his head. "No need."

"You don't mean to sleep on the floor."

"No." The fairy began to shed his clothes, folding them neatly as he went.

Ainsley watched, more curious than anything.

When he had set aside all his clothes, Rue stretched, placed a hand upon the wall, then vanished, leaving behind a gray spider about the size of a thumbnail. It had a few pale speckles on its body.

Ainsley watched the spider scuttle into a corner and begin to weave a web. "You'd better be careful around Warren. He's never met a spider he hasn't tried to squash."

The spider paused in its weaving and rubbed its forelegs together.

Even though Rue had declined the offer, Ainsley had a pallet brought to his room anyway. He didn't need anyone asking questions about their sleeping arrangements and the bed was a bit too narrow for two grown men anyway.

Under the guise of giving Rue a tour of the lands, Ainsley rode with Rue out into the woods and began to explain the various things about which he was not allowed to speak. Rue barely paid attention, since he struggled to steer his borrowed horse.

The normally placid gelding meandered behind Hadley and snorted at Rue.

"What are you doing to Devon?" Ainsley demanded, glancing over his shoulder to see Rue manhandling the reins.

"It doesn't listen."

"You're going to hurt his mouth."

Rue immediately slackened his pull on the reins.

Ainsley gave Rue a brief lesson on how to manage a human-trained horse, which turned out to be different than directing a fairy-trained one. Once he had the gist of it, Rue steered Devon to pace alongside Hadley.

"Does it really hurt his mouth, that metal thing?"

"If you yank on it."

Rue leaned forward and gave the gelding a pat on the neck. "Apologies, dear heart, I didn't know." He turned his attention Ainsley. "You were trying to tell me about what I am not permitted to say?"

"Anything," Ainsley told him.

"At all?" Rue asked, perfectly serious.

"Nothing about, uh...Don't talk about anything that has to do with us, for one. Or about any of the men you've been with, or that you've even been with men. Or that you know any men who've been with men."

"Ah. Well."

"It's a sin here, Rue, and a terrible one at that."

Their ride continued in silence, the snow crunching beneath the horses' hooves. Branches, laden with ice, creaked in the breeze.

"The idea that sin might have a different sort of weight to it here than it does at home may have crossed my mind," Rue said.

"In what way?"

"At home, we consider sins to be grave transgressions against the gods themselves."

"No, that's what a sin is," Ainsley confirmed.

"I don't understand."

"Which part?"

"How taking someone to bed transgresses against your god."

Pushing the words out took more effort than Ainsley had expected. "It's unnatural."

"How could it be?"

The abrupt desire to return to the Otherworld seared through Ainsley's chest. "It is. It's. I don't know, Rue. The only reason to lie with someone is to a make a child. Anything else is." Ainsley couldn't stop himself from rolling his eyes, out of discomfort and embarrassment. "It's a transgression. Self-serving. Wicked."

"We could ride together for days and I don't think I'd understand any better."

"I've lived here my whole life and I still don't understand."

The fairy mused, "Maybe your mother can explain."

"No!" Ainsley shouted. He tightened his hands on the reins abruptly and Hadley danced in surprise. He forced himself to loosen his grip.

Concerned, Rue breathed, "Ainsley."

"No, you can't, Rue, you can't *ever* talk about it with her."

"I'm sorry."

Ainsley continued, tense words barely making their way out through clenched teeth, "It's not just a sin or a crime. It's disgusting; my family would hate me."

"Oh."

Ainsley kept his eyes down. The harsh tightness in his chest and throat didn't fade, the burn in his eyes and the bone-deep sickness in him remained. He tried to think of anything else but failed.

He failed until glowing, cream-colored butterfly danced past his face, trailing golden sparkles through the air. The sight of it took him by surprise, jostled him out of his thoughts. It settled onto Hadley's mane, it's wings slowly opening and closing.

"A king's-crown," Rue pronounced. "Very rare in this world."

Ainsley glanced over to see that the fairy had the fingers on one hand slightly crooked, as he did sometimes when casting magic.

"They're signs of good fortune, you know. If one lands on you, you're surely blessed by the White Lady," the fairy told him. "What a fantastically lucky horse you've got, Sir Ainsley."

An ugly snort of laughter escaped Ainsley's nose.

The butterfly took wing again, fading into mist as it went.

"I don't understand why, Ainsley, but I understand the weight of it. Your family shall have no knowledge of such things from my lips."

Ainsley nodded. For the rest of their ride, he coached Rue on the appropriate way to word how things had been between them; finding a way to avoid both scandal and Rue's inability to lie proved a challenge. By the time they'd figured out what to say, neither of them wanted to speak another word.

They stayed out so long that Ainsley started to lose feeling in his fingers, despite the fur lining of his gloves.

In the stable, he fumbled with Hadley's tack.

Rue fumbled with Devon's as well, though it had more to do with the type of fastenings on the tack.

In the end, they both gave up within minutes, calling for the stable boy to do. Ainsley made a note to slip the lad an extra bit of something good to eat when dinner came.

They stomped the snow off their feet and trudged up to Ainsley's small room in silence. Rue stoked the fire and had it burning bright in no time.

Ainsley stripped off his gloves and flexed his hands in front of the fire. The cold had turned his fingers red and stiff. Holding them out to the fire hurt.

"Here." Rue extended his hands to Ainsley.

Once Ainsley placed his hands in Rue's, the fairy brought them closed to his mouth and whispered into Ainsley's palms. With that and a few gentle squeezes, he brought the feeling and warmth back to Ainsley's hands.

Ainsley left his hands in Rue's longer than necessary, savoring the contact.

"This spell I learned during my first Winter Court. 'Twas the longest by far. An impossible tempest snowed us in. Three weeks, four days."

"I'd have been terrified."

"Oh, terror gripped me as surely as ice gripped the world, gentle knight. If my cousin hadn't deigned to keep an eye on me, I might not have survived."

Unable to help himself, Ainsley wiggled his fingers a little more firmly into Rue's grip.

"Are your hands still cold?" Rue asked.

"No."

A wicked, knowing look flashed in Rue's eyes. He brought Ainsley's knuckles to his lips.

Such a strong wave of longing rolled through Ainsley that he had to step away. More than lust made up this yearning; the need for companionship and understanding and all the precious familiarity that had existed between them had left an emptiness in Ainsley.

And in Rue, too, judging by the sharp look of loss that passed over the fairy's face.

"Not yet," Ainsley said.

Rue nodded.

In a strained whisper, Ainsley added, "And not here, either...Fuck, if anyone walked in on us! Or even *heard* us."

"Heard us?" Rue asked, keeping his voice soft but smiling crookedly. "What would we be doing to overhear?"

"You know exactly what."

"Do I? I'd thought, well, in all honestly, Ainsley, I thought I would have great difficulty ever persuading you to think of me in such a way again. Seeing me as you did, and so many times, it should have soured whatever you found appealing about me."

"I thought so, too," Ainsley admitted. "But here I am, undeterred by the rivers of sick and piss with which you befouled your self and bed."

At the description, Rue winced.

"Anyway." Ainsley glanced around the room. "Do you want to play tables?"

"You'll have to teach me."

Ainsley riffled around in the chest at the foot of the bed and emerged with the board and pouch of game pieces. He pulled the chair and table over closer to the bed, then settled on the edge of the bed.

Rue watched him as he set up the board. When Ainsley began to explain the rules, the fairy listened so intently that he began to frown.

"It's just a game," Ainsley assured.

"What are the stakes?"

"No stakes."

"Games always have stakes," Rue insisted.

"No stakes, nothing to be won or lost except for the game itself. Listen, we don't have to play, but there isn't much else to do."

Rue sat across from Ainsley and studied the game board. "Tell me the rules again."

Ainsley started from the beginning.

Rue played carefully, each move made with serious consideration.

After a while, Ainsley gave up on actually playing and began his own study of the man across from him. Where their friendship, let alone their romance, could go from here required painstaking reflection. It could not, Ainsley knew, grow into anything healthy while they remained in Triviai. Secret relationships never fared well. He also knew he didn't trust Rue enough to return to the Otherworld.

"Your turn," Rue said.

Ainsley selected a piece almost without looking and slid it across the board.

Rue lapsed back into his contemplation of the game.

The desires of the body and heart needed to be set aside. He should, as a matter of prudence, tell Rue to go elsewhere so that Ainsley could think without being distracted.

Except weeks without Rue around had done nothing for his state of mind. Being alone had only brought clarity in the sense that he knew he missed Rue.

No, he decided, for now Rue could stay. He deserved the chance to prove himself a changed man, at least. Ainsley didn't think the threat of drinking overmuch would ever disappear, but maybe it could fade.

"What do I need to change?" Ainsley asked.

Rue looked up, brow knit. "What do you mean?"

"I've given you all these things you need to change, but you haven't given any in return. You want my trust, but I want yours, too. How can I earn it?"

"I don't know."

Ainsley tapped his fingers on the table. "Well. Why don't you trust me? I mean...do you think I'd hurt you?"

"Not physically. And...not intentionally in any other way."

"You always think I'm lying."

"I." Rue sighed. "I don't...it's not that I think you're lying so much as I'm frightened that you are."

Without a clear understanding of the difference, Ainsley kept quiet until he'd thought through his answer better. "Could you put a spell on me to compel the truth?"

"Mind magic far outstrips my comfort with spell casting. I'd likely do some great harm to you."

Ainsley thought a little longer. "What if we bought a truth serum? I think the university mages sell them."

"To what end?"

"You could ask me anything you wanted and know that I meant it."

Rue began to smile.

"If you call me simple, I'll send you away," Ainsley warned.

The fairy only smiled wider. "You have such a straightforward view of the world, Ainsley. I'd only think there was something wrong with the serum."

They returned to silence and contemplation, the only sound that of the game pieces moving on the board.

"What if..." Ainsley began, but his idea felt stupid before he'd even finished thinking it. "Never mind."

"I cannot tell you what you want to hear. I don't know how to unlock whatever it is within me that keeps me wary. But I will try, and I will keep you appraised of my efforts."

"Maybe you should get waylaid by bandits and I can save your life."

Rue laughed.

Before they had finished their first, painstakingly slow game, Warren let himself into Ainsley's room. "Is that tables? I've got next game."

Rue looked up at Warren, his eyes flashing with mischief.

Ainsley warned, "I wouldn't. It can be dangerous to play games with the Fair Folk."

"Well, if you're doing it, how dangerous can it be?"

The grin that spread over Rue's face made Ainsley worry. He had no way to explain how he could dare to play these games with Rue and Warren couldn't. He also didn't know what Rue would do to a mortal for whom he had no affection.

Warren watched them play, actively critiquing Ainsley's moves.

By the time Ainsley lost, he willingly moved aside to let Warren take his spot on the gameboard.

Rue watched Warren settle in across from him with much more than mischief in his eyes. "Stakes?"

"No stakes," Ainsley answered for his brother.

Warren scoffed. "What are you worried about? I'm not about to gamble away anything important."

"Stakes?" Rue repeated.

"I'll bet a penny on it."

Rue looked at Ainsley. "What's a penny?"

"A perfectly reasonable bet for a game of tables," Ainsley said.

"Fine. I'll wager..." Rue looked over Warren. "A good night's sleep."

Warren laughed.

"Two children and an expectant wife, I'd guess it's something you haven't had in sometime."

"How do you wager something like sleep?" Warren demanded.

"Have you forgotten you speak to a prince of the Western Court?" Rue asked. "Some magics are difficult, even impossible, for me, but I am no common thing, capable of nothing more than glamour and trickery."

Warren looked at Ainsley, his brow creased. "Uh."

"Your wager is with me, lordling, not the knight."

Warren hesitated, looking back to Rue, then nodded. "Fine. I accept." He fished a penny out from his coin purse and set it on the table.

Rue set up the gameboard. He played this game with the same slow consideration as before.

Warren couldn't tolerate it as well as Ainsley had. He fidgeted and tried to goad Rue into making his moves more quickly.

"Unsportsmanlike," Rue murmured with a glance up. "I'll double my wager if you remain silent for the rest of the game."

Ainsley tried not to snigger but couldn't control himself. The sound came out ugly and choked and he finally dissolved into giggles.

Warren glowered but didn't say a word. He sulked through the rest of the game, lost, and said, "Huh, well, beginner's luck."

"Was it?" Rue took the penny from the table and peered at it as though he'd never seen a coin before. "I remember this. You used it to get bread."

"No coins where you're from?" Warren asked.

"Oh, coins aplenty change hands in the Otherworld but no one's ever had the gall to hand me a bill for anything," Rue said.

"You don't pay for anything?"

"Not personally, no. The seneschal manages such things," Rue explained. "Does your king carry coin on his person?"

"I don't know what Jannes does," Ainsley said. He couldn't imagine Balor or Corva carrying money around with them.

"Enjoy your games," Warren said and strode away. He nearly kept his irritation to under wraps, but the way he let the door slam fully gave him away.

Rue held out the penny to Ainsley. "You carry such things. Will you watch over this one for me?"

Their fingers touched when he took the coin. "I can't say I'll give my life to protect it, but I'll hold on to it."

Rue nodded. "Your brother doesn't like games?"

"My brother doesn't like to lose."

"You two have that in common, then."

Ainsley snorted. He stowed Rue's penny in his coin purse. "Do you want to play again?"

"Not particularly."

Ainsley flopped back on the bed and stared at the cobwebs on the ceiling. "How many of those are yours?"

The bed creaked when Rue came to sit beside him. He reclined, studied the ceiling for some time, then said, "Only the one in the corner."

"You don't need to sleep there, you know. I had them bring up a pallet for you."

The offer went without an answer.

"Do you like being a spider?" Ainsley guessed.

"I don't dislike it. It's a little harder to keep track of myself."

"Ah."

They lapsed into silence again.

"I used to sleep on a pallet, you know, it's not...I'm not trying to demean you. I know you're a prince, but...Would you rather have the bed?"

"'Tisn't a matter of status, Ainsley. And I don't mean to turn you out of your own bed." Rue remained quiet for a little longer. Abruptly, he confessed, "I'm afraid."

"Of what?"

"Sleeping on the ground like that."

Ainsley frowned and propped himself up on one elbow so he could look at Rue. "You slept on the ground all the time when we were traveling."

"That's different. It's...I don't know how to explain it. I know it's not rational, but there's something about sleeping...I don't know whether it's because we aren't out of doors or because there would be things above me, but it bothers my nerves."

"You should take the bed, then," Ainsley decided. Upon seeing the look of hesitation on Rue's face, he said, "I don't mind, honest, I don't."

Rue rolled onto his side, one arm tucked beneath his cheek. "You don't mind."

"No, I don't mind, I just said that."

"Oh, no, I...I thought maybe if I." He trailed off and ducked his head a little.

"You thought what?" Ainsley urged.

"I cannot lie, thus I thought perhaps if I...if I said, I might be more like to believe it."

Ainsley couldn't help the coo he made nor the soft, delighted smile that grew on his face. The urge to kiss Rue nearly won out, but Ainsley limited himself to placing his hand on the other man's arm. "I'm glad you're trying. It means a lot."

"'Tisn't easy, dear knight, the task you've set before me. I think I might need a fair amount of encouragement."

Ainsley laughed and gave Rue a gentle push. "Don't get cheeky."

Rue smiled, easy and light.

Rue helped himself to the available books. His fascination with them baffled Ainsley. An allegory caught his interest the best. He poured over the text as though it could unlock some secret meaning. The Bible he perused but pronounced he could do without. Luckily, he said it out of earshot of anyone but Ainsley.

He ran out of reading material within a week, though. Cresthill had but four books, including the Bible.

It led Ainsley's mother to say, "I must say, Your Highness, I'm impressed you could read them at all. Even being a prince, I didn't think a fairy would be able to read Latin."

"Oh, blessed are the Fair Folk. We can comprehend any mortal tongue."

"Any language?" his mother asked, eyebrows sky high.

Rue nodded but didn't seem to notice her incredulity. He had nose buried in the allegory again. He had conjured up a small light by which to read. Warren's children persisted in their attempts to touch it. Each time their fingers contacted the light, it guttered, and Rue's mouth turned down a little further.

Thomas had the misfortune to break the fairy's patience.

As he reached up for it again, Rue warned, "Leave it be."

"Or what?" the boy asked, his chest puffed and his chin jutted out.

Suddenly, painfully, Ainsley saw himself in the boy. They had curls to match, though Thomas's had a darker cast, and he shared Ainsley's narrower build.

Rue marked his page with a finger and leaned forward in his chair. "Or what the lad asks, but does he know to whom he speaks? Should I send him to the woods to cut down a switch, or fetch his father's belt?"

"Rue," Ainsley warned.

Ainsley's mother stared, her eyes just as wide as Thomas's.

The fairy continued undeterred, "No, a brave lad, he doesn't fear the switch. Instead should I send rats to nibble off his toes while he sleeps? Worms to crawl up his nose? Carrion birds to pluck out those fair brown eyes?"

Thomas stared up at Rue, his eyes the size of the moon and his jaw quivering.

"Or maybe, wee mortal, I can tell you to leave my light be once more. Does that suffice?" Rue asked.

Thomas nodded.

"Good. Note, though, lad, I'll repeat myself to you but once."

The boy nodded again.

Rue leaned back in his chair and returned to his book.

"Thomas, go play with your sister," Ainsley said.

The boy scampered over to the girl's side and dutifully took up a poppet.

Quietly, Ainsley said, "You don't need to be cruel. He's just a boy."

Rue once again paused his read. He turned to face Ainsley. "I laid not a hand on him."

He spoke with such honest conviction that Ainsley had to reconsider Rue's experiences of cruelty, given that his aunt had once offered him as a consolation prize during a hunt. "I think we're a little tenderer with children than you might have known."

"Ah. Noted."

When Ainsley knew that his mother and the children had other things occupying their attention, he reached over to give Rue's hand a squeeze. If anyone had treated Ainsley like that as a child, he might have grown up to rely too much on drink, too.

The fairy acknowledged the contact with little more than a glance his way. The glance held such warmth and weight that Ainsley moved himself to the other side of the room to avoid touching Rue any further. The world well tolerated touch between companions and comrades, but Ainsley didn't trust himself not to stray too far.

Thomas continued to cast worried glanced towards Rue and scampered away when the fairy rose to return his book to the shelf.

Rue plucked the light he'd conjured from the air and approached the boy.

The boy went stiff, his little body held rigid with fear. When Rue crouched beside him and his sister, Thomas took several steps back.

"You're braver than I, miting. I always feared the switch. One whack across the palm and I'd be weeping."

"I've never been switched," Thomas said. "Seen the smith's boy get it, though. He cried, too."

Rue held out the light to Thomas. "I've finished reading."

Thomas hesitated to take the light. "No worms?"

Rue shook his head. "I'll harm thee not."

After that, Thomas took the light with a smile. He showed it to his sister and carried it around with him for the rest of the day, proudly crowing to anyone who would look, "A fairy light!"

At dinner, Warren said, "Put it away. I don't want to hear any more about it."

"But—"

"Before the damned thing leads you somewhere you shouldn't go," Warren said.

"'Tisn't that kind of light," Rue offered. "It does nothing but shine."

Warren didn't acknowledge that Rue had said anything. Instead, he continued to warn his son, "Do you know what happens to fools who follow around lights like that? They end up lost and alone, or worse. Walked off a cliff or into a swamp."

Rue picked apart the meat on his plate, fastidiously sorting out all the bones from the flesh.

Thomas asked, "Is that true?"

Warren's face soured when he saw that the boy had asked Rue instead of him.

Rue answered, "The light will do no harm, but following unfamiliar lights often proves an unwise choice. Many wicked things among the Fair Folk might delight to see someone led astray and that is not a place you want to find yourself."

"And if you are, always be polite. But never say thank you," Ainsley added.

Thomas glanced towards his father but returned his eyes to Rue. So far, both children had been warned to leave their guest alone by parents and grandparents alike. The household, apart from Ainsley, seemed to regard Rue as they would a badger that had made its way into the castle. He had the potential to cause terrible damage and wisdom dictated that they leave him alone and hope he left of his own accord.

"What else can you make?" Thomas asked.

"Oh, some variety of illusions, small and middling, a flame or bit of ice, should I desire it."

"Lightning," Ainsley reminded.

Rue's whole face flushed at that and he squirmed. "Yes. A little of that, too." He glanced towards Ainsley and looked utterly ashamed of himself. He listed no more of his powers.

Thomas demanded to see all of Rue's tricks, but before Rue could agree or decline, Warren silenced the boy with gruff words and glowers.

After dinner, though, and as their nurse brought the children to bed, Rue tapped Thomas on the shoulder. The toddler, Olivia, had squirmed out of the nurse's arms and provided an excellent diversion.

He crouched beside the boy and opened his hand to reveal a small flame flickering in the middle.

Thomas reached out to touch it and immediately yanked his fingers back, sticking them in his mouth.

"You forgot your light," Rue said. He closed his palm and quashed the flame, then offered over the orb of light.

"Father said to leave it."

Rue, with a bit of fiddling, fashioned the orb into something else. It became more solid, no longer floating in the air but resting heavily in his palm, dull as a common stone and inert. He traced a simple rune over the surface to make it glow again. He traced it another time and it turned off.

"Did you catch that?"

Thomas shook his head. "No, I'm sorry."

Rue handed him the orb. "Keep it safe. You can practice tomorrow."

"Thomas!" called the nurse. She had finally secured Olivia, though the girl seemed likely to escape again.

Thomas hesitated, then clasped his hand around the orb and ran after his nurse. He glanced back at Rue one last time, a grin on his face.

Ainsley gave Rue's shoulder a pat when he stood. "You'll never get him out of your hair now."

"Better to have more than one friend in the mortal realm, even if he's still barely knee-high." He cocked his head to better catch Olivia's screams. "Wild thing, that one."

"Mmm." Ainsley glanced around to ensure that everyone had left the hall. "Who knows what the world will make of her."

"I wonder more what she'll make of it. A girl as fierce as that could bend kingdoms to her will."

"Maybe if she'd been born in the Otherworld. Women are different here."

"The women are different?" Rue asked archly.

"People are different," Ainsley insisted. "There's no..." He lowered his voice to a whisper. "People like me, who might be more at home with the morals of the Folk, we hide or something terrible happens to us."

Rue circled around Ainsley and leaned in close to whisper, "And is that how it should be?" He trailed his fingers along Ainsley's spine, making him draw in a steadying breath.

He stepped away. The hall had emptied, but even if the whole castle stood unoccupied, Ainsley would worry still. When he glanced back, he expected to see hurt on the fairy's face, but instead he found a sly smile and mischief in his eyes.

"Let's walk a bit. I can show you the manor. You haven't been outside the castle much."

"Restless as ever," came the fairy's comment.

Ainsley didn't respond. He headed outside. Rue followed, of course. He conjured another light so that they could see their path better. In the dark, the manor proved even more unremarkable than in the day.

The kennels provided the most entertainment. The hounds greeted them eagerly. A fine, lean hound with a spot of black over her eye lapped at Rue's hand.

"Yes, hello, we've met before, you're right," he told her.

She wagged her tail.

He gave her a pat on the head and scratched behind her ears.

Ainsley gave his attention to an aging hound whose eyes had gone milky. "Nosewise, good boy," he cooed. Nosewise had sired many fine pups and had been the swiftest hound in the kennel in his prime.

The dog gave a slow, contented wag of his tail and nosed up against Ainsley's hand.

They both smelled thoroughly of the kennels by the time they headed back to the castle.

Once in his room, Ainsley stoked the fire and stretched out onto the pallet. Sleepiness hadn't yet quite come over him, but it felt good to stretch and feel the fire on his face. A quick peek towards Rue found the fairy watching him.

Ainsley sat up, extended a hand, and, when Rue took it, he tugged the fairy down onto the pallet with him. He pulled him into his arms, his chest against Rue's back, and rested his chin on Rue's shoulder. The fairy's bones no longer pushed against his skin; food and rest had done him good, though he had never looked anything but perfect. He looked beautiful, no matter what, be he tragic or splendid. "You don't have to stay, not if you're uncomfortable."

"I'd never move again if I could," the fairy confessed.

Ainsley adjusted them, settling Rue between his legs. He hooked his fingers with the other man's, examining the fineness and replenished strength of Rue's hands, the lovely cast of his skin. Like river stones. "I missed you. Even all that time under the hill, we were together but..." He sighed. "I missed how things had been."

Rue remained quiet.

"Why did you think I meant to go without you?"

His grip on Ainsley's hands tightened.

"Was it something I did? Was...was I too restless? Was I careless with you? Selfish?"

"Inexperienced, maybe, but always gentle and sweet in your doing of things," Rue admitted. "But you never hurt me or left me unattended, if that's what concerns you."

"It must have been something."

A long silence stretched between them before Rue finally said, "Good spirits have always eluded me. Somehow, for some reason, there's...there's this emptiness in me, Ainsley. I'm hollow. It's a space I can fill with service to my king, or wine, or some passing lover. But it never stays filled. No matter how sweet or gentle you are, no matter how much I love you, nothing fills that hollow."

Ainsley considered his words. "Does anything help?"

"Idleness makes it worse." He let out a small laugh. "Being too busy makes it worse, too. And sometimes..."

"Go ahead," Ainsley urged.

"Sometimes it is such a small thing, a thing I wouldn't even be able to recall usually, that sets me on this path. Little by little, I grow emptier, food loses its taste, the words on a page dull. A walk on a beautiful day becomes a chore instead of a delight. It can be...oh, it can be Tadgh's teasing, or doing something to disappoint my aunt and uncle, it can be the sight of someone else, beautiful and unmarred, reminding me that I'm not."

Together, they sat and breathed, hands clasped together. The fire crackled to their right. How many times had they nestled together like this, their conversations drawn out deep into the night? They had talked for hours once, but what could Ainsley say to any of what Rue had shared?

"Most times it passes. A few days. A week. Other times, well...you saw. Empty and aching, I do what I can to make others hurt. To make them look at me. Whether they laugh or cry, whether they bed me or hit me, it doesn't make a difference."

"Rue."

"Tadgh says I'm star-touched and maybe he's got the right of it."

"Star-touched?" Ainsley asked.

"Ah, a kinder word for madness, usually, no matter how it shows its face. Usually when parents realize their babe is star-touched they switch it out for one in the mortal realm. Sometimes the realizing comes too late, though, or it's mild enough to manage. Apothecaries have their powders and philters, don't they?"

Ainsley knew how suspect the brews and serums offered by magic workers in Triviai could be and had to ask, "Do they work?"

"Sometimes. For some people. The simplest solution, as far as most care, is a quick ride on a kelpie's back, though."

It took some time for Ainsley to puzzle out how a ride on a horse, no matter how magical, could fix anything; eventually he recalled that kelpie's most often drown their riders. "I haven't got to say it again, have I? Not to hurt yourself."

"No, I'm well bound to that command."

"Have I got to make it more specific?"

"Not presently."

Ainsley tightened his arms around the fairy. He couldn't ever let him go, not at this rate. No matter how ugly those nights at Court had been, they hurt half as much as the idea of being without Rue. Not just separated, fighting, or sleeping in different beds, icy and silent, but fully without him.

This was how love ruined people. It kept people who hurt each other together just as much as it ripped others apart. How disastrous would this bond between them prove? Ainsley hoped something could be done to soothe things, though. There had to be some way for them to return to that safe, warm world they'd had together. Maybe not the exact same one, but something similar.

"I'll help, if I can," Ainsley told him.

"I'll ask, if I know how."

They parted after another long stretch of quiet. Sharing a bed, nice as it would have been, risked a lot. Bedsharing wouldn't have raised a single eyebrow, but Ainsley didn't trust what they'd get up to if they did. The servants kept their ears pricked for any unusual sounds at night and were well known to listen at doors. Many affairs had been so exposed to interested parties in exchange for a few coins.

Still, Ainsley dragged the pallet beside the bed. "Don't step on me when you get up."

"I'll endeavor not to."

As they waited for the weather to warm, Rue passed his time surreptitiously showing off his magic to Thomas and finding creative ways to avoid the truth about himself when Ainsley's family asked a question that tread on dangerous territory.

Had he a wife, or children? What about a betrothed, or at least a sweetheart? Was that usual, in the Otherworld, for a prince to go unmarried? What about heirs?

Rue danced around the truth of things artfully, but even so, Ainsley started to worry. He needed an excuse to leave earlier than he'd told his family he would.

Today, Warren watched the fairy and his children sit together on the rug before the fire, his eyes narrowed.

Rue had enchanted their wooden horse to walk. "A small magic, and harmless," he'd called it.

"Still." Warren's whole face had twisted.

"Peace, lordling, I cannot lie, you know this well by now," Rue scoffed. "I'll undo it should it worry thee too greatly."

"Leave it."

Rue nodded.

"For someone who can't lie, you're awful hard to get answers out of," Warren noted after a few more minutes.

"Ask and I'll answer true. It's all I've done."

"What do you know about this maid my brother loves?"

Rue glanced towards Ainsley.

Ainsley groaned. "Leave it, Warren. It's over."

"My brother, never in his *life* interested in a maid, goes away and falls in love? She must have been exceptional. You've got to know something."

"I know many maidens, but if your brother's heart went to any of them, he never shared it."

Warren huffed and rolled his eyes. "You don't tell your family, you don't tell your friends. I don't trust that, Ainsley."

"It doesn't matter. Anything between her and I is over."

"It's not like you to give up."

"The heart is fickle," Rue added. "Perhaps something changed. Perhaps what was there paled in memory."

Warren grunted. "You've got to know something."

"Perhaps he fell in love with a glamoured old crone and is too embarrassed to tell that he went to bed with a fair and comely maid and woke up with his arm around a toothless hag," Rue suggested.

Warren stared, then laughed.

"Shut up, Rue," Ainsley said and gave the fairy a bit of a kick in the leg. He had to slump down in his chair and stretch to manage it.

Rue seized his ankle and yanked Ainsley out of his chair.

Ainsley landed hard on his ass and had to bite back a curse, given the presence of the children. He didn't need Olivia screaming that her nurse was a rotten bastard.

Rue persisted with his wild guesses, "Maybe he drank a love potion and it's spell has waned. Maybe 'twasn't a maiden at all, but his own reflection in the river and he's too 'shamed to say he'll never love a girl as much as he loves himself. So many things could have happened, why worry about what is done?"

"Which one was it, if you had to say?" Warren asked.

"Oh, those things all passed, but with other men. What I think happened, in truth? I think..." Rue paused to choose his words carefully. "I think your brother's business is his own."

"At least one of you has sense," Ainsley said.

"What my family does is my business," Warren insisted.

"You aren't lord of Cresthill yet," Ainsley reminded peevishly. He reached over and smacked Rue's chest with the back of his arm. "Let's go."

"Where to, my..." Rue swallowed. "Grouchy. Friend."

Ainsley deeply appreciated that Rue had caught himself. He smacked him again, this time in the arm. "Come on." He pushed himself off the ground and when Rue didn't move fast enough, he tapped the fairy's leg with his boot. He headed out of the room.

Rue followed behind, asking, "Where to, I asked."

"Anywhere else."

Ainsley's feet brought him to the stables, though he had no intention of riding anywhere. Sometimes giving Hadley a treat brought him a little peace.

Rue watched as he cut up an apple for the horse, feeding her one quarter at a time. The apple had gone soft with age, but Hadley eagerly munched it regardless.

"This mystery maiden has your brother concerned."

With a sigh, Ainsley slumped against a post. "I shouldn't have mentioned anything."

"Seeking comfort for a wounded heart is hard to fault."

"It was stupid. They'll figure it out sooner or later." He sighed again and slumped harder, as though sulking would fix anything.

Without looking up from his examination of his fingernails, Rue suggested, "Tell them the truth, then, in the way that you can. Your love was unfaithful and sullied what you held so dear with the touch of other men. From what I've gleaned of love and marriage in my time here, your family will be glad you put her aside."

"Mm."

"If you slump any farther down that post, you'll be sitting in horseshit," Rue warned.

Ainsley forced himself to straighten up. He started to say something, but a commotion in the courtyard drew his attention. He peered out of the stable to see what had the hounds barking like that.

Rue came to look too, standing directly behind Ainsley, close enough to be a distraction.

A knight in full armor upon a leopard-spotted horse trotted up towards the castle. Ainsley could have picked that horse out from a thousand others; most knights favored solid-colored horses: sorrels, bays, and blacks. But Alfred had always done things a little differently. He preferred a polearm to a sword and favored his left instead of his right, no matter how their trainers had tried to beat it out of them.

Without thinking, Ainsley rushed out of the stable to greet the other knight. "Fred!"

The knight pulled off his helmet, revealing a flounce of shiny, mouse brown hair. He stared down at Ainsley, his blue eyes not just wide but almost horrified. "Jack?"

Grinning like a fool, he declared, "Aye! What are you doing here?"

"Oh...I..."

"Come on, get off that horse."

Slowly Alfred slid off his mount.

As soon as his feet hit the ground, Ainsley threw his arms around him. Alfred remained stiff in his embrace, which Ainsley should have expected. "What brings you to Cresthill?"

"The king's having a tourney. I, well, I thought to tell your family, in case they'd kept in better touch with you than the rest of us."

Still grinning, but less delightedly now, Ainsley pulled away and put his hands on his hips. "Fred, aren't you a sight."

"No one's heard a whisper about you for months, Jack."

"Oh, well, I've been travelling, haven't I? Guess I could have written a few letters..." Ainsley glanced at his feet. "But how've you been? Why don't you come inside?"

"I just wanted to relay word of the tourney."

Ainsley rolled his eyes. He knew what Alfred worried about, but Ainsley no longer felt that strange, uncomfortable pull towards the other man. The feelings that had haunted him all his youth had evaporated, leaving affection and comradery, but nothing more. "Don't be stupid."

Ainsley took the spotted horse by his reins and led him to the stables.

Rue had remained there, leaning once shoulder against the wall. He watched, his face smooth but his eyes taking in everything.

Following behind reluctantly, Alfred reminded, "We agreed though, Jack. On what would be best."

"Jack?" Rue asked. He absolutely picked apart Alfred with his gaze, not with jealousy, but the way a cat watched a bird.

"Oh, well...The other boys called me that on account of how, well...of how stubborn I was. It's short for jackass," Ainsley explained. Clarity didn't break on Rue's face, so Ainsley elaborated, "You know, stubborn as an ass and all that."

"Clever," Rue corrected. "Clever as an ass. They know what they're doing."

Alfred had stopped short of coming inside the stable; he stared openly at Rue. The look on his face rested somewhere between the guarded suspicion that Ainsley's family showed and the fascinated way that Thomas watched Rue's magic tricks. For good measure, a sprinkling of flushed, awkward lust made its way into the mix, too.

The tips of his ears had turned pink. Anyone else mightn't have noticed it, but there had been at time when Ainsley had noticed everything about Alfred.

"Alfred, this is Rue, a prince of the Western Court. Rue, this is Sir Alfred, a knight of the realm and heir to Rosebridge."

Alfred gave a stiff bow.

Rue smiled at him. "Not the Alfred I've heard about?"

Ainsley wanted to punch him in the arm.

"Heard what?" Alfred asked, the pinkness in his ears spreading.

"Nothing bad," Rue assured. "Stories from Ainsley's youth, nothing else."

The arrival Alfred received from the lord and lady of Cresthill outstripped the one Rue had gotten in terms of warmth. It took no time at all for them to bring up the girl Ainsley had made up, though, asking Alfred if he knew anything about her.

"You've been out traveling, maybe you know where he stopped."

Alfred stared at Ainsley; he seemed aghast. "I."

"It doesn't matter, any of it," Ainsley insisted.

"Why not?" his father asked.

"Because she ruined herself with someone else," Ainsley said.

His parents quieted after that and his mother immediately returned the topic to Alfred's travels.

For the rest of the day, Alfred began odd sounding sentences but never finished them. He cleared his throat incessantly and could barely look at Ainsley. Between the awkwardness, they traded stories of where their travels had taken them. Alfred asked a lot of questions about Rue when he thought the fairy out of earshot, but rarely spoke directly to him.

Finally, at point when Rue had gotten bored and wandered off and the rest of the house had gone to bed, Alfred lowered his voice to less than a whisper, "Is it true?"

"Hm?"

"You knew a maid?"

"Oh. That." A quick glance showed that no one else occupied the hall.

"I thought...you and I, I thought we."

Ainsley thought he would choke on the words before he managed to say them.

He breathed, "I thought we had the same affliction."

It took everything Ainsley had to answer, "We do."

Affliction! God, had he ever been half as uptight as Alfred about things?

"How'd you fix it?" Alfred demanded in that same barely-there whisper. "How'd you manage with a girl? I've tried, you know."

"I didn't."

Again, Alfred looked betrayed. "D'y'mean?"

"I didn't. I haven't been with a girl. There is no girl. It's just...it's just a story." Ainsley fidgeted and wondered when Rue had gone. "Don't tell anyone, though."

"No, I. Same secret, still safe."

"I've." The need to leave overwhelmed him. "We're hunting tomorrow. Get some sleep."

Alfred nodded.

Ainsley left him to sleep in the hall. He and Alfred had slept in halls together when their masters had traveled together. The echoes of a castle late at night had nearly been enough to drive two youths mad, that close to each other, wanting to touch, but frozen by fear and damnation. Every other squire had snuck off with some serving girl, all the knights had found their wenches, but he and Alfred had lain awake, aching, but pretending to sleep.

"So that's the lad you were sweet on?" Rue asked as soon as Ainsley stepped inside their room.

Ainsley yelped, jumped back, then gave the other man an annoyed push. "Scared me."

Instead of letting himself be pushed, Rue snagged Ainsley's wrist and pulled him in. "I was trying to."

"It wasn't funny."

"It was a little funny."

Ainsley stayed in his arms. He did more than stay, he settled in, letting out a deep breath and melting. He hadn't realized how much tightly he'd carried himself.

"Are you displeased with me?" Rue asked.

"Hmm?"

"You kicked me today. Twice. And hit me just as many times. And yesterday, and the day before..." Rue spoke without accusation. "Light as they were, I thought I should ask."

"I..." Ainsley hadn't thought about it much. He had traded similar blows, playful and friendly, with other lads when he'd been younger. A way to get attention.

To feel their flesh against his. It would end in roughhousing, if he was lucky.

He sighed and rested his forehead against Rue's chest. "I'm sorry. It's an excuse to touch you."

"Ah. That game I've played. I know a much better way to wrestle, though." His voice hummed through his chest and came out rough and husky, just as it always did.

Ainsley wanted to roll around in that voice the same as he wanted to roll around on a velvet blanket. He wanted it the way he wanted a breeze on a sweltering day or a hot bath after hours in the cold. A few more words and he'd give in. "I'm sorry."

"Accepted."

Before he did anything stupid, he stepped out of Rue's embrace. "Not here."

"I know."

Ainsley turned away, prepared himself for bed, and flopped down into the pallet.

Rue made his way to the bed more gracefully. He lay on his side, peering over the edge, as he did most nights. "Do you plan to go to the tourney?"

"As soon as I can."

Rue said nothing.

"You're coming with me."

"I haven't a horse."

Ainsley shifted a little, making himself more comfortable. "If...well. If you went home to get one, would you make it back?"

"I don't know."

Not a sip of wine had touched Rue's lips, even as weak as mortal drink was. But he stared after it, watched other people drinking it. His hands inched towards any cup left near him. A return to the Otherworld could spell disaster.

"I don't want to risk it," Ainsley confessed.

"Nor I."

Feeling small and weak, Ainsley asked, "What if you didn't come back?"

"Oh, sweet knight, I would come back but the question is when. Would you be gray by then? Or dead? You can lose years at the bottom of a bottle."

The blankets Ainsley tightened around himself offered no comfort. "I'd hate that."

"Would you like to know something?"

"Hm?"

"That worried me as much as your leaving did. How long would you be away? Would you make it back to me safely? You can die here, my love, in the blink of an eye. In half as many years as I've lived, you'd meet your death."

"Maybe not as soon as that." Ainsley had to say something to get rid of the lump in his throat. He failed to think of anything cheerier and resigned himself to asking something that had been on his mind for a while. "If I went back to the Otherworld...how many years would it be before you wanted me to leave?"

"As many as I live."

"Be serious."

"'Tis monstrous of me, I know, to ask you to abandon your home and family for the sake of staying by the side of a star-touched drunkard, but I would ask it of you."

And it was lustful and wicked of Ainsley to want to forsake his king and his blood just so he could share a bed with another man, but he would do it. Maybe not today, or even this year, but he knew there would come a time when he would trade his life here for a life in the Otherworld. How could he stay in a place that hated him when he had known a world that didn't?

Sitting through masses had once filled him with unease and concern for his soul, but now it sickened him. He couldn't live in his world anymore.

And, he considered, he hadn't much lived in it before. He had imagined a future of duty, a wife he didn't love, children for the sake of reproduction, service to his king and his brother, but never anything for himself.

His dream had been to explore a single country. He had never aspired to anything greater, never hoped to be fulfilled by anything more than the knowledge that he had done what had been expected of him.

He pushed himself up on to his knees. He placed a quick kiss on Rue's cheek. "I'll go back with you, just not yet."

"Hope is such a dangerous thing to give."

"Stop being melancholy." Ainsley almost smacked his arm but checked himself and gave the fairy's arm a squeeze.

"You never told me he was in love with you," Rue accused quietly, his breath tickling Ainsley's ear.

He and Ainsley lingered in one of the smaller hallways before the great hall. Ainsley had stopped short, peeking into the hall to find Alfred seated at the long table. Something about the sight of him made Ainsley want to turn around.

Alfred had acted strangely the past few days. Squirrelly and nervous. They trained together in the mornings and that was about the only time when Alfred had seemed normal. Any other time he and Ainsley were together, Alfred took to stammering and blushing. And sending poisonous glances in Rue's direction.

Ainsley didn't remember him being so nervous. Or maybe he'd been nervous then, too. "He's not..."

"Oh, my sweet knight, you are a perfect fool," Rue breathed.

Ainsley almost leaned back against him. "I thought you weren't going to call me that."

"But you manage it so charmingly. I wouldn't have you any other way."

At that, Ainsley had no choice but to turn him around and smack him in the side. He miscalculated the placement, though. Rue winced and Ainsley knew he must have gotten him in a particularly sensitive part of his scars.

Immediately, Ainsley's eyes bugged. "I'm sorry."

Rue shook his head.

"God, fuck, Rue, I am," Ainsley insisted.

Rue made towards the hall. "We should eat."

Without thinking, Ainsley caught his sleeve. "Come out for a ride with me. I'm not hungry."

Ainsley saddled his horse and brought his bow so he could pretend that they'd gone out looking for game. The last hunt had been unsuccessful. Warren had caught a single rabbit.

They rode in silence for a while.

"Did you have something to say to me?" Rue asked.

"Other than I'm sorry?"

"Other than that," Rue said.

"No. But I wanted to show you something."

He steered Hadley towards a common landmark for the area, a lone and gnarled old apple tree that produced the sourest apples Ainsley had ever tasted. Every child in walking distance had eaten one of those apples on a dare.

They had all played around this tree as children.

Rue stared at the tree for a while, then looked at Ainsley, one eyebrow raised. He watched when Ainsley swung off his horse and put a hand on the tree.

"Come over here."

Rue obliged. "What?"

"All my best memories happened around this tree. I used to think I'd never find anything as good as a summer day chasing each other around this tree, or telling stories, or playing bandits."

"I. Well. Alright." The fairy shifted uncomfortably.

"There isn't anything more to it than that, except, you know...they're not my best memories anymore. Or, I guess, they're a different kind of good." Ainsley sighed. He stepped in close and leaned against Rue. "I just."

After a moment's hesitation, Rue slide his arms around Ainsley. "What?"

"I hate worrying. I hate the way it makes me. I wish—"

"Shh, now, you still speak to a prince of the Otherworld. No wishes."

"It's not fair of me, you know, to have judged your behavior as I did and now expect you to tolerate what I'm doing. Next time I put my hands on you, you should, I don't know...turn them into feathers or something."

Rue snorted. "If you land a blow on me that leaves a mark, I might consider it." He tightened his arms. "Until then, would you think me too wicked if I said I enjoy getting a rise out of you? You're so easy to fluster and I love to see you flustered."

Ainsley contemplated a few answers, trying to think of words to explain what he wanted and how he felt. Words failed him, though. He had always liked himself, for the most part, knowing he could be too proud or stubborn but not counting it as a real fault. He hated this side of himself, he found.

"It's difficult to hide," Rue suggested quietly. "That was the hardest part when I first started drinking overmuch. We hide when people will stop us or judge us or treat us harshly for what we do, whether the fault rest with them or us. It wears at you."

"I hate it."

Rue combed his fingers through Ainsley's curls and cradled his head close against his chest. He pressed a kiss to the top of Ainsley's head. "A few more days and then the road will carry us away."

Ainsley nodded. They wouldn't fare any better at the king's tourney, but they'd at least have privacy on the road. A tent to share and their hours together interrupted, it would echo of what they'd lost.

"What would happen if I made a wish?" Ainsley asked.

"I'd wager nothing good."

Aware of exactly what he did, Ainsley wiggled further into Rue's arms. "But could you grant it? Would you have to?"

"The common fey, if caught, may grant a wish to save themselves. Royal as I am, I am capable of doing such a thing without being caught or threatened."

Ainsley tightened his arms. "But what if you are caught? Have I caught you right now?" he teased.

"If you want anything from me, all you need to do is but speak my name and command it of me," Rue reminded gravely.

"And I hate it."

Rue let out a sigh and rocked gently against Ainsley. He slid his fingers through Ainsley's hair, down his neck, and under his chin. He tilted Ainsley's face up. "Only because you have no idea what I can do to you."

For some ungodly reason, unable and unwilling to stop himself, Ainsley kissed him. That mild threat, the soft gravel of his voice! It didn't matter what magic Rue possessed, he could have ruined Ainsley with those alone. Their mouths melted together, slow and heavy, warm and firm.

Ainsley couldn't breathe with how hard Rue crushed him close, his fingers digging into his clothes, his lips voraciously claiming Ainsley's.

The distant baying of hounds had them shoving each other away.

Chest heaving, eyes flashing, and his lips parted, Rue looked finer than any of the sweetest, rarest fruits that Ainsley had seen in the Otherworld. Better than honey and whipped cream drizzled on a cake.

The hounds grew closer and brought with them the sounds of horses and men's voices.

Rue warned, "Wipe that look off your face, my love, or I may have to take you, others be cursed."

"Fuck, Rue, it's like you want to get caught," Ainsley growled. He hurried to his horse and swung back into the saddle before he could do anything stupid.

With a louche grin on his face, Rue followed suit.

By the time the others had arrived, Ainsley felt sure he had smoothed away any sign that might give them away.

Warren, Domenic, Alfred, the lord of Cresthill, and one of Warren's friends had ridden out, bows in hand.

Ainsley and Rue had left a clear track, the mud churned up by their horses' hooves to color the snow.

"Thought you'd sneak out hunting without us!" Warren reined in his horse a few inches away from Ainsley, putting himself between Rue and Ainsley. "I knew you were sore about missing that deer. You never could lose gracefully."

From a distance, Alfred stared at Ainsley. At Ainsley's mouth.

It made Ainsley shift about in his saddle. He met Alfred's eyes and the way Alfred looked back sent a horrible quiver of fear through him.

Alfred didn't know, he couldn't have. They had been careful, discrete. Hadn't they? Alfred couldn't tell they'd been kissing just by looking at them.

"It must be a family trait," Rue said.

Warren's friend sniggered but did his best to disguise it.

Warren didn't look towards the fairy and directed his scowl towards Ainsley instead. "What do you want to wager I catch something before you?"

"I'm not going to bet with you."

"Because you know—"

"I'll take your wager," Rue interrupted. Every pair of eyes turned towards him. "Against your horse I'll bet a secret."

Warren scoffed. "For my horse? What would I do with a secret?"

Rue began to smile, a sweet, soft smile that made Ainsley's skin crawl. He thought, for a moment, that Rue would lean over to place his hand on Warren's thigh and whisper something sultry into his ear. "A secret about your brother."

Too shocked to react, Ainsley stared.

Alfred began to protest on Ainsley's behalf. "That, that doesn't sound like a sporting bet, if you don't mind me saying."

The offer caught Warren's attention, however. "What kind of secret?"

"No!" Ainsley finally managed. "No, no, trading for my secrets, Rue. Tell him one of your own, if you want to go telling secrets."

"Counter my offer, then, if you find yourself so concerned," Rue said.

"Fine, I do, I'll bet you both. I'll catch the first game..." Ainsley paused to think of what he could wager. "And I'll stake, uh, I'll my tourney fee on it." He had nothing else of value to bet, except for his horse, armor, and sword and he'd miss those more than coin.

"The tourney fee I just gave you?" his father asked.

Ainsley grinned. "You know Warren's a terrible shot."

Before his father could chastise him, Ainsley kicked Hadley into a trot and peeled away from the group.

He spied deer tracks in the snow and called over his shoulder, "And Warren, you can double it if I get a stag!"

"Not on your life!" Warren shouted.

Rue headed off in an entirely different direction from the rest of them; Ainsley saw him strike out and puzzled about it before returning to the task at hand.

A few minutes of stalking the tracks later, Ainsley heard a caw from a branch up and to his left.

The crow ruffled its feathers, showing that familiar flash of white beneath one wing. It took flight and came to land on his shoulder. It took a bit of his cape in his beak and gave an insistent tug. Then it took wing again, wheeling off to the west.

Ainsley headed in that direction, mildly concerned that Rue had some trick up his sleeve.

In the end, there was no trick. Just a stag.

Ainsley took the creature down, though he did it without the usual rush of pride he got from catching game. He'd done it cleanly, a perfect shot.

"Nice and clean," Alfred offered.

Ainsley nodded, then remembered his human manners. "Thanks, Fred."

Warren didn't congratulate him nor scowl with envy. Instead he just stared at the creature.

"I don't want your horse, but you can do the dressing," Ainsley told him.

"Fine."

With a half-hearted grin, Ainsley said, "You can double my tourney fee, though."

"Not fucking likely." Warren jumped off his horse and stomped over to the stag.

Ainsley wondered if his own mood got that foul when he lost at things.

Rue had returned to the group, his hair a little ruffled. The only sign he'd changed shape and likely not noticeable to the others.

"No luck, Your Highness?" Domenic asked.

"It seems Sir Ainsley has luck enough for two." Rue eyed the wound on the stag and the bloody arrow Ainsley had pulled from it. "And the skill, too, it seems."

Queasy memories bubbled to the surface. "I fouled my first hunt." The first deer he'd ever shot had died thrashing while he'd needed to drive a spear through it to end the screaming. He hadn't been able to look at a bow or eat meat for weeks.

"Balor only grants permission to hunt to the most skilled archers. 'Twould offend the Green God, he says, to do anything else."

"The what?" Ainsley's father asked.

"Different realm, Father, different gods," Ainsley reminded.

"Doesn't make it right."

"Lend me your ear, my lord, and I'd share the tale," Rue offered. The slight against his religion didn't appear to offend him. "I could tell you, too, of the goblin deities and the great spirit worshipped by elf-kind."

"No interest, thank you, Highness."

A frown twisted Rue's mouth, but he held his tongue. "Ainsley. I have a secret for you, let's venture somewhere private for the telling of it. 'Tis hardly a secret if seven know it."

"You're going to tell me a secret about myself?" Ainsley followed, though, when Rue began to head back towards the castle.

"A secret about your brother, those were the words you should have marked."

Ainsley doubted that Warren had any secrets. "Go ahead, then."

Rue waited for them to be utterly alone. "He sleeps beneath the blacksmith's roof each night."

"Warren does?"

"No."

He opened his mouth to protest, then reconsidered. "My brother sleeps beneath the blacksmith's roof."

"Yes."

The blacksmith had a wife, two daughters and three sons. Ainsley considered Rue's secret, turning it over in his mind. "Does my father know?"

"His steward slips the blacksmith's wife two silver shields each month for the wee one's care. It must be a weighty love he carries for the boy, or a monstrous secret, because I've seen the shields knights carry in this realm."

Ainsley frowned. "What?"

"Massive things. I don't know if my arm could bear it."

"Rue, shields are coins."

"They aren't. Ainsley, I know what's a shield and what's a coin."

"Gold crowns, silver shields, copper lances."

"The copper ones are called pennies," Rue corrected.

The effort required not to grin or laugh almost outstripped Ainsley's self-restraint. "No, well...Yes. The little round ones are called pennies. Lances are sort of...well, they're more like ovals. And they have lances stamped on them."

"I see."

Rue didn't sound like he understood at all. Ainsley almost asked him what he saw. A tree, or mud, or snow, he would have answered.

Instead, Ainsley went on to explain, "And there's sparks and stars, too, but hardly anyone uses those except for mages and the people who live around the university. They're made of electrum."

"This is tiresome."

"You can name me every songbird in the Western Court, but you can't remember a few coins?" Ainsley teased.

"I can name them for the Eastern Court, too. As for the wilds of the Meridian Court, well, who knows what's sprung up there sing the Obliteration?"

"Could you tell me their songs, each and every one?"

"Perhaps half, if I had my harp to play them for you."

After a quick glance to make sure no one could see or hear them, Ainsley gave Rue's hand a squeeze. "Then a harp you'll have."

"You needn't–"

"You'll have it and you'll play them for me, Rue, and you can play me even sweeter songs while we travel. When I win at the tourney, you can write the sweetest one of all about my skill with a lance."

His tongue wet his lips, vibrant against his lips. "I needn't witness any tourneys to attest to that skill."

"What's the difference between coins and birds?" Ainsley forced himself on to another topic, anything to get the image of Rue's mouth out of his mind.

The question took the prince by surprise. "Is that a riddle?"

"No, it's a question. Why can't you remember the coins?"

"Oh." The word came out flat, uninterested. "Birds interest me and I've precious few experiences with coins."

Ainsley didn't need to steer Hadley towards the stable, she turned that way of her own volition. "Would you like me to ask you a riddle?"

"I'd love it."

"I run but never walk. I murmur but never talk. I've a bed but never sleep, and I've a mouth but never eat."

Rue pondered a while and as they groomed their mounts, he said, "A river."

"Your turn."

"Feed me and I live forever, but a single drink will spell my end."

"Fire," Ainsley answered. By the look on Rue's face, he'd answered too quickly. "Do you want another turn?"

Rue's face contorted, somewhere between embarrassed and prideful. Finally, he admitted, "Yes."

"Then you'll have it."

This time, Rue went quiet, absorbed in thought. Ainsley had nearly forgotten what they were talking about when Rue said, "I have forest but no trees. I have a river but no water. I have mountains but no rocks."

"Uh." No immediate answer came to mind. He thought for a while as they returned inside, shedding their winter clothes and stealing a bit of bread and cheese from the kitchens. Ainsley spied a bottle of wine and almost snagged that too.

It would have been perfect, a hot fire and mulled wine, the two of the nestled together on the pallet in front of the fire. Giggling, trading kisses, their heads pleasantly light.

He left the wine.

Things could be perfect without wine. He didn't need to dry out his mouth and foul his breath or overindulge just to wake with an aching head.

He didn't ever want to taste wine on Rue's lips again, not when he'd tasted them tainted with sick and honey and wine all at once.

And they couldn't do any of those things here, anyway. He shouldn't have been entertaining such stupid notions.

"You haven't guessed." Rue lagged behind him as they returned to their room in the tower.

"Uh. A...uh. A forest but no leaves? Uh, a, the winter?"

"No *trees*."

"Oh." He returned to thinking, trying to puzzle it out up until he settled himself onto the pallet in their room.

Their room. He didn't remember when he'd started to think of it as their room instead of his. Dangerous, that.

Without being asked, Rue blew life into the fire. He lingered beside the pallet, waiting for permission to join him.

Ainsley didn't grant it. He stretched out and batted his eyelashes up at him, feeling luxurious and ridiculous all at once. "Give me a clue."

"No."

"I'll trade you."

"I'm not interested in a trade."

"Don't you even want to know what I'm going to offer?" Ainsley pouted.

Rue stopped waiting. He dropped onto the pallet, his fall carefully controlled. He planted his knees on either side of Ainsley's thighs but held himself so that they barely touched. "Were I to guess, sweetling, I think you have nothing to trade that you won't eventually give me for free."

One kiss in the woods and here Rue was, thinking Ainsley would take him back into his bed without another moment's hesitation.

Of course, he might. The idea tempted him horrendously. He'd spent months untouched even by his own hand.

What had happened to caution? To sorting out his heart and his head? Letting his loins guide his fate would spell his ruin.

But what a fun ruin it would spell. He set his hands on Rue's thighs. In an instant, Rue seized his wrists, pinning them above his head. The fairy still had himself positioned so that their legs scarcely touched.

Heat swelled in Ainsley's stomach and he barely kept himself from arching up against the fairy. "Have you intentions?"

"On occasion I've had them."

"And now?"

"But what of my riddle, dear knight?"

A brief tug against Rue's grip found it unyielding. "How am I supposed to think like this?"

"Like this you're supposed to think of me," Rue admitted. "Would you rather the riddle, though?"

"I." Caution nearly won out. He had no lock on his door and who knew if anything had been overheard. But the way Rue looked down at him, his black eyes glittering and his mouth begging to be kissed, that couldn't be discounted.

When they had kissed in the woods, Rue hadn't tasted of wine or sick, his breath had been clean and warm.

"We shouldn't, Rue." His voice refused to raise above a whisper.

"Then tell me to go."

He couldn't. God, he couldn't. He wanted Rue more than anything but being in this place dredged up all his oldest fears. The inability to choose, to force his hand one way or the other, seared through him and tears pricked his eyes.

Rue released his wrists and sat back on his heels. He stared, horrorstruck, as Ainsley covered his face to hide his tears. Within moments, he gathered Ainsley into his arms. "My love, what is it?"

"Everything," Ainsley admitted.

He had thought himself done with tears. Too many nights he'd spent weeping himself empty. Nights after watching Rue's drunken antics, nights after fights, and nights alone, here and in the Otherworld, desperate for things to be as they had been.

He turned his face against Rue's chest and clung to him. He wormed his knuckles between his teeth and dug in hard.

Rue pulled back and immediately forced Ainsley's hand from his mouth. "What are you doing?"

He sniffed and viciously wiped at his nose. "I don't *want* to cry anymore. It hurts worse to cry."

The fairy brought Ainsley's hand to his mouth and kissed the bite mark. Then he clasped his hands around Ainsley's hand. "Sweet thing, tell me what I can do to help."

Ainsley shook his head.

"We can go back. Tonight. Now, even, should you desire it."

"No, it's...Rue, it's too soon."

"You have my name," the fairy reminded.

"I want you," Ainsley snapped. "Not some puppet."

"If I couldn't drink..."

Shakily, Ainsley told him, "No. I'm not, I'm not just going to order away all your bad habits, Rue. I'll help you manage them, but I'm not going to take that kind of responsibility for your life. It wouldn't be real."

Rue sighed and agreed, "No, it wouldn't."

"Besides." The thought formed slowly, and Ainsley had to think for a bit to make sure he understood what he wanted to say. "Something else would take the place of wine."

"If I ever again lower myself so far as to call you a fool—"

"I'll bite your tongue off if you call me a fool," Ainsley growled, more venomous than he felt, if only to keep the tears away.

Rue shivered. "What finer consort could a prince of the Fair Folk desire? Say it again, dear knight."

"Stop it."

Hurt flashed over Rue's face; he reined it in quickly.

"Wanting you pains me. I cannot have you and it frightens me to even think about loving you within these walls."

"I acted without malice."

Suddenly, in the middle of the day, Ainsley needed to sleep. The food they'd taken lay abandon by the fire.

Rue followed his eye and brought it to him. "We haven't yet broken fast. Perhaps it will help."

Ainsley reached for the cheese, taking the knife from his belt and slicing off a hunk for Rue. He'd attempted to get the fairy his own knife, but all the blades here were made of steel, or worse, iron.

Rue handed him the piece of bread he'd torn off. He speared his cheese on a bit of wood and held it over the fire.

They ate in companionable quiet, their discomfort fading as the meal progressed.

Ainsley told him, "It will be the same at the tourney. Worse, we won't even have a room."

"A tent, then?"

Ainsley nodded.

"Bring it to me and bring me a paint pot as well. I'll work my best magics on it. I'll garner us some bit of privacy."

"How?"

"In my king's army, each general and lieutenant has a tent so enchanted as to keep war secrets safe from those who would steal them. The runes painted upon them fade in the sun, in the rain, in the wind…I think they fade even in the dark, given how many times I repainted them. I know well the runes to paint and possess the magics to give them power."

"And it works?"

"It works well enough that when an ogre took the life of General Talvaius, not a single person heard him scream as the beast beat him to death with his own arm."

The image turned Ainsley's stomach. "Well, I suppose, as long as you swear you have no intentions to murder me..."

Shock showed plain on Rue's face. "Never!"

"Then I'll get you my tent and some paint."

"To murder you," Rue scoffed.

Ainsley liked that he'd offended Rue with the ridiculousness of his suggestion. "Besides, I'm sure that if you were to murder me, you'd do it silently."

"No life I've taken has ever ended in silence. If you find a way to do it without making noise, share with me."

The last piece of cheese went to Rue, though he attempted to decline. He had eyed it for a while and Ainsley had insisted he take it. Rich things called to the Fair Folk, anything heavy with fat or laden with sweetness. The lord of Cresthill served nothing like what the lord of the Western Court had served. They had no cakes or tarts, no honey or sweetened cream. Naught but bread, cheese, and meat, the occasional root.

Gingerly, Rue plucked the cheese from the knife with which Ainsley had speared it. He had burns on his fingers, collected from brushing against hinges, nails, and latches around the castle.

"The night you saved me," Ainsley began.

Rue paused mid-chew.

"You wielded a knife against them, but I thought you didn't carry things as a crow."

The fairy resumed his eating and once he'd swallowed, said, "'Twasn't a knife."

Ainsley waited for a better explanation and when none came, he nudged Rue's foot with his.

"I snapped a branch from the tree."

The quiet brutality of the confession took Ainsley aback.

"You look displeased."

"Surprised." When the look of disbelief remained on Rue's face, Ainsley amended, "Shocked."

"I'd have killed them barehanded if required."

"Why?"

"What sort of man would I be to look on as brigands slaughtered a man unarmored, barely blooded, and retching?"

Such a perfectly fairy thing to do, to ask a question instead of answering one. "That's not an answer."

"I gave it as one."

Ainsley gave up on trying to pull a straightforward answer from him. Rue possessed the ability to be direct and sometimes was even inclined towards it. He would share if he wanted and easily evade if he didn't.

"Because if you'd died, I'd have never gotten to know you."

The confession brought a grin to Ainsley's face. He swooped close to press a kiss to Rue's cheek. Such a small, chaste kiss brought no risk of them losing themselves. It produced such a look of wonder on Rue's face that Ainsley resolved to do it more often when he could get away with it.

Maybe they couldn't rut as freely as they'd like, but that didn't mean they couldn't love each other in other ways.

It took Rue a few days to paint the tent and enchant it. He spread out the canvas on the floor of the hall, crouched over it as he patiently, carefully drew the runes.

Thomas watched, fascinated and asking dozens of questions.

Olivia nearly ruined it by running across the wet paint. She barreled towards it, more concerned with fleeing her nurse than where she ran.

Rue uncoiled and snatched her up with such speed that the girl forgot to scream.

The nurse wailed for her, then clasped her hand over her mouth to stifle the sound. "Oh, my lord—"

"Your Highness," Rue corrected.

"Your Highness," she quavered. "Please, spare the girl, she's...She's wild but she's young. Please."

Ainsley watched, quite liking the haughty expression on Rue's face as he held Olivia. He'd never harm the girl; Ainsley knew that much. More than he wondered about Rue's intentions, he wondered where Warren had found such a young nurse for his children. He had seen their last nurse in the village, her face lined but with enough meat on her bones that Ainsley knew his brother had given her a good retirement.

This new nurse had a fine face and shining copper hair. She had remained quiet around the family and seemed permanently exhausted by Olivia. Ainsley didn't even know her name for certain. He thought it might be Molly or Mary, or even Milly.

"What will you give me for her safe return?" Rue asked.

"Anything." The girl looked close to tears.

"I require two things."

The nurse nodded.

Rue handed over Olivia to Ainsley. "Hold this until I return. Nurse, with me. This must be done elsewhere."

Ainsley bounced his niece on his knee, watching as Rue lead the girl away. Never had Rue shown interest in a woman, not even when he'd been at his most debauched.

"Where are they going?" Thomas asked.

"I don't know."

"Why was Nanny crying?" the boy pressed.

"Because she's scared."

"Is he going to hurt her?"

"I doubt it," Ainsley answered. He did doubt that Rue would offer the girl harm, or that he meant to bed her. Of course, the girl didn't know that. She likely thought the fairy meant to have her.

Ainsley should have intervened. He watched the two of them disappear out of the hall together.

Olivia began to fidget and squirm out of his grasp.

He stood and twirled, tossing her into the air.

She screamed with delight and demanded he do it again. Thomas soon wanted to join in and for the quarter hour that Rue and the nurse were away, Ainsley exhausted his arms launching the children as high as he could get them.

Each time, Olivia stayed put, giggling when Thomas let out a shrieking laugh, then shoved her way back into Ainsley's grip.

Rue retuned with the nurse looking his usual cool and unaffected self. The girl's face had flushed bright red, though she didn't seem unsettled other than that. She had a sort of glazed-over look.

She gathered up Olivia and ushered Thomas away.

"What did you do to her?" Ainsley asked, wondering if he should have been more concerned.

"I asked a few questions."

"What kind of questions?"

"One about you. One about men who are as we are. She barely choked out the words, such was her distaste."

"Rue!" Ainsley hissed.

"She'll remember it differently. All she remembers is that I've demanded something sweet with my dinner."

Sulkily, Ainsley accused, "I thought you didn't do mind magic."

"Illusion is much different from that sort of magic you refer to. I could have told you my name and made you think I'd told you a poem, but I cannot change what you remember to be true." Rue crouched beside the tent and took up his paintbrush again.

Ainsley settled, cross-legged, onto the floor beside him. "What did you ask her about me?"

"No one suspects anything about you," the fairy relayed in barely audible confidence. "I know you worried."

When the household began to assemble for dinner, they left a wide berth around the drying tent. Rue had left it spread on the floor and Ainsley guessed his family would have liked it better if he'd left a moldering corpse instead.

No one asked about the tent, either.

Except for Alfred and he did it quietly, whispering anxious questions about it.

Finally, Ainsley grew tired of deflecting and asked, "Fred, what are you worried about?"

"That you've gotten yourself in over your head."

"Oh, that I've likely done," Ainsley agreed easily. It should have concerned him that he'd broken the heart of a fairy prince, but he, somehow, had fallen back into trusting Rue. Or, at least, trusting that Rue would never do something he considered to be harm to him.

"You should send the creature away," Alfred implored.

Rage washed over Ainsley. "Call him creature again—" A hand on his shoulder interrupted his threat.

"Walk with us tomorrow, Sir Alfred, and I'll ease your fears," Rue offered. "Traveling companions should not provoke this much distrust."

Alfred mumbled an agreement and slunk away, leaving dinner early.

"Fred always mistrusted magic," Ainsley told Rue. "A walk won't help."

"It might."

Despite Ainsley's warnings, Rue insisted on waking early and fetching Alfred from the hall.

The knight woke with a knife in his hand, which only made Rue laugh. He grinned even wider when Alfred donned his armor and took up his gisarme for the walk. He looked faintly ridiculous, walking so heavily armed alongside two men in nothing more than cloth.

As they walked, Rue tried to foster conversation with Alfred, but ended up pulling Ainsley in instead. It didn't seem to affect the fairy's mood much. He had woken determined and deliberately cheerful.

After an hour, Rue paused and looked around.

Alfred adjusted his grip on his gisarme and glanced towards Ainsley.

"We'll travel to the tourney together," Rue began.

"If we must," Alfred answered stiffly.

"I know you bear me some small resentment. I thought I should put your mind at ease. I'd prefer us to be friendly."

"If you want to make friends with me, then you should go back to where you came from," Alfred growled.

"Fred!" Ainsley scolded.

The other knight wheeled to face him. "I don't know why you've thrown your lot in with him!"

"He's my friend." Over Alfred's shoulder, Ainsley saw Rue raise an eyebrow and tried not to make a face.

"More than that, surely," Rue protested.

Alfred's face contorted and turned his head towards Rue. "D'y'mean?" The words barely came out with how hard he'd clenched his jaw.

"Rue, don't," Ainsley warned. An idea came over him, but he knew...or at least, he hoped Rue wouldn't be foolish enough to tell Alfred anything.

"Ainsley told me many things about his youth. About how he wanted things to be, his regrets and yearnings," the fairy began.

"Rue, I'm serious!"

Rue pressed on, his face calm and friendly. "Things in the Otherworld are different. Love can be different."

All this time calling Ainsley a fool and the idiot thought he could win Alfred over with friendly words and stories about a place where men could bugger freely.

"You needn't hide yourself with us," Rue told Alfred.

"I'm not hiding anything," the knight snarled.

Rue snorted and rolled his eyes. He seemed to forget that he taunted a fully armored knight who held a weapon. "A childhood of lusting after another boy and you're not hiding anything?"

Alfred swung the gisarme without hesitation.

If Rue had been mortal, if he'd had even an ounce less of martial training, if Ainsley had left him out in the cold these weeks, Alfred would have struck true. Even still, Rue barely dodged out of the way, throwing himself back and to the side.

His hand automatically went to his hip and his face blanched when he found himself unarmed. "For each blow you land, you'll spend a year as the dog you are, so put down your weapon," Rue warned, his voice heavy with something Ainsley didn't recognize.

Magic, he realized, as he fumbled his knife from his belt. Not the sweet, tender magic Rue had used to ease his sleep or warm his hands, but the kind meant for curses and revenge.

Alfred thrust his gisarme towards Rue, undeterred.

The knife nearly shook out of Ainsley's hand and he gaped as his friend pressed his attack. He tried to say something, say anything to call out.

Another swipe towards the fairy, but this time Rue didn't dodge fast enough. The gisarme's curved blade slid against Rue's upper arm and the fairy hissed, clasping his hand over the wound. Blood seeped between his fingers.

A small wound, it had to be a small one, because he still moved with ease.

"Alfred, stop it!" Ainsley barked. He stepped forward and pointed the blade towards the other knight. A useless thing, meant for fruit and meat, not piercing armor.

"He's bedeviled you. He'll do it to us both," Alfred insisted.

"No. He hasn't, he's never…He's never forced me to do anything. Not once. Put down your weapon, Alfred, please."

The other knight tightened his hand on the shaft of his weapon.

"Please don't make me try to fight you with a fruit knife."

"Then tell him to go," Alfred demanded.

Rue had edged further away from Alfred, his blood dripping down his arm and onto the dirty snow.

"Tell him to go, Ainsley," Alfred demanded again, this time his voice reaching a dangerous whine.

Part of him wanted to finish what Rue had started and tell his friend what the fairy truly meant to him; the other part wanted them to all survive this encounter. He shook his head and tightened his grip on the knife, wishing his hand would steady.

Alfred started to sweat.

"You should take off your armor," Rue advised.

Alfred lashed out wildly at him and made contact again; this time the point of his gisarme jabbed into the meat of Rue's thigh.

The fairy let out a hoarse grunt and nearly fell to his knees. Blood, and plenty of it, flowed freely down his leg. Too much.

That gave Ainsley enough motivation to move forward, taking Alfred by the wrist. "Fred, please, stop this." He attempted to drag him away from Rue, but the knight elbowed him back.

"You're going to turn into a dog, you idiot. Take your armor off before you're a dog with twisted legs," Rue told him. He'd backed himself up against a tree and dragged himself up into the branches, despite his wounds. He perched on a branch that would be out of Alfred's reach.

He ripped apart the tunic Ainsley had lent him and tied the fabric tight over his thigh.

"Do what he says," Ainsley advised.

Alfred shook his head, sweating like a man about to die. He grunted and propped himself up on his gisarme.

Ainsley dropped his knife and began to unstrap the other man's armor. Images of a dog's legs shoved into a man's armor made his stomach bubble.

Alfred swatted him away and the blade of his gisarme passed far too close to Ainsley for comfort.

From the tree, Rue called, "If he's lucky, he'll faint and you can get him out then."

Alfred bellowed and nearly collapsed. His grip on his weapon faltered and he dropped to one knee.

Ainsley saw his chance and took it; he wrested the gisarme out of Alfred's weakened grip and tossed it away from them. As fast as he could, he hastened the knight out of his armor. Alfred fought him at first, but eventually convulsions overcame him. He writhed and bellowed, his bones crackling unpleasantly.

"Tell him to breathe," Rue advised. Bright red soaked into the makeshift bandage around his leg, visible even from a distance.

"Shut up, Rue!" Ainsley barked, hating everything in that moment. He hated Alfred and Rue and himself. He hated this whole stupid world. He tried his best to soothe Alfred, but the man twisted too much to hold and screamed too loudly to hear a single calming word.

Finally, when his bones had finished cracking and fur had finished growing, instead of Alfred, there was a hound. A fine, lean hound that would have been the pride of any kennel. A hound with blue eyes and sleek, short mouse brown fur.

The hound lay on its side and panted.

Rue dropped down from the tree, stumbled badly, and limped over to Ainsley. He stared down at the dog, not an ounce of remorse on his face. "Maybe he'll be better tempered as a dog."

Ainsley leaped to his feet and seized Rue by the front of his tunic. "How could you do that!"

Rue didn't answer, instead staring at Ainsley, wide-eyed and possibly frightened. He stumbled and nearly lost his footing when Ainsley shoved him up against a tree. "I warned him."

"You turned him into an animal!"

Quiet and concerned, Rue asked, "Should I have let him kill me?"

"I would have stopped him," Ainsley insisted without knowing if it was true.

"Your hand told a different story," Rue reminded bitterly.

Ainsley tightened his grip on Rue's shirt and nearly punched him. He hated that he could keep his nerve for this but not to stop Alfred. He shoved that aside and drew back his anger. He needed to stay angry. "What did you think was going to happen, trying to tell him something like that?"

"That we could be friends if he knew."

"Friends? Have you even got any friends, Rue? Do you even know how to have one?" Ainsley snarled. "You don't become friends with someone by dragging out their worst secret or implying that you've fucked their childhood sweetheart."

In a half-whisper, Rue said, "I didn't know you thought of him that way." He swallowed. He sagged against the tree, favoring his right leg. Alfred had gotten him on the left side both times.

"The closest thing either of us had, at least." The bond between him and Alfred hadn't been that of first loves, but it was more than a missed opportunity. More than friends. Or maybe less than friends. Tied together in a mutual terror, two lonely boys with the same secret.

Ainsley let go of Rue's shirt. Shame washed over him; he tried to soothe it by smoothing out the fairy's shirt. "Let me see your arm."

Rue shook his head and tried to sidle away from Ainsley. "It will heal."

"And your leg, too. I've…I've never had to do it, but I know how to sew a wound."

"It will heal," the fairy repeated. He hobbled towards the dog that had been Alfred.

The dog bared his teeth but didn't manage to climb to his feet. The change had exhausted him.

Ainsley took Rue by the arm and tugged him away. "Please. I." He swallowed and forced out the words. "Let me look."

"A dog is a safe animal to be. Not prey, not predator. People will leave him alone or take him in. A dog has enough of a mind that he won't lose himself, but it's not so clever that he'll be too aware of what's happened."

More blood spattered onto the snow.

"I thought…" With his eyes on the ground, Rue's face remained inscrutable, but the way he whispered said enough. "Two years isn't long."

Ainsley pulled him close. Or tried.

Rue remained stiff, his eyes still turned away.

"Rue," Ainsley insisted. "Please."

Finally, Rue sagged enough that Ainsley could help him to sit against a tree.

Ainsley inspected his arm and bound it with another strip torn from Rue's tunic. He tied another one around his thigh. He'd inspect them both more closely in the castle. He hoped the cloth would staunch the bleeding long enough.

"Can you walk back?"

"Have I another option?"

"I'll bring back a horse for you."

"You mean to leave me?" Panic made Rue's voice jump in pitch.

"No, no, of course not," Ainsley said. "No. You can lean on me. We'll make it back."

"And when people ask what happened?"

Ainsley sighed. He rubbed his face. "I'll tie out Alfred's horse. Tell everyone he left early. I'll make up something. We used to quarrel all the time. Broken each other's noses and blacked each other's eyes. My family will believe we haven't outgrown it."

"Then?"

"Then we'll leave. I'll pack and get Hadley and we'll go in the morning. I'll say I want to catch up with Alfred, make amends before the tourney."

Rue's lips pressed together.

"And...you. Can you make yourself seem uninjured? Hide the blood and everything?"

The fairy gave a curt nod.

"Good. Good, do that."

"Ainsley?"

"What?"

"I hate your realm."

The only thing that made sense was to nod. He slipped his arm under Rue's and helped him to his feet. They made slow progress back to the castle.

The dog followed them and growled at Rue the whole time. His growled so long that he started to slaver.

As they grew closer to the castle, Ainsley squared up with the Alfred-hound and warned, "I'll tell the guards you have waterfright if you don't stop that right away."

The hound quieted. He slunk along behind them even as Ainsley left Rue in the stable and hid Alfred's horse in the woods. The dog elected to stay with the horse and Ainsley didn't care enough to argue.

"I'll be back in the morning," he told both beasts.

The horse swished its tale. The dog sat beside the horse, his head raised.

"There haven't been any reports of wolves."

The dog let out soft sort of bark.

An acknowledgement, Ainsley guessed.

Once they left the stables, Rue cast the glamour and pulled away from Ainsley's help. He faltered every so often, his jaw clenched and his breath coming hard through his nose. But the bloodstains and rips in his clothes remained unseen by anyone else.

They parted ways, Rue to their room and Ainsley to flit about the castle, gathering up what he needed and telling people that Alfred had left.

He returned to find Rue on the pallet, staring up at the ceiling. For a moment, he feared that the fairy had died.

"I could use a bit of wine," Rue told him. "Real wine."

Without an ounce of hesitation, Ainsley handed over the wine he'd stolen. They'd need it to clean the wounds, of course, and more to make the stitching go easier.

"Am I held to my two-cup limit?"

"Do what you need to do."

Half the bottle disappeared with alarming speed.

Ainsley cut away Rue's clothes and the makeshift bandages. He examined the wounds as though he knew what to do. The shallow cut on his arm gaped a little but Ainsley had seen dozens of men recover from wounds twice as bad. The one on his leg, though, that had been caused by the point of the gisarme and went much deeper.

He finally settled on washing the wounds with a clean rag soaked in boiled wine and gave Rue the leather sheath of his knife to bite on, should he need it. Through the stitching, Rue maintained a strained quiet, doing little more than grunt or whine around the sheath between his teeth.

Ainsley, however, whispered swears and apologies throughout the stitching. His hands stayed steady enough, though, which was what mattered. When he'd finished with the thread, he smeared a mix of honey and herbs over the cuts.

"Fairies heal faster than humans," he pronounced hopefully as wrapped fresh bandages around the wounds.

Offended, Rue demanded, "Who told you that?"

"I...No one. I just hoped." He tossed the bloodied rags into the fire.

They stank and smoked almost immediately.

"Here, let me stab your leg and we'll see which one of us heals first."

Ainsley settled onto the pallet on Rue's right side and pressed tentative kiss to his arm. He didn't know if Rue hated him for what he'd said and done. Now was not the time to ask, no matter how badly Ainsley wanted to know.

The fairy swallowed what remained in the bottle of wine. "Can't even get drunk. I hate this realm."

"I'm sorry." Ainsley nearly offered to get him more to drink.

"I abhor it."

The following morning, Rue remained in bed while Ainsley snuck out of the castle to hide Alfred's gisarme and armor, then snuck back in to make his farewells. Ainsley returned to find the room they'd shared stuffed with bolts of fine fabrics and furs.

"What's all this?" Ainsley asked, reaching out to feel a bit of pale silver silk.

Rue didn't answer. He closed the door on the finery and began his stiff-legged walk out to the stable.

When they were sure no one was looking, they headed into the woods to retrieve Alfred and his horse. Blessedly, both beasts had remained in place overnight and seemed none the worse for it. Alfred did bark like mad at Rue, though.

"I'll take you to the butcher and have you snipped," Rue warned.

The dog ceased barking, but returned to his low, constant growling.

"Fred?" Ainsley asked.

The dog looked at him.

"Do you want us to take you home? I can explain...well, I can tell your parents something."

Alfred growled.

"What about the tourney?" Rue asked.

"I don't feel like we should go."

"'Twould be suspect if you did not, I think."

"Not as suspect as you showing up on the horse of a missing knight."

Rue reached over and gave the leopard-spotted horse a pat on the neck. From where his hand rested, color seeped out, turning the horse from spotted to blue roan.

Still, Ainsley hesitated.

"I'd like to see you compete."

The idea that Rue wanted to see him at the tourney had never crossed his mind.

"You're always insisting that you don't require saving. I've yet to see any evidence of that. Set my mind at ease and win but a single contest."

What a perfectly crafted goad. He had no choice but to go. "Fine."

"Good, we're agreed. Give me a leg up."

Ainsley helped Rue onto the horse. "His name's Clover."

Alfred snapped at Rue's foot, which caused Clover to shy.

Rue latched on to the horse's mane.

"Alfred, I swear, I'll put you in the kennel!" Ainsley shouted.

The dog glared but didn't attempt to bite again. He slunk behind them as they rode out towards the tourney.

When Ainsley set up camp that night, Alfred refused to go anywhere near the tent. He sniffed at it once, tucked his tail between his legs, and curled up next to the horses. He ignored Ainsley when he attempted conversation, not even lifting his head or opening his eyes.

Rue sat by the fire that Ainsley had built on his own. He hadn't offered to help with anything or spoken much since that morning. He had remained stony all through dinner and now stared into the fire, watching it as though he'd like to set fire to the world.

Ainsley asked, "Are you angry with me?"

"I find myself less than pleased with just about everything at the moment."

"If I gave you something, would it improve your mood?" Ainsley ventured after another long stretch of silence.

"Is it wine?"

"No."

"Something stronger?" Rue asked.

"No."

"Then it is not likely to improve my mood."

Ainsley jabbed at the fire with a stick. "Is it just the pain that's got you wanting to drink?"

Rue didn't answer.

The silence stretched too long. Ainsley couldn't bear it. He knelt before Rue and gathered the fairy's hands in his. "Trees but no leaves, a river but no water. It's a map, isn't it?"

"Took you a while."

"So call me a fool," Ainsley offered.

Rue sighed.

"And if you're angry with me, tell me."

"I'm not...it's not you. It's me. It's this place. I thought I understood the way secrets work here." The fairy twined his fingers with Ainsley's. "You accepted things so easily but..." He glanced towards Alfred the hound. "I imagined he'd be relieved. I didn't think he'd try to kill me. Or that you'd rather me dead than him a beast."

"I didn't say that!"

"What else should I have done, Ainsley?"

"I don't know. I. Well. It isn't every day you see someone turn into a dog, Rue, or that someone tries to kill your friend. Or that a knight of the realm stands by as someone does either of those things. I should have acted. In any capacity." He tucked a bit of pale hair behind Rue's ear. "I wouldn't rather have you dead."

"You mean it?"

"On my honor and everything else I have to swear on." He moved in slowly, giving Rue time to pull back or protest, but he met no resistance when he kissed Rue.

Luckily, Alfred slept, or he would have started barking at them again.

"I actually have two things for you."

"What?" Rue asked.

"It isn't wine."

Rue's mouth twisted, somewhere between a scowl and a grimace.

Ainsley took him by the hand and tugged him towards the tent. "In here."

The reluctance with which Rue followed hopefully indicated more about the pain in his leg rather than his mood. Once he had Rue settled on the floor, Ainsley rifled through his pack, looking for the things he had procured.

Rue seemed to recognize the bundles when Ainsley took them out and raised an eyebrow. "Jerky?"

It took Ainsley a moment to recall that Rue had caught him shoving these into his pack the other day. The hardest part about lying was remembering the lies. "No."

He handed the first bundle over to Rue.

His fingers felt along the length as if to check it wasn't jerky. He peeled away the wrapping to reveal a narrow knife, about six inches and sharp on both edges.

"I had the smith make it. That was all the bronze we could get together. I know you prefer a longer blade."

Rue examined the blade. He even went so far as to conjure an orb by which to examine it. He titled it at all angles and tested its balance. Finally, he pronounced, "A fine blade."

"Good enough for fruit and meat, at least."

"And cheese," Rue added.

Ainsley handed him a sheath.

Rue secured the blade, then handed it back.

"Freely given," Ainsley assured.

At that, Rue accepted.

Ainsley pulled over the second bundle, this one larger. He handed it over to Rue, unable to keep a grin from his face.

The fairy unwrapped it and stared down at the small harp in his lap.

"My mother said I could have it."

Rue trailed his fingers over the strings, plucking each one.

"You'll take it?"

He nodded, turning the harp over in his hands. The pale brown wood bore knotted carvings, too old-fashioned and heavy for the harp of a fairy prince.

Ainsley had searched high and low, but he hadn't found anything perfect enough to give to Rue. All the harps he'd stumbled upon had been poorly made, or too large, or just plain ugly. This harp, at least, had a sense of gravitas. "Good, because that one is not so freely given."

That wide-eyed look of fear came over Rue, same as he'd had when Ainsley had pushed him up against the tree. In the dark of the tent, lit up by a smidge of conjured light, it looked worse.

"I want to hear you sing. Not now, if you don't want, but I'll have a whole song from you." Ainsley grinned.

Rue didn't return his grin.

"Is a song such a steep price?"

The fairy didn't answer. He stared down at the harp, his fingers tracing over the carving. "'Tis a fine harp, Ainsley, old and loved and made with care. It was your mother's?"

"The one she learned on," Ainsley confirmed.

"You want a song for it."

"As long as you're the one who sings it." Ainsley didn't exactly understand why Rue sounded so sad. He scooted in closer and combed his fingers through Rue's hair. "Am I asking too much?"

"You aren't asking enough and that always spells mischief."

"No mischief, no tricks. I promise. I just want to hear you sing. Is that so suspicions?"

"Highly."

Ainsley moved even closer. "Because you don't believe that I could love your voice."

"Yes."

He couldn't help but sigh. "Well, the harp is yours. Sing whenever it best please you. Are you tired?"

"Yes."

"Let's get some sleep, then."

Ainsley rolled out his sleeping roll, as well as Rue's. He settled in on his side and rested his head on his arm. He watched Rue set aside the harp, his fingers trailing over the engraving again.

"Would you believe me if I said you're beautiful?" Ainsley asked.

Rue glanced over.

"What if I said I love you? Would you believe me then?"

Without answering, Rue settled himself onto his right side. His uninjured side, but that made it so he faced Ainsley, too.

"What if I said I imagined our first night alone a lot differently?"

"That I believe."

Ainsley had put their bedrolls close together. Close enough that he could nuzzle up against Rue. "I do you love you. Even if you don't believe it."

Rue snaked his arm around Ainsley's waist and tugged him closer. "Why do such a foolish thing?"

Instead of taking offense at his dismissive tone, Ainsley accepted the question for what it was: a plea. "Because you make me laugh. I like speaking with you. I like the way your mouth tastes and the way your skin smells and the way you move. You've made an effort to be open with me even though it makes you squirm. Because you love me, too, and you loved me enough to stay away when I needed space and to accept when I told you no."

"What a list you've conjured."

"Now pick one."

"Hmm?"

"Pick one, one you know to be true."

Cagily, the fairy said, "I make you laugh."

"Now say the whole thing. Say 'you love me because I make you laugh.' That's what Sir Richard used to make me do."

"Say you loved him?"

"Don't be an ass. I used to get downhearted when someone trounced me, or when I couldn't run as fast, or if my arm got tired too quickly. I'd practice and practice and still lose. He used to make me say 'I'm getting stronger. I'm running faster.' Things like that. Say it enough and you'll start to believe."

For a while, Rue said nothing. When he did speak, the words came out quiet and guarded. "You love me because I make you laugh."

Ainsley kissed him, hoping it served as an appropriate reward for his effort.

The fairy accepted the kiss and slid his tongue into Ainsley's mouth.

Despite his wounds, he pushed back Ainsley's covers and hooked his injured leg over Ainsley, half on top and baring down on him.

The intensity of it almost scared Ainsley. He should have expected it, he supposed, after so long without. He should have responded in kind, but somehow, he couldn't. Nerves, or surprise, or simply too long of making himself act with restraint.

Even Rue trembled, though Ainsley didn't know if that had to do with lust or his injuries. He continued to shake, even as he pressed himself closer to Ainsley, sucking at his throat.

"What about your leg?" Ainsley whispered.

Rue leaned back, propping himself on his right arm. "What?"

"Your leg." He felt stupid repeating it and Rue looked at him like he was addled. "Doesn't it hurt?"

"Not the worst I've felt. And it hurts no matter what. I'd rather be doing this." Rue leaned more weight on his right arm and slackened his left leg, grimacing as he moved it. "Why? Would you rather not?"

"I'd rather not have to re-stitch your wounds." Before Rue could huff or take offense or grow melancholy, Ainsley gave his shoulder a nudge. "Lay back."

He didn't want this to go sideways or to wait for another night. He had thought about this for weeks. No one to intrude or eavesdrop, just them. He needed time to adjust to that idea, though, and he bought it for himself.

He eased Rue out of his clothes, careful just as much as teasing.

With each moment that passed, Ainsley settled better into the knowledge that they wouldn't be caught. The burning look in Rue's eyes helped, as did the quiet sounds of appreciation he made when Ainsley touched him.

It didn't matter where he lay his hands, thigh, chest, stomach, arm, Rue acted as though he'd ached for that exact touch.

Ainsley settled himself on Rue's stomach, one knee on either side of his waist. "You promised you'd be careful with me if you were inside me."

"I promise it still."

"And..." Asking felt callow, especially when Rue had given himself over to this without hesitation. "It will hurt?"

"Only if we do it wrong." Rue slid his hands up Ainsley's arms and drew him close.

Each soft kiss soothed Ainsley's worries. Every touch gave him courage and drew out the long-simmering fire in his core. Tenderness marked each move Rue made, his fingers probing, stirring a deeper yearning within him.

In the end, somehow, Rue yielded everything to Ainsley. The fairy did nothing without Ainsley's initiation, be it through his words or actions. Despite the vulnerability of letting Rue inside him, Ainsley never felt raw or exposed. His nerves jangled somewhat, but not for too long.

They moved together, leisurely and cautious with each other, given the injuries and inexperience between the two of them.

The relief of giving himself over to being Rue outstripped the physical pleasure in some ways. He had worried about what would become of them, of whether he could really love Rue again. The answer proved to be not just 'yes' but 'absolutely.' They moved together, finding their way towards release, not in unison but without the awkwardness that Ainsley had expected after so long apart.

Even after they'd spilled, they didn't part. They remained twined together, unwilling or perhaps incapable of letting go. He fell asleep cuddled into Rue's embrace, his head resting on the fairy's chest and his fingers tracing the unmarred skin beside Rue's scar.

In the morning, Rue woke up him by playing with his hair.

Ainsley didn't think Rue meant to wake him based on the look on his face. Ainsley didn't mind, though. He wiggled up and pressed a kiss to Rue's cheek.

"Did you like it?" Rue asked before Ainsley could bid him a good morning or ask how he'd slept. A plain question without the usual flourish with which the fairy spoke.

Ainsley hadn't yet determined if the way Rue spoke was an affect, a joke, or simply the way he spoke. He switched between plain and poetic, melancholy or jesting, with some ease, but that didn't surprise Ainsley anymore. Rue had a lot of faces and Ainsley knew he hadn't yet seen all of them.

"Mmm. Up all night thinking about that, were you?" Ainsley had liked it, but he didn't know how much he'd liked it. The act, he thought, required revisiting. Several times, if needed, and then he could have a more educated opinion. "Much better than last time we tried to do anything," Ainsley told him.

"What do you mean?"

"A few days before...before you had to take me home, well, you wanted to, uh, I think you wanted to apologize. I'm not sure, really, I couldn't understand much of what you were saying. Anyway, you got on your knees and I started to tell you off, but before I even could, you threw up on my, uh...my legs."

Horror stamped itself on Rue's face. "I didn't," he whispered.

"Mmm, you did."

"I don't remember that."

"I know."

"I'm sorry."

"You were sorry then, too," Ainsley said. The event felt far away and almost like it had happened to someone else. A chuckle escaped him, one born of discomfort rather than humor. "But I liked it. You inside of me, not you throwing up on me."

Rue started to assure him, "If you didn't—"

"Shh, I said I did. Trust me, sweet thing, I liked it." He pressed his lips to Rue's cheek. "We'll investigate some more another night, yes?"

"Whatever please you best."

Ainsley smiled, calm and peaceful for the moment. "And you, too, though."

"Mmm."

He remained in the other man's arms for longer than he should have. Eventually, they forced themselves to get up. They scrubbed up with damp rags, which didn't feel sufficient, especially after all the baths they'd had at Wolfwood and the Court.

A quick peek at Rue's injuries showed them, so far, free of any signs of infection. Nor had last night's activities undone his stitches.

Before the sun had climbed halfway to midday, they had eaten and resumed their travels.

Alfred sniffed around breakfast for scraps, which Ainsley willingly handed over. The dog even wagged his tail once, though after they'd eaten, he returned to his sulking.

Rue hobbled towards his horse and Ainsley had to ask, "How's your leg?"

"Healing."

Fallclere and its university lay between them and the tourney grounds. The closer they got to the university, the more likely they'd find someone who could sell them something to help with the pain. Ainsley steered them in that direction, taking a less direct route. They had time to spare.

Alfred trotted out in front of them, occasionally looking back to see if they still followed. He looked so essentially dog-like when he did that, the image of a faithful hound.

"Will it, uh...being a dog, Rue, will it do something to him?" Ainsley asked.

"Hopefully make him think twice before he swings a weapon."

Ainsley shot him a look.

"I've never experienced anything more than a mild adjustment period when I've come back from being anything but a man, but I've never been any manner of beast for two years."

"So you don't know."

"I'm not sure, which has a somewhat different tenor than not knowing."

Ainsley had nothing to say to that.

After some time longer on the road, Rue let out a sharp whistle.

Alfred responded instantly, pausing and turning around. He looked between Ainsley and Rue, but when he realized Rue had whistled, glowered and returned to walking.

"It isn't sporting to tease a dog," Ainsley chided gently. "Even if he is cleverer than other dogs."

"Is that the popular opinion in this realm, or one to particular to soft-hearted knights?"

Ainsley grumbled, "I'm not soft-hearted."

"You are. Why protest it so? Would you rather be hard-hearted? Is that admirable here?" Rue asked.

"Sometimes."

"At home it is admirable to be clever, or wicked, and aloof from the suffering of others. Misfortune is an amusement. But you never acted like that. Was it wrong of me to assume all of humanity similarly inclined?"

"People are people. They're the same everywhere. Some are good, some are bad, most are neither."

Rue lapsed into contemplative silence.

Ainsley didn't think he had said anything profound or anything Rue hadn't heard before. He gave the fairy space and left to him to whatever deep thoughts he had swirling around in his head.

When they made camp that night, Rue conjured a flame for the campfire and plucked at the harp strings while Ainsley busied himself.

"You didn't have a tent before," the fairy noted without preamble.

"What?"

"When I was a crow. You didn't have a tent then."

"Oh, well, when I was a squire, I shared with Sir Richard. I figured I would buy one with all the coin I earned. I didn't earn it quite fast enough, though, did I?"

"Maybe if you had slayed your quarry..." Rue suggested.

"Oh, well, it's likely enough," Ainsley agreed. "But if I was that sort of knight, I probably also been the sort of knight to put an arrow through demonic birds following me around."

With a snort, Rue returned to plucking at his harp. He would play a few measures, make some error perceptible to himself but not to Ainsley, cluck his tongue, and start over. He persisted all through dinner, long enough that Ainsley recognized the place where he stalled each time.

"It goes 'all around the countryside'," Ainsley told him. "That's the next line."

Rue began to play again, this time carefully making it through the part that usually tripped him up. Before they retired for the night, he'd played the song three times through, better each time. He sang under his breath, too quiet for Ainsley to make out most of the words.

After another day of fiddling, Rue finally sang an entire song, and not the one he'd been practicing. He didn't announce that he'd sing it or do anything to get Ainsley's attention.

"A dish of cream upon the sill, in bed a sleeping maid.
Tonight the fey go trooping by, the sweetest night in May.
My love and I, beneath the twinkling sky, our horses prance and shy.
Tonight we'll dance til light of day.
My love, My love and I, it's he I'll wed and never put aside.
Sweet and quick, I'll make my promise and give him all my play."

Ainsley tried not to stare as he sang. He tried, but he couldn't help stealing glances towards Rue.

"My love, My love and I, we've never gone astray.
A thousand years of dance and song, without an another sweet.
Forever together, he and I, we'll never part our ways.
A dish of cream upon the sill, and honey in a crock.
Tonight, my love, we're to wed, except he's gone away
To a bed where sleeps a mortal maid, a bed that isn't mine."

Rue stopped playing.
"Go on," Ainsley urged.
"You mightn't care for the next part."
"Rue, please."
Rue licked his lips and continued his playing.

"A snarl of hair and stones for eyes, she'll never be as fair.
A mortal maid is dull indeed, no matter how much cream.
My love, he says I can't compare to his new dear
When it comes to hearts and minds.
I curdle her cream and send flies to steal her prayers
And still he will not come.
I curse them both to never laugh, but there's no snare
To come between a prince and his true love."

They rode in silence. Ainsley kept on hoping for another verse and Rue must have waited for something as well.

Eventually, Ainsley said, "That's my song?"

"Do you deem it a fair meeting of your terms?"

"I should have gotten you a finer harp." It had nothing to do with the song and everything to do with Rue's voice and what it meant for him to sing not just a line or verse, but three of them for another person.

"'Tis finer than any harp I could have hoped for."

They glanced towards each other, then looked away. An unusual bloom of shyness overcame Ainsley. He edged Hadley closer to Clover and reached across the gap to link hands with Rue. They hadn't seen anyone else on the road and Ainsley didn't anticipate that they would.

Ainsley said, "When we go back, promise you'll bring your harp when we travel."

"Are you asking me for a formal oath?"

"No, nothing like that."

"Then I'll take your request into consideration."

Such a fairy answer. It nearly pleased Ainsley to hear it. He kissed the back of Rue's hand. "If I win the melee, will you write me a song of my own?"

Rue evaded the question with one of his own. "What exactly will happen at this contest? I think it might be different from sport at home."

"There's the melee, the jousts for sure, there might be an archery contest. I don't know if Roderick has invited any mages, but there might be single combat between them, too. We'll be pretty near the university, so I think there's a fair chance of it."

"And you mean to enter all of them?"

"Mmm, I don't see why not. Well, not combat with the mages, of course."

"Will there be women in attendance?"

"Certainly. Ladies go to find suitors. They'll give their ribbons to those they favor."

Rue sniffed, somehow making it exquisitely arrogant. Ainsley couldn't have guessed at his thoughts, but he did enjoy seeing him look so prideful.

"Will you be swooning in the stands?" Ainsley asked.

"Likely not, but perhaps if you impress me, I'll reconsider."

Alfred spotted the traveler before either of the men. He barked and circled back around the horses. He ran back towards the traveler when Ainsley and Rue failed to be impressed. Three days on the road had found them utterly unaccompanied. It hadn't surprised Ainsley, given that winter still clung to the country. The spring equinox had not yet come to pass, and the air still had a nip to it.

Rue stared at the cloak-swaddled figure ahead of him.

The stranger glanced back, face hooded, and seemed to be eying Alfred.

Ainsley extracted his fingers from Rue's grip.

"A woman," the fairy pronounced. "Or a man slighter than even you."

"Alfred!" Ainsley called.

The dog didn't heed him. He went on barking until the traveler turned towards him, a crackling bit of lighting cupped in one hand. At that, the dog crouched and growled.

"Call off your beast," the traveler warned.

"Alfred, stop it," Ainsley warned. He pulled up his horse alongside the traveler and hopped off Hadley. He put himself between Alfred and the traveler.

He caught a peek at the face under the hood. A handsome, broad face with ochre skin and rich brown eyes. Almost certainly female.

"My lady—"

"Get away from me."

Ainsley put up his hands and kept his distance. "I don't mean you any harm. I'm sorry about Alfred, he's, well, he's a little high-strung."

"Get it under control before I do it for you."

Alfred let out a whine and tucked himself behind Ainsley. Ainsley resisted the urge to pat the dog on the head. "We really don't mean any harm."

"Then go."

If wisdom had numbered among his virtues, he would have gone. Instead, he said, "I think we're headed in the same direction."

Her eyes narrowed. "So?"

"It might be safer to travel together," he offered.

"Ainsley, does she look like she needs protection?" Rue asked.

"Well, I..." Ainsley glanced between Rue and the woman, at a loss for words. "I."

Without dismounting, Rue glanced over the woman. The spell she'd conjured drew his attention best. "An impressive bit of spark and conjured by a mortal, too. She could knock you off your feet with that."

"And yours, too," she warned.

Rue laughed at that. "Come along, Sir Ainsley, before you really irk her."

Ainsley moved back towards Hadley, but not without a few more glances at the woman. He couldn't help it; not much older than him and female to boot, Ainsley hadn't encountered a mage like her before. She had to be a mage; witches didn't conjure lightning.

"Ainsley, lest I start to doubt your fidelity," Rue warned.

All at once, Ainsley went hot and cold.

"My cousin would like be disappointed if you went after another."

The woman glanced between them.

"My companion has given his love to one among the Fair Folk," Rue explained haughtily. "My cousin bid me watch after him."

It flattered Ainsley a little that Tadgh had done any such thing. He also appreciated the incredibly fey manner in which Rue had twisted the truth. To the woman, he said, "It's true, you needn't worry after my intentions. My heart rests quite comfortably in the hands of another."

"It wasn't your heart I was worried about."

A laugh jumped out of Ainsley's mouth. "Well, everything else rests comfortably in my love's hands too."

She cracked a smile.

"Ainsley, knight of the realm, at your service, my lady." He gave a small bow.

The woman clenched her first and dispelled the lightning in her hand. "Sama."

"Are you headed towards the university?"

"Only past it. I'm off to the king's tourney."

More excited than he meant to show, Ainsley asked, "Do you plan to fight?"

The spectacle of mages battling always drew Ainsley in more than one between jousters or swordsmen. He understood those things, but magic always surprised him.

She snorted. "No, just saving the lives of the fools who do."

"A healer!" Ainsley exclaimed.

Sama frowned at his eagerness.

"We headed just this way hoping to meet one."

"Did we?" Rue asked.

She asked, "Why, which one of you caught what?"

"No, Rue...he ended up on the wrong end of a blade. It's, well, it seems to be healing right, but it pains him."

From atop Clover, Rue protested, but Ainsley shushed him.

Sama shifted the pack she carried and glanced over the two of them. Likely appraising their clothes and belongings before she named a price. She asked Rue, "How much does it hurt?"

"As much as it should, I imagine."

"Rue, don't be difficult. You can't even get up on your horse alone." Ainsley turned to Sama. "Can you help?"

She twisted her mouth, then looked up at the sun. "We can discuss it over a meal."

They ate first. Sama repelled most of Ainsley's attempts to learn more about her and Rue seemed put-off that Ainsley had taken it upon himself to find him a healer.

After they ate, Rue reluctantly peeled down one leg of his hose to show Sama the wound on his thigh. She peered at it, pronounced it adequately cared for, and offered to sell him a salve to help with the pain.

"I've no coin but a penny," he told her.

"I'll pay for it," Ainsley offered. "How much?"

She produced a small, sealed jar from within her pack. "A crown."

Ainsley laughed. "Four lances."

"Do you know what this is?"

"A scam, if you're asking a crown for it," he answered. "Five lances and Rue will sing you a song."

The sound that Rue produced startled Ainsley, Sama, and Alfred as well. The hound let out a small, concerned growl.

Sama countered, "A shield and bugger the song."

"He's got a lovely voice."

The look Sama gave Rue could have curdled milk. "Aye, and he's a fairy, and I've got no use for any sort of fairy trickery. A shield and that's it."

"Seven lances, two pennies, and Rue will sing you a song."

"I said bugger the song."

"So seven lances?" Ainsley asked, producing his coin purse.

"And ten pennies."

He counted out the coins and passed them to her.

She handed over the jar of salve, but not before she'd tucked the coins away.

Once he had it in his hands, Ainsley knelt before Rue as though about to pledge fealty. "O, wondrous prince, I beseech thee, tell your cousin of my good deed. I'm desperate to know I've pleased my love." He held up the jar as an offering.

"I'll certainly relay this, though I'm not sure your love will be at all impressed by this sort of tomfoolery." Rue took the jar, treating it more like an obligation than a favor.

Ainsley giggled at the look of sheer irritation on his face. Maybe Rue wasn't the only one who liked to get under people's skin, or maybe Ainsley had spent too much time among the Fair Folk. He pushed himself back to his feet. He turned towards the made to find her face somewhere between amused and irritated. "Sama, we share a destination, you're welcome to travel with us."

"I've managed well enough on my own."

It took every drop of effort Ainsley had not to take offense. Some deep part of him wanted to accompany this woman safely to her destination. He forced himself to give her a smile. "Safe travels, then. And don't be a stranger if you spot us at the tourney."

"Safe travels."

She shrunk in the distance as they rode way.

Rue glanced back at her a few times. When she'd grown small, he noted, "You wanted badly for her to travel with us."

Ainsley almost denied it but recalled how little faith Rue had in his honesty in the first place. "Knights are supposed to safeguard women. I haven't been able to manage very many knightly things."

"She didn't seem to need safeguarding."

"Or want it," Ainsley conceded.

"Will you be attempting to safeguard all the women you encounter?"

The vaguely prickly way Rue asked prompted Ainsley to ask, "Is it going to upset you if I do?"

"If I were a woman, I'd consider it quite rude to have some perfect stranger trying to safeguard me."

"Well, I'm not a stranger. I'm a knight."

"And I am a prince, but I don't think a title makes me any less strange or more trustworthy."

The idea of Rue doing anything untoward towards a woman struck Ainsley as vaguely ridiculous.

"Or what of Tadgh? He's the Crown Prince, that's a weighty title. Would you trust his intentions towards a stranger?"

"I think fairies have different sorts of intentions. It's not as though I'm going to trick her into giving me her firstborn."

"Says the man who believes that people are the same everywhere. Either they are or they aren't, I don't believe it can work both ways."

Stumped, Ainsley set to contemplating. He didn't manage to figure out much.

After a while, Rue took pity and continued, "Intentions, be they mischievous or romantic or altogether evil, would frighten me if I were traveling alone."

The strangers he'd encountered while traveling alone had done him no harm with one exception. That exception had nearly cost him his life. "I'll leave them alone, then, unless they appear distressed."

"Much less intrusive."

"Says the man who followed me around for weeks without introducing himself."

Rue had the decency to look chastised.

"Speaking of firstborns, what do fairies want with human babies, anyway? In all the stories—"

"Stories, Ainsley, are just that."

"That's what you said about that Snow Hag and it wasn't just a story at all. Why do fairies take mortal babies?"

Rue shrugged. "There's as many reasons as there are fairies. Some cannot conceive a child of their own, others wish to hold further leverage over a particular mortal. Some seek a servant or concubine that cannot resist their glamours. Some of the Folk think of human babes in the same way you might think of a puppy. Shall I continue?"

"I suppose not."

They came up no more travelers that day, nor did Sama catch up with them. At night, though, Ainsley thought he saw another fire winking in the distance. He sent up a small prayer for her safety, then turned his attentions to Rue. He had to bully the fairy into using the salve he'd purchased. It took a liberal application of guilt, as well as sliding his fingers up Rue's thigh, to get him to agree.

Alfred watched as judgmentally as a hound could while Ainsley spread a thin layer of salve over the wound.

Rue let out a small, whimpering moan. His eyes fluttered closed.

Ainsley felt the muscle of Rue's thigh soften as the tension melted out of him. "If it hurts you so, then why put up such a fight about the salve?" he asked.

"Because you've already seen me in such unbecoming ways. I thought I should try not to seem utterly contemptible."

Ainsley translated, "You were trying to impress me?"

"I was trying to impress you."

That deserved a kiss and Ainsley gave it freely. "I've found you impressive from the start."

He would have done more than kiss him, but Alfred started to growl. Ainsley pulled out of the fairy's arms to scold him. By the time he'd quieted the dog, Rue had pulled his hose back up and started to take food out of their packs.

The hound stared at Rue, his lip curled.

Rue offered him a bit of dried meat and Alfred snapped at him. Rue yanked his hand back. "If it bothers you so much to see him with another man then maybe you shouldn't have wasted your chance with him."

Alfred dropped into a low stance, hackles raised and his lips pulled back from his teeth in an ugly snarl. He looked like a true beast.

"Go ahead, keep growling at me. It won't change a thing about the past," Rue snapped.

"Rue, don't fight with him."

"Why not? It is unsporting?" The questions came with a bit of snark, but no small amount of genuine curiosity as well.

"No, it's futile."

Rue didn't argue. He shot a nasty glance at Alfred, then made a show of turning his back on the dog and returning to making dinner.

No matter how much Alfred growled and whined, Ainsley didn't let the hound determine how close he got to Rue. He had to hide from the eyes of humans, he wasn't about the hide from a dog, too. By the time Alfred was a man again, Ainsley would be on his way back to the Otherworld. He had accepted that they would have to keep Alfred with them until he was a man again.

"Do you think we could bring him to the Otherworld? Could someone else fix him?" Ainsley asked.

Without looking up from his food, Rue answered, "I don't know. Why?"

"Two years is a long time to have a dog that hates your lover."

Rue paused, almost went back to eating, then set his food aside. "What do you mean?"

"I don't much fancy him barking every time I kiss you."

"You mean to keep him."

"What else am I supposed to do? Let him wander the wilderness on his own? Even if he's a dog now, Alfred's been my friend since I was a boy."

Rue stood and approached the dog. Alfred growled, but Rue ignored him. He took the dog's face in both hands. "Alfred, I ask thee not for love or acceptance, or even tolerance. Turn a blind eye to us and find peace in your heart. Do this and the curse I've laid upon you shall be lifted regardless of how much time has passed." He released the dog and wiped his hands on his shirt.

Alfred slunk away, apparently displeased.

"Could you do that the whole time?" Ainsley asked.

"One can always add a proviso to a curse should one consider it fitting. But it must fit the curse, too."

"Ah."

"I tried to make it as easy as I could, but I don't know if he'll manage it."

Ainsley gave the fairy a pat on the arm.

The addition of the proviso did little to improve Alfred's attitude towards Rue in the following days. Maybe as a dog he couldn't understand it or maybe he harbored too much ill-will.

Maybe, Ainsley thought, Alfred needed to meet someone else. Falling in love with Rue had effectively scrubbed every trace of angst concerning Alfred from Ainsley's heart. Maybe it would do the same for Alfred. Of course, considering that Alfred was currently a dog, Ainsley didn't know how that would work. He couldn't set him up with a member of either species, really.

"Rue?"

The fairy didn't answer, too busy plucking at his harp. If Clover hadn't had the sense to follow along with Hadley, Rue probably would have gotten lost days ago.

"Rue!"

Without looking up, the fairy hummed, "Hmm?"

"Did you fancy me when you were a crow?"

Rue's head jerked up. "What?"

"I mean, you did an awful lot of preening."

"Of course, I fancied you, I stalked you across miles of countryside."

Ainsley rolled his eyes. "But I mean, well, was it carnal?"

"We weren't exactly inhabiting compatible forms at the time."

"Alright, what about crows? Did you fancy other crows?"

At that, Rue stared. "Are you asking me if I've taken animals to bed, Ainsley?"

"Uh. Not exactly." His cheeks heated uncomfortably; he wished he hadn't broached the subject in his thoughts let alone aloud. He scrambled for anything else to say.

"Are you asking me if I've wanted to?"

Too fast, Ainsley asked, "Do you think it's going to rain? It's cloudy, isn't it? Sort of looks like rain."

"It might rain," Rue answered. He didn't return to their previous subject. Within minutes, he had returned to plucking at his harp.

Given enough time and silence, Rue's plucking usually turned into a song and Ainsley had taken to keeping quite in the hopes that Rue would sing something. A common theme in the songs he chose seemed to involve losing a lover to a mortal or taking a mortal lover and cursing them for some slight or betrayal.

The song Rue sang now ended with a mortal youth cursed to wander the moors beneath the full moon as the beast he'd shown himself to be in the eyes of the fairy maid he'd wronged.

"That's a werewolf," Ainsley pronounced when he'd finished singing.

"Hmm?"

"She turned him into a werewolf."

"Oh. I suppose it can be taken that way, can't it?" Rue asked.

"I don't remember all the songs at Court being this dire. Is there something on your mind?"

Ponderously, Rue answered, "Yes," but declined to elaborate any further.

Even cautious and roundabout questions failed to provoke a more elaborate answer. It wasn't until the middle of the night, long after they'd twined themselves together, that Rue said anything further.

Ainsley had half fallen asleep, knowing he should get up to relieve himself, but too content in Rue's arms to move.

Out of nowhere, Rue said, "All the songs about mortals and the Fair Folk go that way. At least, all the ones I know. It worries me somewhat."

It took Ainsley a few moments to puzzle out what he could mean. "In what way?"

"That we might be incompatible. Long-term, anyway. Mortals who visit the Otherworld tend to keep their stays brief and those who don't tend not to fare well."

Ainsley pulled himself out of Rue's arms. "We're going to talk about this, but I've had to piss for the longest time."

Rue followed him out of the tent, tending to similar needs. By the time they returned to their bedrolls, they'd woken more fully. Rue sat cross-legged with a fur pulled over his lap. He watched Ainsley's every move.

He looked too serious. Borderline morose, in fact. It wouldn't do, especially not for a conversation like this. Ainsley turned aside his fur and crawled into his lap, taking great care to avoid the injury on his thigh. He settled his head against Rue's chest and pulled more coverings over them both.

"Now," Ainsley pronounced. "Tell me."

"Of mortal lovers who've fared well in the Otherworld, I know little. Of Fair Folk who adjust to life in the mortal realm, I'm similarly uninformed. Exile is a grave punishment."

"Well, we aren't staying here," Ainsley told him. "I'm not spending my whole life pretending not to love you."

"Even as dear to me as you are, I managed to treat you badly. What would those who bear you no love do, if they could?"

"You gave me your protection."

"And I couldn't even keep you safe from myself."

The sound of Rue's heart anchored him. Constant, without end, without pause. "I won, though."

"What?"

"I beat you, Rue. I won that contest."

"You didn't play fair, my love," the fairy reminded.

"Don't make it sound like I cheated. I made my moves carefully. And I won." Ainsley worked at keeping his voice even. Becoming accusatory wouldn't do this conversation any favors. "I'd win again, I think."

Rue, to his credit, didn't argue. "I hope you win against me every time."

"I hope the occasion never arises again."

Rue let out an unusual, strangled sound, maybe a groan or a laugh. He tightened his arms around Ainsley. "You are inescapably straightforward."

It felt like a compliment.

The king had selected the town of Ilseworth as the location for the tourney. Ainsley had attended half a dozen tourneys here as a squire. The town boasted a large, flat meadow perfectly suited to a melee; the mayor was also rumored to be a friend of King Jannes's brother-in-law.

The tourney didn't start for a few days yet, though Ainsley spied a few other knights milling about the public square.

He'd greet them later. He had more important things on his mind now.

Namely, a bath. Ten days without one had not seemed so terrible before he'd been afforded the luxury of a hot one every day.

Rue, to his credit, hadn't complained once. He'd heated a bit of water for them each morning, conjuring the water when fresh water hadn't been available.

Even from a distance, Ainsley could spot the prostitutes that lingered outside the bathhouse. Some of them local, more of them trickling to find work among the tourney attendees. He kept his head down as he walked past them. Women who offered themselves for sale always churned up a deep discomfort him in. He'd never understood why, any more than he understood why he had hated the easy tavern girls who'd flirted with the other squires.

"Two pennies," offered one particularly scrawny and rough-looking woman.

Ainsley ignored her.

"Two for whatever you want," she cajoled. "One for a bit of suck."

He beelined for the owner of the bathhouse, eyes resolutely on the ground.

The whore placed herself in his way, still naming prices, but she fell back once he shouldered past her.

Rue tugged on his sleeve. "Give me my penny."

The request took him by such surprise that he swung around. He stared up at Rue, abruptly reminded of their difference in height after so long usually riding or sitting beside him. "What for?"

Rue held out his hand palm up. "For that woman."

"Rue, she's a whore."

"I'm aware."

"What do you want with a whore?" he demanded, unable to explain the hideous surge of jealousy he felt. Rue had never gone after a woman; he wouldn't go after one as ugly and low as this one.

"My penny, Sir Ainsley, before I take it."

With a huff and a scowl, Ainsley dug out a penny and shoved it into Rue's palm. "Watch out for pox."

"Oh, lambkin, if Folk could get pox I'd have it ten times over." The prince approached the whore.

"Two for anything you like, even for whatever you are," she told him.

Ainsley wanted to spit on her. Despite himself, he couldn't stop watching their exchange. Even as he paid the owner of the bathhouse, he kept glimpsing over.

Rue placed the penny in her hand. "Forgive my friend, he sometimes lacks manners."

"Enough for a suck," she told him. She nodded her head towards a more secluded area.

"The coin is freely given."

She frowned at him.

"If receiving alms disquiets you, feel free to do someone else a good turn in exchange," Rue told her. While the woman continued her confused frowning, he turned away and returned to where Ainsley had stood and watched him.

As they entered the bathhouse, Ainsley asked, "What was that about?"

"You pushed her."

Sheepishly, Ainsley insisted, "She wouldn't have moved."

"With all your concern for the woman we met on the road, Ainsley, I'm surprised at you."

"That's different."

"Different indeed. You'd foist your assistance upon a woman who had no need for it and push around that unfortunate creature."

With the distinct and uncomfortable feeling that he'd displeased the fairy, Ainsley asked, "What would you have had me do?"

"Say excuse me, at least. Poor thing. She looks about ready to starve to death."

"Well, she…it's." Ainsley struggled to figure out what had the fairy in a huff. "Am I supposed to feed every hungry mouth in the country? There's thousands."

"Thousands."

"Mm."

"And your king allows it?"

Ainsley asked, "No one goes hungry in the Otherworld?"

"Not that I've ever seen."

As gently as he could, Ainsley reminded, "You also never paid for anything or even handled a coin."

The righteous indignation went out of Rue. "Still, you didn't have to push her," he sulked.

There was no arguing that. "You're right."

They found a corner of the bathhouse without too many others. While Ainsley stripped, Rue took the time to cast a glamour over his scars. He currently drew stares without them visible and Ainsley didn't blame him for wanting such a thing out of the public eye.

Before he set to washing, Ainsley sank in up to his chin and soaked. Eyes closed, he tried to shut out the sounds of the other bathers.

Women and men traded propositions, laughing and flirting and splashing at each other.

He wished a plague on every goddamn one of them. How could everything be so easy for them?

"Hmmm, what a pair," cooed a voice.

He peeked one eye open to find a woman, much comelier than the pitiful wretch outside, crouching beside Rue.

"Have you come to fight in the tourney?" she asked.

"No," Rue answered.

She gave him a smile. "No? You look like you'd fare well on the field. A strapping fellow like you. Whatever sort of fellow you are."

Ainsley wanted to shout at her to go away.

"Hardly broad enough to be strapping, I think I'm much better classed as lean," Rue corrected.

The woman laughed, tucking a blond curl behind her ear. "Funny, too. You could use company, I bet. How long on the road to get here? Must have been lonely. I can find a friend for your friend, too."

"Ah, my friend is here to enter the tourney. His strength is better spent on the field than in bed if he hopes to win."

The woman looked him over, her lips quirked off to one side. "Win? If I were him, I'd sit it out altogether. Poor little lad might get stepped on."

Ainsley had not been so aware of his stature in months. Shorter and slimmer than most men, he'd worked hard for every ounce of strength he had. He worked hard to maintain it, too. He washed himself more aggressively than a few days of travels and lovemaking truly deserved. Scrubbing and sluicing away all the dirt, sweat, and whatever else his skin had accumulated improved his mood.

"Oh, for shame. Don't underestimate such a fine specimen because of his size. It's all about what one does with one's assets," Rue scolded.

Heat pricked the tips of Ainsley's ears. He dunked his head underwater to give his curls a last rinse.

"I would wager the lad wins at least one contest."

"What do you wager?" the woman asked.

"Ah, there's the problem. Without coin, I can offer nothing but boons and favors."

At that, the woman's interest clearly waned. "What about you, little man? Anything more than favors in your pockets?"

"Not enough to waste on someone like you."

The flirtation on her face vanished altogether. "I'll watch for you on the field. Maybe someone will knock you on your ass. I could use a good laugh."

When she'd gone, Rue assured, "I find your size deeply appealing."

"Shh, with that, people are about," Ainsley grumbled.

"Do you think they're listening?"

"I don't know. Maybe. It's always better to assume they are."

Rue sank lower in the water. "I despise this realm."

With how abject the other man looked it took all of Ainsley's restraint not to embrace him. He settled for patting him on the shoulder. "Wash your hair. You'll feel better."

Dutifully, Rue scrubbed at his hair.

Someone splashed into the water beside them. "Jack!" the big man greeted him.

In the dim light of the bathhouse, Ainsley had to squint. "Curtis!"

"Alfred found you, then? He wanted to make sure you heard about the tourney."

"Mmm. Yeah, he did."

"You two come here together?"

"Uh. Alfred, he and I got into it. He took off, you know how he is."

Curtis snorted. "Mmm. Always was a funny sort. Anyway. Everyone thought something had happened to you. Good to see you're all in one piece."

"Oh." Ainsley didn't know what else to say.

Curtis shot a narrow-eyed look towards Rue. "George and Michael are here, too. We can catch up with them. You'll have to tell us what kept you so hard to find."

Rue gave Curtis a once over, then returned to washing his underarms.

"I was questing."

Curtis laughed. "I can't wait to hear what kind of quests you had. Save some damsels, did you?"

"What about you, Curt? What did you get up to?"

Curtis snorted and told some meandering story about catching poachers that ended with him bedding one of the poacher's daughters.

Ainsley didn't care much for level of detail Curtis gave. He didn't much want to know about the squeaks and squeals of the knight's conquest. Something about the way he described the girl felt wrong. Slippery and seedy, the story churned up the same sort of discomfort as the bathhouse prostitutes.

He wondered what Curtis would say if Ainsley told a story like that, one about a poacher's son instead. He wondered how badly Curtis would beat him for it.

"Is this a custom for knights here?" Rue asked.

Curtis scowled at Rue. "What?"

"Holding men's lives hostage in exchange for bedding their daughters?"

"She was *grateful*–"

"That you didn't kill her father. Mmm. I know exactly how I'd be feeling." Rue sat up straighter.

"Who do you think you are?" Curtis demanded.

A large part of Ainsley wanted to sit back and see how this played out. He leaned back against the edge of the pool, resting his elbows on the ledge.

"Someone with a little more decency than most men in this realm."

"This realm?"

"Mmm. Miserable place full of miserable bastards."

Curtis surged upwards, sending water sloshing.

Rue stood more slowly. He looked fantastic, his skin glistening wet and his face dripping with disdain. "I name you a foul thing–"

"No curses," Ainsley warned.

Both men looked towards him. Rue looked irritated, but dumb confusion scrawled across Curtis's face.

"Curses?" Curtis echoed.

"What about a very minor curse?" Rue asked.

"You know this thing?" Curtis demanded.

Ainsley nodded. "Curt, this is His Highness Rue, prince of the Western Court and one of the Fair Folk. Rue, this is Sir Curtis, of Westfall."

The thickness with which Ainsley laid on Rue's titles gave Curtis some pause. He'd been ready for a full out brawl a moment ago and now he just cast a particularly scorching look towards Rue.

"What are you paling around with fairies for?"

It took a while of careful consideration for Ainsley to decide on his answer. "I've fallen in with them. Quite badly, too."

"You owe him something?"

Ainsley shook his head. "Not quite. I took a lover among them and Rue's taken it upon himself to keep me in line on my love's behalf."

"Ainsley, you do your love a disservice. The concern is with keeping you well, not in preventing you from taking others to bed," Rue assured.

"So I can take others?"

"Do you want to?"

Ainsley let out a soft chuckle. "Who could compare to my love?"

"Comparisons are made with ease."

"Then who could compete?" Ainsley said.

Curtis glanced between them, his nose wrinkled.

Ainsley glanced at Curtis. "My love is a wonderous sight to behold, Curt, you have no idea how mad I've gone for her."

"Gone pretty mad by the looks of it," Curtis grumbled, not too seriously.

The other two had effectively dashed the quiet, calm mood of his bath.

Ainsley hauled himself out of the water, dried himself, and pulled on the fresh set of clothes from his pack.

"If you can shed your nanny, the boys and I will be at the tavern tonight," Curtis told him.

"Should I expect this sort of welcome from all your fellow knights?" Rue asked once Curtis had left.

"I don't think so."

"Because so far two out of two isn't good odds."

"It's excellent odds, though, isn't it?"

"Beg pardon?"

"Excellent odds that they won't like you," Ainsley explained.

"Sometimes I want to pinch you."

Ainsley flashed him a smile. "You know, you can't just go around cursing people."

"To curse him was not my intent. I only meant to singe his eyebrows off. And maybe some other bits of hair, too."

"Don't do that either."

"Are you commanding me?" Rue asked.

"No. Just asking you not to go getting in brawls with everyone who looks at you sideways."

"I'll resort to a quieter treachery, then."

Ainsley didn't point out that Rue had misconstrued his request. The fairy had known exactly what he'd meant and would only resort to some well twisted reply if confronted. Besides, Rue had the right to defend himself if provoked.

They retrieved their horses and Alfred, then staked out a site for their tent near the tourney grounds.

As night began to fall, Rue pronounced, "Go meet up with your friends."

"Oh, I...Are you going to come?"

"No, my love, I'd rather not."

"Don't let Curt get to you," Ainsley urged. "He's just, uh, he's a little bit of an idiot."

"I'm not worried about Curtis or the opinions of any of your friends, if the rest are anything like the ones I've met so far." Rue produced his harp and plucked a few strings. "Far and away have you been from your kind, sweet thing, and you should go to carouse with them. Questions they'll ask and if they ask them of me, twisting the truth will grow tiresome."

No one had set up camp anywhere near them, so Ainsley felt entirely safe swooping in to give Rue a quick kiss. "I won't stay out late."

"Don't make promises you're not like to keep."

"I'll try to keep myself reasonably together," Ainsley amended.

"That's more like it. Enjoy yourself."

Rue sent him on his way with a pat on the arm and a gentle push away. The sound of harp strings followed him away from their camp.

So did Alfred. The hound trotted alongside him, his tongue lolling out of his mouth.

It took no time at all to find the other knights. They had gathered themselves around the central most table in the local tavern. Well into their ale already, the majority of them roared at the sight of Ainsley. Several took it upon themselves to embrace him.

"Jack!" George cried while giving Ainsley's shoulders a shake. "Curt says you're here to compete."

"Course I am, George, what else am I supposed to do? Wave at you all from the stands?"

They laughed at that.

One of them placed a mug of ale in his hands and another, maybe Michael, asked him about the dog.

Ainsley glanced over. "Oh. Alfred."

"You named your dog Alfred?" Curtis asked.

"Uh. Well. It's the name he came with."

The big man wrinkled his nose and rolled his eyes but didn't question it any further. "So. What's this about you and some fairy girl?"

Ainsley sipped his ale to buy time. "What about her?"

"She's got someone following you around? Bit odd, don't you think? Especially a bastard like that one."

"Oh, no, Rue isn't...He's not a bad sort, honest. They do things different in the Otherworld is all." The ale had gone stale, but he took another sip anyway. A few mugs and he wouldn't mind the taste, he knew that much. "He's good to travel with. Handy in a pinch."

"What's that? You worried he's listening in?" Curtis teased.

"No, just." Ainsley squirmed. He didn't know when lying had become so much harder. "We might be family someday. No good to have blood there."

A few of the others still had their wits enough about them to turn towards him. He'd misspoken somewhere but didn't know how.

"What?" he asked, eyes lowered.

"Family? You mean to wed a creature?" George asked.

Demanded. He hadn't asked or inquired. He'd demanded, his lip curled.

"I. Well. I don't see why not." He couldn't marry Rue, he knew that. At least, he didn't think he could marry Rue. Nor did he know if he wanted to marry Rue, but he thought their relationship warranted being called more than friends.

"Well, you're not a witch or a madman for starters. Do your parents know? They can't possibly approve."

"It wouldn't be a common creature; I'm not talking about some peasant or merchant's daughter."

"Oh, a proper fairy *lady*!" George laughed. "With spiderwebs for a gown and moonbeams in her hair?"

If George had ever seen one of the Fair Folk, he wouldn't have laughed. If he had seen Corva in her gowns of mist and fog, he would have begged for the right to kiss her foot. If he'd come across even the commonest of fairy maids, his heart would have leapt in his chest.

"Royalty," Ainsley told them.

George, Michael, and Curtis laughed.

"Can't you see it? You chasing around a brood of little pixie princes!" George declared. "You know what, Jack? You take any girl that will let you. Everyone thinks they're going to marry their first decent lay."

The other men laughed and drank to that.

Ainsley forced himself to do the same. It didn't matter if they thought he was lovestruck or addled. He drank down the rest of his ale and hoped no one would notice the redness in his cheeks. Or, if they did, blame it on the drink.

Alfred paced between the men, nosing their hands and sniffing their faces. His tail wagged occasionally, but more often than not, he would pause and glance towards Ainsley, unsure about something.

It had to confuse him, being around his old friends.

In the hopes of soothing the hound's nerves, Ainsley scratched behind his head and patted his flank. Alfred leaned into his pets and slurped at his fingers.

It felt normal until Ainsley recalled their exact circumstances.

The other knights traded stories about their quests, the beasts they had slain, the bandits for which they'd collected bounties, and the women they'd bedded. Michael told of a pair of vampires he'd slain and showed off the ring he'd taken from one of their corpses. George complained of the wife that waited for him at home and several times mentioned how badly he hoped he'd planted a son in her instead of a daughter.

In the corner, a youth played a lute and sang of dashing knights and pretty maidens. His voice, sweet and high, matched his willowy limbs and smooth cheeks. He couldn't be much older than fifteen. A few years ago, Ainsley would have been destroyed by the very sight of the lad.

A serving girl worked up the courage to kiss the lad's cheek. They both blushed, hardly able to look at each other

An unbecoming riot of anger surged through Ainsley and it took him a moment to realize that he didn't hate the girl for having kissed that particular boy. He hated her because she could do what he couldn't.

He gulped down the rest of his ale just so he had an excuse to get up and get another. He had no desire to sit through anymore of his friends' tall tales. He decided against another drink and ducked outside. No one noticed but Alfred. The dog remained by his side as he leaned against the wall of the tavern.

The idea of returning to the Otherworld called to him and he badly wanted to go. Rue would take him without hesitation. Better to risk being trapped there than to remain here and realize what a beast he was. Pushing around destitute women, hitting Rue, standing by while people he cared about hurt each other.

Rue had named him so many things, gentle and sweet and kind. Ainsley didn't feel like that at all, not now.

He was just frightened and angry.

George barreled out of the tavern, startling Ainsley out of his contemplations. "Sick already?"

"Just needed air."

"Barely drank anything," George continued.

Ainsley thought about arguing, but George had started to slur his words before Ainsley had even arrived. He'd have better luck arguing with a post.

"Wee little thing, though, you never could hold your drink." George crouched down and took Alfred's face in his hand. "Handsome dog, huh. Look at you."

Alfred wagged his tail.

George lavished attentions on the dog, roughhousing and getting him riled.

Ainsley had half a mind to tell the truth, but George gave the dog a final pat and said, "Downright strange of you to name the dog Alfred."

"I didn't name him."

"Two of you. Always..." George trailed off, eyes glassy. "Always doing whatever it was you two did. Fighting. Whispering.”

Alfred circled around George and nosed his palm.

“That's enough.” George pushed the dog away. “Always was an odd one, Alfred. Funny. Him and Umber both.”

“Umber?” Ainsley had never noticed anything unusual about Umber, a knight some years older than them. He'd been quiet, but never rude or awkward. Just withdrawn. People had chalked it up to losing a hand.

“Oh, definitely. I mean, Alfred I always suspected, but Umber. Well. We *knew* about Umber.”

Alfred slunk away from George.

Ainsley gave the dog a pat on the head. “Knew what?”

“That he was a pervert. That's how he lost his hand, you know. Got caught giving his cock a pull.”

“Christ, George, if that makes someone a pervert, you're the worst of them. Surprised you've got any hands left.”

“Pulling it behind the weapons shed, watching the lads wrestle.”

Ainsley rolled his eyes. “Seems like thin evidence.”

“Aye, well, wasn't the first time he'd been found out doing something like that. They started with a finger. When he ran out of fingers, they took the whole hand.”

He straightened up. “I could use a drink.” He left George outside and got himself another drink. Maybe it would ease his boredom and discomfort.

He tried his best to brag and carouse with his friends, but they didn't find any of his exploits in the Otherworld particularly impressive. They didn't care about finding shards of ancient relics or surviving the intrigues of Court.

The story of the bell finch impressed them the best. They seemed to like that he'd turned the weaknesses of fairies back against them.

“Counting seeds? That really works?” Michael asked, maybe too eagerly.

Ainsley shrugged. “Worked on her, didn't it?”

“I thought that was vampires, though, counting things,” Curtis countered.

George pointed out, “Mmm, but they're both unnatural things, aren't they? Iron works on all sorts. And silver, sometimes.”

“Either way, if I'm ever up against one of those things, I'll take steel over a handful of seeds any day,” Michael said.

The other knights chorused their agreement.

Ainsley stood, claiming a headache and the need to sleep. They teased him but let him go without any real difficulty.

“Ainsley!”

He turned back.

“What about your dog?” Michael asked.

Alfred had remained with the knights. He panted happily and his tail swished lazily against the floor.

"He'll find his way back when he's ready." He didn't think Alfred was the sort of dog to come when called and he didn't want to embarrass himself arguing with the hound in front of the others.

He returned to the tent to find Rue already tucked inside his bedroll. He stripped and sidled up to him.

The fairy huffed at being woken and rolled over. "Thought you'd be out later."

"Mmm."

"And come home drunker."

Ainsley butted his head against Rue's chest.

Rue slung an arm over his waist and pulled him closer. "Sleep?"

"Sleep."

Sleep avoided him, though. He tossed and turned until Rue demanded to know what had gotten him worked up. Without hesitation, Ainsley immediately regurgitated every thought and feeling he'd had since seeing the women outside the bathhouse.

Rue took in all the information without a peep, laying on his side with his head resting on his arm. Finally, when Ainsley told about what had happened to Umber's hand, Rue said, "You'd think he'd have stopped doing that where he could get caught."

"That's not the point!"

Rue closed his eyes, stretched delicately, and nestled back against his arm. "An ill-timed joke, my love. Forgive me. I hoped to lighten the mood."

"Easy for you to joke, you're not..." The rest of the thought eluded him. He wanted to accuse Rue of having nothing at stake, but he had as much at risk as Ainsley.

"Envy I well understand. Our love should be as freely displayed as any other. But this other thing, this...agitation. Nervousness. Whatever it is. I don't understand that."

"I'm afraid."

"Of what, though? You've warned me thoroughly away from any topic that might give us away. We have privacy within these walls. No one can see or hear us. Alfred cannot tell anyone. You've demonstrated that you can pretend not to love me in the public eye. What do you think will happen?"

"I don't know. A thousand things." He drew his knees to his chest and rested his forehead on his knees. Endless scenarios played in his mind, all of them unlikely. No one would barge into their tent or sit outside of it, waiting for a breeze to ruffle the flaps enough to let sound escape. Rue had meticulously minded himself in public, especially since his attempt at sharing with Alfred; he would never accidentally place his hand somewhere suspect. And Ainsley's nerves frayed as soon as he heard an interloping voice, no matter what they were doing.

Rue sat up and wrapped his arms around him. His voice came, rough and quiet, and made the hairs on Ainsley's arms raise. "If the stars misaligned and shone misfortune upon us, if unfriendly eyes did witness what they would call sin...what then? You think I would let anything happen to you? I went to battle against trolls mounted on war-cats, you think I quiver at the idea of some mortal on a horse?" He pressed his lips to Ainsley's cheek. "For you, I would fight every knight in the realm without flinching."

The words should have comforted him. "But Alfred—"

"Ainsley, if I had wanted Alfred dead, he would be dead, not a hound. But Alfred is your friend and, given how unfavorably you took his transformation, I'm glad I let him live. If he had turned his weapon towards you, it wouldn't have mattered how badly you thought of me afterward, I would have killed him."

The declaration weighted heavily on Ainsley.

"I enjoy your company too much to ever have it taken away by any hand but your own."

In the middle of thinking that he didn't know what he would do if anyone tried to hurt Rue, Ainsley realized he did know. He would uselessly stand by, shaking and pleading. He would watch with his guts in his throat. "I want to go home."

"And where do you call home?" came the cautious question.

"I. Back to Wolfwood. I want to go now."

"Before the tourney?"

"Yes."

"Ah. Well. If that's what you want..." The fairy trailed off wistfully, leaving some unspoken desire hanging in the air.

"You don't want to go." The idea that Rue would want to stay in Triviai didn't exactly make sense.

"I should have liked to see you compete. And I should have liked to see you do it with my ribbon."

"I can't—"

"Oh, you'll brag endlessly of your lover among the Fair Folk but can't twist the truth a little more and pretend it's her ribbon?" Rue teased. He moved away from Ainsley and rummaged through his pack for a while. He produced a ribbon. "It's yours, whether you compete or not."

With the ribbon between his fingers, Ainsley knew he had to compete. "Fine, but we'll go right after."

"Whatever please you best."

He could feel embroidery under his fingers. "I can't see it."

"Inspect it upon the morrow."

A whine escaped him before he had the sense not to act like a child.

Instead of conjuring a light, Rue kissed his cheek. "You woke me up." He huffed.

"Wounded as I am, I should be resting, sweet knight. Even now, I...Oh, such a weak constitution...I might even faint." Rue pretended to swoon into his bedroll.

His antics provoked a smile. Ainsley nestled in beside him. Little pleased him more than when Rue fooled around. "How is—" Ainsley began.

"It's healing. I'll keep you apprised of any changes."

The preliminary jousts for Ainsley's camp began the following day. He donned his armor and Rue fastened the green ribbon so that it showed prominently. A closer inspection in better light showed sprigs of parsley embroidered in the silk. Rue had grinned when Ainsley had gaped at the design.

"The herb did you so many favors last time. I thought you might need it."

Given that more than a year had passed since his last tilt, he fully expected to be unhorsed by every opponent. He reconsidered as he took better stock of the other knights in his camp. Maybe he'd do decently, given that some of the knights had too many years and at least two had horses they couldn't manage.

"Impress me, Ainsley, and I'll consider writing you a song."

A stallion screamed a few yards away.

Ainsley watched as the horse broke free of the squire holding his reigns.

Clover flicked one ear and Hadley let out a snort that sounded nervous to Ainsley's ears.

Alfred barked.

Ainsley glanced over and the dog barked again, wagging his tail and circling around them.

Rue reached out to give the dog a pat.

Alfred immediately dropped into a slinking crouch and bared his teeth.

When he noticed Ainsley watching, Rue asked, "Haven't you got somewhere to be?"

They parted ways, Rue and Alfred towards the stands, and Ainsley towards the other knights. Alfred would have swept at the tilts, likely. He'd unhorsed nearly everyone he'd ever come across.

As he waited for his turn, he couldn't stop himself from scanning the crowd. He spotted him easily enough: gray-skinned, finely dressed, and in the same spot every time, with enough room for another person left on either side of him. Alfred proved more difficult to track. The hound would pop up here and there, sometimes circling around a particular knight, other times pacing about in front of the stands.

Michael yanked on Ainsley's ribbon. "Oh, so she's real? Or did you learn to stitch that yourself?"

Ainsley's face went hot. "She's real."

"Fairies are little, aren't they?"

"Not all of them."

"But littler than humans, right?" Michael asked. "Figure that's the only way for you to find a maid that isn't head and shoulders taller than you."

He gave Michael a mild shove. Once he would have argued that most women were in fact shorter than him, but the need eluded him now. "What about you? Is someone cheering for you?"

"A whole gaggle," Michael boasted. "If I wore a ribbon for each one, I'd look like a Maypole."

The image made Ainsley chuckle.

In the distance, a stallion let out a terrible shriek.

Ainsley and Michael rolled their eyes. Bringing a stallion to a tourney was one thing but bringing a horse that couldn't be managed was another.

"God help whatever whelp got stuck squiring for Ivan," Michael pronounced.

"Is that Ivan?"

Michael nodded his head. "He ought to know better than to bring that thing anywhere *near* another horse."

"Christ, do you remember—?" Ainsley began.

"Oh! That bay mare of Richard's! The beast went after her so badly we all thought you were next!" Michael recalled.

Ainsley had felt badly about it afterward, but as soon as he'd seen Ivan's stallion charging towards Richard's palfrey, he had fled. The horse had been frothing at the mouth and shrieking. "The son of a bitch bites, you know. I didn't want any part in that."

"Oh, no, I'd have been running right along with you."

They traded old stories back and forth, waiting for their turn. Talking helped stave off nerves, but once Michael was called, Ainsley started to grow anxious.

Michael performed well but tweaked his shoulder in the last round. When Ainsley pointed him towards the tent that the healers had set up,

Michael shrugged off the suggestion.

When it came time for Ainsley to joust, he swung into Hadley's saddle, gave her a pat on the neck, and checked the stands for Rue one last time.

This time the fairy had people closer to him and seemed to be speaking with some of them.

Sweating under his armor, Ainsley fidgeted on his horse. Would Rue think badly of him if he lost? And, conceivably worse, it would hurt. He didn't relish the memories of the times he'd been unhorsed. He'd broken ribs and even bruised his tailbone once. One time his foot had gotten caught in the stirrup when he'd fallen and Hadley had almost trampled him.

He worried so much that he almost missed the mark to charge. He kicked Hadley into action and lowered his lance, his heart thundering and his stomach churning up acid into his mouth. The impact of his lance against the other shield rippled up his arm. His nerves settled, too, as he hadn't met with any extreme pain or humiliating loss. He had done this so many times growing up that it only took him a few rounds to puff out his chest and lift his chin.

It took him three matches before he unseated an opponent. Once he had, he couldn't help but strut around between matches. He fell easily back into bragging with the other knights, remembering exactly what it was like to be eighteen and full of himself. They applauded each other, jeered at the losers, and soothed each other's egos when one of them lost.

Ainsley didn't win any prizes, but he did reasonably well. Better than a lot of others, and damn decent considering how long it had been since he'd tilted.

He peeled away from his friends when the matches ended to find Rue.

Alfred found him first, barking and circling around him.

He patted the dog and sought out the fairy.

Rue sidled out from among the crowd carrying something he hadn't had in the morning. He flashed a grin at the people with whom he'd been sitting and headed towards Ainsley. He once again tried to pat Alfred but yanked his hand back before the dog could snap at him.

"What's that?"

Rue tied the coin purse to his belt. "We've been invited to join the lord and lady of Davenport for their meal."

"We have?"

"Mmm."

"Why?" Ainsley demanded.

Rue shrugged. "She likes to talk. I lent her my ear."

"And what's that?" Ainsley nodded towards the coin purse.

"I placed one or two bets."

"One or two? That's it?"

Rue gave him a smile better saved for when they were alone. "At least one or two. Come, you'll want to scrub up before we join them. I can smell you from here."

The fairy headed towards their tent.

Ainsley hurried after. He couldn't tell if he'd impressed Rue or not and badly wanted praise. He wanted Rue to admit that he wasn't as useless as he seemed, that he wasn't delicate and in need of protection.

Rue didn't offer anything to that effect. He conjured a fire, set a pot of water to heat, and tugged on one of the leather straps of Ainsley's armor. "This needs to go."

"Did..." Ainsley began. Directly asking his opinion felt pathetic.

"Hmm?"

"What did you think?"

"You placed well."

"I know I placed well. What did you think?" he pressed.

Rue checked the water and dipped in a rag. "Are you going to undress?"

Scowling, he stripped, took the rag, and washed himself.

Rue gathered up his clothes, shook the dirt out of them, and gave his underthings a rinse in the hot water. "Have I told you how abominable it is that you don't wash your clothes?"

"I wash my clothes."

"Not nearly often enough."

"We haven't all got entire wardrobes full of things we don't wear," Ainsley snapped.

"Would you like them? I can send for them."

He thought of the diaphanous tunics, skin-tight hose, and slippery silk robes that Rue had waiting for him in the Otherworld. Beautiful and striking as he was, Rue would look gorgeous if he'd had the confidence to wear anything that left his scars visible. "You know I'd look ridiculous in them."

"I don't know that at all. I am very willing to let you try them on and find out." He wrung out Ainsley's linens and spread them out to dry.

Ainsley gave himself one last scrub to make sure he hadn't missed any particularly sweaty areas. He ducked into the tent to fetch his other set of clothes.

Rue followed and tied shut the tent flaps.

"I can't see—"

"What's to see?" Rue asked. A hand skimmed up Ainsley's back.

He reached around and curled his fingers around Rue's hand, drawing his arm around himself.

Rue settled both arms around him and placed his chin on top of Ainsley's head. "You performed admirably. If every threat in the world came mounted on horseback and bearing a lance, I'd count you safe and sound."

Ainsley snorted.

"It appeared that you enjoyed yourself better with your friends today. Do you still want to hasten back home?"

"I..." He hadn't thought about it. "I don't know. Ask again after the melee."

Rue hummed a non-answer. He kept his arms around Ainsley. "I understand a little better now, this custom with the ribbons. I think I'd understand all together if I could have told anyone that I gave it to you." He slid his hands down Ainsley's side and pressed a kiss to his shoulder. "I'll settle for declaring my love in private for now."

"For now?"

"Such worry clouds your brow, I can hear it in your voice. Let me take those worries away."

"Might be impossible."

"Will you deny my attempts at reprieve?" Rue asked. "So many ways there are to ease the burden you carry." His hands moved even lower, fingers digging into Ainsley's hips. "The calm will burn away like morning mist, but while it lasts, you'll mark it wonderful. Let me, my love, grant me one chance."

To hear him plead like that made Ainsley fidget, filled up with squirming desire. He badly wanted to turn and press himself against Rue, but when he tried, the fairy held him firm.

"Grant me permission, Ainsley."

"Yes."

Rue knelt, his hands sliding down Ainsley's thighs as he went. He pressed a kiss to the swell of Ainsley's rear.

He flinched, not exactly sure how he felt about what he thought Rue might do next. The intimacy of the idea overwhelmed, no matter what they'd done together before.

He felt a little puff of air against his skin as Rue snorted.

"Turn around then, if you're so worried."

Ainsley turned and took a step back. "I. I'm sorry, it's just—"

"Shh, plenty of time to try plenty of things when you're ready. Come back over here, unless you think I can turn into a frog as well."

The jest effectively killed the unease that had bloomed in Ainsley's belly. He moved back towards Rue.

This time the fairy kissed his belly.

Ainsley leaned into that kiss instead of flinching from it.

Rue placed kisses all over, on his hips and thighs, on his belly and even trailed his tongue across Ainsley's skin here and there. Before Ainsley could beg for anything, Rue wrapped a hand around Ainsley's length and began to leave kisses there, too. He used his lips and tongue with maddening slowness. Any slower and Ainsley might have lost interest, but Rue managed to string him along so that the frustration was exquisite instead of upsetting.

Need got the better of him though, and he begged, "Please, Rue."

The fairy drew back. "Please what?"

"I want to spill."

"Not yet."

Ainsley didn't know what to do with that answer.

"Don't worry, love, you'll get there. Just not yet." Rue pressed another kiss to his hip, comforting more than carnal, then returned to his slow, steady attention to Ainsley's length.

The longer it lasted, the less control Ainsley had over himself. He began to thrust hard and in earnest, his fingers knotted in Rue's hair. He came undone when he spilled and let out a hoarse cry. It wasn't until that powerful rush faded that Ainsley realized how firmly he had gripped Rue's hair.

He released the other man, who sat back on his heels and wiped his mouth. Ainsley tried his hardest to fit his thoughts into a coherent sentence. "I...was that...Should I not have done that?"

Instead of answering, Rue took Ainsley by the wrist and urged him into a kneel. His hand shook, his grip infirm.

"Rue?"

"Had I wanted you to stop I would have made it clear." His words came out unevenly, his breathing ragged.

Ainsley wanted better reassurance. He had horribly disheveled Rue's hair and the need to fix it came over him. He couldn't though, no matter how he smoothed it. The style would need to be taken out and redone entirely. "I'm sorry."

Rue brought his other hand to Ainsley's mouth and murmured, "Taste this."

Unsure what he'd find, Ainsley touched his tongue to Rue's hand to find it coated with seed. He hadn't expected it and he fought his instinct to recoil. He wrapped his hand around Rue's wrist and licked a larger swath of it clean.

Rue let out a small, sweet laugh and pressed his mouth to Ainsley's. "Such a fine thing you are, my love, I'd keep you by my side forever."

"You mean that."

"I mean it."

Forever. For a human it meant decades, but what did it mean to one of the Fair Folk? Rue had already lived longer than any of Ainsley's grandparents. Forever, to him, might mean centuries. It could mean a thousand years. A thousand years with a man who didn't trust him, that he didn't trust. A thousand years of hoping Rue didn't fall into a melancholy or start to drink again and knowing that it would someday happen again.

He couldn't make himself believe that Rue would always be sober and lighthearted. Rue had never tried to sell that story, either.

Ainsley knew how to handle those things better now. Maybe the next time would be easier.

Or maybe it would be worse. But it would be better than sending Rue away to face the next time alone.

"Hawthorne Gilrhys Escher."

Rue's face twisted at the sound of his true name. Pain, fear, betrayal flooded over each feature.

"I love you. All of you, as you are."

The fairy waited, tense. Waiting for some command.

"That's it, no orders or demands. I love you, your true self."

"What a sentiment, dear heart. Did you have to scare me half to death in the proclaiming of it?"

"I think I did."

Rue snagged him around the waist and dragged him into an embrace. He buried his face in Ainsley's shoulder. "It's a secret thing, that, not meant to used so."

"How do you know?" Ainsley asked. "You've never loved anyone before. Maybe fairy wives and husbands go to bed cooing each other's true names."

"I'd be willing to bet that most who wed among the Fair Folk never reveal such a thing to each other."

Embarrassed that his declaration had gone so awry, Ainsley sulked, "So tell me not to do it again."

"I'll beg you to do it again. By all the stars, Ainsley, I've never been so loved."

They knelt together, clasped in each other's arms, for a while longer. Eventually, Ainsley voiced, "We were invited somewhere."

"Then we should go."

"One more kiss."

Rue gave him three.

They joined the lord and lady Davenport at their banquet table. Dozens of others joined them as well, some of them knights and some of them spectators. A cheer that Ainsley had in no way expected went up at the sight of them. He looked over to see a grin on Rue's face. He greeted lords and ladies as though he'd known them for dozens of years. They greeted him just as warmly.

"How did you make such friends?"

"You win enough to bets to impress but not enough to fleece them. Throw in a handful of pretty magic tricks and enough flattery to sicken even Tadgh—and you mortals are easy to flatter! I should have found more sporting prey..." He glanced around the diners and found something that made his eyes flash. "Now there would be a true hunt."

Ainsley followed his gaze and found that it had lighted upon the king. At the sight of Jannes, Ainsley's stomach did the same star-struck somersault it always did.

"Would you like him, dear heart? I could get him for you so easily." The question came so quietly that Ainsley almost mistook it for his own thoughts.

"Shh, with that," he scolded when he recovered from the suggestion.

"These words are for your ears only, you needn't fret. In a crowd no one will notice."

Still, having Rue whisper those sorts of things into his ear wouldn't end in anything good. "I said shh."

"Whatever please you." Rue peeled away from his side and went to speak with Lord Davenport.

Ainsley followed. A few people stopped him to praise his performance in the jousts and wish him luck in the melee tomorrow.

One young lady batted her eyelashes at him and asked about the lady who'd given him his ribbon. "Is she your true love, Sir Ainsley?"

"I'd be tempting the fates if I said yes."

"Did she watch you tilt today?"

He had to say, "No," no matter how he wanted to brag that his lover had watched and praised his performance.

"Such a shame. She's lucky to have someone like you."

He grinned. "I'll let her know."

"Ainsley!" Rue waved him over to a pair of empty seats. He had a cup of wine in his hand already.

The sight shouldn't have sent such a wrenching nausea through Ainsley. He clamored to Rue's side.

The fairy appraised the look on his face. He took another cup from the table and handed it to Ainsley. "Two, we agreed. Or would you prefer something else?"

Two. A perfectly reasonable number of drinks to have, especially given the relative weakness of mortal wine compared to that of the Fair Folk.

Rue waited, utterly still but somehow looking dejected.

To ask him to never drink again wouldn't stop Rue from drinking, but it would make him hide it. Ainsley couldn't see denial spelling anything but disaster and mistrust.

Ainsley nodded. "Two." Perfectly reasonable. And it was only mortal wine.

Rue gave him a small, terse smile.

The restraint needed to keep his hand from reaching over to squeeze Rue's arm almost alluded him. He tried to think of some way to offer verbal reassurance, but they all sounded like warnings instead of comfort in his head.

Lady Davenport interrupted their uncomfortable quiet. She placed her hand on Rue's arm and said, "Your Highness, His Majesty wishes to make your acquaintance."

"Whatever for?" Rue asked.

"Visiting royalty often do us other the courtesy of greeting our monarchs," she explained. She cast puzzled look Ainsley's way. "To pay their respects."

"Do they now? Am I required to pay something?" Rue asked.

"I..."

"Lead on, my lady. I'll deign to look upon your mortal king."

When Lady Davenport nodded and turned away, Ainsley jabbed Rue in the ribs and hissed, "Stop that."

Rue widened his eyes and placed a delicately posed hand to his chest. He looked the picture of a sweet and innocent prince come to tour a foreign land and desperately unsure of their customs. "Have I offered offense?"

"You can't just use questions to pretend you don't know what you're doing."

"You think me so callow? Have I done something to cause you to think of me so poorly? I would make amends for any misstep, Sir Ainsley, if you require it."

Ainsley rolled his eyes and prodded him to follow Lady Davenport.

"My lady, can you tell me how I should greet the king?" Rue sidled up to her.

She gave Rue several quick notes on how best to greet Jannes. When they arrived before Jannes and Aurelia, it became immediately clear that Rue had asked so that he could do the opposite of what she had advised.

He gave no bow, not even at the neck, when presented to Jannes. He did not lower his eyes or soften the haughtiness of his expression.

"May I present His Majesty, the King," Lady Davenport announced. Her eyes darted towards Rue and her face paled at the sight of him so undeferential.

"Jannes," Rue said.

Ainsley nearly jabbed him again.

Rue availed himself of an unoccupied seat beside Jannes. "I'm told you sought an audience with me, mortal king." He leaned in, resting his chin on his hand.

"I sought...!" Jannes began.

Lady Davenport mumbled several fragmented sentences.

"Your husband invited this creature here?" Jannes asked.

She stammered so badly that Ainsley took pity and intervened, "To dinner, yes, Your Majesty, but Rue comes to the mortal realm as my...traveling companion."

"Surely not my only purpose here, Sir Ainsley," Rue drawled.

The initial flare of irritation and worry faded and left Ainsley with a wicked idea. Whatever game, whatever intrigue Rue now played at could be played in more ways than one.

"Of course not. How terrible of me to forget. Your Majesty, my friend seeks songs. His dearest hope is to return to the lord and lady of the Western Court and play for them all he collects from far and wide across the lands. If you had a harp, he could sing you the sweetest song ever heard by mortal ears."

The turning of tables did nothing to upset Rue. Instead, he grinned, leaned back in his seat, and announced, "Oh, yes, fetch me my harp and I will sing. Such an enchantment my song will weave that any other song will be ruined for all who hear it."

Jannes cleared his throat. "Maybe some other time."

Rue sipped his wine. "If you seek not songs then what would you have of me, o king?"

"Visitors from the Otherworld are a rarer sort of creature than what we usually host in these lands."

"Oh? And what are the common ones?"

"Vampires, demons, werewolves," the king listed with a bored wave of his hands. "Base things, all of them, and foul."

"We have precious few of those things in my realm. Never have I met even one. Though I think I might like to." He glanced at Ainsley.

"Count yourself lucky," Jannes told him. "I wonder if the fairy folk will prove pleasanter."

"Pleasantness to the senses is not always the same as pleasantness to one's health or spirit," Rue pointed. "Ainsley, are you going to sit or just stare at us?"

"I haven't been invited."

"Did you expect it hand-delivered and sealed?" Rue asked. He plucked a blade of grass from the lawn beneath them. He curled in his fingers with a sweeping motion around the grass and then released the grass towards Ainsley. It fluttered to him and wiggled its way between his fingers.

When Ainsley lifted his hand, he found an envelope nestled within. He broke the seal and scowled at the flowery message penned inside.

Rue nodded towards the seat next to him.

Jannes motioned to it as well, seeming to understand that the usual courtesies had been set aside for the madness of a fairy prince.

Ainsley sat. He took a large swallow of wine and then regretted it. He needed his wits about him, especially if some whimsy had struck Rue's mood.

"What is it you want to know about the Fair Folk?" Rue asked.

"Tell me first of your lands," Jannes requested.

With an extravagant gesture, Rue threw an illusion into the air before them. It showed a map, a portion of what Ainsley knew from the maps he'd studied. It showed a vast swath of forest grown around a slender river that ended in a swamp, as well as a sketch of a low, long manor surrounded by gardens.

"Emberhall, the keep of Prince Kerrigan. My father and brother to Queen Corva, lady of the Western Court."

"Impressive—" Jannes began.

"What's that?" Ainsley asked at the same time, pointing to the black patch in the middle of the forest. "Beg pardon, Your Majesty."

Jannes waved a hand.

"A crater, carved out by generations and generations of experimentation and testing." Rue frowned at the map. "Of magic and alchemy alike, that crater has seen its share. My mother once told me that in that very spot did King Abies execute her brother Joran. That, she said, was how she met my father."

Ainsley checked to make sure Jannes had nothing to say before he asked, "Execute him for what?"

Rue waved a hand as though Joran had done something trite. "Being too dangerous. He kept drinking all these...outlandish potions, imbuing himself with elements and magics not meant to live within a corporeal form. They'd lock him up, dry him out, and he'd be guzzling potions and elixirs down again as soon as he was freed." He glanced at the map. "But you asked about the lands..."

He waved a hand and the map changed to show not just the whole of the Western Court but the entirety of the Otherworld. The three courts of the Fair Folk shared a large continent. In the southern sea sat a chain of island labeled the Ever Isles. Above the courts, in the north, a series of caves marked the homes of the giants, which Ainsley had heard about before.

Jannes pointed to the Wilds of the Meridian Court, decorated with sketches of crumbling ruins in some places, but with warnings in most. "What's this?"

"Ah. That, that is all that remains of the Court of the High King of the Otherworld. Once, the kings of the other courts pledged fealty to him, but when he tread on dangerous ground with the Devil—"

"The Devil!" Queen Aurelia gasped.

"Aye, some business about wishes and deals and things gone sour between the Great Beast's realm and ours...the Beast and all his Fallen laid waste to the Meridian Court. Some millennia ago, but neither the Meridian Court nor relations between the Folk and the Fallen ever recovered."

"Still at war with the Devil?" Jannes asked with a little too much gleam in his eye for Ainsley's liking.

Rue shook his head. "No, not at war, no. The Devil left the other courts alone and for that, we've kept the peace."

"Even with all the mages in the university and all the soldiers in Europe, I wouldn't want war with the Devil," Aurelia said.

"We are always at war with the Devil," Jannes pronounced.

Ainsley shifted. He had no fondness for the Prince of Darkness but had rethought a lot of church teachings during his stay in the Otherworld.

"Bad enough that he leaves his bastards all over..." the king grumbled.

His wife refilled his wine. "Oh, let's not talk of such dark things now, we're making merry."

"What's in the Ever Isles?" Ainsley asked. He reached up towards the illusion and his fingers glanced over the spell, making them tingle and it ripple.

"Elves. They keep to themselves."

"Oh." The disappointment in his voice sounded spoiled, even to him.

"Reclusive, not unfriendly. People do visit the Isles," Rue rushed to assure him. He moved his hand towards Ainsley but diverted safely to a carafe of wine and refilled his cup. He returned his attention to Jannes. "Seek thee a history lesson?"

"Your land's monarchs."

With a roll of his eyes and scoff, Rue launched into a brief history of the lords and ladies of the Western Court. He managed to make the extravagant, dizzying splendor of being fairy royalty boring but far above Jannes. His eyes flicked between Ainsley and the king every so often.

He finished his second cup of wine and a servant approached to refill it for him. He waved them away. "I'd have something that suits my palate better."

"Oh?" Jannes asked.

"Wine is dryer here. Water suits me fine for now."

Ainsley gave Rue's foot a nudge with his own.

The fairy nudged him back without looking his way.

The queen asked her husband's permission to be excused after the first course. "My head..."

"Again?" Jannes asked. He diverted all his attention towards her, cupping her delicate face in one of his large hands.

Popular rumor made it well known that Queen Aurelia suffered from debilitating headaches. Theories as to the causes ranged wildly.

"A little rest and I'll be right as rain." She gave her husband a smile.

"There's healers camped nearby, Your Majesty," Ainsley pointed out.

The king waved away his offer. "Every healer in the kingdom's seen her. I'll walk you to our rooms."

She shook her head. "I'll lie down in Lady Davenport's tent for a while. I really do think a bit of rest will do it today."

Jannes kissed her hands and gestured for a maid to attend the queen.

Rue watched them walk away. "This happens often?"

The slam of the king's fist upon all the table startled everyone nearby into silence.

They all turned to look at him.

Jannes demanded, "What business is it of yours?"

Rue assured, "I asked without ill intent."

"Of course," the king growled. "Tell me you weren't about to offer something."

"An offer of aid—"

"Is not aid if it comes with a price."

"Precious few things in life come without a price," Rue told the king, though he didn't say it unkindly.

"And I know enough of fairies to know that your price is not one I would pay. Fairies always grant things in underhanded and twisted ways."

"Always," Rue scoffed. He leaned back in his chair, his arms crossed loosely across his chest. It lasted for only a moment. He propelled himself out of the chair. He waved a hand when Ainsley began to stand as well. "No need to follow."

Darkness soon swallowed up his form as he walked away.

Ainsley remained, scrambling for anything to say. "He...Your Majesty, if it isn't too bold..."

"Speak."

"Rue isn't a bad person. Custom differs in the Otherworld, and maybe some of the Fair Folk delight in tricking mortals, but he isn't like that."

"Oh?" the king asked. He trained his eyes on Ainsley, the green of them glimmering in the light of torches and conjured orbs alike. "How is it that a mortal knight comes to know a fairy prince so well? Common folk embroil themselves with creatures often enough, but usually good breeding keeps noblemen above their sort."

"He saved me." All the ways in which Rue had saved Ainsley could never be explained, not to the king, but they all counted. "In our realm and in his."

"A debt, then, binds you to him." Jannes nodded as though it clarified matters. "Of course, it does."

"It's...it's not like that. He's not holding anything over my head, I'm not coerced into traveling with him. He's a decent man and if he offers aid, it's because the plight of others moves him, not because he hopes to gain from it." The words, too fiercely spoken, came up like vomit.

Jannes appraised him. "You think highly of the creature."

Ainsley shook his head. "It's different than that. It's..." He sighed. "I don't know. He's strange and changeable, but he isn't dangerous. He isn't evil."

The conversation between them died. Neither of them made any effort to rekindle it. The gulf between a king and his knight had never been so vast, Ainsley thought.

Above them, the illusion Rue had cast faded then blew away in scraps when the wind picked up.

The wind continued to bluster. The diners began to scatter when thick clouds rolled in, blocking the moon and stars.

Still, Rue hadn't returned.

Ainsley snatched one of the conjured orbs and carried it with him as he set off to look for the fairy. He headed towards the tents, knowing well that Rue liked to listen in on other people. He called it discovering things and took offense when Ainsley called it eavesdropping.

He kept a lookout for rabbits and crows, too, but didn't think Rue was keen on changing shape with his leg still healing. He stuck to the outskirts, shadowy places where Rue would go unnoticed better.

Before he'd searched half the camp, a woman's scream ripped through the air. Like every other knight in the area, he bolted towards the sound. By the time he arrived, a dozen others had circled around the entrance to the Davenport's tent. He could see a dark stain spread across the carpet laid over the tent floor.

More immediately concerning to Ainsley, several of the king's personal guards had Rue, disheveled and naked, bound in a net of fine metal mesh. He knelt, shuddering and hunched, and Ainsley saw red marks appearing on his skin.

He shoved through the others and began to tear at the net, recognizing the links as iron.

The guards pushed him back. "He killed the queen."

"Don't be stupid!" Ainsley snapped. "There's blood all over that tent and not a drop on him!"

The guards seemed somewhat cowed by that.

It gave Ainsley the chance to throw the net off Rue.

"He tried to fly away. Turned into a bird, he did," one of the guards insisted.

"Aye, and what would you do if you found a murdered woman? Go for help as fast as you could." Ainsley hesitated to touch Rue, scorched as his skin was. The iron net had burned away the glamour he kept over his scars, too, leaving the vast swath of burns visible to all. Of course, the king's guards had iron nets. Iron worked against more than just fairies. "Rue."

Rue remained kneeling and bent over, but his posture loosened. Into the ground, he panted, "Sir Ainsley, finally your turn to save me."

A quick look around revealed a pile of clothes some yards from the tent. Rue must have spied the blood and taken wing. Must have.

Instead of going for the clothes, Ainsley threw his cape over Rue. He placed a hand on his head. "Are you going to be alright?"

He didn't answer.

Without moving from Rue's side, Ainsley glanced inside the tent and wished he hadn't.

With her throat ripped so thoroughly that Ainsley saw bone, the queen lay sprawled on the tent floor. Blood splashed the tent walls and soaked deep into the carpet. The front of her gown had been torn open, though Ainsley didn't know if that meant she'd been violated, too.

He didn't want to know.

A bit of vomit pushed at the back of his throat and he forced it down. He kept himself firmly between Rue and the guards. His hands possessively clutched at Rue's shoulders.

Lord Davenport, pale and sweaty, mopped his face with a rag. He had one arm around his wife, who had her face covered with her hands and turned into her husband's chest.

The crowd around them chattered, loud and frenzied, until suddenly it went silent.

Jannes didn't have to shove through anyone, they all parted for him. He didn't look like a king just then. He had his tunic unbelted and his hose sloppily tied. A stain down the front of his hose suggested he'd been mid-piss when he'd heard the screams.

He bellowed when he saw his wife, a wordless, curdling sound that made Ainsley tighten his grip on Rue. He strode into the tent, bloodying his shoes, and began hurling things about. One of the things he threw came too close to Aurelia's body and he screamed again, falling to his knees beside her.

He touched her for a moment, then drew his shaking hand back from hers. When he stormed away, her arm flopped against the ground.

The king grabbed the nearest person and demanded, "What happened!"

"I don't know, sire, I don't. We all came running."

He seized another, demanding answers and tossing aside anyone who couldn't provide them. The fourth he seized, a guard, pointed towards Rue.

"No!" Ainsley shouted. "No, it wasn't anything to do with him."

"That thing!" Jannes barreled forward.

Ainsley sprang to his feet, placing himself between the king and Rue. It felt like tossing a bit of hay before a charging steed. He put out his hands to stop him, though it only made Jannes push him back. "Your Majesty, on my life, I'll vouch for him."

The king gripped Ainsley by his shirt and lifted him off his feet. Magic cracked all around him, magic he had called up with a few harsh words.

"He *can't lie*, he's a fairy," Ainsley insisted. "Ask him anything and if he answers, it's the truth."

Jannes shook him. "By God, if you're lying...!"

Behind him, Rue stirred. He glanced back to find the fairy climbing to his feet, the cloak clasped with one hand. "A fairy cannot lie. I didn't kill her. Put down the knight and I'll tell you what I saw."

Jannes dropped Ainsley, who barely caught himself. "You'll tell me...!" the king raged. "You'll tell me, or I'll rip you limb from limb."

"I left dinner to clear my head. You'd irritated me and I felt badly for the woman. I walked for some time and thought to make the offer to her. Let her make her own choice, I decided."

"You dared—"

"Do you want to know what I saw or not?"

The king quieted, but still seethed. All around him, magic lashed through the air. It said more than words ever could.

"I walked towards the camp, asked directions, and spied a man, head down, unsteady on his feet. Filthy, too. Drunk, I thought, so I gave him a wide berth. I passed him and some moments later, a woman screamed. Lady Davenport, I think. The man I'd noticed ran. Away, though, not towards the sound. I took wing—"

"Took wing," Jannes echoed.

"I became a crow. I thought to follow him. As he fled and I changed, someone threw a net over me and dragged me over here." He cast a baleful look towards the guards. "Had I not been so detained, the man would be yours by now."

"Was this man a creature, too?"

"Perhaps. Pale and dark haired. Disheveled. I cannot say whether he was human or not."

Jannes threw back his head and let out one last horrible scream. The magic he'd conjured knocked several people aside and set fire to nearby tents. He panted, his broad chest heaving. "Take them both. To the town jail."

"I—" Rue began.

"Now!" Jannes hissed.

The guards and several on-looking knights rushed in.

The stance into which Rue settled and the way he curled his fingers worried Ainsley. The man had gone against things fiercer than mortal guards. He'd kill them all, or turn them into beasts, or work some other terrible curse on men who'd done nothing but obey their king.

Ainsley grabbed on to Rue's arm. "Let them take us. Please."

Rue surveyed the guards. "I'll go, but not without my clothes."

One of the guards scooped them up.

Another gave Ainsley a rough shove forward, hard enough to make him stumble.

Before Ainsley had righted himself, Rue lunged forward, slamming a palm into the man's chest. The blow burned a hole in his leather jerkin and knocked the man on to his ass.

The others around them leveled weapons towards Rue, but it was he who delivered a warning. "I go because this king acts out of grief and because Sir Ainsley has asked me to. I am a prince of the Otherworld and we have gone to war over less. Tread carefully."

Ainsley edged between Rue and the weapons. "We'll go, we will, but don't make this difficult."

"Then go." One of the guards nodded towards Ilseworth.

The group made their way forward, all of them twitchy and uneasy.

The town had one jail cell beneath the market hall. Manacles hung from the walls, but the guards didn't bother to chain them. They tossed in Rue's clothes, gingerly ushered in their captives, still nervous around Rue, and locked the door.

Ainsley remained still once the door closed, unable to see in the absolute darkness of the stone chamber.

A cozy, golden glow gave some relief as Rue hung an orb in the air. He tousled Ainsley's hair and stroked his cheek, then stiffly knelt to gather his clothes.

"How's your leg?"

"Changing shape didn't do it any favors, but it's not opened again."

"And what about your skin? That iron..."

"Mmmm. That I could have done without." He straightened and began to don his clothing. He had to brace himself on Ainsley a few times while he pulled on his hose. "I could do without all the iron in this place."

"Does it hurt you even from this far?"

"Too close, too small a space. It...it fouls the air."

Ainsley took the orb from the air and surveyed the cell. He selected the corner farthest from the manacles to rehang it. With a gesture, he called Rue over.

The fairy folded him into his arms.

It felt like permission and so he crumpled into the embrace.

"Come sit."

They eased into the corner together and Ainsley burrowed deeper into Rue's arms. The sight of the queen so thoroughly murdered remained in his mind's eye. The gleam of bone and deep, tacky red of her blood. He hadn't ever wanted to see the queen's breasts, he'd never thought about her in that way, but now he saw nothing else that her naked, blood-spattered breasts.

She had children, two little ones who wouldn't understand.

And Jannes! What madness would befall a man who had seen his wife so?

"Was it a man?"

"A man as you are or a man as we both are?" Rue asked.

It took Ainsley some thinking to puzzle out his meaning. "Was he human?" he clarified.

"I do not believe so. He had uncommonly fair skin and when he ran, he moved in a way I have not seen a mortal move."

Unbidden, the image of a vampire ripping out the throat of Aurelia came to him. Had she felt each ravage? Had he slaughtered her while she slept?

Or maybe it hadn't been a vampire. Demons tended towards unnatural paleness, a trait from their father.

Or maybe it had been an anemic werewolf or a white-skinned member of the Fallen, or something else altogether. All the different types of creatures had never been accurately captured and confusion with the nomenclature had to do with it. Devil's spawn, fallen angels, and the denizens of Hell all shared a name and confusion often arose when finding the difference between ghouls, ghosts, and wraiths.

The thought of all of this sickened him. He pressed closer to Rue as though the fairy could offer him something better.

Rue locked his arms around him. "A horrible thing."

"Horrible," he echoed.

Beneath his cheek, Rue's chest moved more shallowly than it should have. The iron labored his breathing, perhaps, or the stress of recent events coupled with his injuries new and old. When Ainsley asked after his health, he said, "I'm tired, my love."

"Then go to sleep."

"I don't want to."

Ainsley straightened up a little. "Why not?"

No answer came. Perhaps Ainsley hadn't needed to ask. Rue had never pretended to be unaffected by the things he'd done as a solider, just better accustomed to the aftermath. Maybe a slaughtered woman, unarmed and innocent, disturbed him more than the slaying of enemy soldiers and bandits.

"I." The word hung in the air, barely breaking the silence. "Ainsley, I went to offer her help. If I hadn't dallied so long fuming about her husband, if I hadn't stopped to spy outside the tents of others..."

"You couldn't have known."

"But if I had made haste."

"Rue, there are dozens of people camped here tonight. Any one of us might have saved her if we had been closer, but none of us were. Not her guards or her husband or the sworn knights of her realm. We all failed her."

"You do me a kind turn, Ainsley, but you do not ease the ache in my heart."

He pressed a kiss to the fairy's temple. "I'm sorry."

Sounding miserable and desperate, Rue whispered, "I want a drink."

"It won't help."

"I want it anyway."

Ainsley crouched before the fairy and cupped his face in his hands. "If you must have it, my love, I won't stop you and I won't think less of you for it."

Rue sniffled and turned his face into one of Ainsley's palms.

"But consider the price. You've done wondrously these past months and I think you're happier for it."

He sniffled again and wiped his nose on his sleeve.

Ainsley kissed his forehead and didn't offer any other advice.

Rue scrubbed at his eyes.

The numb misery of what they'd seen soaked into them as they waited for someone to return. Eventually neither of them could remain awake any longer. Beneath Ainsley's cloak, they twined together and fell into uneasy dozes.

They both jolted awake when the cell door slammed open.

Rue threw out an arm in front of Ainsley's chest as soon as his eyes opened.

Two guards bearing torches stared at them from the doorway.

Jannes loomed behind them, clutching a grisly prize.

"You say you cannot lie," the king declared.

"I cannot," Rue confirmed.

"I have no reason to believe that."

"'Tis well known about fairies." Rue didn't manage to keep the condescension from his voice.

Ainsley scooted away from Rue.

"If you wish to test it, send the guards away and I'll grant you three questions."

Jannes waved away the guards.

Rue stood. "Any three questions you ask, I'll answer without twists or evasions, so long as you swear not to tell a single person what you glean." He offered his hand.

Jannes shook his hand.

"The deal is made," Rue declared at the meeting of their hands, his voice tinted with magic.

Jannes yanked his hand back. He rubbed his palm against his hose. "Why did you come to Triviai?"

A banal question that made Ainsley's heart speed anyway.

"I had to bring Ainsley back."

The normalcy of the answer made Jannes scowl. "And why did you stay?" the king pressed.

"I hoped to reconcile with the lover I had wronged."

Jannes bared his teeth in the semblance of a smile. "A lover," he scoffed. "What lover?"

Ainsley had expected the question as soon as Jannes had sniggered but hearing it and knowing the answer still made him flush all over. His hands grew clammier and he wanted to press his hands over his ears and hide his face. Any other time Rue could have twisted out of the truth.

Carefully, Rue asked, "Is that your third question?"

Jannes's eyes narrowed. Hesitance had betrayed them, especially when Rue had answered so easily before. "Name your lover."

"Ainsley." Rue pronounced his name with warm pride.

Surprised disgust showed itself on the king's face. The answer must have satisfied him that Rue couldn't lie, though. He lifted the severed head he had brought with him and shoved it into Rue's face. "Is this who you saw fleeing last night?"

"No."

Jannes threw the head so hard that it dashed against the wall beside Ainsley.

He scrambled away from it and grabbed on to Rue's arm.

"You will bring me the head of the one you saw," Jannes told him. "Or—"

"Or nothing, o mortal king. A threat moves me not."

Jannes rounded on Ainsley. "You. Knight."

Ainsley's voice wavered and he couldn't stop shrinking behind Rue. "Your Majesty?"

"Take your damned creature and fetch me the thing that killed my wife. Fail and this is the last quest you'll ever have as a knight of my realm."

"I'd do it without threats, sire," Ainsley reminded meekly.

"Go."

Rue strode out but Ainsley couldn't go. He had long esteemed his king and he hated the way Jannes looked at him now.

"Sire," he said.

"Go," the king snarled.

Rue turned back and tugged at his hand. "Come along, gentle knight. We must find Alfred."

The camp had suffered greatly between last night and the morning. Many had fled and the charred remains of Jannes's wrath fluttered about the ground. The table from last night had not yet been cleared and showed evidence of animal plunderers.

Alfred waited for them at their tent. He let out an anxious whine and nosed Ainsley's palm when he arrived.

"It's alright, Fred."

He gave a weak wag of his tail.

Ainsley scratched behind the dog's ears.

Rue clasped his hands behind his back and stood square with the dog. "Sir Alfred."

Alfred's head swung toward him.

"Your king has tasked Ainsley with finding the queen's murderer. Your assistance would not go unrewarded."

The dog lowered his head and hunched his shoulders.

"Can we set our differences aside for this?" Rue asked.

The serious regard with which he addressed the dog would have made Ainsley chuckle any other time. Now, it made him add, "Please, Fred. The queen's dead."

The dog let out a quiet harrumph.

Rue accepted it as agreement. "Come, Sir Alfred, we must find something that has the killer's scent. Ainsley, take down our camp, prepare the horses."

Rue returned with a bit of blood-soaked carpet in his hand and scrape on his cheek.

Ainsley didn't need to ask what had happened. What remained of the tourney camp raged with rumors and vitriol. He'd heard no less than four knights swear to cut down any creature they came across. Ainsley sincerely hoped their anger would fade and that unnatural folk would have the sense to hide for a while.

"Ainsley."

"Hmm?"

"I have erred."

The somberness of his tone made Ainsley worry. "Drinking?"

He shook his head. "I bound your king so he could not repeat what he learned, but I did not consider things carefully enough."

"I don't follow."

"The guards listened outside the door when I named my lover."

"Oh." It should have affected Ainsley more. He should have felt something. Anger, terror, anything more than mild irritation.

"I know you counted this a grave secret. I had no intentions to lower you so in the eyes of your peers."

"It wasn't your fault."

"It was."

Ainsley sighed. "I don't hold you accountable for the eavesdropping of others. Have you what you need to track our quarry?"

Rue nodded.

"Good. The sooner we find him, the sooner we can leave this place behind."

The fairy regarded Ainsley warily. "I thought you'd be angrier."

"I..." Ainsley glanced around the camp. The life he should have lived. The one he should have wanted. "When accusations fly, I'm sure my knees will shake. But I knew I couldn't stay. I knew the lie wouldn't hold."

Rue nodded. They didn't speak much as they followed Alfred.

The hound led them westward with his nose to the ground. Every so often, he glanced back to check if they still followed, but other than that, his pursuit remained absolute.

Half a day's ride brought them deep into the thick woods around Ilseworth. Alfred paced in front of the mouth of a small cave. He glanced anxiously between them and the cave.

Rue dismounted and held up a hand for Ainsley to wait.

Ainsley ignored him. He swung out of the saddle and drew his sword.

The fairy frowned at him. "I'd have you wait."

The mouth of the cave stood about five feet tall and three wide; they would have to stoop to enter it. A small bit of sunlight came through the canopy overhead, but not enough that they could see inside the entrance.

"You should make a light," Ainsley answered.

With a grumble, Rue produced a light and held it up.

Ainsley linked hands with him and tugged him forward.

Leaves and other bits of debris littered the floor of the cave. Something had disturbed it, but whether it had been an animal or their quarry Ainsley couldn't tell.

Rue held the light up high and strengthened it. More light revealed a dark smear of something on one of the rocky walls. He brought the light closer and nodded towards the smear. "To my eyes, that resembles a hand."

Ainsley held up his hand near the stain for comparison. "Maybe."

Further inspection of the cave showed more and increasingly smaller smears on that side of the wall. Something had shuffled along this side, turning aside all the litter from the floor. Thirty feet back, they found the end of the blood and the disturbances, but no creature to accompany it.

Ainsley knelt before the widest cleared swath on the ground. He picked through the litter and found a few things of interest. A scrap of fabric, a coin, and a crumpled strip of paper.

The coin Ainsley recognized as a spark, one of the coins commonly used by mages. He smoothed out the crumpled strip of paper and found it covered in lines of arcane runes. The paper had blood on it, long dried, and ragged edges.

"Do you know what this says?" Ainsley asked, holding the paper up to Rue.

The fairy shook his head. "Should I?"

"I thought you could, uh...comprehend any mortal tongue?" Ainsley said. "Wasn't that it?"

"'Tisn't a mortal tongue, that. Arcane runes weren't designed by mortal hands."

Ainsley sighed. "Our best chance is the university. Either this creature is a mage or had dealings with one." He knotted his fingers in his hair and tugged. It hurt, but not enough. He tightened his grip.

Rue crouched beside him and untangled Ainsley's fingers from his hair. "Sweet thing, what has you so distressed?"

He grasped too hard on to Rue's hands, but the other man didn't pull back or flinch. "I want to go, Rue. I hate it here."

"I'll take you now."

"No, we've got to find who did this. Find the right one or they'll be taking heads from every creature they come across." He couldn't get the severed head Roderick had shoved towards them out of his mind. Nor could he rid himself of the image of that head dashed against the wall. He didn't want that fate for anyone else.

Rue kissed Ainsley's knuckles. "Then let us make haste."

Ainsley nodded.

Armed and armored men filled the roads as they hadn't before the tourney. Every group they came across demanded to know Rue's business in the mortal realm and every time, Ainsley roared at them. He made it no secret that Jannes himself had set them on this quest and promised that the honor would be his.

Bluster usually cowed those who eyed Rue suspiciously. Drawing his sword dissuaded the rest.

When they came to an inn, Rue offered to pay for a night indoors. Ainsley had avoided inns since they'd left the tourney grounds. He wanted to be away from people as much as possible. Those they'd encountered on the road did nothing to change his mind.

Today, Rue insisted, "I won enough to coin to pay for it and so badly do I yearn for a soft bed."

"Soft beds you won't find in a place like this."

"Softer than the ground, surely."

Ainsley conceded the point with a shrug.

"Ainsley, please. A bed is all I ask."

He couldn't stop himself from regarding the inn suspiciously. "Then a bed you'll have. Tonight, at least."

Rue exchanged coin for a bed and a meal. He paid with an odd sort of strutting that Ainsley took as pride. He had asked a lot of questions about coins lately. Teaching him the names and values of the coins had provided something else to think about so Ainsley had done so willingly.

"Are you showing off?" Ainsley asked quietly while the innkeeper had his back turned.

"If you are watching and there are others about, I am almost certainly showing off."

Despite being in full view of the entire inn, Ainsley beamed at him.

"Especially in this realm. It would be one thing if you held one of my peers in higher esteem than you do me, but if I paled in your eyes compared to a mortal, well...could shame kill a man?"

"Oh, now you're being mean!" Ainsley's smile widened. He couldn't help it and didn't want to. Smiles had been hard to find recently.

The innkeeper glanced between them.

After a hot meal, Ainsley and Rue retired despite the earliness of the hour. Rue expressed his disappointment that the inn lacked a bathhouse; the innkeeper had claimed their tub was currently being used for laundry and thus couldn't be rented.

"Every inn has a bath at home," Rue sniffed.

"We aren't at home."

Rue caught Ainsley's face in his hands and kissed him. "Hearing you call my world home is so precious to me."

Ainsley had his doubts that the Otherworld would ever truly be his home, but he didn't share them. He kissed the tip of Rue's nose. "I had such a fantastic trip planned for us..."

"You *have* one planned, my love. A delay means nothing when we will have so many years together."

High spirits had found the fairy again it seemed. For a few weeks following the queen's murder, gloom had hovered over them both. Ainsley had put it aside a little sooner, but he had traded it for bitterness instead of cheer.

Each distrustful look cast towards the fairy had heaped onto Ainsley's bad mood. He worried that rumors had spread about Rue's connection to the queen's murder and about their involvement together. It wouldn't take long for it to become well known at court, which meant that any knight they passed might have heard.

Rue embraced him and turned his face into the crook of his neck. It made some of that bitterness melt away. A feather-light kiss on his cheek dissolved even more of it.

He went willingly when Rue pressed him into the mattress and left kisses on his lips.

There and nowhere else did he kiss Ainsley. His hands didn't move to explore any part of Ainsley's body. He slid down Ainsley and rested his head on his chest. His chin pressed into the bones of Ainsley's chest but not enough to hurt. He fixed his gaze on Ainsley's face.

He combed his fingers through Rue's hair. "Is a bed all it takes to make you this happy?"

"I love you."

"I love you, too."

"Tell me what you planned for us," Rue requested. "Where will we go first?"

"Oh...I don't know anymore. I think I want to change a few things."

"Why?"

"Because we're different than we were. Apart and together," Ainsley said.

"Tell me where it is that calls you now."

"The sea."

Before the sea had appealed to him casually, but now he could think of nothing else. So many stories spoke of the vastness of the ocean, the lull of its waves, the treachery of its depths. He had to see it, wade into the waters, and know that the enormity of the seas could swallow him.

"Months upon these waters fair, months so far from you, my dear," Rue sang quietly. "To your bed I must return, for your arms I'll e'er yearn..." He pushed himself up to kiss Ainsley. "But there's no kiss so sweet as sea-salt spray, no way I can stay ashore when the sea calls to me til my heart grows sore."

"Oh, no sad songs, Rue," Ainsley insisted.

"How do you know it's sad? You didn't even let me sing a whole verse."

"I've never heard a song about the sea that wasn't sad."

"The Blue Lady does tend to work in ways so few can understand. Her love is vast, but it is different," Rue admitted. "What will we do at the sea? Make love in the sand?"

"Sounds scratchy."

"Make love on the rocks, then? The sea spray making our skin glisten."

Ainsley snorted.

"How about in a boat?"

"I might get seasick. I've never been on a boat."

"In small and cozy seaside villa with gossamer drapes and feather pillows. The crash of the waves coming in time with the movement of our bodies."

Ainsley chuckled. "Sort of sounds like you have something on your mind, Rue."

"In hypotheticals only at the moment, my gentle knight. Tonight, I want you to tell me of all the wondrous things we'll do together."

He sounded so peacefully earnest that Ainsley shared what he'd planned for them. Rue listened as though Ainsley told dreamy tales of romance. He indulged every suggestion Ainsley made and never once said he didn't want to go where Ainsley planned.

Eventually, their conversation moved away from travel. Rue crawled beneath the covers and nestled up to Ainsley's side.

The door had no lock and Rue had cast no spells to keep their conversation from the ears of others. Somehow, Ainsley didn't care. A few months ago, he would have jumped at every footstep that fell in the hallway, he would have flinched away from Rue each time he heard another person's voice but not tonight. It didn't matter to him anymore what reputation he garnered. It didn't even matter if the rumors reached the ears of his family. Not right then, anyway. Someday, he knew, this could come back to bite him in the ass, but he couldn't make himself care.

The night offered a wonderful respite from the rest of the world.

The morning didn't treat them as kindly. The innkeeper and his wife scowled at them. Ainsley assumed he and Rue hadn't been discrete enough. They had stayed up all night giggling and kissing without any effort to keep their voices low.

Or maybe that Rue was a creature provoked their ire enough.

Either way, they left that inn behind them. Knowing he'd likely never set foot within those walls again comforted Ainsley.

Rain came around midmorning, at first a gray and miserable drizzle that soon turned to a full-blown tempest.

Alfred nearly lost his mind barking at nothing and racing around in circles.

Ainsley and Rue dismounted and led their horses to lower ground off the road. Mud squelched its way into Ainsley's boots and spattered his hose. The rain soaked through to his skin. As uncomfortable as he was being soaked, the violence of the skies above him preoccupied him more. He spied no shelter and lightning cracked perilously close to them.

He could taste it in the air. He flinched each time lightning flashed or thunder rumbled.

Rue took his hand. An unpleasant tingle slithered up Ainsley's arm and made his teeth ache. He recognized it as magic but couldn't fathom its purpose.

Rue told him, "I can keep us dry or I can keep us safe, but I haven't the strength to do both for long. I hope you don't mind that I elected to keep us safe."

"Mmm, well, as long as you can make me a fire later, I suppose I can forgive you."

Rue curled his fingers tighter around Ainsley's. "Cheeky."

Ainsley grinned.

Sodden and chafing, the mud sucking at his feet, Ainsley did not find the walk pleasant in any way. He resigned himself to the rain and thought of warm and dry things. Unbidden, thoughts of Rue's cousin came to mind, thoughts of watching him dance through the rain. It felt like it had happened a thousand years ago.

"Can I tell you something?" Ainsley asked.

"Always."

"You mustn't tell anyone."

Rue nodded gravely.

"I sort of miss Tadgh."

Rue laughed. "You and I might be the only ones to ever utter such a sentence."

"I wonder how he's doing. Do think he misses us?"

"I...I don't know. Perhaps. He is a creature of strange whims, but I think he gets lonely."

Courtiers had always surrounded Tadgh and their circle had never lacked merriment, but Ainsley didn't doubt Rue's guess. "He's sort of peculiar about things, isn't he?"

"Which things?"

"Touching people."

"He actually quite likes to touch people. Sometimes. It's the kind of touching that bothers him."

Ainsley nodded. He'd known that. He didn't understand, exactly, but he didn't understand most things about Rue's family.

"He simply isn't inclined to such things in the same way others are. So affected by the Blue Lady he is. If he wasn't the Crown Prince, it wouldn't chafe him so. Everyone wants to cozy up to the throne and they think getting him into bed is the best way to do it."

"We shouldn't go to Court," Ainsley declared after a few quiet moments passed.

"We shouldn't," Rue agreed cautiously.

"But maybe Tadgh could come to visit us. I can't imagine he's doing anything important."

"You should word it exactly that way when you invite him," the fairy suggested.

An impossible amount of water had soaked them, but when the rain passed Ainsley almost wished it hadn't. Being wet in the rain had somehow been pleasanter than being soggy in the sunshine. His clothes bunched and twisted horribly. Wetness had lent a stronger quality to their scent, too.

He smelled like a sodden sheep.

Soon enough they came to an area the rain hadn't touched. No clouds loomed in the distance and the sky above shone a perfect, clear blue.

Rue had kept a hold on his hand the entire time, though the tingle of his magic dissipated. He tugged Ainsley to a stop. "Let's eat and dry off."

If they pressed, they could make it to the university by nightfall and he told Rue as much.

The fairy didn't release him. "It won't take long. An hour, maybe less. We'll still arrive tonight." He pressed the issue with an earnestness Ainsley hadn't expected.

"Is this about more than getting dry?"

"I am not ready to face an entire city of humans so quickly. I would savor a little more time without such scalding looks. And one more chance to hold you in my arms. I suspect you might not be so relaxed with so many eyes on us."

Christ, he really didn't miss a thing, did he? All the times Ainsley had thought Rue unconcerned with and far above the way people around him acted, he'd noticed everything.

"We might need more than an hour then."

Rue snorted.

They spread out their clothes and tent to dry in the midday sun. Rue cast a spell to aid in their drying, then began to rummage through their packs to find a quick meal.

Sunshine and a soft breeze soothed Ainsley. He rested his head on Rue's shoulder when the fairy sat beside him.

Rue handed him a strip of dried meat.

What a sight they'd be if anyone passed them.

"Magic is hard for humans?" Rue asked.

"Uh..."

"You have to study it."

"Oh. Yes. I think, uh, I think some of us are better than others. Fairies don't have to study magic?" Ainsley asked.

"Have to? No. Each of the Fair Folk have their powers, strengths and talents...That which we lack we can supplement with learning, though that depends more on intelligence than our other magics."

Ainsley nodded. It confirmed what he'd gleaned. "Could I learn fairy magic?"

Rue opened his mouth then closed it. "Hmm." He tilted his head and glanced over Ainsley.

Ainsley did not like being studied like that all. He felt like a bug before a cat. "What?"

"Do you want to learn magic?"

"I...No, I don't think I'd be any good at magic. It's a lot of studying and reading and I, uh, well, I don't want to end up inside out."

"Mmm." Rue slid an arm around Ainsley's shoulders and pulled him close. He kissed his curls. "I said intelligence, lovely thing, and there are many kinds. The monks who serve the White Woman cast magic that requires neither runes nor incantations."

"Oh."

"We can visit them if you like. They reside in a monastery along the Tadgh."

Ainsley began to gnaw on his strip of meat. "Maybe. Probably."

Rue trailed his fingers along different parts of Ainsley's skin. He hummed softly.

Alfred, who had mostly ignored the two of them for days, huffed and let out a small yip. The rain and the way he'd shaken himself off had ruffled his normally sleek fur.

Ainsley fished out another strip of meat and tossed it his way.

The dog snapped it up and wagged his tail as he chewed at it.

"He seems in a better mood," Rue mentioned.

Alfred didn't cast a baleful look towards Rue or growl.

"Maybe he's tired of being a dog," Ainsley suggested. "Or maybe being a dog has made him nicer. Dogs are usually nice if you're nice to them."

In the full light of day, Ainsley could see that the burns left by the iron net had completely healed. Not a single scar remained from the ordeal. For Rue's sake, Ainsley counted it a blessing.

"You know all those clothes you don't wear?" Ainsley asked.

"Decide you want them after all?"

"No." He twined his fingers with Rue's. "I want you to wear them."

"I..."

"At least once. Even if it's only for me."

Rue squirmed, which he almost never did.

"Are you blushing?"

The fairy's cheeks darkened further. He gave no answer.

Ainsley pecked him on the cheek. He shoved the rest of the dried meat into his mouth and rummaged through his pack for a comb. He undid the braids in Rue's hair, which had been ruined by the rain, and combed out his pale gray locks.

He'd watched Rue braid his hair dozens of times, but apparently watching wasn't enough to learn. He fumbled his way through and ended up with results worthy of a child.

Unbidden and deeply unwanted, the image of Roderick gripping Rue's severed head by his pale hair sent a roll of nausea through him.

He sighed and combed his fingers through to undo the braid. "I like your hair down, anyway."

"Do you?"

"I like it no matter how you wear it," Ainsley confessed.

Rue turned and snagged Ainsley around the waist. He pulled him into his lap and kissed him. He held him close like that for some time, tender instead of amorous. Rue's affections had run warm instead of hot lately, which Ainsley didn't mind at all.

They tarried a bit, then pulled apart and dressed.

Alfred trotted happily alongside the horses.

As the light faded, Rue replaced it with a few of his conjured orbs. They bobbed and danced above him as he rode, bathing him in a silvery light.

They passed through the gates of Fallclere, the city which surrounded the university. Rue did not draw so many stares as he did elsewhere and they ones he did draw lacked the same hostility. The doors of the university would be closed to visitors at this hour, so they stabled their horses and took a room at an inn in the shadow of the university.

The common room of the inn buzzed with a quantity of magic Ainsley hadn't felt since he'd been in the Otherworld. He had visited the university in his travels with Sir Richard and hadn't noticed it then.

Rue glanced around the inn and appraised the patrons. "Mages, most of them, I assume."

Ainsley gave the crowd a cursory glance. "Likely." He noted a relative dearth of creatures. Mages, even with all their pretention and obsessions, tended to treat creatures a little better than most. It had to do with their curiosity and urge to study all things magic, Ainsley assumed.

He spotted a familiar face, handsome and ochre, but when he looked that way again, she had gone. He squinted and scanned the crowd again.

"Ainsley?" Rue asked.

"I thought I saw someone."

"Anyone of note?"

He shook his head. Now he didn't even know if he had seen her. Wishful thinking, maybe. Even as brief as their interaction had been, Ainsley knew Sama better than he knew any other mage.

They tucked themselves into a quiet corner of the inn. People still eyed Rue as he ate. Some openly stared.

The fairy pretended not to notice their stares or the snippets of conversation he must have been able to catch.

Ainsley caught a word or two every so often, but usually it was nothing more than the word 'fairy.'

Alfred rested his head on Ainsley's lap, begging for scraps.

Ainsley gave them over and stroked Alfred's ears when the hound returned to beg for more. "There isn't anything left for you."

Rue offered a bit of crust to Alfred.

The hound's eyes darted towards the crust and he took it without a snap or a snarl.

Rue risked giving him a pat on the head and Alfred tolerated that as well. A small smile worked its way onto the fairy's face, and he lifted his chin.

"I didn't know you wanted him to like you so bad," Ainsley said.

"He's your friend, Ainsley, of course I want him to like me."

Ainsley wanted to take Rue's hand. He settled for nudging his foot under the table. "Tomorrow we'll go to the university, I'm sure someone there can help us. At least with reading the spell." He didn't know what they'd do from there, but it was a start.

Rue nodded as though Ainsley had pronounced something wise.

"Knowing what kind of spell it is should help. Might even be able to point us towards the mage who wrote it. I mean...maybe. Do you think so? I think so."

The fairy glanced up. "I have faith, Ainsley."

"Faith in what?"

"A great many things, dear heart," Rue answered.

Ainsley ate a little more and tried to organize his thoughts. He didn't manage to organize much. As they walked to their rented room, Ainsley glanced back to find that Rue had gone. He searched the inn and spied a bit of pale hair disappearing around a corner.

He hurried after him and found Rue pulled into a corner with the same person Ainsley had glimpsed before.

"Hey!"

Sama and Rue turned towards him.

The mage conjured fire and spun towards Ainsley. She pushed Rue behind her. "Stay back."

Ainsley unsheathed his sword. "Release him."

He hadn't expected mages to go after the queen's killer. They generally didn't get involved in much unless they could turn a profit or research something.

Had Jannes put out a bounty?

Utterly unbothered by Ainsley's blade or her flame, Rue placed a hand on Sama's shoulder. "Fear not, Ainsley. She has something she wants to tell me."

Ainsley gripped the hilt tighter. He'd never fought a mage and didn't relish the idea of trying to parry a fireball. "Could be a ruse."

"I'll meet you in our room, fair knight," Rue told him.

Ainsley stayed put.

"Go. You'll hear her shrieks should she try to do me harm."

Sama raised her eyebrows and gave Rue a look somewhere between amusement and concern.

"Go on," Rue urged with a warm smile.

With that, Ainsley sheathed his sword and went to the room they'd rented. He did it with half a dozen glances back and no small amount of trepidation. Once in the room, he paced. He couldn't still himself.

Rue entered some minutes later leading Sama by the hand. He secured the door behind them. With a wave of his hand, he sent half a dozen small golden orbs to light the room.

"What?" Ainsley asked.

"What she had to share I thought would be better shared with us both," Rue told him. "And I thought it would be best if we could assuage her worries too."

"What worries?"

"The good mage is convinced you intend to bring my head to the king, as has been the fate of too many creatures in recent weeks," Rue explained.

At first, he took offense, but the mage looked worse than she had on the road to the tourney. Haggard and pinched. Even now, she positioned herself between Ainsley and Rue.

"Is it that bad?" Ainsley asked.

Sama nodded. "Three vampires missing, at least one of them taken by a knight. Two demons set upon last week and they wouldn't have escaped if they hadn't been together."

Ainsley sat on the bed. "I don't plan on bringing Rue's head anywhere his body doesn't go."

"Will you bring me to your king whole, then?" Rue asked with false and wide-eyed concern.

Ainsley snorted.

"You should go back to the Otherworld," Sama insisted to Rue.

"I cannot yet. Ainsley has been set upon a quest and means to see it through. I remain here as long as he does."

"What could be more important than your life?" Sama demanded.

Ainsley produced the strip of paper he'd found in the cave. "We're tracking the queen's true killer."

"Then track him on your own," Sama insisted. "Being here endangers your friend."

"We traveled the whole way here from the tourney without trouble," Rue said.

She reminded, "Because you traveled with a knight. Any other you came across probably thought the same thing I did. If you go wandering off alone, another one will be waiting to grab you."

The mage's fears had firm foundations, Ainsley couldn't deny that. He'd worried the about same things. "How did you get back here so fast?"

"What?"

"You were at the tourney, but you've been back here long enough to know all the happenings in Fallclere."

A mage on foot couldn't have outstripped two men on horseback, even if they had tarried somewhat.

"I..." Sama faltered. "I know someone who can move between places with more ease than most. He knew well the urgency of the situation. I had to warn people."

Ainsley asked, "He can move between places?" He glanced at Rue.

Rue shrugged. "I brought you between your world and mine, but Folk don't oft move in such ways within a realm. Only between them. I've heard that the Great Beast moves so with ease."

Ainsley looked at Sama. Mages usually looked down on magics other than arcane, but people from all walks of life ended up trafficking with the

Devil if driven to it.

"They beheaded the first creature they came across," she reminded without denying Rue's postulations. "So long as he had dark hair, it was match enough for them. Do you know how many creatures have dark hair? And how quick the descriptions get skewed? It will be open season on all of them soon."

"What do you care what happens to creatures, anyway?" Ainsley asked.

"I care because they're people," she snapped. Her cheeks darkened as she continued, "I am a *healer*. Not that I expect you know what it means, blood-soaked as hands like yours are like to be."

"Ah, peace, good mage," Rue soothed. "Ainsley has proven himself a friend to creatures, not a threat to us."

"I..." Blood throbbed in Ainsley's ears. Sama's accusations pinned him somewhere between shame and anger. He shoved the strip of paper towards her. "I need to know what this spell is. We found it in a cave where the killer stopped."

She took the paper. As she read the runes, her eyes widened and her lips parted. She shoved it back towards Ainsley. "Dangerous magic, that. I've never seen a spell like it end well."

"What is it, though? And can you tell who wrote it?" Ainsley asked.

"I." She looked at it again. "It's a reworked version of Torvel's Cantrip...they all are, but this one's meant for humans, not animals. Torvel was a healer, but he had a queer bent to his work. Rumors said he was half-fey with the way he twisted things." She glanced towards Rue, who seemed to take no offense. "He worked enchantments for crippled men to walk but worked them on a single horsehair they had to keep on their person. He would heal the blind but do it so they'd see things that weren't there, too. His cantrip, well...he used it as a joke, as far as all accounts say. A wicked trick to play on lords who mourned a favorite horse or hound, but he only ever cast it thrice."

Torvel sounded like one of the Fair Folk; that or an absolute madman. That aside, Ainsley had no better idea what kind of spell he'd found. "But what is it for?"

"For bringing dead things back to life."

Ainsley understood why she'd danced around the topic. He stared at her, then looked to Rue. The fairy, he hoped, had more experience with these kinds of magics. He might know what to say, because presently all Ainsley could do was blink.

Rue's face remained unchanged. He scratched at one corner of his mouth. When the other two remained quiet, he looked at Sama and raised an eyebrow. "Well?"

"A horse, a cat, a sow, Torvel cast it on all those things and all the beasts had to be slain again. Since his day, others have tried to fix it but the closest anyone who ever came to having it work right ended up dead. He traded his life for the hound's, although the hound came back more or less fine by all accounts."

"I." Ainsley took the strip of paper back from Sama and stared down at it as though he would be able to read it now. He frowned and seated himself at the foot of the bed. It couldn't be possible. Conjuring a bit of fire or water, healing a wound, or casting an illusion made sense to him, but this? This was impossible. "So." He looked at Rue.

"You believe someone cast that cantrip on a man?" Rue asked Sama.

She nodded. "Someone would have to be desperate to do it, though."

"Desperate and well-versed in magics, yes?" Rue asked. "I assume this is no trifle for students or mages of middling talent. 'Tis a difficult art at home."

"I couldn't cast it, that's certain."

"Mmm." Rue crossed the room and placed a hand on Ainsley's shoulder. "Don't look so sad, Ainsley. It means our search has been narrowed."

Ainsley shook his head. He didn't know what he'd expected to learn in Fallclere, but he'd hoped for something more straightforward than necromancy.

Even the very word made him shudder.

The dead should have stayed dead, everyone knew that. Even vampires didn't spend more than a minute or two actually dead and half of them still didn't take well to the transformation. Even demons couldn't often be persuaded to bring back things that had passed. Rumor said even the Devil himself wouldn't do it. Ainsley had always thought mages far above such types of magics.

"Who would be so desperate?" Rue asked. "Surely mages know each other's business the same as any other guild."

"We've all lost somebody at some point," Sama answered. "I'll ask around and come back tomorrow night."

Ainsley said, "Much appreciated."

Sama moved toward the door and paused before she opened it. "You two should stay out of sight. And if you can't manage that, at least stick together."

"Oh, like sap on treefox's snout," Rue vowed.

When she had gone, the fairy sat beside Ainsley. He put an arm around Ainsley and pulled him close. "Such news would have gladdened you, I thought."

"I don't know anything about necromancy."

"Ah. I know preciously little, but I think this news changes little about our original plan. How many things continue to live when their head is separated from their body?"

The idea of beheading anything made Ainsley swallow. He had avoided thinking about it so far. His throat tightened.

"I can do it," Rue offered softly. "You needn't raise your blade or even watch if it upsets you."

Once Ainsley would have taken offense, insisted that he could slay a beast as well as any other knight. Now, though, he nestled deeper into Rue's arms. "I should be braver."

"Killing has nothing to do with bravery. The most awful of cowards can kill someone. Sometimes the braver thing is not to kill anyone at all. The harder thing, too." Rue kissed his temple.

It sounded like something his mother would say, which did nothing to alleviate the ache in his chest. How badly would chaos spread if they couldn't find this killer? What would become of Jannes and, in turn, what would become of the kingdom?

He tried to turn his thoughts to other things but failed. He sunk further and more firmly into his worries about king and country, the effect of this upheaval on his family, and how much it would ache to leave them behind.

Surely, Rue would bring him back to visit whenever he asked. Last time had been a misunderstanding.

Whether his family would want to see him was another matter, especially once the stories about him and Rue spread.

Distantly, Ainsley became aware of Rue's fingers unlacing his clothing, loosening his belt, and he allowed it to happen. He lacked the will to resist. Whatever the fairy wanted tonight, he could have, but without Ainsley's participation.

Without a word or gentle caress, Rue stripped Ainsley of his garments and lay him down on the mattress.

A sigh escaped Ainsley's lips. His eyes fluttered shut and he put an arm over his face to keep out the light.

Rue leaned over him and pressed him deeper into the mattress. The slither of glamoured fabric against his skin awakened him to the reality of the situation. The fairy kissed his cheek.

If he protested, Rue would pull back. If he even so much as turned away, Rue would stop. Wouldn't he?

Rue withdrew, pulled up the blanket, and tucked Ainsley in. "I'll be awake a while longer, my love, but you should rest."

Ainsley shook his head.

"You won't rest? You look exhausted."

He felt cold and unnerved. Rue had done nothing. He'd never even had intentions to do anything. Ainsley understood that but still, something sat wrong inside him. "Don't go anywhere."

"For once, sweetling, I find myself the restless one. A short walk and I'll return.”

“Rue, please,” Ainsley whined.

“Sama’s warnings rattled you, didn’t they?”

“That they did. The necromancy does nothing to soothe my nerves.”

The fairy stretched out beside Ainsley. “If my love requests my presence, then have it he shall. What strength would I need to resist him?”

“Tell me everything will end well.”

Rue admitted, “I...I cannot promise that.”

“Tell me something else, then. Something that will lift my spirits.”

Rue nestled closer and pressed his lips to Ainsley’s temple. He began, “The Black God witnessed the birth of the Blue Lady and the White Woman. In his heart he felt joy at their creation. Together they made a happy family. When the Green God arose from the earth, he felt joy then, too. They exulted together. The Blue Lady and the White Woman loved this young new god. They doted on him, told him of all the world’s wonders and beauty.

“They laughed together, the three of them. The Green God danced with them and raised his voice in song. The Black watched and found the joy in his heart cooling. He could not dance as they did, feather-light and graceful, and his voice rumbled when he tried to raise it in song. He grew melancholy.

“This did not escape the others. The White Woman brought him warmth and told him jokes, she played her flute for him and held him close. The Blue Lady sang for him and brought him to bathe in the sea, to lay upon the sands and gather wave-worn stones. She told him stories of the heroes to come and the marvels the world would see. The Black God’s heart grew no lighter.

“The goddesses asked, ‘What troubles you, friend?’ and he replied, ‘Our new companion. He is more pleasing, more beautiful, and sweeter than I. He is young and I am ancient. I am tired. I cannot dance or sing. I only exist.’ The goddesses could give no reply to soothe their oldest friend, no matter how they tried.

“The Green God overheard the goddesses speaking among themselves. He went to the Black God and found him lying beside the River Tadgh, buried in the cool mud of its banks. He crouched in the mud beside him. ‘I can teach you to dance,’ he said. ‘Dancing will not mend my heart,’ said the Black God from his wallow of mud. ‘Then I shall go,’ said the Green God, tears in his eyes. ‘I know I have disturbed how things should be.’ He knew that he could not stay and watch the sadness his existence had created in another.

“The Black God could not abide this. As the Green God walked away, he lifted himself and cried, ‘Stay!’ The Green God looked back. ‘Why?’ he asked. ‘Because if I cannot feel joy, I at least wish to see you feel it,’ answered the Black God. 'I have taken your friends,' said the Green God. 'My friends,' said the Black, 'Have taken you. They have your love and I cannot.'

"The Green God returned to kneel in the mud. He took the other god's hands. 'You have my love. But you are greater, calmer, and more beautiful than I. You are ancient and I am barely here. I dance and you do not join me. I sing and you do not raise your voice. Surely my love makes no difference to you.' The Black God, in all his eons of life, had never felt this way before. He had never been so lost for words. He said, 'I cannot dance.'

"The Green God smiled. 'But I can teach you, though only if you leave the mud.' They stood together and washed the mud from their skin in the waters of the Tadgh. They washed each other's skin. The Green God taught the Black God a dance, then, too, but not the kind he had taught to the White Woman or the Blue Lady. From that dance rose the first tree in the Otherworld."

Ainsley had known how the story would end almost from the moment Rue had started to tell it. He gripped Rue by the front of his shirt and pressed his head against the other man's chest. The story hadn't lifted his spirits, though it should have. A happy ending, a sweet one, for the pair of gods.

"What troubles you?"

"Do they love each other still?" Ainsley asked.

"They will love each other always," Rue assured.

Ainsley sniffed.

"I think you are overtired, my love, and burdened by your quest. Sleep would serve you well and I can aid you in the finding of it."

"Don't go."

"I won't go," Rue promised. He slid his fingers beneath Ainsley's chin. "Would you like to sleep?"

"No dreams."

"Only sweet ones." Rue pressed his fingers to his lips, then rested them on Ainsley's temple.

As Rue had promised, Ainsley dreamt of light and meaningless things that night.

He woke to find Rue still beside him and still dressed. Still in his boots even, though the glamour he used to make his hand-me-down garments seem finer had faded.

Rue rolled on to his back and stretched. He opened one eye, saw that Ainsley was awake, and nestled up to him. "Fell ye better this morn, dear heart?"

"Yes." Whatever strange mood had settled over Ainsley last night had gone and he prayed it wouldn't return. He wasn't well suited to weather such unusual emotions. He liked things straightforward. It had been so long since anything in his life had been straightforward.

"Then may I make a request?"

Ainsley nearly told him he could have whatever he wanted, but the fairy conceivably could have asked for anything. "Tell me your request and I'll consider it."

"I want to see the university. I know the mage bid us stay out of sight, but to come so close to the one interesting thing in this realm—"

"The one interesting thing!"

"You, my love, are a person, not a thing," Rue soothed. "Take me to see the university. Magic here is foreign to me and I would return home with a little more knowledge of it, if I could."

"Promise not to wander away."

"I swear."

"And no showing off, either, no matter how flashy the mages get."

Rue's mouth twisted a little. "I'll try."

"Promise, Rue," Ainsley insisted. "Mages like to study things and they like to study uncommon magics most of all. Things are...they are not how they should be right now, and I worry."

"Far be it from me to make you worry more. I'll refrain from showing off."

"Good."

Rue hooked one leg over Ainsley's hips and dragged him closer. "Unless I think some mage has eyes for you, then I might not be able to stop myself," he teased.

Ainsley pressed closer to him. "Wise of you to be concerned. My affections are easily bought with magic tricks."

"Ainsley."

"Walks through gardens and flowers buy me, too."

"You'll hurt my feelings," Rue warned quietly.

"Let me rest in your arms beneath a tree and you'd have bought my heart altogether." He gave Rue a kiss, then pulled back. "Let's go see the university. I won't be a knowledgeable guide, but I'll try."

Rue stayed true to his promise, he remained within arm's reach of Ainsley as they toured the university. The halls, libraries, and workshops were open to visitors so long as they stayed quiet and kept their hands away from everything. Rue struggled with both those requirements. He asked Ainsley ceaseless questions and tried to touch everything.

Only in the laboratories did he keep his hands firmly by his sides and balled into fists. He lingered in the doorway, eying the cauldrons and flasks.

Ainsley peered over the shoulder of a young woman grinding dead beetles in a mortar and pestle.

She noticed him spying and gave him a smile. "Can I help you?"

"Sorry, I didn't mean to bother you."

"You aren't," she assured. "They don't really kick people out for asking questions."

"Oh. Well, then, what are you making?"

"If everything works out, it will be a cosmetic," she said.

"A, uh, a magic one?" he guessed.

"Hair coloring that doesn't wash out as fast."

He glanced back to see Rue barely inside the doorway. "Rue, do you want to color your hair?"

The joke didn't land. Rue's answer was a terse, "No."

The fairy's answer came so sharply that Ainsley returned to the doorway. "What is it?"

Rue shook his head. His gaze danced over the equipment in the room again.

"Alright, well. Let's go somewhere else."

"No, you were speaking with that young lady over there. Carry on."

Ainsley glanced back to see that the mage had gone back to grinding her beetles. "I don't think she'll mind me leaving. Come on." He placed his hand on Rue's elbow and pulled him into the hallway. "Let's go back to the libraries, I think we missed a few aisles. And besides, you'll be able to get more answers out of the books than you've been getting out of me."

"You've answered my questions admirably given your relative knowledge on the subject."

The careful arrangement of his sentence and minuscule pauses as he spoke told Ainsley that Rue had taken the utmost care not to call him stupid. He gave Rue a reassuring pat on the back.

Rue leaned his left arm on Ainsley's right shoulder, a position that indicated comradery more than intimacy. "Perhaps you can answer this, good knight: why are all the books in this place chained to the walls?"

"So people don't steal them."

Rue wrinkled his nose.

"No thieves in the Otherworld?" Ainsley guessed.

"But who would steal a book?"

"Books are expensive."

Rue blinked.

"Oh, that's right, I forgot, you've never had to pay for a thing in your life," Ainsley teased with an exaggerated eyeroll.

Rue leaned on him even harder, bearing down with enough weight that Ainsley sagged.

Ainsley faltered, giggled, and gave the other man a push. "Get off."

"Or what?" Rue snagged Ainsley and put him in a headlock.

Ainsley snorted and wiggled out of the headlock. "You'll get us kicked out, you know!"

Rue swept him up and threw him over his shoulder.

"Rue, really! Before we get in trouble."

Rue placed him back on his feet. "Fine. Take me somewhere to eat. I've grown weary of..." He faltered. "This *dungeon* of a place."

"Of course, my prince, whatever you command." Ainsley gave a mock bow.

Rue placed his hand under Ainsley's chin and lifted him out of the bow. "Never bow to me, Ainsley, even in jest."

He looked so serious that Ainsley had to joke, "What if I knelt instead?"

With a dolorous sigh, Rue drew him in to an embrace.

"What is it?" Ainsley asked.

The fairy shook his head.

"Don't do that. Tell me. Not telling me things gets us in trouble."

Rue tightened his embrace. "My father," he began, then faltered.

Ainsley waited even though they were perfectly visible to anyone who entered the hallway.

"He was angry when I spilled the flask. So angry. It took him so long to put the fire out. I don't know if he was...drunk or punishing me or if he just wanted to watch something burn, even if it was me."

Ainsley had no comfort to give. He squeezed Rue a little tighter. "Let's get something to eat."

Rue stepped back and nodded.

Outside, Ainsley combed the street vendors for something that would make Rue happy, or at least, distract him for a little while. He found a vendor that offered pies both savory and sweet. He paid more than he should have, but only because the vendor had one berry pastry left and he didn't want to risk someone else buying it. He managed to buy it without Rue noticing; it wasn't much of a feat, the fairy still seemed out of sorts.

They brought the pies back to their room. Once Rue had finished the savory pie Ainsley had given him, Ainsley handed him the still-wrapped pastry.

Rue peeled back a bit of wrapper and frowned.

"Oh, I've never seen you frown at something sweet; your heart must be heavy indeed."

Rue set aside the pastry, still mostly wrapped. "I'll save it, if it's all the same to you."

"It's yours, do with it as you will." Ainsley shrugged but couldn't completely hide his disappointment.

As he heaved yet another impressive sigh, Rue flopped back onto the bed. He stared up at the ceiling.

Ainsley lay beside him and rested his head on Rue's chest. "What are you thinking about?"

"I worry you'll think me mad or daft or both."

"Won't know unless you tell me."

It took some time for Rue to answer. He murmured, "Sometimes I want to...to just be a spider for a while. Crawl into a safe, warm little corner and build a web. Wait for food, hope no one clears away my home. Watch and rest and...exist."

"If you really want to turn into a spider you can. You can even sit on my shoulder like you did when you were a crow."

That made Rue smile. He ran his fingers through Ainsley's curls. "What if I crawled up into your curls and ate all the lice?"

"I don't have lice!"

Rue leaned in and inspected his curls. "I don't know, you should let me crawl in there and check. Lice seem to be ubiquitous among mortals." He used his fingers to pantomime a spider's crawl over Ainsley's scalp.

"Oh, and you're all so high and mighty in the Otherworld that you don't get them?"

"*I* certainly don't. Perhaps more common Folk might be so unfortunate, but if one of the royal fey ever had lice or crabs or a hint of pox, I've never been told of it."

"Sounds like bragging."

"I'd rather be a braggart without lice than a humble man with them," the fairy declared and sounded exactly like his cousin.

Rue's fingers worked more firmly into Ainsley's scalp, then migrated lower. Soon enough, Rue had Ainsley turned over on his belly while he kneaded his fingers into his neck and shoulders. He slipped his hands inside Ainsley's tunic, his fingers warm and hard as the pressed into the muscles of Ainsley's back. It hurt, almost, and drew long, deep sighs out of Ainsley.

When he lowered his attentions even more, to Ainsley's rear and thighs, Ainsley had to say, "Now you're teasing."

"Then roll over."

Ainsley hurried to comply.

Rue settled himself on Ainsley's thighs. He made quick work of the laces on Ainsley's hose and nearly made even quicker work of Ainsley himself. Firm, slicked fingers and a handful of kisses had him undone in minutes.

It went so quickly that once he'd spilled, Ainsley blushed and started to stammer an explanation.

"Shh, now." Rue kissed him again.

"It's just—"

"Did you enjoy it still?" Rue asked.

"I...Yes."

"That's all that matters."

Ainsley urged him so that Rue crawled up his body and straddled his chest. They worked together to pull down Rue's hose, their fingers brushing against each other.

Rue looked down at him, a smile on his lips. He brushed a thumb over Ainsley's cheek, then his mouth.

Ainsley kissed pad of his thumb.

Rue's eyes burned as he looked down at him.

Ainsley put his hands on the backs of Rue's thighs and pulled him forward. He took Rue into his mouth.

Rue took control of things from there, having his way with Ainsley in a manner that almost bordered on careless in his need and single-mindedness.

Ainsley felt vaguely used but in the best way possible. He liked it, liked the abandoned look on Rue's face. He liked being the focus of that powerful desire.

After he spilled, Rue leaned in to place a lingering kiss on his lips. His mouth tasted warm and sweet, and his lips were gentle, a far cry from the needful way he'd taken Ainsley's mouth. "Did you enjoy that, too?" he murmured into Ainsley's mouth.

Ainsley swallowed the question and answered with a kiss.

Someone slammed on their door.

They stared at each other, frozen for a moment.

Rue stood first, slowly, and went to the door, conjuring clothes for himself as he went. "Yes?"

Ainsley scrambled into his clothes and to hide any sign of something untoward. He kicked Rue's actual clothes into a corner and smoothed out the bed covers.

"It's me," Sama called through the door.

Rue glanced over and met Ainsley's eyes.

Ainsley nodded.

Rue opened the door.

Sama let herself through the door. "I have a name for you."

Ainsley tried to say something, but his mouth had gone dry. He licked his lips and tried to tame his hair.

Sama glanced between them.

Ainsley's cheeks burned hot.

Rue leaned against the door and rolled his eyes. He mouthed, "It's like you *want* people to know."

Ainsley widened his eyes and set his lips firmly, hoping it would dissuade any further comments.

"I have a name for the mage you seek," Sama repeated.

Ainsley nodded. He gestured for Sama to have a seat on the room's one chair, but she made no move to do so. "Please."

"Lady Marion Duverger."

Ainsley shook his head. "The Duverger family lost their title and their holdings years ago. The..." he trailed off and had to think. "The lord there now is Hamish Russel. One of the queen's brothers. Jannes gave the holding to his brother-in-law for good service in a border campaign, I think"

"Their offense of this family must have been great," Rue said. He leaned against the wall, arms crossed.

"They conspired against the last king. Some say they even tried to have him killed and that it was them that cursed Roderick the Younger with madness."

"Oh, this realm has mad princes, too?" Rue asked, a small smile curving one side of his mouth.

"He cannot even speak. Rips his hair out, they say, and wails all night," Ainsley said.

Rue looked even more amused.

"Roderick...the Elder, not the Younger," Ainsley clarified, "Jannes's father even had them sack their keep. There's been bad blood between the Duvergers and the Stautons for generations, since the Stautons took the throne and broke an engagement with a Duverger maiden."

"So we should perhaps visit this Marion?"

"The castle's in ruins. The whole family fled the country to avoid the axe," Ainsley explained.

"Not Marion, she came back to study magic," Sama said. "Under a false name, it was such a scandal."

"I never heard that."

"It was before you were born unless you've been in the Otherworld for a long time. About forty years ago. And mage gossip tends to stay, you know, with the mages."

Ainsley sighed.

"The castle, then? Even if it is ruins, well, a mage of skill could make that livable, no?" Rue proposed. He glanced at Sama.

She confirmed, "Aye, a good mage could live anywhere in comfort. By all accounts, to have done this spell, Lady Marion must be an excellent mage."

"We'll go first thing in the morning. Or...We'll get directions first thing in the morning."

"I'll get you an old map, the university has plenty of outdated ones. The new ones will only show the Russel keep," Sama said.

Ainsley nodded. After a moment too long, he remembered to say, "Thank you."

"Have you eaten?" she asked.

Rue grinned, then covered his mouth. "Yes, milady, and I have a pastry that still requires my attention."

She nodded. "Good. Well. Good luck. And, honest to God, *hurry*. Before more creatures lose their heads," she urged.

"Of course," Ainsley assured.

"At prime, tomorrow in front of the university," she said, then left.

Rue remained leaning against the wall. He stretched, rolling his shoulders. "In the saddle again so soon."

"Is that a lament?"

Rue straightened up and stretched his arms above his head. "Pfff, I like as not need it after so long idle at Court." He reclined on the bed and retrieved the pastry. He peeled back the wrapper and turned it over in his hands. He sniffed it. "What sort of berries are these?"

"I think he said it had bilberry jam."

Rue took a bite. "This summer I'm going to take you to the fyssberry festival."

"Oh."

"Your fingers will be stained for weeks." He gave the pastry a once over. "This isn't bad. Tadgh might go, he might bring the little princess. It is good luck for children to have something dyed with fyssberries. It will like be good luck for you too, you may be a child still to the Green God."

Ainsley didn't know if he should take offense. "Are they for eating, too?"

"Only if you like to see things that don't exist. Fyssberries grow in a half dozen colors but none of them should be eaten by men who wish to keep their wits. Every weaver, dyer, and tailor will attend the festival if they can. The fields of fabrics drying in the sun, blowing like a thousand banners in every color you can imagine..." He broke off a piece of pastry and offered it to Ainsley.

Ainsley accepted it.

"If we go to the Ever Isles, you'll want lighter clothing. 'Tis hot there. A lot of elves go about in nothing at all." Rue finished the pastry and sucked a speck of jam off his finger. "Prime. Is that an early hour?"

Ainsley nodded.

"To bed?"

"It would be wise."

"I miss our lazy mornings."

"Soon."

Rue kissed him. "Soon," he agreed.

They reached the ruins of the Duverger castle with little incident but a slight delay. They had come across a corpse of what Ainsley guessed to be vampire, headless and strung up in a tree. Ainsley hadn't been able to ride past in good conscience. They'd taken down the body and buried it. Rue had crouched in front of the mound of fresh-turned earth for a while and when he stood, white flowers had circled the grave. Ainsley had given the ring of flowers a wide berth as they'd departed.

He wished he could give the ruined keep the same sort of distance. Half the castle had tumbled down into a heap of stones and wood, remnants of the battle the Duverger family had lost in their final stand against Roderick the Elder.

The burned-out and crumbled remains of wooden structures dotted the surrounding land and brambles had overgrown the road to the castle.

They tied Hadley and Clover a distance from the ruins.

"Fred?"

The dog looked at him.

"Watch the horses. Bark if anyone comes."

Alfred gave a soft *wuff* of confirmation.

Ainsley patted his head.

The hound's tail wagged. He settled himself next to the horses, tail still wagging as Rue and Ainsley headed toward the ruin.

Ainsley kept glancing back.

Rue took his hand. "You're sweaty," he accused.

Ainsley pulled his hand away and dried his palms on his hose. He loosened his sword in its sheath. He wished Alfred wasn't a dog; he was a good man to have in a fight.

Rue took his hand again. "You're shaking."

"I'm *frightened.*"

Rue tightened his fingers. "My knight, you are safe with me."

"Have you ever fought a mage?"

"No."

"Then how do you know?"

"Perhaps now is not the time best suited to shaking my confidence," Rue answered. "Maybe there will be no one to fight. This place...does not smell lived in. It smells of death, and filth."

"Perfect," Ainsley whispered.

Rue drew his bronze knife, released Ainsley's hand, and moved first into the ruin. He stepped over a low pile of stones and ducked beneath a charred beam. He moved like a river over stones.

Ainsley couldn't fathom how Alfred had ever landed a blow on him, let alone two.

Rue breathed, "Old death. And fresh."

Ainsley stayed close behind him.

The wide, sweeping tracks of a robe or gown, or something dragged, marked a clear path for them to follow.

Ainsley drew his sword and reminded himself to breath.

Rue silently picked his way through the rubble.

Ainsley followed less silently, his steps scuffing even when he tried his hardest. He'd forgone his armor in favor of the chainmail shirt Rue had given him long ago, knowing steel wouldn't protect him against magic. He'd never even dreamed of owning enchanted armor.

They moved deeper into the castle and the signs of destruction became less apparent, only scorch marks on the stone and rubble on the floor. As the rubble lessened, the trail became less distinct. The deepest part of the castle, despite the smell, looked habitable. A pile of wood by the fireplace in the great hall, new rushes on the floor, bundles of herbs hanging on the wall.

Well. New*er* rushes. They needed to be changed, and badly.

In what must have been Lord Duverger's solar, they found the source of the smell permeating the previous rooms.

A body, the throat slashed and ripped as Aurelia's had been, but swarming with maggots and discolored from rot.

Ainsley covered his mouth.

"Weeks," Rue murmured. He stepped closer, his head tilted. He moved horrifically close to the body and poked at the cloth and bedding with the tip of his knife. "Bedclothes, I think, and long hair." He slid the blade under something and lifted it. "A necklace. Gold and ruby." All of his pronouncements came whisper soft.

Ainsley gagged, bile flooding his mouth. He couldn't swallow it. His whole body twitched.

Rue turned to him.

He hurried to a corner, braced himself against the wall with one arm, and retched. He dropped his sword. The sound filled the room.

Rue made a soft sound of pity and disgust both. He approached Ainsley with a waterskin then froze.

Ainsley had seen it too and heard a desperate clawing, the sound of nails against floor.

Something else moved in the room. Behind them.

They both stilled, eyes wide.

A creature emerged from beneath the bed, wide-eyed and streaked with filth. It scrambled out, writhing, teeth bared.

Rue positioned himself in front of Ainsley.

Ainsley snatched up his sword.

The creature crouched on all fours in front of the bed, eyes darting around the room. It bared its teeth again and growled at them. It made a tentative movement toward the door.

Rue moved to cut it off.

It retreated.

Dirty, gaunt limbs showed beneath its rags and human eyes glared out from a tangle of black hair.

Brown eyes. Plain, unremarkable brown eyes. No hint of red to show unholy heritage. Its teeth, plainly displayed, lacked fangs to mark it as a vampire.

It had filth crusted on its fingers and face and long, ragged nails.

It backed itself into a corner, wedged as far as it could go.

Rue glanced back at Ainsley. "I can manage, if you like to excuse yourself."

Ainsley shook his head.

Rue nodded and stepped forward. He flicked his fingers toward the creature.

It stiffened. Its eyes bugged. A horrendous shriek escaped its mouth as it tried to move but couldn't.

Rue approached and it started to keen, high and terrible. He grabbed the thing by the hair and bared its throat.

A thick collar of pink scars showed plain on its throat, starting in the place towards which Rue angled his blade.

It stared at Ainsley, howling and wailing.

Crying. Tears streaked down its face, clearing a path in the grime.

"Rue!"

Rue glanced back. "Do you need to leave?"

"Let it go."

"It's the thing we seek," Rue reminded. "I recognize the face."

The creature continued to keen, snot bubbling out of its nose.

"I think it's just a lad."

Rue raised an eyebrow.

"Oh, let him go."

"Ainsley."

"Rue, please, look at him."

Rue looked down at the creature with distaste. He frowned. He released the creature's hair and stepped back. He sighed and put his hands on his hips. "You, thing, can you speak?"

The creature blubbered and squirmed as much as Rue's bonds allowed.

Ainsley sheathed his sword and approached. "Put your knife away."

"No."

Ainsley frowned at him.

"You might be a soft-hearted fool, my love, but I don't have any intention of letting that thing get it's claws in me."

Ainsley crouched in front of the creature. "Your spell will hold?"

"It shall."

"Give me your waterskin."

Rue handed it over.

Ainsley dribbled water over the creature's hands.

It watched, breathing hard through its nose in short puffs.

Normal human hands, thin and knobby from malnourishment, with overgrown nails. Ainsley cleaned the creature's hands and used his knife to pare the nails, for safety as much as hygiene. He wiped the lad's face with a cloth, smearing away layers of grime and old blood around his mouth, as well as the fresher snot and tears.

Rue remained standing, watching with a strange look on his face. "What are you doing?" he asked finally.

"Wouldn't you feel better if you were clean?"

"Ainsley, we're meant to kill this creature, or have you forgotten your king's demand?"

"He said to bring him the creature. And this isn't a creature, it's lad, a human boy."

"Young perhaps, but not a child," Rue pointed out. "And that thing...Ainsley, that thing was dead not long ago. Look at his throat, no man could survive that."

"We'll bring the king the mage's body. She's more culpable than..." Ainsley looked at the creature, which had gone still, but still snuffled.

"A revenant," Rue supplied. "Mindless, likely. Nothing comes back from the grave intact."

Ainsley looked at the revenant. "Are you mindless?"

The creature met his eyes. He swallowed, a labored movement. He wet his lips with a tongue, perfectly pink and human.

His breath stank.

Ainsley covered his mouth. He held up the waterskin. "Are you thirsty?"

He opened his mouth.

Ainsley tipped in a bit of water.

The revenant swallowed greedily.

"Ainsley, your king is *not* a merciful man."

"We'll bring him the mage."

"And what will we do with this thing?" Rue asked.

"I don't know. I don't. I just...We don't know what's left of him. If he acted of his own will or if..."

Rue sighed. "Go to the horses and fetch a length of cord."

Ainsley eyed his knife.

"You'll find the thing unharmed when you return."

Ainsley hurried to fetch cord from the horses.

When he returned, Rue bound the creature's hands, then tied a loose collar and leash about the creature's neck. He addressed the revenant, "This knot will only tighten. It will choke you if you fight it. Do you understand?"

The thing didn't nod or speak, but he looked at Rue the same as he'd looked at Ainsley.

Rue waved a hand toward the creature.

He loosened from the tense ball in which the spell had trapped him. He fell forward to his knees and remained curled on the floor, prostrate before them.

"How, my love," Rue began, "do you plan to get this corpse to your king?"

"We'll need a shroud. I'll...I'll see if there's a cart somewhere, too, or something to make a stretcher..."

Rue nodded.

Ainsley stood.

The revenant moved.

Rue's hand went for his knife.

Ainsley took the leash Rue had fashioned. "Stand up. You can help me look."

The revenant stood slowly.

Ainsley could discern his features better without the grime. Wide-eyed and hollow-cheeked, his age was hard to guess. Between fifteen and seventeen, younger if he was tall for his age. Not likely older. "What's your name?"

Rue scoffed.

Ainsley shot him a look.

"Rude thing you are, asking an enchanted creature its name. Even a dead one," Rue scolded as he riffled through a chest of linens.

Ainsley amended, "What can I call you?"

The revenant didn't answer. He swallowed, the same labored movement as before.

"Well, think while we go," Ainsley proposed and started walking. He kept a hold of the leash but wanted to release it. It felt obscene.

They wandered the grounds but found nothing of use. He could see the spires of Hamish Russel's castle on a hill not too far in the distance. The ruined keep sat on a smaller hill, likely the tallest one available on the property before it had expanded through marriages.

Ainsley went back to Rue, who'd wrapped the mage's corpse in several sheets and bound it with a length of cord. "What if we went to Lord Russel?"

"Hmm?"

"Someone in that manor would have a cart to sell and it's a shorter trip there than to court."

"Very well. Am I expected to carry this?" Rue eyed the mage's corpse.

"We'll lash it to a horse."

"I meant out of the castle."

"Can't you use magic?"

Rue narrowed his eyes.

"You are a Prince of the Western Court, after all."

"You're trying to goad me."

Ainsley gave him a smile. "I'd be so terribly impressed, my love."

"Tender-hearted *and* manipulative. So many faces does my lover have. What stars did the sky see when he was born?" Rue threw his hands over the corpse as though casting a net. A shower of thin, golden lines descended, and he lifted the bundle by those threads.

Ainsley was impressed.

The revenant seemed less so. He moved away.

"Don't worry," Ainsley soothed. "He won't hurt you."

"Don't promise it that, Ainsley."

Ainsley ignored him. "Come on."

The revenant walked in front of Ainsley to the horses, glancing over his shoulders every few steps to look at Rue.

Alfred growled at the creature, hackles up and teeth bared.

The revenant growled back.

"Stop it," Ainsley warned them both.

Rue lashed the corpse to his mount and Ainsley tied the revenant's lead to Hadley's saddle.

He led the mare by the reigns as they made their way to the castle. It felt wrong to ride when the others walked.

Night fell as they walked. Rue lit their way with conjured lights that the revenant regarded suspiciously.

Ainsley offered him assurances that the lights wouldn't do him any harm. He even plucked one from the air and showed it to the creature.

"See? Just a light."

The creature let out a rasp of a word. "Star."

Ainsley grinned. "A star! It does look like a star, doesn't it! Rue, did you hear that!"

"Don't make a pet of the thing, Ainsley. Your king is not a merciful one."

Ainsley stopped walking. "Why are you being like this?"

Rue stopped, too. "Because you don't get attached to things you are leading to the slaughter!"

Ainsley looked at the revenant.

"Your king will kill it, or it will kill something else and I'll be back where I was, a knife to its throat."

"Then what should I do?"

"Let me kill it before losing it will break your heart."

Ainsley shook his head, not able to believe the callous way Rue spoke.

More softly, Rue explained, "You are a sweet and kind and you love broken things, and dangerous ones. You allied with witches and a werewolf and walked for miles with a *dragon* around your arm."

"And none of them hurt me."

Rue sighed.

"I'm not a good knight, Rue. I can't kill things, especially not ones that haven't hurt me."

Rue approached. He took Ainsley's hand. "I think that makes you an excellent knight. You go on being an excellent knight, a beautiful thing of love and light and mercy. I am not that sort of man. I'll be swift. I can...I can put it to sleep, a sleep that even a blade won't wake. Let it die during a pleasant dream."

"No."

"It's better than your king will give."

The revenant made a noise, a quieter version of his keening from before.

"It killed two people," Rue reminded.

"Fewer than you have. Only one more than I."

Rue sighed. He kissed Ainsley's knuckles.

They resumed walking.

They arrived late at the castle, but not too late to find people awake at the inn. Ainsley left Rue and the creature outside, explained the situation to the innkeeper, and left with directions to the wainwright.

He returned to Rue to find him with his knife leveled at a local and his foot on the back of a second.

The revenant crouched on the chest of a third man. He had an ear between his teeth.

"The king has put out a reward for the head this creature," Rue explained.

"And it will be my reward," Ainsley told the men. He drew his sword to emphasize the point. "Unless you really wish to disagree? Three on three is better odds."

The man put up his hands. "I didn't know, milord, I didn't know they belonged to anyone."

"Go."

The man went.

Rue let up the other man.

"Get up," Ainsley told the revenant.

The creature stood and stepped off the man.

"And spit out that ear."

The revenant shoved the ear into his mouth and swallowed.

Ainsley grimaced.

"Hungry," the creature rasped.

Ainsley glanced at Rue.

"Oh, two words, you've the thing nearly tamed. Do you think it would eat out of your hand?"

Ainsley took Hadley's bridle and walked away. "We've a wainwright to find."

"And a bath!" Rue called as followed.

They procured the cart from a wainwright upset at being bothered at such an hour. He quieted his complaints when they overpaid for the cart and agreed to purchase his grizzled old nanny goat to pull it.

Once they had the corpse in the cart, Ainsley returned to the inn and asked after a bath and stabling their animals. He gave Alfred a few strips of jerky and asked him to watch over things in the stables for him.

Ainsley overpaid for baths and a room, too, but this time to buy the innkeeper's compliance with letting a fairy and the revenant stay in his inn. Ainsley swore the creatures presented no danger a dozen times.

Ainsley scrubbed up quickly, the less soiled of the two of them, and then Rue took his turn, reheating the water to his liking.

After he bathed, Rue reclined on the bed and said, "We should sleep in shifts."

Ainsley peered into the bathtub. Not too dirty at all. "Come here," he said to the revenant.

He hesitated.

"Come get clean."

"Oh, Ainsley," Rue sighed.

Ainsley ignored him. He gestured for the revenant to come over. He untied his hands.

Rue sighed even louder and when Ainsley lifted the collar over the creature's head, he said, "If it lays a hand on you—"

"He won't," Ainsley said, keeping eye contact with the revenant.

Brown eyes met his, quiet and complaint.

"Undress, get in."

The revenant obeyed, stripping off his rags to show a painfully thin body marked here and there with the same thick scarring as his throat. It looked like something had gnawed at him. On his chest he had a newer wound, still dark and angry, with sutures still in. A clean line, not ragged like the others.

"I can take those out." He'd done it on Rue's leg not too long ago and knew these stitches needed to be out weeks ago.

The revenant ran a hand over the wound. "Heart."

"I'm not going to hurt your heart. Just take the threads out." Ainsley pointed to the black silk threads.

He touched the threads.

Ainsley took the small fruit knife he'd used on Rue's stitches. He held it in the fire for a moment, then waited for it to cool.

The revenant winced and whined as he cut and pulled out the threads but didn't fight the process. Bits of paper came out along with the stitches.

"Now in the bath," Ainsley said.

He stepped into the tub gingerly and sank in. As soon as he sluiced water over his skin, dirt clouded the water.

Ainsley handed him the soap.

He understood what to do with it and set to scrubbing, maybe a little too viciously.

Ainsley washed his back for him and tried to help him with his hair.

In the end, he had to cut out the worst of the knots and mats.

Ainsley gave him a shirt and pair of hose.

They'd have to see about shoes somewhere in the morning.

Ainsley looked him over. He smiled at him. Skinny and scared and perhaps slightly mad, but he looked like a youth, not a monster.

The revenant smiled back, an odd baring of his teeth, like he hadn't done it in a while.

"What can I call you?" Ainsley asked.

He shook his head.

"I've got to call you something."

"No name."

"Ever?"

He shook his head. "*No*," he insisted.

"If he's so chatty, ask him what's got him killing women," Rue proposed.

The revenant looked at the fairy. "*Makes me.*" His voice didn't sound right. Thick and labored. The scars on his throat must have gone deep.

"So much for mindless," Ainsley said.

Rue sat up, "Who makes you?"

"*Her.*"

"The mage?" Ainsley guessed. "Marion?"

The revenant nodded.

"How?"

"Name," the revenant answered. He touched the wound over his heart. "Heart."

Rue glanced at Ainsley.

Ainsley shrugged. "I know precious little of magic." He dug the spark they'd found in the cave out of his purse. "Is this yours?"

"Spark." The revenant's eyes focused on the coin. He touched it. "Spark..." He took the coin out of Ainsley's fingers. He squeezed it, eyes closed. He pressed his fist hard against his face. He dug his teeth in.

"Hey!" Ainsley said. He put his hand on the revenant's arm.

He shouted and pulled away. He hit himself in the head, loud enough that Rue stood up.

"Back up," the fairy said.

"Think!" the revenant insisted. He hit himself again.

Ainsley approached.

Rue grabbed his arm and pulled him back. "Leave it."

The revenant dropped into a crouch, then to his knees. He hit his head hard enough against the floor to draw blood. He collapsed into a loose heap, then sat up all at once, blood streaming down his face. He stood and lurched toward Ainsley.

Rue stepped in his way.

The revenant grabbed him instead. "Fairy."

Rue drew his knife and placed it to his throat.

"Wish, wish, wish," the revenant whispered.

Ainsley put his hand on Rue's wrist. "Rue, don't hurt him."

"No wishes," Rue warned.

"Wish!" the revenant insisted. Each word it spoke came out labored.

"Can you help him?"

"Help him? He's *dead.*"

The revenant dropped to his knees in front of Rue. He clasped his hands. "Wish."

"Please," Ainsley insisted.

Rue sighed. He took his hands back from the revenant. "What's your wish?"

"Think," he answered.

"This is a bad idea."

"Think," he pleaded.

"I don't do mind magic."

The creature took Rue's hand and pressed it to his skull. "Wish. Think."

"I'll try." Rue knelt beside the creature. He skimmed his fingers over his scalp, then withdrew them to peer at it. "He has runes carved into his skin here."

"Think," the revenant repeated piteously.

"Think," Rue agreed. He glanced up at Ainsley. "This thing was dead. It is possible that letting it think again will make it much more dangerous. Unstable."

"If...if he's dangerous, we'll do what we have to," Ainsley said.

Rue stood. He paced and hummed to himself. He poked at the revenant every so often, peering at the wound on his chest and the runes on his scalp. He muttered under his breath and finally said, "I'll try to break the spell on his mind. It might break one keeping him alive." He looked at the revenant. "Do you understand? This might kill you?"

The revenant nodded.

"Magic doesn't work right on dead things. They're not of my realm," Rue reminded. "And neither is the spell already upon it."

The revenant said, "Please."

Rue placed his hand on the creature's head and drew him close, almost into an embrace. He whispered something Ainsley couldn't make out into the revenant's ear.

The revenant sagged to the floor and began to sob.

"What did you do?" Ainsley asked.

Rue shrugged. He stepped back from the sobbing form as though it disturbed him. "He wished to think. I granted him thought."

"Yes, but...Just like that?"

"I bestowed what I could to lift the bindings on his mind, but...I cannot undo the other harms done to him. I don't do mind magic. There are those who might serve him better in the Otherworld but..."

Ainsley crouched beside the weeping revenant. "We'll have to bring him."

"Have to?" Rue asked.

"What?"

"Ah, nothing. Nothing. My love means to return home with a dog *and* a ward. I thought we might take in a foundling someday but...I imagined something smaller. Sweeter-faced."

"He's just a lad."

"Not so much younger than you," Rue pointed out.

Ainsley sighed.

Rue sat beside the two of them on the floor. He pulled a blanket down from the bed and draped it over the revenant. "You are young yet and this...this wretched thing represents an unknown burden of unknown length."

"Am I alone in this, Rue? Do you wash your hands of us?"

"Of course not." Rue took his hand and kissed his palm. "Of course not, but I don't foresee any part of this being easy."

"It will be better at home."

Rue offered no agreement.

Ainsley put a hand on the revenant's back.

He closed into a tighter ball. He cried himself to sleep.

Ainsley and Rue slept in shifts. At dawn, Ainsley went out to buy breakfast, as well as refresh their provisions for the trek to Jannes's court. He returned, arms full, to find Rue and the lad staring at each other.

The revenant had the blanket wrapped around his shoulders.

Rue sat on the end of the bed.

Ainsley asked, "What?"

"Tell him what you told me," Rue said, still looking at the revenant.

"Marion Duverger fed me to a dog." His voice came less labored than before, but still raspy and unsettling.

Ainsley opened his mouth, then closed it.

"Then I woke up and the dog was dead and I was..." The revenant touched his chest. He dug his fingers in, massaging the area. "I was..." His eyes went wide. He buried his face in his hands and pulled his hair. He let out a solitary wail.

Ainsley took a step forward.

Rue warned, "He bites."

Ainsley froze.

"He's done this exact thing five times far."

Ainsley set down the things he'd purchased. He extracted a slightly worn pair of turn shoes and tossed them toward the revenant. "Put those on."

"Marion Duverger fed me to a dog," he began, his face still hidden. "Then I woke up and the dog was dead and I was..."

"Are you hungry?" Ainsley asked.

He lifted his head, eyes fixed on Ainsley's face. He swallowed. "Fed me to a dog."

"Put your shoes on. Wash your face. Then we'll eat."

He reached for the shoes. "I woke up."

Ainsley handed Rue a roll and a piece of cheese.

Rue looked at the small chunk of cheese.

"Do you want it all now or do you want some for later?"

"I want to go home."

"Soon," Ainsley promised.

Shoes in hand, the revenant approached Ainsley, eyes on the food.

"Shoes, then wash your face," Ainsley told him.

"I was dead," he repeated. Wobbling on one leg, he pulled one shoe on. He nearly fell when he switched legs to put on the other.

Ainsley pointed to the water pitcher.

The revenant splashed some water over his face, then returned to Ainsley. He extended a hand, palm up. "Fed me. To a dog."

"It's bread."

The revenant scowled. "A *dog*."

"Bread."

"Fed me!"

Ainsley waited.

"Fed me, fed me...!" The youth gnashed his teeth. He bit his knuckles. Rue stood.

"Bread," he finally said. "She fed me to a dog! Bread, bread...a dog."

"I think he's worse," Rue said.

Ainsley gave the revenant a roll which immediately disappeared down his throat. He showed him the cheese. "Cheese."

"I was dead."

"I know."

The revenant met his eyes. "She fed me to a dog."

"I know. Do you want some cheese?"

"I know," the creature echoed.

"Yes or no?"

"No. Yes. Yes!" he said. He devoured the cheese with resounding speed.

"You gave him a bigger piece," Rue pointed out.

"He was dead," Ainsley scolded.

"I was dead," the revenant agreed. He placed his fingers over his heart, digging in again, but not as hard this time. "I was."

"She fed you to a dog," Rue said.

"To a dog," the revenant said. He touched his mouth, pushing around his lips. He pulled on his bottom lip. He grunted. "Dead."

"Still no name?" Ainsley asked.

He shook his head. "I was. She makes me."

"A new name," Ainsley proposed. "No spells. Something to call you."

He shook his head.

"Think about it."

"Think. I was dead," the revenant repeated with almost a tone of scorn.

Ainsley started to pack their bags.

When he saddled their horses, he saw a circle of teeth marks on Rue's forearm. No broken skin. "Did...did he hurt you? Badly, I mean."

Rue sighed. "I startled him."

Ainsley touched his hand. "We're doing the right thing."

Rue circled an arm around him and pulled him close. He kissed his forehead. "You're so *confident*." He returned to checking Clover's tack, then went to harness the goat to the cart.

The revenant stood by, his hands bound at Rue's insistence, and the cord around his neck again. He'd accepted the bonds peacefully enough, though he had insisted several times that he'd been fed to a dog during the process.

He didn't seem to mind Alfred, though.

Alfred, however, wouldn't get within six feet of him.

The horses didn't like him either and neither did the goat.

Rue didn't go near him either.

Ainsley began to wonder if they detected something he couldn't. Animals and unnatural creatures had better senses about these things and though Ainsley had developed a small sensitivity to magic in the Otherworld, he didn't feel anything odd about the revenant.

He smelled a little bit. Not fetid or even really unpleasant, but a distinct earthy smell that another bath or two might have banished. Maybe sweet water would have done him well. He had a strangeness to his gait, a tight dragging of his feet but every so often he'd rock up on his toes and walk like that for a few steps, always appearing to be on the verge of tripping. He glanced over his shoulder constantly and whispered to himself, mostly about how he had died.

At one point, he stepped walking to watch a flock of bird and the cord around his neck nearly strangled him.

Ainsley only noticed when he let out an awful squawk. He reined Hadley to a stop and leaped off to undo the cord. He couldn't unwork the knot and slipped his knife out of his belt to cut it.

When the blade touched his skin, he let out a delicate whine and flinched.

"I won't hurt you," Ainsley promised. "Stay still."

He froze in place, not even breathing until the cord slithered down his chest to the ground. He touched his throat.

Ainsley put his knife away. "See?"

"See," the revenant echoed. His breath smelled like moss, nowhere near as foul as the day before.

Ainsley smiled at him.

He smiled back. He held up his hands, still bound. He raised an eyebrow.

Ainsley untied those, too.

Rue sighed.

"Come walk with me," Ainsley said to the revenant. "Have you thought about a name yet?" He took Hadley's reigns and tossed them to Rue, knowing the mare would shy if the revenant came too close.

"No name."

"A *new* name."

The revenant shrugged.

"Thomas," Ainsley suggested.

He shook his head.

"Oliver."

He shook his head.

Ainsley went on listing various names, ranging from those of squires he'd known to family members to ones he'd heard in ballads.

"Those are all *awful* names," Rue called over his shoulder after Ainsley had offered about two dozen and the revenant had refused all of them.

"I don't hear you making suggestions."

"Look around, the world is *full* of suggestions."

"I see a goat and two horses and a lot of trees," Ainsley said. "And a stuck-up prince."

"Oaks." Rue pointed to a flock of birds. "Sparrows. That river we passed? What was that called again?"

"Greenpass."

"And there, a patch of clover."

"The horse is already called Clover."

"Daisy, sorrel, daffodil, buttercup, we pass hundreds of wonderous things and you want to name him after some common man."

"He *is* a man."

"I was dead," the revenant insisted with a tone of refusal. He shook his head.

Ainsley didn't know what to make of that, so he ignored it. "Let's put the name thing aside for now."

The revenant nodded.

"So. Do you...do you remember anything else? Before you died?"

He nodded.

"What do you remember?"

He licked his lips. He swallowed, then pressed his lips together hard. "It."

"Hmm?"

He tugged on his lip and pulled downward. He repeated the movement several times with force.

Ainsley warned, "Careful."

"Careful," he echoed. He repeated the word several times under his breath. "Too careful."

"Hmm?" Ainsley glanced at him.

"*Too* careful," he insisted. "I...I was *careful*. Uh. Uh. Too much."

"Nervous?" Ainsley guessed.

He smiled. "Nervous. I was nervous. I was dead...Uh." He frowned.

"Woke up."

Their conversation continued in a similar manner for a while. Ainsley couldn't often understand what he meant but he knew that the revenant had something to say.

The revenant stopped walking. He squinted at a willow tree, then headed toward it.

Ainsley followed.

Rue sighed. "Don't..."

Ainsley kept going.

The revenant threw himself down beneath the boughs of the tree, grinning up at the boughs from his back. "Willow."

"It is," Ainsley agreed.

He put a hand on his chest. "Name."

"Willow?" Ainsley asked.

He nodded, a tranquil smile on his face. "I woke up."

Ainsley called, "Rue!"

Rue brought the horses over, resignation on his face already.

"We could eat," Ainsley proposed.

Willow rolled over on to his side. "I eat bread."

"And ears," Rue said.

"And ears," Willow repeated with a grin. He winked at Rue.

Rue pressed his lips together, then a smile spread across his face too. He sat beside the other two.

Willow reached over and poked the round bruise he'd left on Rue's hand.

"You did that."

"He bites," Willow told him.

"Not exactly behavior becoming of a gentleman."

Willow shook his head. "Not a gentleman."

"Clearly not," Rue agreed.

Willow wrinkled his nose and twisted his mouth as if thinking hard. "Marion...Marion said..."

Rue and Ainsley waited.

He bit his hand and pulled at his mouth. Finally, he said, "A secret. She said she would keep my secret. But first I had to help her."

"Help her what?" Ainsley asked.

Willow shrugged. "She fed me to a dog."

"Likely a ruse," Rue said.

"Hmm?"

"It seems whatever the mage did to him needed to be done to something dead. What better assassin than one who bends to your will and cannot think?" Rue said. "If caught, even under torture, it cannot tell your secrets. Even with the spell undone as best I could, well..." Rue looked over

Willow. "The results are...tenuous."

Willow stretched out. "Bread." He reached toward Ainsley's pack with his eyes on Ainsley.

Ainsley divvied up a midday meal between the three of them while the horses and goat grazed. Alfred stretched out in the sun near the horses and snapped up whatever scraps came his way.

Every so often, a breeze would waft the stench of the mage's corpse toward them.

Willow scarfed his food and then wandered around the willow. He ran his hands over the bark and branches. He peeled up bits of moss from nearby stones, then lay down and covered himself with the sections of moss, all his exposed skin.

Ainsley watched him.

He folded his hands together on his chest as though in prayer. A few moments later, he peeked on eye open.

"What are you doing?" Ainsley asked.

"Thinking."

"Strange way to think."

Willow sat up. Most of the moss fell off his face. "Remembering."

"Your life?"

He shook his head. "I was dead."

"I don't know if that's a good thing to remember," Ainsley said.

"It was..." He closed his eyes. He smiled. "Warm. Rocks in the sun. Feet by the fire. Nothing and everything." He flicked one last piece of moss off his face.

The nostalgic disquiet made Ainsley take Rue's hand. He'd likely given up his chance for a peaceful afterlife because he'd never repent these sins.

Maybe he could forget a god that would condemn him. Maybe Rue's gods would accept his prayers better than his own ever had.

Willow looked at their tangled fingers. He rolled over from where he'd lain to sprawl in front of them. He walked his fingers toward their hands, then over them. "Secret." He winked.

"The winking sort of disturbs me," Rue confided softly to Ainsley.

Ainsley nudged him with his elbow.

"Secret, secret..." Willow mused.

"What's your secret?" Ainsley asked.

He rolled onto his back and placed one arm behind his head. "I..." He put his fingers inside his mouth and ran them over his teeth. He tugged on his lip and scrunched his eyes closed. "Helena. Margaret. Peter." He opened his eyes then winked at Rue. "Gregory. Thomas. Eleanor."

"And they are?"

Willow grinned. He sat up. He rubbed his fingers together. "Sparks and stars."

Rue raised an eyebrow.

"Evenings for rent," Willow said.

Ainsley frowned. "What do you mean?"

Rue made a face, his lips pressed into a line and turned down at the edges. "Don't ask questions you don't want answered," he advised.

Ainsley rolled his eyes and bit back a remark about how Rue never answered his questions anyway. The fairy had done much better speaking openly and Ainsley knew better than to take that lightly.

Willow fished a spark out of his shoe. He placed it in Ainsley's hand, then indicated that Ainsley should give it back. Once Ainsley had placed the coin into his palm, Willow kissed him, quick and transactional.

Ainsley froze.

Alfred let out a sharp bark.

"Five sparks in a star, one star for whatever you want," he recited in the most normal cadence Ainsley had heard from him yet. He sounded like he had said it hundreds of times.

Rue covered his mouth to hide a snigger.

"How old are you?" Ainsley demanded.

Willow returned the coin to his shoe. He shrugged. "I think it's just a lad."

Rue took Ainsley by the chin and tilted his head from side to side. "A kiss from a dead man. What luck could come from that?" He smoothed his thumb over Ainsley's mouth. "Many would count it an ill omen."

Ainsley pulled back. "Ew."

Willow darted in and pecked Ainsley again.

Rue cackled.

Willow dissolved into giggles.

Ainsley glanced between the two of them. He smacked Rue as he stood. "We have places to be!"

Neither of the creatures moved, too busy laughing.

"Both of you."

Rue dragged Ainsley down beside him and kissed him much more deeply than Willow had. "Whatever luck it brings we'll share it."

Willow, when he stopped laughing, patted Ainsley on top of the head. He approached Hadley, who shied away from him. "Horse." He held out his hand.

The horse flattened her ears.

"I wouldn't," Ainsley warned.

Willow stepped back looking a little wounded. He regarded the horses. "She fed me..." He shook his head and put his hands on his hips. "I...Horse. Mmmm. Stable!" He smiled. "A stable, a stable."

Rue kept his arms around Ainsley, his eyes on Willow. "You dislike those who trade such favors for coin," he stated quietly.

Ainsley glanced at him. "I don't—"

"You do."

"I don't...I don't dislike them."

"Hate felt too strong a word. But you act with contempt."

Ainsley wanted to argue. He could have argued, lied and blustered his way out of the accusation. "It's not their fault. It's everyone who goes to them."

"Ah."

"Years and years of people being able to buy what I'd never have."

"Clearly you could have had it, if wretches like that sell themselves as well."

"But never the way other men could," Ainsley pointed out. "I'd never be able to brag about it. I'd never be able to say, 'oh if you'd seen the cock on him you wouldn't think I'd overpaid!' or anything like that."

"And you wanted that? To go to whores and boast to your friends about your conquests?"

"No. Not like that. But...But it always chafed me that I couldn't." Ainsley sighed. He didn't know if he could express the loneliness of hearing other people brag about awful things they'd done and then keep his tamest wishes a secret. "I don't know how it is in the Otherworld, the rules for these sorts of things, but a foot soldier could come back from a skirmish and brag about how he'd raped six or seven women, everyone would think it good fun for him. If I'd said I'd even kissed another lad...well. It wouldn't be so fun."

"So you haven't changed your mind about him?"

"D'you mean?"

"I thought his former profession might sour you to his cause."

Ainsley shook his head. "No."

Rue kissed the side of his face.

Willow paced around the horses in a wide berth as Rue and Ainsley readied their mounts and packs. He mumbled words related to horses and stables to himself.

The more he spoke the easier the words sounded, though his voice never smoothed out.

Ainsley wondered if it had to do with the scars around his throat. He didn't like thinking of what a dog could do to a man's throat.

It brought to mind gore of the queen's murder. The gleam of bones through the blood.

And Willow had done that to her.

He mounted Hadley and tried to do his best to think as they rode. Rue had given him good counsel and he'd ignored it. He shouldn't have gotten attached to Willow, but that had happened almost before Ainsley had realized.

How had he looked after he'd killed that bandit? Retching and bloody, surely nearly as awful to behold as Willow had been.

He sighed.

Willow hung back as they walked. He moved closer when Rue took out his harp, as close he could get without spooking the horses.

That night as they camped, Rue let him examine the harp.

Three nights later, Rue and Willow scrapped over the last bit of cheese. Ainsley had left it unattended by the fire, turned his back for a few minutes to check on the animals, and whipped around when he heard Rue shout and Willow yelp.

Rue had the revenant by the ear.

"Come now! Are you children?" Ainsley demanded.

"He bit me," Rue said.

Willow snarled.

"Let him go."

Rue released him.

Willow shoved the fairy.

Ainsley wrapped an arm around Willow and pulled him back.

Willow twisted in his arms and bit Ainsley's throat.

Ainsley grunted and shoved Willow to the ground. He clapped a hand to his neck and found it wet, though with spit, not blood.

Willow sprung back up but didn't make toward Ainsley or Rue. He bolted toward the forest, crashing through the brush and into the trees.

"Are you alright?" Rue asked. He probed the bite with gentle fingers.

Ainsley wiped the bite with his sleeve. It felt tight and swollen. "It's fine, it..."

"He didn't break the...oh. Just a little, right here. Should I kiss it better? Or clean it, at least. Have we wine to boil?"

"I've got to go get Willow."

Rue shook his head. "He can't go far. Don't you hear the river?"

"Fred?"

The dog lifted his head.

"Come help me find him."

Alfred trotted over. He sniffed around and ate the piece of cheese that had fallen to the ground in their tussle. He wagged his tail.

"Help me find Willow."

"I'll get him," Rue said. "Sir Alfred?"

The dog circled around Rue. He nosed the fairy's hand, then put his snout to the ground. He headed to the forest.

Rue followed the hound. He called, "Wash that!" over his shoulder as he went. He conjured an orb of light.

Ainsley scowled. He heated water and cleaned the bite. It would leave a nasty bruise for sure.

He glanced at the horses and the goat, then around the camp. It wouldn't be wise to leave this unattended.

No one had ever called Ainsley wise.

He headed into the woods, or at least, he tried. He couldn't see much. He stood at the edge and called, "Rue!" but got no response.

He stomped back to campfire.

Alfred returned first, wet and pleased with himself.

Rue followed not to long after pulling Willow along by golden cords that bound his hands to his waist.

Willow had scratches on his face and blood on his mouth.

"What did you do?" Ainsley asked.

"He did that to himself. The thing is in a *state*."

Willow howled when he saw Ainsley.

Alfred growled at him.

"Fred, leave it."

The dog slunk over to the fire and curled up.

Ainsley approached Willow.

He tried to step back but Rue kept a hold on the cords that bound him.

"Come sit," Ainsley urged.

Willow let out another awful howl.

Ainsley took him by the arm. "Come sit."

Willow collapsed at his touch, curling onto the ground and placing his forehead near Ainsley's feet. He let out a wet, choking sound, somewhere between a sob and a groan.

Ainsley glanced at Rue.

"Be careful," Rue warned.

"Untie him?"

"And if he flees again?"

"Then I'll go get him this time."

Rue smiled and let out an amused snort. He waved a hand and the bindings vanished.

Willow buried his hands in his hair, tearing at it.

Ainsley knelt and pulled his hands away, but the creature resisted, twisting against Ainsley's grip. Ainsley held him so hard he thought he'd break the poor thing's wrists.

After several minutes of twist and howling, Rue knelt, too, and placed two fingers against Willow's temple.

The revenant slumped.

"He's asleep," Rue explained.

Ainsley took the opportunity to wipe clean the creature's face. "He really did this to himself?"

"I cannot lie."

"I know, but..." Ainsley sighed. "He was that upset over cheese?"

Rue touched the bite on Ainsley's neck. "I don't think the cheese represents the true source of his disquiet."

"Oh."

"Last time he became upset, sleep seemed to serve him well."

"Do you think..."

"Go ahead."

Ainsley asked, "Do you think he's truly mad?"

"Mmm." Rue looked over the sleeping youth. "I...I would say the lad is star-touched without a doubt, but...but when I called him mindless, I likely spoke too soon. He has suffered. Died a terrible death, come back to what so far seems a terrible life. And, well...the world could not have treated him too kindly before he passed."

"Likely not."

"He may need help we cannot give."

"Don't ask if you can kill him."

Rue shook his head. "When we return home, I'd like to ask Tadgh for his opinion. He may have a better sense for what Willow needs."

"Perhaps."

"He picked a good name for himself. Willow. More like to bend instead of break. Strong roots." Rue brushed his fingers over the revenant's brow. He whispered something Ainsley couldn't understand into his ear.

Ainsley placed his hand over Rue's. He kissed the fairy's cheek, certain he'd said something kind or helpful. He had to tease, "No cursing people."

Rue kissed him. "Not this time. The creature's given me no offense."

"He bit you."

Rue bobbed his head from side to side. "Ah, can we hold it against a kitten to use its claws?"

"I love you."

"And I you, sweet knight. The most delightful of all mortal creatures I've found. Your world holds so precious little for me and it so vast. Imagine if I had flown by..."

"No."

Rue raised an eyebrow.

"I won't imagine it."

Rue put an arm around him and snuggled close. They sat beside the fire for a while, quiet and comfortable. Just before they turned in for the night, Rue asked, "Was that really the last piece of cheese?"

Ainsley snorted. "Yes."

"You aren't holding out on me?"

"Have I ever?"

"The opposite, sweet thing. I could have taken you to bed after one kiss, methinks."

Ainsley elbowed him lightly. "Maybe."

"How is it that you made it so many years untouched? Such a beautiful thing and so eager."

Ainsley shrugged. "I guess..." He stopped to think. He looked at Alfred to make sure the dog still slept. He well knew that if he had pushed things a little more with Alfred in their youth, he could have gotten him into bed. Well. Maybe not into a bed. Probably just Ainsley shoved up against a wall or bent over a barrel.

"Hmm?"

"I never wanted to be with someone who...who'd be ashamed of me. Of us. I never wanted to have to hide and I couldn't have hidden if I loved someone. So...So I suppose I decided it would be better never to love anyone."

"What a tragedy that would have been." Rue kissed him. "Sleep?"

Ainsley glanced toward Willow.

"He'll remain like that until I wake him," Rue assured.

"Fred?" Ainsley called. "Fred!"

The dog lifted his head.

"We're going to bed. Keep an eye on him."

The dog crawled a little closer to the fire and settled his head on his forelegs.

"Thank you, Fred." He gave him a pat on the head, then headed toward the tent.

"Sir Alfred," Rue bid the dog goodnight with a bow of his head.

Alfred licked Rue's hand when he gave the hound a pat.

Rue brought a blanket out for the revenant, then came to nestle with Ainsley for the night.

In the morning, Ainsley emerged from the tent to find Rue standing just outside of the entrance, still and quiet.

"What—"

"Shh."

Ainsley came to stand beside him.

By the ashes of the campfire lay two men. Willow had not moved, still beneath the blanket Rue had placed on him. The other man Ainsley had not seen in what felt like forever. Alfred had curled up against Willow in the night and now had an arm slung around his waist, his face pressed against his chest, slid under the blanket with him.

"The air did hold a chill last night," Rue murmured. "Without fur, he must have grown cold."

Ainsley asked, "Why do I need to be quiet?"

"I fear your friend's state of mind if he wakes in such a manner."

"But the curse is broken."

"The terms never spoke of acceptance. Only turning a blind eye."

Ainsley stepped around Rue. "Willow won't wake?"

Rue shook his head.

Ainsley crouched and rolled Willow away from Alfred. He used the blanket to cover Alfred, who wore nothing. Once he'd put a decent distance between the two men, he gave Alfred a nudge.

Alfred didn't wake.

Ainsley slapped his side. "Fred!"

Alfred woke with a shout. He rubbed his face, then froze. He sat straight up and touched his face, the top of his head, then stared at his hands. "Jack."

"Fred."

"Jack!" Alfred cried with a grin. He grabbed Ainsley by the shoulders. He gave him a shake. "Jack!"

"Aye, Fred, you got your head out of your ass."

Alfred let out a crow that had a rather doggish quality. He stood, clutching the blanket to himself. "Oh, Christ, I smell like a dog."

"Well," Ainsley said.

Rue tossed a pack toward Alfred. "This was yours. Hopefully, you have soap and a change of clothes. You remember where the river is?"

Alfred stared at Rue, a mixed expression on his face. Confusion, vague recognition, distaste...Then it smoothed away. He gave Rue a half-smile. "Thanks."

Rue pressed his lips together. He gave a curt nod.

Alfred gathered his pack and made for the woods, unsteady on just two legs.

Rue touched Willow, who woke with the same kind of start as Alfred.

Willow looked around, wild-eyed. He grabbed Ainsley's arm and shook his head, lips pressed together. His jaw trembled.

"Oh, now, shh," Ainsley soothed, afraid he'd start hurting himself again.

"Sorry," Willow whispered. His fingers dug into Ainsley's arm. "Sorry."

"It's not nice to bite."

Willow nodded. "Sorry."

"I'm not angry."

Willow threw his arms around Ainsley's neck and squeezed hard. Almost too hard. He sniffled.

Ainsley patted his back. "No more biting."

Willow pulled back and nodded eagerly. "No more." He crossed his heart.

Alfred returned, scrubbed and dressed, and started asking a lot of clarifying questions about the things that had passed since his transformation. It seemed they had neglected him to fill him on the finer details of things.

He didn't, for instance, know why they had a dead body in a cart.

Ainsley explained as best he could.

"And the...that. That wretch." Alfred kept his voice low and cast his eyes toward Willow. "You can't mean to...to, what? Keep him from the king."

"I'd see him through this quest alive," Ainsley said.

Alfred shook his head. "That thing's not right, Jack. Can't you feel it? Something...God, he reeks."

"No, he doesn't. He's...He's a little...He's got a scent about him but it's like after it rains, not like a corpse." Ainsley felt confident saying that considering how familiar he'd become with the scent of a corpse in recent days.

Rue had thrown heaps of pungent herbs and flowers onto the car to help the smell a little.

Alfred insisted, "He reeks. He's dead and dangerous."

"Fred, give it a rest. Are you hungry?" Ainsley offered as a distraction.

"Aye, I could do with more than scraps for once!" Alfred scolded but he did it with a smile.

Rue busied himself around camp, taking down the tent and tending to the animals.

Willow spent most of breakfast tugging at his lips.

"Why do you do that?" Rue asked him.

"Helps."

"Hmm?"

Willow bit his tongue, rubbed his nose, and tapped a fingernail against his teeth. He managed, "They don't come out. Thinking. I'm...I'm *thinking* but..." He pressed his fingers against his lips. "Not talking."

"Oh."

"Some...thinking. Some thinking..." Willow sighed. "Thoughts. Thoughts. One thought." He circled one finger around and round to indicate a rotation or a spiral and with each circle, repeated, "One thought."

"I understand," Rue said. "I've had thoughts preoccupy my mind once upon a time. Some of them still show their face."

Willow kept circling his finger. "Two thoughts. I was dead. She makes. I was dead. She makes me. Three thoughts. She fed me to a dog. I was dead. She makes me."

"Someday we may yet find peace for you. These things all came to pass recently. Even a lesser horror might preoccupy your mind but those horrors? Such things challenge us."

Willow stilled his finger. He touched the newest bite mark on Rue's hand. "I was…"

"I acted unbecomingly. Your need exceeds my own."

Willow traced the scratches he'd given himself. "I…I scared you."

"You concerned us both," Rue said.

"Don't get attached to things you are leading to the slaughter," Willow reminded.

Rue smiled. "It was good advice. My love so seldom takes good advice that it might not be difficult for some to mistake him for a fool."

"I heard that!" Ainsley called.

"Did I offend thee, my love?" Rue asked, wide-eyed with what must have been false concern.

Ainsley rolled his eyes. He tossed Rue his pack.

Rue caught it with ease. "Give us a kiss to soothe our nerves."

Alfred coughed.

Ainsley gave Rue a kiss anyway, though he did it with a strange twisting in his gut.

Alfred walked away.

Rue watched him mount Clover. "It seems I'm to walk."

"It's my horse!" Alfred reminded testily.

Rue raised an eyebrow.

"Take Hadley. I'll walk for a bit," Ainsley offered.

"I don't want to take *your* horse."

"Go ahead," Ainsley urged. "I'll walk with Willow."

"Should I worry where your affections lie?"

"Rue, he's only a lad!"

"A seasoned one," Rue reminded.

Willow winked at Ainsley.

"I can't tell if you're really jealous or just being an ass," Ainsley told the fairy.

Rue gave offered no answer in either direction. He did spend a good portion of the morning's ride playing the harp, so Ainsley didn't worry too much about his state.

That evening, Rue played a tune he'd picked up in a tavern, a two-person song meant to be sang by a man and a woman. People played it most at May Day and weddings, though sometimes a bawdier version came to life in rowdy taverns.

Sir Richard had favored that bawdy version after a long time on the road or on a campaign.

Rue sang the first verse softly to himself, a young man's proposition to his sweetheart.

Willow answered with the second verse, the woman's response to her suitor, though he sang the more scandalous version. He did a saucy bit of a jig with it, too, pantomiming lifting a skirt and winking at Rue.

Ainsley snorted.

Alfred looked positively scandalized.

"Oh, he can sing but he cannot talk," Rue noted dryly.

Willow rubbed his fingers together. "A star for anything you like. Some people liked me a lot." He touched his hair. Then he reached over to tug on Ainsley's curls, playful more than painful. "I'll be anything you like." He did that saucy jig again. "I was..." he sighed.

"Dead?" Rue guessed.

Willow shook his head and flapped a hand at him. "I...I was." He touched Ainsley's hair again. He sighed. He twirled his fingers around one of Ainsley's curls, his elbow resting on Ainsley's shoulder. "Peter...Hair like this. Helena, eyes like the sky. Margaret likes to use a lance."

Ainsley raised an eyebrow. "A lance?"

"Jousting with her thighs."

"Oh."

"And...And Thomas." He continued to play with Ainsley's hair. "I think it's just a lad."

"I'm sorry," Ainsley said.

He hated to think how Willow had been used and wondered how badly he'd been treated. He'd heard enough of details from knights and squires who'd bought time with a prostitute to guess that Willow's clients had not always treated him carefully.

Willow shook his head. "Thomas," he sighed dreamily. "Thomas...played nice. He." He tilted his head to think. "Thomas went home. He..." Willow quieted but stayed leaning against Ainsley.

Rue played a different song.

Willow knew that one, too, and sang along. As he sang, his voice came more easily than Ainsley had heard yet.

After a half-hour, Willow said, "Thomas sent letters. He sent coin. He..." He sighed. "He said 'come home with me.' I didn't go. A secret in a city is safe. A secret in a castle is...*dangerous*. Nervous, nervous, I was nervous."

"I'm sorry."

Willow shrugged. "No more letters. Thomas...Thomas takes a bride, makes a babe. I..." He pressed a hand to his stomach. "No babes live here."

Ainsley said, "Of course not, Willow, you're not a lass."

"Not a lass," Willow echoed sadly. "Gowns and wigs and rouge...But not a lass. It's just a lad."

"Did...Did you want to be a lass?" Ainsley asked. It would have made sense; people who wanted to change their bodies like that hung around the University in the hopes that magic could aid their cause. Such people flocked there, living safer together in Fallclere than they could most anywhere else.

Rumor said some mages could do such good work that no one would ever know their clients had been born with different bodies. Such folk would set out from Fallclere with new names, new garments, and a newly invented past.

Ainsley had heard once that the Queen's sister, who had reportedly died abroad, actually now lived a jolly life as a lesser lord in a holding on the border of France.

Willow answered, "No."

"I...You know, I wouldn't...It's not my place to judge that sort of thing," Ainsley assured.

Willow shrugged. "I was...I am. I am..." Suddenly he smiled. "I am the sun. I am a shadow. I am a petal, a dew drop. I *am*. And I am not."

Ainsley didn't know what to make of that.

Willow stopped walking, his face tilted back to the sun. "I am vast and lovely. I am anything I like." He spread his arms.

Ainsley looked at Rue.

"Some riddles cannot be answered except with what lies in our hearts," Rue answered. "That's what Balor said, anyway, when I asked him why he favors gowns."

"I don't know what that means either."

"It means...It means that Willow is. And he is not." Rue somehow possessed an understanding of what the revenant meant. Or, at least, he understood better than Ainsley did.

Alfred had ridden ahead of them.

"So..." Ainsley glanced at Willow.

Willow smiled. "I am and I am not and that is all I ever have been." He sounded so confident when he said it. "I am Willow."

"That you are," Ainsley agreed.

Willow peeled away from Ainsley and sidled up to Rue.

Hadley gave him a sideways look and flattened her ears but didn't shy. Willow had spent the last handful of nights carefully approaching her with oats in his palm.

He requested, "The Lady's Hart?"

"Hmm?" Rue asked.

Willow sang a line.

Ainsley wondered what his voice had sounded like before a dog had ripped his throat out. Not that he sound sounded unpleasant presently, but Ainsley suspected he might have had an actively good voice once. High and clear.

"Teach it to me," Rue said.

Despite the sour look on Alfred's face and the even sourer stench that came from the mage's corpse, Ainsley felt good about the things to come. Each day Willow's words came a little easier and maybe by the time they reached Jannes's court, he'd be able to relate a coherent story to the king.

After Rue put his harp away, Willow tried to make conversation with Alfred.

Alfred wanted no part in it.

Willow didn't seem to understand. He would wander away for a while then return with a clearer version of what he'd said the first time. He tried to tell jokes or pointed out things he saw. At camp that night, he picked a flower and showed it Alfred, telling him proudly, "Daisy."

Alfred scowled.

"Willow, come sit," Ainsley called.

Willow went, though he did glance at Alfred over his shoulder. He sat, dropping an armful of daisies and wildflowers into his lap.

"We'll be at court in a few more days. Have you ever been?"

Willow shook his head. "Lords and ladies, never the king."

"It...it will probably be better if you stay close to me—"

Willow scooted so they sat thigh to thigh.

Ainsley chuckled. "And not talk too much. I mean. To strangers."

Willow nodded. "Keep your head down?"

"Yeah."

"Nose clean?"

"That too."

Willow rested his head on Ainsley's shoulder, his eyes on his hands. His fingers worked to weave the flowers into a chain. "I was...I was pretty in a gown. Wool right over your eyes. Thomas thought..." He sighed. "Thomas thought I could pretend forever."

"Thomas was noble, right?"

Willow nodded.

"Are you?"

Willow laughed so hard he doubled over.

"No. A little house in the manor." He sighed. "Thomas..." He touched his chest. "His heart is bigger than his brain."

"It happens to the best of us."

Willow resumed his flower chain.

Sometime later, he stood, knelt before Rue, and offered him a crown woven of daisies and wildflowers. "My prince."

Rue stared. His lips parted slightly.

"Tell him it's freely given," Ainsley advised softly.

"Freely given," Willow echoed. He peeked up at Rue.

Rue took the crown.

Willow pointed. "Put it on."

Rue placed the crown upon his head, his cheeks a little darker than usual.

Willow put one on his own head, and then placed a longer chain around Ainsley's neck. He approached Alfred, who'd watched the whole scene playout with a curled lip. With the same tentative approach that he used with the horses, Willow held out the crown. "Fred?"

"I'm not your friend."

"Fred, he's harmless," Ainsley scolded.

"Harmless!"

Willow flinched. He clutched the last chain to his chest.

"Harmless," Alfred shouted again. "This wretch wasn't even harmless when he was alive and you're going to say it when you know he's killed two women? After he bit you?"

Ainsley pursed his lips, not sure what to say. Alfred had these moods. He gestured for Willow to come back to his side. "He didn't mean to bite me. Not really."

Willow scuttled to sit beside him.

"Oh, he didn't mean it! And he didn't mean to ravage the queen. He didn't mean to bend over for a few pennies or—"

"That's enough," Ainsley interrupted.

"You'd do better off putting it in the cart."

"I'm not going to do that."

"That's because you're an idiot, Jack. You always have been."

"Fred, don't—"

Alfred stood up. "Don't tell me what to do!"

Ainsley wrinkled his nose.

"If I wanted advice from...from...!" Alfred shouted and kicked his pack.

Ainsley had never been gladder that he'd hidden Alfred's gisarme, especially with how he'd used it last time.

"Go for a walk, Fred."

Alfred stormed off.

Rue clucked his tongue. "I fail to see what you liked about him *at all*."

Willow answered, "Nice legs. Shiny hair."

Ainsley pressed his lips together. "Go on, eat, why don't you?"

Willow placed the last flower chain on Alfred's pack. He chewed his strip of jerky without his usual fervor.

Rue came to sit next to Ainsley. He smoothed his fingers through his curls and kissed his cheek. "He's not a...He's not the pinnacle of friendship."

"He was the only friend I ever really had."

Rue hummed.

"Go ahead and say it."

Rue shook his head. "It doesn't need saying. Do you need to go after him?"

"No, he'll come back when he's cooled off."

Alfred didn't come back until morning. He returned stone-faced with a stout branch in his hand.

Willow approached him before Ainsley could warn him off. He caught a blow to the ribs for his trouble. He crumpled with his arms wrapped around himself.

Ansley had his sword in his hand before he'd thought about it. He didn't make it over in time to stop the blow to Willow's back, but he parried the third. "Fred!"

Alfred kicked the creature at his feet. "You should have killed it. The fairy's right. Keep it away from me or I'll do what you can't."

Ainsley leveled his sword toward Alfred. "Maybe you should...Maybe you should go home, Fred. I don't think this is the right kind of quest for you."

"Quest!" Alfred roared. "You think you're on a quest. You *idiot*. You always were the *stupidest* lad I knew. Runty and weak and stupid. Richard should have sent you home."

Ainsley lifted his chin. "Get on your horse and go."

Alfred kicked Willow again, hard enough for him to cry out.

Ainsley dropped his sword and tackled Alfred.

Alfred's branch made solid contact with the side of his face, hard enough to blur his vision and rattle his teeth.

They wrestled, but Alfred had the clear advantage, still armed, not to mention heavier and more vicious.

He let out an awful howl once he turned Ainsley onto his back.

Willow had launched himself onto Alfred's back and buried his teeth in the meat of his shoulder. He shook his head like a wolf at a carcass. When he pulled back, Ainsley could see sharp teeth, too many for his jaw, crowding his mouth.

Blood leaked down his chin and jaw, spattered his face.

Alfred screamed, a hand clapped to his shoulder.

Ainsley scrambled away from him and dragged Willow away from Alfred, slipping his arms under Willow's and securing his hands behind his neck.

Rue came running into camp, half laced into his clothes. He snatched up Ainsley's sword and blocked the blow meant for them. He swept Alfred's legs out from under up and placed the tip of his sword against his throat. "I liked you better as a dog."

Alfred glared up at him.

"I'm going to step back. You're going to get on your horse and go. If I see you again, you'll think my last curse a kindness." Rue stepped back.

Alfred immediately reached for the branch that had fallen from his hand.

Rue stomped on his wrist. "My love, do you still count this man a friend?"

"Don't kill him."

"If he does anything but get on that horse, I will."

Ainsley sighed.

Rue moved back again.

This time Alfred had the sense to run to Clover. He clambered on to the horse bareback and galloped out of the camp.

Rue watched him go, eyes narrowed. He dropped Ainsley's sword and examined his palm. He sighed at the burn. "Does any of that salve remain?"

Ainsley nodded. He released Willow, who'd stopped struggling.

The revenant dropped to his knees, his hands pressed to his mouth.

Rue sat down abruptly. He rested his head on one knee, drawing in small, slow breaths. Eventually, he curled onto his side.

Ainsley watched the two of them struggle, afraid to take his eyes off either of them. His own head and one side of his face throbbed as well, and he could feel that Alfred had loosened at least one of his teeth. He glanced around to see if his pack was nearby. He darted over to grab it but paused when something crunched under his foot.

He looked down to see a pile of human teeth, roots and all.

He glanced at Willow, who'd settled cross-legged onto the ground, his palm filled with blood and lumps, his other hand searching inside of his mouth. He pulled out an overlong canine, root and all, and placed it among the other teeth in his hand.

"Christ," Ainsley breathed.

Willow glanced up. He cleared his throat, spit a gooey mouthful of blood, and gave Ainsley a tight smile.

"What happened?" Ainsley brought his pack over and crouched beside him.

Willow spat again. He lifted one lip to show new, human teeth pushing the beastly ones out of his gums.

"Doesn't that hurt?"

Willow nodded. He pulled out another sharp tooth. He continued the process of removing teeth and spitting blood for nearly an hour.

Ainsley did what he could to tend to Rue, washing the burn on his hand and coating it with salve. He tore strips off a tunic Alfred had left behind and bound his hand.

"What a fucking mess," Ainsley muttered.

"I want to go home," Rue whispered.

Willow sat there, his palm full of bloody teeth.

"Does...Do your teeth always do that?"

Willow shook his head. "She fed me to a dog." He touched his throat. "It's...I. The woman in the tent...She made me. Marion made me do it to the woman in the tent but..." He swallowed. "But I did it to Marion when she tried to kill me again."

"Can you control it?"

Willow bobbed his head side to side. "Don't know yet." A dribble of red spit trailed down his chin and dripped onto his lap. He wiped his chin with the heel of his hand and dried it on the grass.

Ainsley offered him the water skin.

He rinsed his mouth and spat a final time. He buried his teeth, human and otherwise, in a small hole beside the campfire, then held out his hands for Ainsley to drizzle water over. "Are you angry?"

"Fred attacked you."

"No more biting," Willow reminded.

"This is different."

Willow dried his mostly clean hands on his hose, then sat beside Rue. He touched his arm. "I liked him better as a dog."

Rue patted Willow's leg.

"You don't get attached to things you're leading to the slaughter," Willow told him.

"You don't give flowers to a man who tried to kill you," Rue offered.

"Didn't try that hard," Willow pointed out.

Ainsley tried to stand but had to sit back down before he'd even fully righted himself.

"What fine prey would we make for interested party," Rue mused as he flopped onto his back. Puffy white clouds reflected in his eyes.

Ainsley reached over and dragged his sword closer.

"Should I envy how readily you defended our new companion?"

"It was a little different this time."

"Count the ways for me."

"Fred wasn't fully armed and armored this time. I had more than a knife," Ainsley began, "I didn't think I could talk him out if it. Willow didn't do anything to provoke him—"

"Provoke!" Rue pushed himself halfway up. "You think I provoked him?"

Ainsley opened his mouth.

Rue's face split into a grin, unable to hold a serious countenance any longer. "How I love to see thee flustered, dear heart." He lay back down. "I'll be fit to travel soon. Come lie with me."

Ainsley lay down, not next to him, but with his head on Rue's stomach.

Willow scooted a little closer.

"If you must," Rue said.

Willow placed his head on Rue's thigh. He took Rue's hand and placed it on his face. "Face hurts."

Rue left his hand where he placed it. "I imagine it must. Two sets of teeth within a morning?"

"Ribs hurt. Back hurts."

"Poor thing."

"Better when I was dead."

"How bleak," Rue said.

"Warm. Everything and nothing and..." He sighed. "I hate this."

"You'll like the Otherworld," Ainsley assured. He rolled over and rested his arms on Rue, then his chin on his arms. "Unless. I mean. Do you want to come with us? Do you have a family to go back to?"

Willow let out a bitter snort and gave Ainsley a nasty look.

"I don't know which question earned me that awful look you just gave me," Ainsley told him.

"Go with you."

"You don't want to go?"

"No. Not. No...Go back to family?" Willow sighed and shook his head. "Impossible."

"Then you want to come with us," Ainsley clarified.

"*Want* to go. I...have to go. Nowhere else. Fed me to a dog, dead, secrets...Have to go. Yes?"

"I won't make you."

"I might," Rue said.

Willow frowned at him.

"Oh, what a price you'd fetch! How many riddles could you break, impossible quests now fulfilled with a dead man walking? The wicked things of Court would love to make you weep..."

Willow sat all the way up.

"Rue, don't...Don't scare him." To Willow, Ainsley said, "Don't listen to him, he likes to get a rise out of people."

"Wicked creatures, we fairies be," Rue vowed. "Fit your foundling with bells and berries, fair knight, if ye mean to keep him well."

"You're *strange*, you know that, don't you?"

"Mind thine manners, sirrah, or you could lose my favor."

"Aye, Your Highness, consider them well minded. Grave warning, that, I'd be a fool not to mind it."

Rue reached over and tweaked his nose. "I saved you again today."

He flinched, his face more sensitive than usual. "Ouch. Alfred wouldn't have killed me."

"Know thee that for sure?"

Willow wrapped one of Ainsley's curls around his finger. "Saved me."

"You have blood under your nails," Rue told him.

Willow examined his nails. He made a face, then started to scrape them out with his teeth.

"A bath, I think, will be our first order of business in Wolfwood," Rue mused.

Willow let out a fair approximation of a wolf's howl.

"Maybe two or three..." he added more softly.

Willow nodded his agreement. He tugged on his own hair. "Needs it."

"Mmm, you're like as not to give Ainsley lice. I'll have to put both of you out to be sheared."

"I don't have lice!" Ainsley protested.

"Keep cozying up to Willow and you will."

Willow giggled and repeated, "Willow will."

Rue sighed. "What luck have I to have garnered two fools in this awful realm?"

Ainsley rolled his eyes.

Rue dragged Ainsley closer to him. He nuzzled against his throat. "I count it the most wonderous of luck to have you, my love. I wouldn't trade you for the wisest of men."

"I wouldn't trade you for a wise man, either."

Rue squeezed him tighter.

Willow stretched and yawned. "Horse?"

"Oh, soon. I'm not ready to get up," Rue said.

"Nap?"

"Go ahead."

Willow yawned again. He curled up against Rue's side, reminding Ainsley of a cat.

In the middle of the night, Ainsley woke up Rue, shaking the fairy and demanding, "Do you hear that?"

Rue nestled his face further into his arm. "Hmm?"

"Listen."

A whimpering sort of moan came from outside the tent.

"It's only Willow."

"I know, but—"

"He does it most nights," Rue assured. "He always stops."

Ainsley pushed him. "I feel bad enough making him sleep outside and you're saying he moans like that every night?"

"Let the poor wretch cry; what else can we do?"

"You don't even check on him?"

Rue pulled a blanket over his head.

"Rue!"

Rue sat up. "If he's doing anything other than laying out there crying..." Rue trailed off, brow furrowed. "Though he does sound a little more miserable than usual." He crawled out of the tent.

The light he conjured showed Willow, his tunic stripped off and blood on his hands and smeared across his chest.

Ainsley swore under his breath, grabbed the light, and went over to Willow. The earthy smell that came from him had doubled at least. "What happened?"

Willow looked up, his face smeared with blood, too. He shook his head and let out a plaintive whine, his lips pressed together.

The scratches on his face looked worse than they had yesterday. Ainsley couldn't tell if he'd scratched himself again or if the blood had come from somewhere else.

Rue crouched beside him.

"Help."

"What happened?"

Willow touched his chest. "Heart."

"Let's see..." Rue fetched a bowl and rag, then conjured and heated water. He wiped Willow's face first.

The scratches bled like they were fresh and had gone red around the edges.

Rue frowned.

Ainsley sat down, not sure what to do.

Rue cleaned his chest to show that the incision on his chest had gone red, too. Blood oozed out as soon as he wiped it away. "This might need stitching again."

Ainsley insisted, "It was healed."

"Did you scratch at it?" Rue asked Willow.

"No." He shook his head. "It...it hurts. Everything hurts."

Rue peered at the wound. He poked it. "You didn't open this?"

"No!"

Rue sighed. He looked at the scratches on his face, then examined the scars that littered his body. Not so pink now, more the reddish-purple hue of wounds still healing. He sat back on his haunches and let out a sigh through his nose.

"Hurts."

"I know," Rue said. He cupped Willow's check and gently wiped at his scratches again.

Ainsley rummaged through his pack to find the salve he had purchased for Rue's leg.

Rue took his hand back. "The mage's spell may be...It may have been imperfect."

"What's that supposed to mean?

Rue looked over Willow one more time. He leaned close to whisper to Ainsley, "It may not hold."

"Don't say that."

"My love..."

"Don't say that!"

Rue nodded. He wiped the freshest blood from Willow's chest. "We can stitch it shut again. Maybe all that excitement with Alfred opened it again."

Willow's jaw quivered. "I was dead."

"Ay. Know thee of any doctors for dead men?" Rue asked.

Willow started to sniffle.

Ainsley scowled at Rue. "Here, come here. Stop crying." He showed Willow the jar of salve. "This will help the pain."

Willow flinched away a few times as Ainsley applied it. Halfway through, he scooted back. "Worse."

Ainsley glanced at Rue.

Willow scrunched up his face. "Ugh!"

"Don't rub it!" Rue immediately warned and grabbed Willow's wrists. "And don't scratch it."

"I didn't!" Willow squirmed and rubbed his check against his shoulder.

"Stop," Rue said.

Willow glared at him.

"Stop and let me look at it," the fairy insisted.

Willow went still.

Rue inspected his face, moving the light closer. "'Tisn't a healing salve, my love?"

"What?"

"It's only for pain?"

"Oh. Yes." Ainsley checked the instructions carefully penned onto the clay jar. "Just for pain."

"Look at his face."

Ainsley glanced between the scratches he had treated and the ones he hadn't. "We should put more on."

"It hurts!" Willow insisted. He tried to pull his hands back.

"Let me try something else," Rue said.

"What?"

"Magic brought you to life, yes? And that's a salve made by a mage. I don't know much about the magic used in this realm, but I know it takes a mighty power to bring one back from the Lands Beyond."

"I'm dying?"

"I don't know. Do you want to die?"

Willow shook his head. "No. Help."

"I'll try. I'll...do what I can."

"Please."

Rue smoothed the pad of his thumb over one of the scratches the salve hadn't mended. It went as though he wiped away dirt, leaving nothing but a thin, pink line.

Willow scrunched up his face but didn't flinch or otherwise move away.

"Healing run in the family?" Ainsley asked.

"Not for me. I didn't...I didn't use my power with the intent to heal. I gave a bit to him. His body did the rest. Or. The spell that raised him did the rest...Something did the rest. I don't know the truth of it. These are my best guesses."

"Did that hurt as bad as the salve?" Ainsley asked.

Willow shook his head. "Itchy." He touched his face where Rue had touched it. "Feels better now."

"Wonderful."

"Can you...Can you fix that?" Ainsley asked, nodding towards the wound in Willow's chest.

"We should sew it first."

Willow whined.

"Ainsley will hold your hand if you need comfort," Rue offered.

Willow didn't catch the sarcasm and grabbed Ainsley's hand. He didn't let go even after Rue had stitched the wound shut again.

When he had closed the wound, Rue put an ear to Willow's chest. "Sounds like a swamp."

"What?"

"Your heart. It sounds...wet."

Willow frowned.

"Like footsteps in mud."

"Rue, really," Ainsley chided.

Rue cupped Willow's face in his hands and touched his forehead to the revenant's. He closed his eyes and whispered in that language Ainsley could never understand.

The magic that passed between them warmed the air, a honeyed breeze that circled the two of them and tugged at Ainsley's hair.

When Rue pulled back, the incision had lost its redness, but still looked fresher than it had when Ainsley had taken the stitches out.

"Does it still hurt?"

"No."

Ainsley wanted to hug him. He wanted to hug both of them. He handed Willow the tunic he'd shed. "Come into the tent?"

Willow and Rue looked at each other.

"I feel bad leaving him out here all alone. Especially without Fred to keep an eye on him."

Rue pointed out, "It will be crowded."

Willow gave a half-hearted eyebrow waggle. "Cozy, cozy." He pulled his tunic over his head.

In the tent, Willow curled himself into a ball under a blanket.

Ainsley couldn't get back to sleep. He tossed and turned several times.

Rue threw an arm around him and squeezed him tight. "Go to sleep."

"I can't."

"Then at least stay still."

"Rue, is he going to be alright?"

"I cannot say, dear heart. I'd advise you not to think about it overmuch."

Ainsley grunted.

"If he dies, know at least you've done him a greater kindness than likely most in his life."

"I hear you," Willow said without moving.

"Are my claims unfounded?" Rue asked.

Willow didn't answer.

Ainsley slept uneasily that night, dreaming of dark things he couldn't recall when he woke.

Willow seemed in better spirits that morning that he had the last few days. He tugged on Ainsley's sleeve, pointed to his cheek, and said, "Look!"

"They're healed," Ainsley said.

Willow shook his head. He ran his palm over his cheek. "Beard."

Ainsley took a closer look. "Peach fuzz."

Willow wrinkled his nose. He rubbed his cheeks. "Haven't shaved in..." He stopped to think. He dropped his hand and put them on his cheeks. "Since I was alive." He looked around. "What month is it?"

"May."

"Uffff." Willow looked around. "May!" He sighed. He stretched and reached for a piece of bread that Rue had left unattended.

Rue smacked his hand. "No manners, this thing!"

Willow made a face at him. "I'm hungry."

"*Ask.*"

"Please?"

Rue handed him the heel of bread.

Willow scarfed it.

Later, he ran off and returned with an armful of wild greens. He offered some to Rue, who took a sprig of parsley and tucked it behind Ainsley's ear.

In a few days' time, Ainsley smelled the city before he saw it. Or, more specifically, he could smell the tannery.

"By all the stars," Rue murmured, looking at the river, which had lost its clarity a while ago.

"No filth in the Otherworld?"

"I've traveled our lands and by Green God and the Black, I never smelled anything so foul as this aside from a battlefield."

"Magic?" Ainsley guessed.

"Like as not. You have mages, though, in this world. Couldn't they do something?"

Willow rubbed his fingers together. "Mages go where coin bids. A shield says Jannes doesn't smell it."

"Ah."

Ainsley stopped walking.

They'd almost reached the city gates.

He couldn't make himself take another step.

"What's wrong?" Rue asked.

"I..." He looked over Willow.

For all his progress, the revenant still looked wild, dangerous, and hadn't quite reclaimed full control of his body. He'd kept that strange gait and often dropped into a crouch when startled. He growled, too, and bared his teeth, and Ainsley thought he'd eat another ear if given the chance. The collar of scars around his neck didn't aid his cause.

"He looks..."

"Like what he is?" Rue guessed.

Ainsley nodded.

"I can fix that. With your permission?" He turned to Willow.

Willow shrugged.

"What would you like to look like?" Rue asked.

Willow glanced down at himself. "I like me."

"A disguise."

"Oh...Mmmm." He crossed his arms. "Uh." He tousled his own hair. "You pick."

The changes Rue made didn't alter Willow's appearance overmuch. He lightened his hair and hid his scars; he gave more a life-like shade to his skin. He looked like any other peasant lad.

When Rue finished, Willow gave a spin. "Good?"

Rue nodded.

"You, uh. You might to want to look a little more human too," Ainsley pointed out.

Rue raised an eyebrow. "I can assure you, dear knight, that I don't."

Ainsley decided not to argue. He'd bring it up again if the guards gave him too much of a hard time getting inside the city gates.

Halfway there, Ainsley thought Willow's hair looked darker again and a few minutes later, it had returned to its usual black.

"Rue, you've got to leave the glamour on him."

"I didn't dispel it."

"Then why's his hair gone dark again?"

Rue poked and prodded the revenant. He even peeked at the cut on Willow's chest, then pronounced, "He absorbed it. What wee spongy lad thou art."

Willow snorted.

Ainsley bit his lip. He didn't feel right bringing Willow into the city undisguised, but he didn't want to leave him alone either. Not when every knight in the kingdom would take his head at the first chance they saw.

"Fret not. It's a small magic and one I can reapply easily enough as the need arises," Rue assured. He placed a hand on Willow's shoulder and the illusion resumed. "I'll be vigilante. Stay near me, yes?"

Willow nodded. "Yes."

At the gates, the city guards peeked at the body in the cart, shirts pulled up over their noses.

One said, "Ugh, if I have to look at one more dead body, I'll quit."

"Are there many bodies to look at these days?" Ainsley asked, wondering if some illness lurked within the city gates.

"Every knight and his brother coming in with a dead creature to show the king."

Ainsley nodded and urged Hadley onward, sick to his stomach with how many had died for Jannes's revenge.

He gave his name again at the castle gate. The sound of hammers and saws filled the air here; magic tickled his nose, too. Ainsley could glimpse the king's half-built palace. Jannes meant the marble palace to replace the small, ancient castle in which all his ancestors had dwelled.

Once inside the castle, Ainsley understood the king's desire for a new home. Cramped by narrow walls and low ceilings and in near total dark, Ainsley almost reached out for Rue's hand on their walk to the great hall. Instead, he rested it on the hilt of his sword.

He knelt before Jannes's throne and tried not to look at Aurelia's empty one. He tried not to think of Willow's mouth crowded with beastly teeth tearing her throat apart. He swallowed.

A few titters went through the crowded courtiers when a servant announced him.

Rue nodded his head to Jannes, but he neither knelt nor bowed.

Willow sunk to his knees and stayed there, eyes on the ground.

"What brings you before us?"

"I fulfilled the charge you gave me, Your Majesty."

"Many knights have come before us these past weeks to tell us they've found the creature that murdered our wife." Jannes gestured toward a pile of skulls beside his throne. "Why should we believe you any better?"

He placed the shrouded corpse before the king, the stench nearly making him vomit. "This is the body of Marion Duverger. She sent an assassin to kill your wife."

Jannes didn't look impressed. "That could be any body. We can tell from the smell it's too far gone to recognize."

"Ask Rue," Ainsley suggested mildly. "He cannot lie."

Jannes sneered, "Right. Your prince."

"I'll answer your questions, mortal king, should it please you to ask them," Rue answered.

"Fine, then, fairy. Step forward."

Rue remained where he was. "What would you like to know?"

Jannes asked, "Is that the body of Marion Duverger?"

"Ainsley spoke true. That is she and it was she that sent your wife's killer."

"And what of the creature she sent? Did you apprehend it?"

"The wretch was dead before we reached her castle. She fed him to a dog," Rue answered.

Jannes leaned back in his throne. "Hm."

"Sire?" Ainsley asked.

"I've been told otherwise."

"By whom?"

Jannes glanced to his right and called, "Sir Alfred?"

Ainsley groaned.

Alfred stepped into the great hall.

"Is the creature you spoke of among us?" Jannes asked.

Alfred pointed to Willow. "There it is. Disguised but that's the bastard."

"Sir Alfred, I warned you," Rue called. His voice rang clear and true above the general chatter of the court.

"Not now," Ainsley hissed.

"I gave my word."

"Yes, but can't it wait?" Ainsley demanded.

Jannes waved a hand in their direction. "Guards, take the creature."

Willow clambered to his feet and grabbed Rue's arm.

Ainsley stepped in front of them. "Your Majesty, please."

"You meant to conceal this creature from us," Jannes accused.

"He's just a lad, he didn't...He didn't do it by choice."

"It's a dead thing," Alfred said, "They called it a revenant."

"Sir Ainsley, step aside. You've brought us the creature and we...we will turn a blind eye to what we know. Do not make this difficult," Jannes said.

Ainsley eyed the advancing guards. "I can't let you kill him. He's not wicked."

Rue put a hand on Ainsley's shoulder. "Come mind your ward, my love. I'll see this managed."

Ainsley shook his head. "This isn't—"

Rue's fingers tightened on his shoulder, not painful but reassuring. He asked, "Do you trust me?"

"I." Ainsley glanced again at the advancing guards. "Yes."

Alfred moved further into the room, a glaive in his hands.

"Take them all. Alive or otherwise," Jannes called to the guards.

Ainsley drew his sword, keeping a hold of Willow as he circled, trying to decide what would be the best course of action.

Half a dozen guards advanced in unison with spears and shields.

It would be a bloodbath.

"Bite them?" Willow asked.

"Stay by me," Ainsley insisted.

Willow tightened his grip on Ainsley's arm.

Ainsley looked for Rue, but he'd vanished.

Not half a minute later, the fairy reappeared behind Alfred, twisting the glaive out of his hands. He used the pole to knock Alfred to the ground. "Sir Alfred, you...you are the basest of creatures, a mortal man. Any other form would be a gift. I bind you, Alfred of Rosebridge, from doing harm to others. When you reach for another with ill intent, you'll known the pain your actions would have brought."

Alfred roared and went to swat at Rue, but curled in on himself, grunting with the effort of trying to reach other man.

Jannes had launched himself off the throne by that point. He flung a spell towards where Rue stood, but by the time it reached him, Rue had gone again and the fire whizzed over Alfred.

The glaive clattered to the ground.

A crow wheeled through the air and lighted on Ainsley's shoulder. It tugged at his hair.

"That's not helpful!" Ainsley said.

The guards had gotten close enough that Ainsley could have touched the points of their spears.

Willow had all but sealed himself to Ainsley's side, his chest fluttering and his eyes darting to the faces of the advancing guards. He whined.

Once or twice, Ainsley tested their resolve, trying to knock away a spear, but it had little effect.

The third time he tried to knock away a spear, the guard jabbed back and he barely parried it.

Rue took flight again, this time landing on the guard and pecking at his eye.

The guard dropped his spear and clapped a hand over his eye.

Ainsley seized the opportunity. He grabbed Willow and dragged him through the opening, shouldering the guard so he fell.

The other guards hurried to pivot.

Jannes sent another spell their way.

Rue, a man again, knocked away the king's spell. "I'll kill them if you like, my love. I think I could manage it."

"I..." Ainsley looked around. Rue had offered so casually to take the lives of nearly a dozen men and Ainsley believed him when he said he could manage it.

Just as easily, Rue offered, "Or we could flee."

"That. Let's do that."

Willow nodded eagerly. "No more biting," he agreed.

Rue waved his hand and a wave of choking black smoke filled the room. The guards began to hack and cough, and when Jannes attempted a spell, he choked and wheezed.

Holding on to each other, they fled into the narrow halls of the castle, back the way they came, and barreling through servants and courtiers alike.

"Hadley!" Ainsley said.

Rue let out a laugh. He dragged Ainsley close and circled an arm around his waist. "I love how much you love your horse!" he cried, then kissed him.

If Ainsley didn't know better, he would have thought Rue was having fun.

He didn't actually know better, he reflected.

Weakly, he answered, "She's a good horse."

Rue took his hand again and continued sprinting out of the castle.

They made their way back to Hadley, dodging stable boys and grooms. Most of them hurried out of their way, having no disillusions how their cloth and pitchforks would do against steel.

Ainsley helped Willow on the horse and turned to look for Rue.

A spotty groom brandished an iron hay hook in Rue's direction.

Rue twirled his knife, sizing up the groom.

"He's just a lad, Rue, leave him."

Rue glanced over his shoulder.

The groom took the opportunity to lunge.

Ainsley grabbed Rue around the waist and pulled Rue back before the youth could make contact. "Don't try to play the hero," Ainsley warned when he saw the groom winding up for another swing.

The youth didn't take the warning. He made a wild swing toward them.

Ainsley smacked the groom's hand with the flat of his sword hard enough that he dropped the hook. He kept his sword pointed at the groom. "I'd run if I were you."

Rue sent a flicker of lightning toward the youth's feet when he didn't flee.

The spell sent him running.

Ainsley climbed onto Hadley and Willow wrapped his arms tight around his waist. A crow took Rue's place and tugged one of Ainsley's curls before it took off through the stable. He followed the crow through the city gates, barreling past the guards that called for them to stop. He rode Hadley hard, too hard, until Rue lighted on the branch of a tree and called to him.

Beneath the tree, Rue conjured a doorway made of twisting branches and flower petals. He asked, "Are you ready to go home?"

Ainsley glanced back.

No one had followed them, but it wouldn't take long for anyone to figure out where they'd done, or for Jannes to gather reinforcements.

"I can never come back."

Rue shrugged. "Don't be dramatic."

"Nice, coming from you," Ainsley snapped.

"Do you think your parents would sell you out to the king?"

"No!"

"Then you can come back to visit the only thing you have worth visiting," Rue assured. He placed a hand on Hadley's neck. "Let me take us home."

Ainsley nodded.

Rue took Hadley by the bridle and led her through the doorway.

Willow squeezed Ainsley tighter as they passed through the doorway, his cheek pressed hard against Ainsley's back. When he saw Wolfwood, he gasped. He slipped off Hadley's back and pressed his hand to one of the house's walls.

Ainsley climbed off Hadley and watched Willow roam around the courtyard, inspecting everything with the wonder of a child.

"Go take care of her. I'll keep an eye him. And I have to tell Dora!"

Ainsley groomed Hadley and got her settled into a stall, then made sure she had food and water. He found Rue and Willow in the kitchen with Dora, who'd already set food before Willow.

Willow gobbled it like he'd never eaten before. At one point, he dropped a half-eaten oat cake onto his plate and started to weep.

Ainsley looked to Rue. "What...?"

Rue shook his head. "Don't fret. It's not such an uncommon reaction to our fare." He glanced at Dora, who nodded in confirmation.

Dora did look over Ainsley. "Is that the same one as last time?"

"He is," Rue said.

"Mortals, you know, they all look the same. Plain things. I never understood the fascination," Dora said. "Begging your pardon, Your Highness."

"Oh, he's such a sweet thing. How could I resist?"

Ainsley blushed.

Willow wiped his eyes and resumed eating the cake, still sniffling.

Rue had Dora prepare a room for the revenant, but he fell asleep in the stuffed chair in Rue's room that night. Freshly bathed and smelling, for once, more of soap and herbs than moss and earth, he'd wiggled into one of Rue's robes and curled up in the chair.

He had sighed and hummed happily to himself until he'd fallen asleep.

"Will you ask Tadgh to come look at him?" Ainsley asked.

"You can ask him well enough yourself. I suspect he's fond of you."

Ainsley sat on the bed. "I think he is. He did give me his blessing."

Rue's thin eyebrows shot up. "When?"

"Right before I challenged you to a drinking contest."

Rue's eyes went wide and his jaw went slack. "By all the stars, I knew it hadn't been just the parsley! I knew it!"

"You never said anything."

"I didn't consider myself in a position to ask." Rue sat beside him.

"Mmm."

"I..." Rue swallowed.

"Go ahead."

"Go ahead, he says," Rue tutted. He leaned against Ainsley. "Staying away from drink is one thing when the wine is weak as what we serve to children. It was...Mere months had me undone last time I came home."

"Aye."

"I'm ashamed of how I behaved and...I'll do it again. I always do it again."

Ainsley put his arm around him. "Shame gets us nowhere but deeper in the hole."

"Are these wise words from my beloved?"

"Rue, I'm trying to be serious."

"Apologies, dear heart."

Ainsley tried to gather his thoughts again. "Don't be ashamed. It's pointless and makes you feel worse. Just...Be proud of what you can do. Acknowledge what you can't do on your own and ask for help."

"I'll try."

"And be honest with me."

"I'll try." Rue sighed. "But 'twill undo me again. I can't promise it won't."

"I know, love."

"You know." Not a question, but a statement meant to reassure himself.

Ainsley nodded.

"And you love me anyway."

"And I love you anyway," Ainsley confirmed. He kissed his cheek. "Are you ready for bed?"

Rue shook his head. "Show me the plans you made for us."

Hand in hand, they walked to the library.

It took three weeks from when Ainsley sent the letter for Tadgh to arrive at Wolfwood. He came without forewarning and as unaccompanied as Ainsley had ever seen the prince. He brought only his daughter and her nurse. Despite the small number of people, he came with a cart packed with bundles and chests. He arrived in the early morning, finding Rue and Ainsley in the courtyard with their weapons.

Willow watched them, whistling and making leery comments from where he balanced on the gold-weighted stone. He liked to sit there. He liked pretty much anything laced with magic.

He'd burrowed into the mud of the Tadgh at one point and emerged as hale and hearty as Ainsley had ever seen. Still pale and laced with scars, but definitively improved. The wound on his chest had healed to nothing more than a smooth, pink slash.

He'd crowed with joy when he'd had to shave.

Ainsley had needed to show him how to shave with the grain of his beard instead of against it.

Tadgh called, "Pup!" as he dismounted.

Ainsley spun to see him. "Tadgh! Uh. Your Highness."

The fairy grinned. "I'm surprised to see you. What could a man as miserable as my cousin have done to convince you to come back here?"

Ainsley glanced at Rue. "He always calls me a fool. I guess I must be. Especially if I had to ask you for help."

Tadgh tittered. He turned to Rue and said, "Cousin, no surprise to see you home with two foundlings."

Rue looked at the cart. "You brought a lot."

"Our lord and lady found their stay here somewhat dull last summer. They seek to hold the Summer Court in another venue when the days grow hot. I asked permission to use Wolfwood as...as a safer haven for my princess."

"Court trouble?" Rue asked.

"One or two foiled assassinations. An attempted kidnapping. Easily enough diverted but..." Tadgh glanced around until his eyes lightened on his daughter, safe in her nurse's arms. "But she is precious to me."

"Woeful would it be to have her come to harm," Rue agreed.

Tadgh watched his daughter, then sighed and placed a hand on his hip. He looked at Willow. "Anyway. Tell me about your other foundling."

Willow had hopped off his stone and made his light-footed yet shuffling way over to Ainsley. He'd placed his chin on Ainsley's shoulder and murmured, "Sweaty."

"Then don't lean on me."

Willow sniffed him. "Yuck."

Ainsley gently elbowed him off, but Willow returned within a moment. He always found his way close to someone, making contact with Rue and Ainsley, flirting with them, though he did these things more in a way that asked for attention and affection than any kind of carnal response.

"Come here," Tadgh said to Willow.

Willow didn't move.

"Go ahead," Ainsley said.

Willow looked to Rue for confirmation.

Rue nodded.

Willow stood in front of Tadgh, his hands loosely clasped in front of him and his eyes on the ground.

Tadgh circled him. "Always bringing home these pathetic boys..."

"Willow's not a boy," Rue mentioned.

Tadgh raised an eyebrow.

"I am. And I am not," Willow offered softly.

"Ah. What do I call you?"

Willow shrugged. "Willow."

"But in reference to you?" Tadgh asked.

Willow shrugged again. "Anything but late for supper."

Tadgh snorted. "Very well. Tell me your tale, Willow, and I'll see if I can lend any sort of aid."

"She fed me to a dog. I was dead."

Tadgh's face changed, from haughty to pity to curious all in a few seconds. He tilted up Willow's chin to peer at the scars around his throat. "Are these from the dog?"

Willow nodded.

"Brutal." Tadgh glanced over the rest of Willow, his eyes darting over the visible scars.

Willow had helped himself to the thin, revealing clothes in Rue's wardrobe. He grinned at himself in the mirror when he wore them and walked around with his chin held high.

"Finally found a use for them," Tadgh noted. "You'd do well take a page out of this wee thing's book," he said to his cousin.

Rue rolled his eyes. He went over to his niece and took her from the nurse. "Come along, Acorn, I'll show you your new home."

The baby gurgled at him.

"She's gotten big," Ainsley noted.

Tadgh nodded toward Rue. "Go give her the tour with him. I wouldn't trust him not to bring her to the library and skip all the interesting places."

Willow grabbed Ainsley's sleeve.

Ainsley patted his arm. "He's not so bad," he assured the revenant.

Willow nodded, his fingers finding the iron knife he wore on his belt anyway. "He's here to help."

"He's here to help," Ainsley agreed.

"That is the hope," Tadgh said. "I have to say, for a dead man, you look quite well."

Willow glanced vaguely around. He touched his chest, tracing the scar over his heart. "She...She fed me to a dog and I...I woke up. I woke up...A dog didn't do this. She did."

"It would have to be a clever beast indeed to leave that kind of mark. I confess, I don't know much about the magics of the human world, but I am a fair hand at healing," Tadgh explained.

"It's...Being here makes it better. The...Rue says magic makes me alive. This world is..." Willow looked around. "This world *is* magic. I can feel it."

"Fascinating. Will you walk with me?"

Willow nodded.

Ainsley headed inside to find Rue in the library with Merremia, as his cousin had predicted.

He kissed Rue on the cheek.

"Oh, you are sweaty," Rue noted.

"I'll meet you in the baths once Tadgh comes to retrieve the little one. Although...God, she is big! Has it been so long?"

"Babies grow fast. Children are rare treasure but rarer still in this realm and they are children for so precious few years."

Ainsley touched the baby's hand.

She grabbed on.

"She is sweet."

"I..." Rue swallowed. "I never imagined Tadgh as a father. Too vain and selfish, too easily distracted. Even when he showed her to me, I thought he would abandon her within the week. But now her spirit is our spirit."

"It will be nice to see her grow up," Ainsley said.

"I." A few tears slipped down Rue's cheeks. "I want her to be happier child I was. Than Tadgh was."

Ainsley wiped Rue's cheeks. "She will be."

"You don't know that."

"I do."

"Did your father drink?"

"Not the way you mean. But we aren't our parents. You'll do better than yours."

"You don't know that either. The last time I saw her I was...I was so soaked in wine I could barely stand."

Ainsley sighed. "I don't know a lot of things. But I know you're a good man. You'll be a good uncle. Hmm?"

"I'll be a good uncle," Rue whispered.

Ainsley patted Rue's thigh. "And...You know. Maybe someday you'll be a good father."

"Ainsley, you're going to make me cry."

"Maybe it's my turn to make you cry for once."

Rue sniffled. He scrubbed his eyes with the back of his hand. "I can't apologize enough times."

Ainsley said, "Good thing we can't do it by accident. I think you'd die of shock."

Rue let out a wet chuckle.

By the time Tadgh and Willow returned, Willow had lost some of his nervousness. He came over to Rue, peered down at the baby, and said, "Now she's sweaty, too."

"Can you help?" Ainsley asked.

Tadgh took his daughter back and settled into a stuffed chair. "Willow doesn't need helping...Or. Well. I think he needs a lot of help in other ways, but the magic of this world will give him life that your world could not have sustained. His roots can draw what it needs from our world."

"Strong roots," Rue noted.

"It's a good name. You gave it to him?"

"He picked it himself."

Tadgh smiled at Willow. "Oh, not so mad as he seems, then. And he...He does seem a hair star-touched, cousin, have you noticed?"

"She fed me to a dog," Willow reminded sourly.

"You mentioned a few times," Tadgh said. "I think you also mentioned that you were dead."

Willow squinted at Tadgh. "Same thoughts. Over and over."

"Better than they were?" Tadgh asked.

"Sometimes."

"I don't think he'll get any less dead," Tadgh continued. "He might get more dead if that…That *thing* inside his chest stops working."

Willow touched his chest.

Ainsley tugged on Rue's sleeve. "Ready for a bath?"

Rue sighed and dragged himself out of the chair.

Ainsley scooped him up and threw him over his shoulder. "I've captured you."

"Ainsley!" Rue scolded.

"Perhaps your cousin can save you."

"No, no, I thoroughly wash my hands over whatever happens between you two in the baths," Tadgh said.

Willow tittered.

Ainsley carried Rue along to the baths and said, "Poor Rue, captured by a marauding knight. What fate might befall him?"

"Put me down."

Ainsley put him down and kissed him. He rested his arms on Rue's shoulders. He smiled at him. "You're so wonderful."

"Say it again."

"You're wonderful, Rue. I…"

"Go ahead."

Ainsley embraced him. "I'm so glad to be home."

Rue squeezed him tight. "These walls would be empty without you."

Ainsley kissed him.

"Pick me up again."

"What?"

"Pick me up."

Ainsley lifted him but didn't throw him over his shoulder this time.

Rue locked his legs around Ainsley's waist. He pressed his mouth to Ainsley's and let out a long sigh.

It took them a while longer to get to their bath and when they did, they needed it much more than they had before.

"Do you think Tadgh will send us on any quests?" Ainsley asked idly as Rue washed his back.

"Not a month away from your last one and you're ready to ride out again?"

"Maybe just a small quest," Ainsley suggested. "I am a knight, after all. I'm supposed to go on quests."

Rue scooted closer and kissed his shoulder. "So impatient. You'd ride out today if someone set an adventure before you, wouldn't you?"

"No."

"Mmm."

"I wouldn't!"

"We have such a long and lovely summer in front of us, dear heart, and so many years. Let's not rush. Not…"

Ainsley turned. "Not with Acorn to watch over?"

"She has so few years to be a child."

Ainsley smiled. He touched Rue's face. "I'll be mindful."

Rue smiled back.

Ainsley didn't know what else to say. He could only smile at him. He'd get restless eventually, he always did. For now, though, it felt so good to have come home, really home, to a place where he could be not just whatever he wanted, but who he was without wanting to be anything else.